# FATE AND ANGUS McGRATH

# FATE
# AND
# ANGUS
# McGRATH

Jean Jardine Miller

JM PUBLISHING

Library and Archives Canada Cataloguing in Publication

Jardine Miller, Jean, 1945-
Fate and Angus McGrath / Jean Jardine Miller.

ISBN 0-9731376-2-2

I. Title.

PS8619.A735F38 2004     C813'.6     C2004-905550-X

Cover and text design: Design and Copy Consultation Services.

Jardine Miller
- publishing what is significant to today
Limehouse, ON  L0P 1H0

PRINTED IN CANADA

*To the memory of my mother, Gladys Jardine, who used to tell people that her little girl wanted to be a novelist when she grew up, instilling in that little girl the desire to never stop writing.*

# PROLOGUE

It was the fact that Angus had shared Byron's birthday which consumed my thoughts as I read the obituary Megan had prepared for the funeral director.

*McGRATH, Angus Michael, suddenly August 26th. Beloved son of Michael McGrath and Judith Rowan. Brother of Stephanie and step-brother of Justin. Sadly missed by step-parents, aunts, uncles and cousins, all of whom will have a special place for him in their hearts forever. In lieu of flowers, donations to the Spellhaven Recovery House, Guelph, Ontario will be appreciated.*

And, when I finally did get my mind around what I was reading, I could only inwardly cry out "Why?"

Why now? Now, when he had finally seemed to be getting his life together? I wondered if Alan and Danny or Jayne knew about the donations request or if Megan had taken it upon herself to openly admit – explain? – her cousin's addiction problems in this way. Well... I wondered about it for a fleeting few seconds then my obstinate thoughts were back, once again, fighting against accepting the too early death.

Hugh had worked so hard to win his confidence, during his convalescence at our house over the summer. And he was thinking logically at last, learning to have patience... not that Hugh was taking any credit for that – you're pretty much forced to learn patience when you have a shattered right leg! He seemed to be in touch with his emotions, assessing, evaluating – no longer exhibiting the irrational impulsiveness that had always characterized his behaviour. Just a few days ago, Hugh had been saying that we had every reason to think the kid would make it this time...

"So, I'll tell him to fax it to the *Victoria Times Colonist*, then, and the *Sun Province*?" Megan was confirming with Judith.

I was glad Megan had volunteered to come with us to the funeral parlour. She was being of far more use to Judith than I was. I wondered if Judith too, while steeling herself to select her son's coffin, was remembering the day he was born...

Byron had been four years old, pleasurably exhausted and sleeping off the excitement of his first real – complete with twenty other four-year-olds, party games and too much to eat – birthday party when Michael called with the news. The baby had been born at 2:30 pm their time – just as the birthday party was ending here I remember thinking, although why, I don't know... just some quirky mental reflex that causes me to immediately start calculating the time difference when I'm speaking to somebody in another time zone. Sometimes I get a mental picture of being asked what so-and-so had to say and my not having the slightest idea – except that it was at exactly 11:25 am Eastern Standard Time which meant that it had to be 8:25 am Pacific Time or 3:25 am the next day in Sydney, Australia and that it must have been important to call from there, at that time, since it's hardly a good time for a cosy chat.

"Congratulations," I said. "That's wonderful. And, Judith – she's all right?"

"Just great," he replied. "We're calling him Angus."

I was silent.

"Marilyn?"

"I'm sorry. You took me by surprise. Don't you think that might be tempting fate?"

"It was my grandfather's name too, you know, and the name of many other ancestors, most of whom, from what I know, lived to a ripe old age."

"Well..." I said, not knowing how to react, "it's your decision. Anyway, I'm really happy to hear that everything's okay and tell Judith 'Congratulations' won't you. Can you give me the room number... and what's the postal code?" I wanted nothing more than to end the conversation – the children were always a good excuse and they'd likely start fighting any minute anyway. So, I lied, "I hear an argument in progress downstairs. I'd better go... Byron had his birthday party this afternoon – he's asleep, but Danny and Megan are helping me to clean up... or, at least, that's what they're supposed to be doing."

"I'll let you go then." He sounded about as glad as I was to get off the line. "We'll send you some pictures... Tell Byron 'Happy Birthday' from us and say 'Hi' to Danny and Megan. 'Bye, Marilyn."

"'Bye, Michael... and congratulations." I said.

Judith sent us photographs of the new-born Angus a couple of weeks later. They were in the mailbox when we arrived home one evening. It was not surprising, somehow – maybe because he already had his name – that he looked more like his late uncle and namesake than the older Angus's own sons did, although Megan swore that his eyes and forehead looked exactly like Byron's in *his* baby pictures. Byron, himself, vehemently denied it, but he was four and considered himself unique. Danny avoided looking at the pictures, on the grounds that he wanted to do his homework before supper so that he could watch *The Brady Bunch* on television afterwards. For Danny, it was still too painful to see his late father's features mirrored in the infant face of this new young cousin.

# DANNY

Danny turned up the volume on his still shiny new cassette player to drown out the giggles coming from his sister Megan's room next door. Megan – about to graduate from grade eight – had brought her friend, Nicki, home to see the graduation dress which had been purchased the day before, after what sounded to Danny like a totally awesome waste of time. His ten-year-old brother, Byron, had told him, in no uncertain terms, what a jerk he was for not getting home before Mom and Megan had gone to the shopping mall. Even junk food, in the mall's food court, had not made up for the hours of trailing around dress shops with his mother and sister. Privately Danny couldn't see why Byron was not allowed to be alone in the house – he and Megan had been at his age, but his mother said it was different when there were the two of them. She'd have known if they got up to anything because – and, at some future date, they'd have to set her straight on that point – they'd have told tales on each other, whereas who knew what Byron would get into on his own? It usually fell to Megan to look after Byron but, in this case, Danny had been told to be home by three and had still not made it by four, necessitating

Byron having to go to the mall. Byron still thought Danny was a jerk.

The girls were, amid the giggles, experimenting with hairstyles and make-up for the graduation. With a year of high school behind him, Danny felt superior to his sister although, if he were honest, he'd have to admit that his own graduation, last year, had been pretty exciting. Sure, they'd all – the boys, that is – played it down, acting like it was no big deal, but it had been exhilarating getting their diplomas, showing their parents stuff around the school and then going to the dance afterwards. Nadine Elliott had let him walk home with her and kiss her on the porch before her mother had yelled from an upstairs window for her to get inside and to bed. She'd acted like he didn't exist ever since...

"Danny!"

The album had come to an end and he heard his mother's voice through the open window from the garden where she was weeding the flower beds.

"Dan-*ny*..."

He reluctantly got up from his previously prone position on his bed and went to the window.

"I've been calling you for the last ten minutes," she shouted up to him. "You were supposed to wash the car – remember? I don't pay you an allowance for lying on your bed listening to that noise you call music!"

"Okay, Mom. Okay – I'll be down in just a minute. I forgot, but I will do it... really."

"You'd better or there'll be a fine."

His mother had a system of fines and bonuses which was supposed to motivate them to earn their allowances. Most of the time she forgot who had done what and just handed out the set amount anyway. He had a job lined up as a Parks and Rec. day camp counsellor starting next week, when school was finished, and would be done with the whole allowance system for the summer – and, hopefully, for ever more if he could find a permanent part time job in the fall. It would be easier after his sixteenth birthday, but that wouldn't be until February. He wasn't really old enough for the Parks and Rec. job but, since they'd accepted him for counsellor-in-training last year and he'd done lots of volunteer work both before and since then, they were sort of obliged to give him a job this year.

He passed his sister's open door on the way downstairs. The girls were too engrossed in making up their faces to notice him. Byron, looking surly, came in at the back door as he reached the kitchen.

"Hey, Byron – want to help me wash the car?" he asked his younger brother.

Byron stood for a moment undecided whether to accept the offer – a desirable one, since he was not allowed to use the garden hose by himself – or continue his vendetta with Danny over the shopping incident yesterday. Fooling around with the garden hose proved too much of an inducement.

"Sure, Danny," he said, "I get to rinse, though. And it'll cost you a dollar!"

Danny wondered how Byron had learned to drive such a hard bargain at such an early age. "Okay," he shrugged. "Best take your running shoes off, though – remember you made Mom pretty mad when you walked all over the house in soaking wet shoes last time."

Byron removed his shoes, using the toes of one foot to yank the heel of the other out of its shoe, and peeled off his socks. Ben, his cocker spaniel, appeared from nowhere to grab a running shoe.

"Get back here, stupid dog!" yelled Byron, diving after the dog. "They're new – you can't have them..."

Danny side-stepped to prevent the dog from running into the hallway and grabbed the running shoe.

"Okay, Ben. Drop it. I *said*... drop it."

He yanked the shoe from the dog's jaws, as Ben attempted to get a better grip on it, and threw it to his brother. Byron stuffed both shoes and his socks into the broom closet.

Danny shook his head but decided not to comment. "Okay – ready?" he asked, opening the kitchen door. "Let's go!"

. . . . .

The next morning Danny slept in until everybody was out of the house. He was finished with school for the year, so it was best to hold off getting up until the bathroom and kitchen were no longer in demand. Then, freshly showered and dressed, he fried eggs and bacon which he took outside to the table on the patio to eat in the morning sunshine.

He had finished and was watching a fat black squirrel sitting in the strawberry patch, eating the ripest strawberries, when the phone rang. The squirrel fled to the nearest tree as Danny got up and went into the house to answer it.

"Hello."

"Danny? Is that you, Danny?"

"Yes."

He didn't recognize the voice.

"Danny – it's me, Michael – your Uncle Michael..."

"Hey! How are you, man? It's been a long time – I didn't recognize your voice..."

In fact, he hadn't seen or heard Michael for at least three years. Years before – before his father died and before Michael had gone to Edmonton – his uncle had been an integral part of his life. Michael played for the Toronto Maple Leafs then and they'd had season's ticket seats in the golds. His father would take him to Saturday night games at which he generally fell asleep before the end of the game. He remembered the awe of the kids at school when they found out his uncle was Michael McGrath... then there was his eighth birthday – just before his father died – when Michael had arranged for the kids invited to his birthday party to watch a Leafs' practice where they could actually talk to their heroes. Every kid in his class had offered to be his best friend forever if he could be invited...

"I'm at the airport, Danny. I'm just getting a rental car, then I thought I'd come over there... Okay with you?"

"Sure, Uncle Michael..."

"Michael's fine – now you're almost grown up. You've finished school, I guess, for the year?"

"Yup..."

"And your Mom's at work and the other kids're at school?"

"Yes..."

"So let's you and me have a man-to-man, eh?"

"That's great Uncle – Michael. I'll expect you in half an hour or so – right?"

"About that. See you, Danny."

Danny hung up the phone and went out to collect his breakfast dishes from the patio table. A visit from Michael was just about the last thing he'd ever expected. His uncle had retired from the NHL a little over two years before when recurring shoulder injuries had ended his career. When Danny, Megan and Byron had visited their Grandma McGrath, the Christmas before last, she had told them that Michael and Judith had moved to Vancouver and Michael was working for an insurance company. They'd heard nothing since then, although Mom had – as she usually did – sent Christmas and birthday gifts to his little cousin Angus on his, Megan's and Byron's behalf. Although Mom hadn't drawn attention to it, he'd noticed that there had not even been a Christmas card in return – well, he'd noticed, then forgotten about it. In fact, he hadn't really thought about Michael for a long time. He used to think about him a lot in the first few years after his father died, but that was only natural, he supposed. An eight-year-old kid, he'd lost his father, then his uncle within months of each other. Mentally, he must have been hanging on to those memories – afraid to let them go – then, as time went on, they had gradually ceased to be constantly on his mind. Michael was still firmly positioned as the hero of his childhood – that perception would never change – but he never really thought about him any more. Well, he had no choice now, had he? Michael was on his way over. Would he recognize him? Would *Michael* recognize *him*? After all, he was the one who had likely changed the most – he had been twelve-and-a-half three years ago when they visited Michael and Judith and little Angus in Edmonton, before heading to Jasper, then down to Banff National Park on their summer vacation. Michael had joined him and Byron, and the dog, Ben, in the tent they had pitched on his back lawn and they'd talked nearly all night. It had been fun – for him, anyway. Byron had been pretty bored – he'd still been a baby in the good old days, after all.

Danny stacked the dishes in the dishwasher and put on some fresh coffee then, calling Ben to come with him, went out to the front porch. He sat down on one of the rattan chairs there and put his feet up on the railing. Ben wriggled underneath the chair and lay down in the shade.

He thought about the years before his eighth birthday. Michael had been his favourite uncle long before the fact that he was a professional hockey player – a Toronto Maple Leaf, had any significance for him. Of course, his only other uncle (unless you counted Michael's sisters' husbands which Danny did not) lived in Australia and was hardly in a position to complete. He had to admit that the reflected glory had been a big factor in their relationship by the time he went to school and discovered that staying up on a Saturday night to watch your uncle play hockey on television was not the prize for good behaviour in other kids' homes that it was in his. Then, by the time he was in grade two, the Summit Series had made hockey so high profile, that – as Michael McGrath's nephew – he was as exalted among his classmates as if he played on Team Canada himself. It wasn't long before everything changed, though. Sure, the kids had been told to be nice to him because his father had been killed, but they seemed to forget that his father was Michael McGrath's brother and that the tragedy was his, too. Of course, Michael wasn't playing well! After the disastrous Stanley Cup season that year, it felt almost as if the cry to drop McGrath had originated from Danny's grade two classroom at Islington's Twin Oaks Public School.

Danny awoke from his reverie with a start as a red Ford pulled into the driveway. Ben scrambled out from under the chair, barking ferociously.

"Shut up, Ben," Danny said sharply, grabbing unsuccessfully at Ben's collar.

The dog half tumbled down the steps and dashed, still barking, to the car. Michael opened the door causing Ben to jump away backwards. Danny picked him up.

"Guess he doesn't remember me," Michael said, getting out of the car. "So how's things, Danny?"

"Great! Shut up, Ben." Danny shook the dog who was growling deep in his throat. "He'll be all right when he gets used to you. Come round the back. I just made some coffee." He led the way to the patio at the back of the house and tentatively set Ben down.

"You go and get the coffee and I'll attempt to renew acquaintance," Michael said, sitting down at the patio table and putting his had out to Ben. "Come along, Ben. You remember me don't you, old boy? I know it was only a one night stand, but it's hardly sociable to forget the people you've slept with..."

Danny grinned as he went into the house for the coffee.

By the time he returned with two mugs of coffee, Michael was scratching Ben's ears and Ben was favouring him with the adoring look he reserved for family members.

"He's a suck, really. He always acts like that when somebody comes, but I don't think he'd be much use if it was a burglar or something." He put the coffee on the table and sat down. "You do still take it black, right?"

"Sure. How come you remembered?"

"Probably because I copied you. When we visited you in Edmonton, I was just starting to drink coffee and you drank it black, so I thought that was the macho thing to do."

"That's a joke..."

"No kidding. Kinda dumb to admit it... but, there you are."

They both attempted to sip some coffee and found it too hot. Michael put his mug down.

"So how was the first year of high school?"

"How come you remember this was my first year of high school?"

"I'm in insurance nowadays – you have to know a bit more arithmetic than you need to in hockey."

They both laughed.

"School was okay. I have a job as a camp counsellor next week, so this week's for taking it easy. How long are you here for? It's Megan's graduation tomorrow night. She's hoping to get the art prize. She's accepted for the School of Visual Arts next year."

"She always was the artist, wasn't she? Remember how miffed you were when she won that Easter Bunny colouring contest in the newspaper that year?"

"Yeah. I was pretty jealous. I thought I was so grown up – I was the one who went to kindergarten – and I remember really resenting all the attention she got. Then you came over and took us both down to the Dairy Queen for ice cream and gave us a long lecture about people having different talents and the importance of being supportive of your sisters and brothers, etc."

"You remember that? I thought it all went over your heads."

"Most of it did, but a lot stayed with me. I've been Megan's champion ever since, but I still haven't found out what my talent is."

Michael laughed. "Diplomacy, perhaps?"

"You never know. Anyway, how's life after hockey? Or should I exercise some diplomacy there?"

"Oh no, no. I'm used to it now. I'm no Gordie Howe – it was just too tough on the old bod after all the years of constant punishment. I'm just glad I had the experience of playing with the Leafs in the glory years. And the Edmonton years – helping to build a new team – were good. I have a hunch my son's going to wish I'd hung on long enough to play with Wayne Gretsky – he'll be the next hockey icon, you wait and see. Anyway, I lived the dream of thousands of Canadian kids for seventeen seasons – so I'm not about to complain."

"So what are you doing? Grandma told us you were in insurance..."

"That's right, Danny – insurance, the graveyard of all old hockey players."

"I thought–" Danny began, when his uncle fell silent.

"You thought professional hockey players made so much money they could just sit around doing nothing without having to worry about putting bread on the table when their careers were over? That's what they all think – all those kids dying to make it to the NHL. But the reality is a broken down body and very little money to fall back on. Oh, there's the players' union now and a decent pension plan, but my career had already peaked by the time that got going, and before endorsements could be counted on to boost the kitty, for that matter. It's all wrong you know, Danny. Starry-eyed kids are signed up – their education interrupted, never to be finished – made to think they're really something with all the adulation and hero worship, then they're spat out unqualified for anything."

Michael was silent. Danny didn't know what to say.

" Sorry, Danny," Michael said, finally, "I'll climb down off my soapbox while you go get me a refill, okay?"

Danny took the mug and went into the house. He wished Mom were here. He really didn't know how to handle this. Michael was obviously very upset about something. He sounded so bitter – not at all like the fun uncle he used to be. Suddenly he felt resentful – who did Michael think he was anyway? He's more or less excused himself from my life for seven years – nearly half of it, more than half of it really when you consider you don't exactly know what's going down anyway for the first three years of your life – and now he turns up and lays this on me. He poured coffee into the mugs, then stood looking at them not wanting to go back outside.

"Hey, look – I'm sorry Danny." Michael slid open the screen door and came in. "I didn't mean to come on the bitter old man like that. The truth is I'm really quite happy in the insurance business – I just wish I'd known a lot more about insurance before. The problem is that my wife isn't happy about it." He paused and Danny immediately guessed what was coming. "Judith's left me for somebody else – guy with a real career and a decent, steady income. And…"

"I'm sorry, Uncle Michael. Really I am." Danny didn't know what to say now. This really was turning out to be a man-to-man chat and he wasn't ready for it! "Um – here's your coffee. It got a bit strong sitting in the pot while we were out there talking." He took his own mug over to the kitchen table and sat down. "What about Angus – where's he?" He could have kicked himself once he realised what a painful question that must be for Michael.

"He's with them. What can I do? A kid needs his mother more than his father at age six. Would you guys have wanted to leave your mother when your parents split up?"

"It was a bit different. Mom didn't go off with anybody and we didn't need to be brain surgeons to figure out that Dad couldn't look after us." He paused, then asked, "Does Grandma know?"

Michael shook his head. "No – that's what I'm here for. Only I haven't summoned up the courage to get myself there yet." He grinned and looked once again like the Uncle Michael Danny used to know. "Hey, let's cheer up – chuck this coffee down the sink where it rightfully belongs and go out to lunch somewhere. You can help me get ready to face your grandmother, okay?

. . . . .

Danny felt an immense relief when Michael dropped him off before driving up to the Newmarket home of his older sister – Danny's Aunt Laura – whose house had recently been partitioned to create a granny flat for her mother. Michael had never been to the house, not having visited Laura and her family since they had moved there, and was relieved when Danny confirmed that Grandma's part was completely separate from the rest of the house. He also convinced him to phone her first since she was getting quite old and frail now, which was the reason she had agreed to live at Laura's in the first place. Michael said he couldn't imagine his mother being old and frail but, then, he hadn't seen her since he retired from hockey and went to Vancouver to live. He went to the phone in the restaurant lobby to let her know he was in town and would be up to see her in the late afternoon. Danny had asked the waiter to bring the bill while Michael was out at the phone and pretended he thought they were ready to go. In fact, he figured Michael would have another beer and had visions of him being stopped by the police on the way to Newmarket. Well, to be honest, he was imagining worse than that after what Michael had been telling him. His uncle seemed a little surprised, when he came back to the table, but took out a credit card and put it down on the tray with the bill. He just talked about how much Newmarket had probably changed since he was last there while they waited for the waiter to come back.

"Guess I *am* a diplomat," he told Ben, letting out the dog who had been shut in the house while they were gone. Ben didn't seem very interested and ran off to sniff around for a good place to relieve himself. "Here, I'll get your leash and we'll go for a walk."

Walking along the road to the hydro right-of-way, he thought about all the things he had found out from the talk with Michael – things he'd only been half aware of or had no idea about at all...

Michael had been mostly worried about how Grandma would react to his and Judith's separation. Apparently she'd gone ballistic when Danny's father and mother had split up and still blamed his mother for his father's death. Then, there was the impetus for the little intrigue with the bill – Michael had told him that his father's fatal accident had been caused by drunk driving... his father had been bombed when he got into his car that night.

These revelations had not really surprised him. Perhaps he had actually been aware of them, at some subconscious level, all the time. There'd always been an icy politeness when you referred to Mom when speaking to Grandma McGrath and vice versa and he'd never known for sure why that was. It must have been really tough for Mom all these years – encouraging them to visit Grandma, ensuring that they did, yet really wishing she didn't feel obliged to insist on it.

They reached the hydro right-of-way and Danny let Ben off his leash.

"Come on, Ben, let's clear our heads..." he shouted to the dog as he began to run across the grass. He ran until he developed a stitch in his side then threw himself down in the grass, rolled over and lay with his hands behind his head. Ben lay panting beside him.

He didn't really remember his parents' separation as having any great impact on his life. It coincided with the time when he was riding high on the wave of Michael's popularity after Team Canada beat the Russians and the Leafs were still the team that every little kid fantasized playing for. Nearly everyone in his class wanted to be his best friend and both he and Megan were invited to so many birthday parties that their mother would laughingly say that she couldn't keep up with all the gifts she had to buy. Their lives were very busy, then, and possibly the only difference had been that he and Megan – Byron was too little for his father to feel comfortable about taking him with them – saw more of their father than before although, in retrospect, that may have had as much to do with the fact that he was, by that time, working for the family firm rather than because of the separation. Those months up to and including his eighth birthday party at the Gardens had passed on a cloud of euphoria. Then the accident had happened.

"Hey, Danny! Danny!"

Ben jumped up and tore away across the hydro field before Danny sat up to find his brother and two other kids coming towards him. Because of the long lunch, it didn't feel like time for them to be coming home from school yet. He wished he'd thought of it and gone somewhere else – he did not feel like listening to a bunch of hyperactive ten-year-olds.

"Hey, Danny! What are you doing lying in the middle of the hydro field?"

"I was taking Ben for a run and decided to lie down in the sun and rest – anything wrong with that?"

Byron shrugged. "Guess not. Come and play baseball with us?"

"Here?"

"No, in the park. Some other kids got out early and have gone ahead to make sure nobody starts using the diamond before we all get there."

"I have to take Ben home," Danny said, getting to his feet and starting to walk away.

"Well, pardon me for living," said Byron, witheringly, "I didn't know you'd got too big to play baseball with us."

"Oh, knock it off, Byron. Aren't you supposed to come straight home from school anyway?" He quickened his pace. "Come on, Ben. Let's go." He began to trot with Ben at his heels.

"Come on, guys," he heard Byron saying behind him, "never mind my jerk brother…"

He decided not to go home, however, but to walk over to the new apartment complex where his friend, Shawn, lived. Maybe they could go swimming in the apartment pool.

· · · · ·

"You know who showed up this morning?" Danny said, as he and Shawn got into the elevator to go back up to Shawn's apartment after their swim.

"Who?"

"My uncle – Michael. Remember…?"

"Sure, the hockey player – whatever became of him?"

"What?" Fame sure was transient. "Oh – he lives in Vancouver now. He gave up hockey a couple of years ago."

"He can't be that old, can he? I mean, I remember how he kinda lost it after your father died…" – Shawn was never very tactful – "but he could still play pretty reasonably, couldn't he?"

"Well, he's pushing forty – he was a Leaf all the times they won the Stanley Cup in the sixties, you know. Anyway, he's had some pretty bad shoulder injuries and didn't play much in his last couple of seasons."

They reached Shawn's floor, got out of the elevator and walked along the passage.

"You wanna stay for supper?" Shawn asked, as he unlocked the door.

"Sure. I don't feel much like going home at the moment. I shouldn't have brought Ben here, though."

Ben, who'd been left in the apartment, greeted them by jumping wildly up on his hind legs.

"It's okay. My Mom's always saying that that's the one thing she regrets about moving to an apartment – not being able to have a dog. She'll give him all the left-overs. Here, throw us your things and I'll put them in the laundry bin. There's pop in the fridge."

Danny passed his borrowed swimming trunks and towel to Shawn who took them into the bathroom, while Danny got two cans of pop from the kitchen and took them out onto the balcony.

"So what did your uncle have to say, then?" Shawn said when he came out of the bathroom and followed Danny out to the balcony.

"Oh, he's pretty uptight. His wife's gone off with some other guy and taken their little kid and – well, I guess life after hockey's not too wicked. He took me out to lunch – I think he just needed a sounding board before he went to my grandmother's. He's worried about telling her because she doesn't approve of divorce but he's afraid not to... in case she hears it from someone else and makes an even worse scene – worse than she would if he told her, I mean... He must have got it over with by now. I wonder what happened...?"

"But *your* parents were divorced weren't they?"

"Actually they weren't. They'd only had a legal separation for a few months before my dad was killed. But that's what makes it worse – you see, my grandmother figures my mother drove my father to drink. He was polluted when he smashed up his car and got killed, you see. Michael says that it had nothing to do with my mother – my dad was always drinking and womanizing. That's why Mom wanted out in the first place. Then he tells me about all the other family skeletons and it's all so weird because the McGrath women – my grandma and my Aunt Laura and my Aunt Frances – always act like their shit doesn't stink. I mean, I always felt like they looked down on us – Mom and us – Byron, Megan and me, I mean. You'd think it was Mom who'd done all the drinking and running around. And, you know the really *really* stupid part?"

"What?"

"The company they own – McGrath-LaPlante – guess what they make?  I never even knew until Michael told me – rubber-based medical devices. And you know what the most profitable rubber-based medical device is?"

Shawn shrugged.

"The key word's *rubber*."

"You mean they make *safes* – condoms?"

Danny nodded.

"Isn't that a laugh? Oh, they make other stuff as well – surgical gloves and things..."

"You sure it's not a joke. I mean, I'm not trying to pretend I'm some kind of an expert or anything..."

"Oh, you wouldn't know it as a brand name. Some British company owns most of *them*. McGrath-LaPlante co-packs – makes stuff for other companies."

"Well, you're sure gonna get popular fast."

"Don't be an ass – we don't have anything to do with it now. I know for a fact that they made my Mom sell the shares she inherited when my Dad died, back to my Grandma McGrath. Well, not made her exactly – she wanted to get away from the McGraths anyway, I guess. Don't you go telling anyone what I've told you, Shawn – I don't want guys thinking I can get them free condoms when I can't..."

"You there, Shawn?" The apartment door slammed and Shawn's mother was calling from the hallway. "Well – hello, Ben, your master over here to use the swimming pool again, then?" She called through to the balcony, "Hi there, Danny..."

"Hi, Mrs. Ellis."

"Hi, Mom," said Shawn, "is it okay if Danny stays for supper?"

"Of course, but it's only tuna casserole. Just put the oven on for me and then I need the two of you to run down to the car and bring the shopping up for me. Here's the key. And, Danny–"

"Yeah?"

"Call your mother and let her know where you are when you get back up here."

"I was going to."

"Good. Shawn usually forgets to call me."

Shawn took the keys and the two boys went down to the underground parking garage to get the shopping for Shawn's mother.

·  ·  ·  ·  ·

By the time Danny arrived home, he had decided to say nothing to his mother of the conversation with Michael beyond the fact that his uncle had taken him for lunch and was visiting Grandma McGrath because Judith had left him and taken Angus with her.

She had never told any of them about the reasons for splitting up with their father or anything about their father's death other than the fact that he was killed in a car accident. So Danny figured that it was best to let her go on thinking that he knew only what she had told Megan and himself, at the time, and reinforced later when things had to be explained to Byron, who had not yet turned three at the time of their father's death. He decided that he'd make a determined effort to be nicer to her and not goof off when he was supposed to be home to look after his little brother – like on Saturday. She must have made an lot of sacrifices for her children and probably been pretty hurt by the attitude of the McGraths over the years.

## MARILYN

I remember the day my mother-in-law died because it was the day I would have liked to celebrate as the tenth anniversary of my life as a single parent, despite the fact that there was nobody to celebrate with. That was before Laura called me, of course. Things were slow that day and I had a lot of time to mentally review the events of ten years before. Maybe it wasn't so much that things were slow as that I was, finally, at a point in life where I could start to think about moving on. Even five years before, I had had enough of the personnel industry and looked forward to the day when I could risk trying something else without endangering my ability to support myself and my children. The days of channelling a large portion of my earnings into childcare costs were past and, now, with Byron in junior high school, I could surely start thinking about being my own person again. At least, I thought I could...

I'd started working part time for the personnel agency when Megan was old enough to attend the nearby co-operative nursery school. By working in the mornings while Danny and Megan attended the school and taking my turn as a helper at one of the afternoon sessions each week, I managed to earn enough money, after paying the children's fees, to ensure that we had food to eat and clothes to wear in the face of my husband's erratic contributions to the household finances. Later, after Byron was born and I found a reliable baby-sitter for him, my hours gradually increased until, by the time the older children were both at school all day, I was earning enough money to manage alone when the time came. And the time came quite quickly after that. When your children start asking why you don't know where Daddy is or when he's coming home and why he's too tired to play with them when he *is* home, you know that – quite apart from how they feel about him – they won't have too much respect for you, either, by the time they're old enough to know what's going on – if you allow the situation to continue, that is.

While I hadn't recognized it until I had two infants and no room to manoeuvre, my husband, Angus, had been in a permanent state of adolescence since I'd first known him. I must have had an outsize inferiority complex. Today, I suppose, it would be described as being totally lacking in self esteem; people don't seem to talk about inferiority complexes any more. Whatever the reason, I was flattered by his attention and it took a few more years of growing up before I realized that the attraction wasn't so much due to his being as madly in love with me as I was with him, as it was to my insistence on the fanciful notion of maintaining my virginity for the marriage bed. I was a romantic. At least, that's how I saw it then. Hindsight sees it more as being blissfully ignorant and unimaginative, but we hadn't yet received the benefits of women's liberation in the early nineteen-sixties. We were really still fifties' people with all those double standards that men enjoyed firmly in place. I sometimes swear that women like my mother-in-law actually liked being martyrs. I realise that few women in that era of the respectable philanderer had the earning potential to embark upon separate lives for themselves and their children, but there are many who actually see their miserable lives as an accomplishment.

Nine years of the kind of lifestyle that was the pride and joy of Isabel McGrath had been enough for me. I never met *her* Angus McGrath, father of Laura, Frances, *my* Angus McGrath and Michael and progenitor of several grandchildren including my own three children and the newest Angus, now safely ensconced on Vancouver Island with his mother and stepfather. *Her* Angus had succumbed to the excesses of his male-dominated era in a hotel room in Montreal by the time I met his son. The official version of his death was that he had suffered a fatal heart attack while there on business. The details involved the obligatory wild partying of a three day convention of medical devices manufacturers, followed by sexual gymnastics with the twenty-three year old receptionist from the company's Montreal office and, depending upon who was telling the story, various snide remarks about testing the integrity of the company's products. Since then – for the last twenty years – Laura's husband, Dennis LaPlante, had been running McGrath-LaPlante without benefit of a Montreal office, Laura's strategy for a successful marriage being to ensure the removal of all temptation – though, quite frankly, I doubt that Dennis ever had the genetic proclivity required to compete with the reputation of the McGrath members – *double entendre* intended – of the company.

Laura called, that day, just as we were finishing supper. It was almost a reinforcement of the reminiscences I had been unable to get out of my head all day.

"I thought I should let you know, Marilyn, that Mother passed away this afternoon."

"I'm so sorry Laura," I said, trying – as I usually did on the rare occasions when I spoke with my ex-sister-in-law – not to let her condescending air get to me. "Is there anything I can do?" There was a long pause. I decided that she wasn't pleased with my offer but tried to convince myself that she was just upset and the silence was not a reflection on me. "Have you called Michael?" I asked for something to say.

"Michael's on his way. He booked a flight for this afternoon after I talked to him yesterday. We thought he'd be in time to see her and, perhaps, make his peace with her before – before she went."

I wondered how Laura managed to continue to sound like a relic of the last century despite, surely, having had to confront today's world in bringing up her daughters during the two decades when social and economic change had more impact on attitudes and behaviour than ever before. I had not seen the girls since they were in high school and beginning to chafe a little under the constraints imposed by their parents, but they'd both been through university since then and, as far as I knew, were relatively normal. I tried to think what to say and wished Megan or Danny had answered the phone instead of Byron. Laura would have communicated her news directly to one of them and I'd have had a chance to prepare myself for talking to her.

"Well... perhaps I should let you go, but please will you or Frances – or Michael – let us know when you've made the arrangements..."

"Of course," Laura said. "We'll talk to you tomorrow."

The three children watched me as I put down the phone.

"Grandma McGrath died this afternoon," I said.

They were not terribly close to Isabel McGrath although I had done my best, since their father died, to encourage them in maintaining a relationship with his family in spite of Isabel's coldness towards me. I had also ensured that they had all three visited her during her final hospitalization.

"Will we be going to the funeral?" asked Byron.

"By-*ron*," said Megan, reprovingly.

"Well, I've never been to a funeral and, it's not like it's a big surprise. I mean, she was old and everything..."

"Knock it off, Byron," said Danny, glaring at his younger brother.

"Sor-*ry*," Byron stood up. "May I leave the table?"

"You haven't finished your pumpkin pie," I said. It had been Thanksgiving the previous weekend and we were still eating our way through the three pumpkin pies Megan had made.

"I've sort of... had enough..." He looked at me, pleadingly. "Okay, Mom?"

"Okay," I said. "But finish your homework before you watch TV."

"I've finished, but I'm going to my room."

He left the room and we heard him slowly going upstairs.

"There's no need to get mad at him, you know," I said to the older two. "He doesn't know how to behave – he's *has* never been to a funeral before and it's not as if he really even knew her very well. You two knew her a lot better than he did."

"Only because we were supposedly old enough to go and stay overnight when she still had the house," said Megan.

"He stayed overnight with her, too."

"Not as often as we had to. He was always too hyper and you'd say he was better off in his own bed, remember?"

Megan, with all the wisdom of sixteen, was going through a phase of being highly critical of her younger brother's upbringing.

There were constant implications that his was a life of ease and luxury compared to the supposedly rigid standards that had been imposed on her and Danny. I decided not to let myself be provoked.

"Let's not get into that now, Megan." I said, mildly, "I'm going to need some support from you and Danny."

"What d'you mean?" asked Danny.

"Well – you're surely both old enough and smart enough to realise that my relationship with the McGraths is not exactly warm and cosy. I've never discussed it with you because I didn't want it to impact on how you got along with them."

"What you mean is you think you should go to the funeral..." Danny grinned, "and you need us to protect you from the McGraths, right?"

"Yeah – sort of..." I said and we all three laughed.

"P'raps we can go with Uncle Michael," suggested Megan. "I mean, he's been a bad guy, too, the last couple of years as far as Grandma was concerned..."

"That's a little different though. *He* got mad at *her* because she put Judith down for breaking up their marriage. She was all into standards to be maintained and stuff like that and thought that marriage was forever, regardless of what happened, and expected Michael to hate Judith because she'd left him. But he didn't see it that way. I mean, he was hurt and upset and everything, but he wasn't about to have her acting as if Judith was some kind of Jezebel so he told her not to expect to see him again until she was ready to apologise."

"And she wasn't into apologising, so he's a black sheep, too – so what's different?"

"Okay, guys," I said, "this is Uncle Michael's business, not ours.

He's on his way, by the way, according to Aunt Laura, and he was actually expecting to get here before Grandma died. Now I'd appreciate you loading the dishwasher and cleaning up here while I go up and talk to Byron and... hey, guys, thanks in advance for protecting me."

. . . . .

Danny was as good as his word at the funeral and never left my side. Megan, at my insistence, did go and talk to her cousin Angela, Frances' daughter. Angela was a few months older than Danny and the three of them had played together as young children. While they didn't often see each other, Megan and Angela would call each other now and again to catch up on each other's lives. I noticed flowers from Judith and Angus and was glad Judith had been so thoughtful – it sort of reinforced the fact that we, one time in-laws, were decent, caring people. Michael said he was glad we had come and that he'd give us a call later. Frances acted as if she and I were the good friends that we had once been – many years ago when we were new mothers together – and talked at length about what a blessed relief her mother's death had been from the cancer that had progressively invaded her body during the last year. Laura asked us back to her house but we'd already agreed to go home from the cemetery, so I invented a test for which Danny had to get back to school and she looked quite relieved.

"I thought we weren't going to have to go back to school," Byron said when we were all in the car and driving away.

"No, I said we'd go somewhere for a late lunch," I replied.

"But you told Aunt Laura that Danny had to be back at school this afternoon."

"It was a little white lie, Byron," I told him. "I was expected to find some excuse not to go to Aunt Laura's and you didn't really want to go all the way up to Newmarket, did you?"

"Guess not..."

"Look... you'll understand better when you're older. Now, where are we going for lunch?"

The question of where to go for lunch occupied most of the drive home and we ended up at the local Swiss Chalet.

"Who was that old, old man in the wheelchair, Mom?" asked Byron when we had ordered our lunch and been served our salads.

"I don't know. Why?"

"He was at the hospital when we went down to see Grandma."

Two weeks ago, after Angela had phoned and told Megan that their grandmother had been taken to hospital, I had driven the three children down to the hospital to visit her.

"He was? Then I expect he's an old friend or business acquaintance."

"You know who I think he is?" said Megan.

"Who?"

"Uncle Dennis's father. He looks just like him – except older, of course."

"You're right," Danny told her. "That guy who was looking after him is Uncle Dennis's nephew, Alan. Remember, Mom, they were at Grandma's once when I was staying there, when I was about ten, and Aunt Laura and Uncle Dennis were there and Aunt Frances and Angela. Angela and I were supposed to do those jig saw puzzles Grandma always gave us to do, but we got bored and spied on them, pretending they were KGB agents or something – we were big on espionage at the time, remember Megan?" He didn't wait for her to reply. "Anyway, I imagine it was actually a shareholders' meeting or something."

"I expect so. I never met any of the LaPlantes – except Uncle Dennis." I said. "Your father wasn't involved with the company until he went to work there after we separated. He was always determined not to be, but I think your grandmother talked him into it at that point."

Actually she had called in the loans she had made to him over the years, to finance the various enterprises that he never managed to get off the ground, and he had no choice but to contribute a McGrath presence at McGrath-LaPlante. The odd thing was that he had actually done quite well in those few short months, before the accident, and landed two key accounts. Perhaps things would have turned out a lot differently if she had made that particular move some years before.

Byron had been waiting patiently to continue his story.

"The nurse wasn't going to let us see Grandma when we went up. She said she'd had enough excitement for one evening. We were going to go down and wait for you to come and pick us up, but she called us back because Grandma told her to. And you know what Grandma said when I went in? Danny and Megan were still talking to the nurse. You know what?"

"No, what did she say?"

"She said it was those LaPlantes the nurse should have kept out. But not to mind because they were going to get the shock of their lives if they thought they were going to run the McGraths out of McGrath-LaPlante. I didn't get it at the time, but I think I do now."

"What do you think she meant, then?" I asked.

"That she'd fixed it – in her will or something – so that they can't run the McGraths out of the company."

"I think you've been watching too many movies –" I began.

"I think he's right, Mom," Megan interrupted. "She really did seem sort of satisfied that day. I thought she was just glad to see us, but now I'm not so sure."

"Why didn't you tell us about this before, Byron?" asked Danny.

"I forgot! You guys came in and you were making a fuss about how the nurse said we were not to excite Grandma and we were only allowed a few minutes and everything. So I forgot all about it until I saw the old guy in the wheelchair and the other one. Is he some relative then?"

"Not to you. No." I said. "The McGraths and the LaPlantes started the business in the eighteen-nineties – that would be your great, great grandfather, his son and Uncle Dennis's grandfather. Cindi and Jayne are the only ones related to both the LaPlantes and the McGraths because your Aunt Laura married Dennis LaPlante. That's really all I know about them. Oh, except that I do remember that Uncle Dennis's brother, who would be – Alan, did you say his name was, Danny?"

"Ah-ha."

"– Alan's father who died when he was quite young – before I met your father. He and his wife were killed in a plane crash in Nevada or somewhere and the boy was brought up by his grandparents."

"And, now, Alan is the Crown Prince of McGrath-LaPlante," said Megan, "or thinks he is... I wonder what Grandma had up her sleeve."

"I expect she's left her shares to Michael or something with some kind of provision that will ensure he takes some active role in the business," suggested Danny.

"I don't know about that." I said, "Michael might not be as well off as he was in his hockey days, but I can't see him working with the LaPlantes. Anyway, it doesn't concern us, so let's talk about something else."

The next day, I discovered just how much it did concern us.

$$\cdot \ \cdot \ \cdot \ \cdot \ \cdot$$

Michael phoned me at about eleven-thirty that morning.

"Do you have plans for lunch, Marilyn?" he asked.

"No," I responded, puzzled. "Are you asking me to lunch – or doing a survey on what personnel counsellors do at lunch time?"

He laughed. "I have to talk to you about something. Can you meet me at – let's see, what's around there? How about Black Angus?"

I wasn't really crazy about steak at lunch time but it was probably easier to meet a retired hockey jock who hadn't lived in Toronto for many years, at a place he knew. I could always have a light supper.

"Sure. Okay," I said.

"Twelve-thirty?"

"I'll be there. Do you want me to make a reservation? We keep the number handy here."

"Thanks. See you then – and, Marilyn..."

"Yes?"

"Don't take any personal phone calls until after I've seen you. Maybe you can ask your receptionist to screen your calls."

"Why?" I asked – to say the least – astonished.

"You'll understand when I see you. Trust me – it's only an hour. I'd get there sooner but I'm car-less. I drove down with Laura. So, I'll use the subway. I could get a cab, but it seems a bit silly."

"Okay, Michael," I said. "I'll see you at twelve-thirty."

I only had to walk a couple of blocks along Bloor Street, but he was there ahead of me. He smiled and rose from the table as the *maitre d'* led me over.

"Hi there." He leaned across the table and kissed me on the cheek. "I've just ordered a beer. Would you like something to drink?"

"I'll just have a glass of white wine," I said as the waiter arrived with his beer.

"A glass of white wine for the lady, please."

"So what's going on?" I asked, as the waiter moved away.

"I'm  sorry if I came across – well, like –" he grinned, "like Harold Ballard ordering the guys not to talk to the media, but – you see – I didn't want Laura or Dennis to get hold of you before I'd told you…"

"Told me what?"

The busboy brought a basket of fresh bread and butter and the waiter arrived with my drink.

"Are you ready to order?" he asked.

"Just give us a few minutes." Michael told him. "Cheers." He raised his glass.

"Told me what, Michael?" I asked again, after raising my glass and then sipping my wine.

"Well, Laura and Frances and I and my brothers-in-law and a few assorted LaPlantes had a meeting this morning at Merv Connor's, the McGrath lawyer – you remember him?"

"I remember him," I said, remembering another meeting in the offices of Conner, Taylor and McDermott nearly ten years ago. "Look, Michael, so you had the –" I thought for a minute, then came up with, "– the Reading of the Will, or whatever you want to call it. What's it got to do with me?"

"A lot, I'm afraid." He paused as the waiter hovered near again. "Look let's order first. Do you want salad?"

We ordered our salads and steaks.

"Did you ever know anything about the share structure of McGrath-LaPlante?"

"Only that Isabel commanded me to return Angus's shares when I inherited them as his next of kin. Oh – she paid whatever they were valued at and, at the time, the money was of more use to me than shares in a family company that I knew nothing about anyway, but it was a royal command all the same."

"Yes, I remember." The waiter brought the salads. "Can you bring another Export, please?" he asked him.

We both nibbled some lettuce leaves until Michael continued. "You see, originally, back in the late eighteen-nineties, the first Angus McGrath – well, I don't know if he was the first exactly, there were likely a whole line of them. Anyway, the first Angus and Everton LaPlante owned the company fifty-fifty as a partnership. Angus's oldest son – also called Angus – worked with them, but wasn't part of the partnership. Things took off and they incorporated. Angus and Everton each had forty per cent of the stock, Angus, the son, ten and Everton's brother the other ten. The shares have stayed divided evenly between the two families but the McGraths – except for a few years during the war when Denny LaPlante took over because my father was overseas and my grandfather in poor health – always ran the company until my father died. As you know, he died unexpectedly and there was no McGrath in place to take over. There was a LaPlante though who had his MBA and had taken his place in the company and worked there for several years... and was really the best person to be the CEO despite his relative youth. It would probably have happened the same way if my father hadn't died. Dennis was the obvious person to succeed him."

I nodded. Angus was still in university when his father died and Michael was in Junior A expecting to be drafted by an NHL team. The Angus I knew was certainly not temperamentally suited to running the company however much his parents chose to fondly imagine he was.

"My mother always expected Angus, eventually, to come into the company in some capacity." Michael continued. "So when he did, finally, start working there in sales it really made her day – she had plans for him to have a seat on the board and everything. Then he was killed. The reason she was so spooked about you having stock was because Laura was married to Dennis and – to Mother's mind – that made her shares virtually Dennis's, so she wasn't about to let the McGrath holdings get depleted any further by you having my brother's."

"So Dennis, his father and his nephew have or control all the original LaPlante shares and assume they have Laura's in the bag, too, and your mother was determined not to let them run the McGraths out of McGrath-LaPlante?" I asked. Michael drew his eyebrows together in a puzzled frown. I laughed. "Not my terminology – a remark she apparently made to my son."

"Danny?"

"No, Byron. He had no idea what she meant, but after seeing the LaPlantes at the funeral yesterday, he was reminded of it and told the rest of us." I wondered whether to tell him the rest of the children's fantasy but, instead, said, "So she expects you to become the new McGrath half of McGrath-LaPlante?"

"No." Michael shook his head. "She expects you to."

At first I thought I'd not heard him right and re-played the conversation in my mind.

"What do you mean, Michael. I have nothing to do with McGrath-LaPlante. Isabel hated me. She held me responsible for her son's death, remember?"

"I'm not about to pretend that isn't true, Marilyn. But you have to remember, at that time, women of her generation thought the women's liberation movement was nothing more than a gang of redneck lesbians. They firmly believed in being the woman behind the –"

"– the respectable philanderer. I know, Michael, I never held it against her. I just wasn't about to live my life that way and I got out. Angus's death could have happened any time before or after I made that decision. I knew that then and I know it now – I've never allowed what she thought to bother me. But it doesn't alter the fact that that *is* what she thought – so what are you saying about me becoming a McGrath-LaPlante McGrath? I'm not even a real McGrath."

"I think what actually happened is that during the last couple of years, she started to look at things differently – after the house became too much for her and she moved into the granny flat at Laura's, she saw more of the LaPlantes, including the old man who perhaps really does want to run the McGraths out before he kicks off. There was Alan progressively working in different areas, learning the business the way Dennis had before him and, quite obviously being groomed to eventually take over from Dennis. That was not as apparent when her only contact with them was at board meetings. Then she and I had the difference of opinion over Judith. It was probably Judith doing what for Mother was the traditional form of marriage break-up disgrace – *going off with another man*" – he mimed quotation marks – "that made her start to see you differently. Maybe she even came to admire you for – well, for being your own person and not letting what happened get your children mixed up or emotionally disturbed – whatever."

He was silent for a moment. The waiter arrived with our steaks.

"Then, of course, you have to remember when Laura and Dennis were married, everybody expected my father to be running the company for many years to come and for Angus to join the firm after university – in other words, there was no shortage of McGraths. But that's not the way things turned out."

"Why not you, Michael?" I asked. "Why did she never try to get you to join the company – when you retired from hockey, I mean?"

"That's easy. Judith was from out west and wanted to live there. We'd been in Edmonton for nearly five years – long enough for me to think twice about living in Toronto again. I thought about it after Judith and I broke up, but I realized I was happier staying where I was – in insurance you build up your sales to suit yourself. I wouldn't want to be in a situation where the level of productivity of other people was dependent on how well or badly I did. Besides my hockey pension – for what it's worth – and my McGrath-LaPlante dividends are enough for my own needs, so I only need to earn whatever I contribute to Angus's upbringing and education – I mean, I'm not motivated to be an ace salesman and I'm not qualified for anything else – well, there's the assembly lines or something, but production was always the LaPlantes' stronghold. By that time Mother wasn't speaking to me, anyway."

We both paid serious attention to chewing steak for a few minutes.

"To get back to the current situation," Michael said. "My grandfather was *his* father's only surviving child, so he had inherited the entire block of McGrath stock, half of which he transferred to my father when he took over the management of McGrath-LaPlante after the war. Then, when he died, he left the other half equally divided between his grandchildren. Without getting into all the arithmetic, my mother has left all her stock – the twenty-five per cent that was my father's and the six-point-two-five per cent that was my brother's – to you in trust for Danny, Megan and Byron."

"I see," I said in a small voice. "Laura and Frances and the LaPlantes must be furious."

"Yes, but not as furious as they are about some of the conditions."

"What do you mean?"

"You are to be the new Director of Human Resources at McGrath-LaPlante –"

"But –"

Michael held up his hand. "Hear me out. If, for reasons beyond your control – i.e. somebody in the company objects – the entire block of shares goes to the Canadian Cancer Society with the proviso that they cannot sell them for fifty years. Obviously there are no saints at McGrath-LaPlante falling over themselves to pay more than thirty percent of the company's dividends to the Cancer Society for fifty years, so you get the job..."

"And, if I don't take it –?" I already knew the answer.

"– the shares go to The Canadian Cancer Society," we echoed each other.

"Did you enjoy your lunch?" asked the waiter, appearing out of nowhere. I looked at my empty steak board and realized that I didn't remember eating anything.

"I think I'd like a cup of coffee, please." I said.

. . . . .

I met with Merv Connor, at the Willowdale offices of Connor, Taylor and McDermott, at ten-thirty the next morning. He gave me the details of my children's inheritance. Isabel's McGrath-LaPlante stock was to be held in trust for them until, in each case, they earned a university degree. I knew that this was more because Isabel did not approve of the age of majority being lowered to eighteen than because she valued the education involved. The dividends were to be used to pay for the tuition fees and living expenses required for their post secondary education. Perhaps, I thought, she hadn't believed that I'd invested the payment she made me for Angus's stock for just that purpose. Meantime I was to become the McGrath factor both on the board and within the management team at McGrath-LaPlante. The current Vice President Human Resources was soon to retire and Merv Connor was of the opinion that this was what had given Isabel the idea of using me as a kind of stand-in McGrath for a few years until one or more of my children was old enough join the firm. She appeared, he told me, to be in no doubt about my ability to do the job.

"That's all very fine, Mr. Connor, I'm quite sure I can do the job, too, but that's not the point, is it?" I said. "Nobody at McGrath-LaPlante is happy about my having the job – the last thing they want is a – well, a surrogate McGrath holding the fort until some real McGraths are available. I know for a fact that old Denny

LaPlante was at the hospital just last week attempting to find out what arrangements Isabel had made – poor old lady's dying of cancer and he and his nephew are down there making like a flock of vultures... Whichever way you look at it, though, they probably figured they'd seen the last of the McGraths – both LaPlantes and McGraths assumed she would leave everything divided equally between her three surviving children. Frances and Michael would most likely have sold all their shares, at whatever the fair market value is, to Dennis or Alan, and got on with their own lives and Laura's practically a LaPlante anyway. Instead, they're stuck with me – virtually an outsider – holding more than thirty per cent of the stock in trust for my children, the oldest of whom is unlikely to be ready to take his place, as they all so picturesquely put it, for at least five or six years. It hardly makes for a warm and cosy situation!"

"Isabel held the fort for over twenty years, Ms. McGrath. She was not active in management, I grant you, but she maintained a McGrath presence in that company while both her sons – first your late husband, then Michael – failed her. She, in fact, transferred her hopes to her grandchildren some time before her cancer was diagnosed."

"She did? Then why didn't she let her family in on her plans? And avoid the ill-feeling which is going to result from this–this crazy will."

"My honest opinion, Ms. McGrath, is that she felt the shock value would provide the company with a much needed shake up. She was determined to put the McGrath back into McGrath-LaPlante, so to speak, and to do so she had to find a means to empower the McGrath heirs – your two sons. She included your daughter in the program because she thought you might just let all the money go to the Cancer Society if she didn't! And last, but not least, she admired you."

"She didn't even like me."

"No, she didn't. But she admired the way you were bringing up your children, the fact that you had made a career for yourself and, while she would never admit it, your courage in striking out on your own."

"Oh," I said. "It doesn't really have anything to do with courage, does it? I'm lucky enough to have come of age at a time when socio-economic realities enabled women to be accepted as people, rather than adjunct to a husband, and to support their families. I would have liked her to know that – I mean, to have known that I was aware of that..."

"I think she knew. She became a lot more introspective during her later years but pride prevented her from making amends. I think, perhaps, you should regard this opportunity – because, whatever else it is, it *is* an opportunity for achievement – as Isabel's attempt to – shall we say – extend the olive branch?"

"Perhaps you're right... I intend to give it my best shot, anyway."

It's funny – until that point, I had been primarily concerned in finding some way out of the predicament. Now, I found, to my surprise, that I was beginning to see it as something closer to an irresistible challenge.

## MEGAN

Her mother would flip – she just knew she would. But there was no way she could *not* tell her. They had always been open and honest with each other and, quite apart from that, her mother must see him almost every working day and talk to him and everything. There was no way she could have asked him not to say anything – God, he would have thought her so immature! So she'd have to tell Mom and she was bound to object to her going out with him – just on the age thing alone without even getting into the whole LaPlantes and McGraths bit.

Megan picked up the phone again and dialled her best friend Nicki's number.

"Guess what?" She said as soon as Nicki's father had yelled upstairs for Nicki to pick up her extension.

"What?"

"He's asked me out – to dinner and to see *Cats!*..." she paused, then added, "...on Saturday."

"You're joking." Nicki had been hearing about Alan LaPlante's maturity and good looks and interesting conversation for the last three days since he had, according to Megan, danced with her for almost the whole evening at the McGrath-LaPlante Christmas Party.

"No. I just got off the phone. Nicki what am I going to tell my mother?"

"I dunno. Just tell her, I guess..."

"Nicki, what would your mother say if you told her you had a date with someone of thirty? He may even be over thirty – I don't really know."

Nicki was silent, then she said, "I see what you mean. But it's not as if she doesn't know him – I mean, it's not like he's some wild stranger who might take advantage of your youth and naivete or ... you know, the kinds of things mothers think. Like, they've got to see each other at the office the next day..."

"The day after."

"What?"

"The next day's Sunday."

"Oh. Well, you know what I mean." Nicki, said impatiently. "She can hardly suspect him of having ulterior motives, can she? I mean what kind of jerk would seduce someone's kid when he knew he'd have to say *"How was your weekend?"* on Monday morning? I mean, he's not a jerk, is he?"

"Of course he's not." Megan thought for a minute. "As far as that goes, I'll be a lot better off than going out with creeps like Doug Jamieson or Billy Buxton," she continued, "You don't spend the evening constantly fighting off hands, coming at you from all directions, with a mature man."

"I thought you *liked* Doug..."

"He's all right – as a *friend*. But you know how those guys are – they're not really interested in your *mind*, they don't *listen* to what you're saying, they're too busy looking at your boobs to make eye contact. Alan talked to me like he was interested in my mind – he didn't even look at my body."

"You sure he's not gay?"

"Don't be stupid!" Megan said, angrily. "Why would he ask me out if he was gay?"

"Maybe he's after your shares. Don't you remember before your grandmother left her shares to you guys, you used to say that those people were trying to get control of her company – well, isn't he one of them?"

"Oh, that was just Byron and his crazy ideas. And Grandma McGrath, maybe – she was pretty weird. But it wasn't really like that at all. And it's his company, too, anyway. And I don't get to even own my shares until I'm through school and we don't even have our applications in to OCA yet. He knows that, too. We talked about it. He told me how a kid he used to go around with went to OCA and that he really envied him. He more or less had to go to Western – his grandparents expected him to..."

"What about his parents – didn't they have something to say about it?"

"They died when he was just a little kid. His grandparents brought him up."

"Oh. So what's his friend do now?"

"He went commercial after he graduated. Took a course in graphic design at Sheridan and went into advertising."

"Him, and everybody else. What a pain... I hope they don't try to turn us commercial."

"Well, people do have to eat, Nicki," said Megan mildly. "Anyway, I'd better go. I still have the end part of my essay to finish and I guess I'd better talk to my Mom before she goes to bed, or should I leave it till the morning? Telling Mom, I mean – not the essay."

"I don't know. *You'll* have to decide. I've got to go – *my* Mom's yelling up the stairs at me. See you tomorrow. 'Bye."

Megan put down the phone. She made a half-hearted move towards the homework on her desk, then lay back on her bed instead. The fact that Alan had called her was so reassuring. She felt warm all over. She had been so afraid he had just been being polite in spending so much time with her at the party – that he'd found it useful, like a good excuse for not mingling with the employees or something like that. But her cousin – and his cousin, too – Jayne had been there without an escort, so he could easily have hung out with her if that had been the case. Jayne was a CA now and was something or other, Megan wasn't sure what, in the accounting department at McGrath-LaPlante. Basically, she thought, I know next to nothing about McGrath-LaPlante and Alan is going to think I'm pretty irresponsible seeing as in three and a half years I'll own ten point four-and-a-bit per cent of the stock. He was hardly going to be into talking about the company but she'd have to see what she could find out from her mother before Saturday so that she wouldn't look stupid if something did come up.

"Are you still awake in there, Megan?" Her mother called softly to her, from the passage, on her way to bed.

Megan sat up startled. "Yes – just finishing my essay," she said.

"Well, it's ten to eleven, so don't stay up too long – you won't be able to get up in the morning. Good night."

"'Night, Mom. I just have a couple of sentences to write and I'll get to bed."

· · · · ·

The next morning Megan told her mother that she was going to see *Cats* with Alan LaPlante on Saturday evening. Beyond asking her if that had been him calling last night, her mother expressed no opinion. Megan felt a little mystified and considered asking why she wasn't complaining that he was too old for her, but decided that it probably was not a good idea to bring up his age unless her mother mentioned it first. That night at supper time, she waited until her brother, Byron, had left the table and nonchalantly asked her mother if she'd had a good day at the office. This, unfortunately, did not elicit any information on McGrath-LaPlante mainly because her mother was surprised at the sudden interest in her welfare. Megan rather wished she'd shown a bit more interest in her mother's job before. Maybe she should phone her brother Danny, who was in his first year at Western, and quiz him. He'd be able to set her straight since he was all gung-ho about eventually getting an MBA and being president of McGrath-LaPlante at some point in the future. He'd even worked there, filling in for vacationing shipping and receiving employees, during the last two summers. He'd know all about it, but he might not be too crazy about her going out with Alan. He kind of had this thing about fulfilling his grandmother's wish to put the McGraths back into McGrath-LaPlante. God, this was stupid worrying about the McGraths and the LaPlantes. Her mother had said it was all nonsense anyway. She was just glad that Grandma McGrath had had the obsession because she had ended up getting a job that she enjoyed out of it. Danny was an idiot.

On Friday evening, Megan and Nicki went through Megan's wardrobe in infinite detail before deciding what she should wear. It was a difficult decision because they agreed that she needed to look mature, which eliminated a lot of her clothes, but, at the same time, not so much that it *looked* as if she was trying to look older. She needed to look quite comfortable going out with an older man. But, as Nicki pointed out, he must like her – the real Megan, so they mustn't lose sight of that. They finally decided on a blue heavy jersey tunic-style dress with a single string of little natural pearls – because the dress had 'the classic simplicity that was basically ageless and the pearls were youthful yet sophisticated'. Nicki had her mother's car and, once Megan's wardrobe had been decided upon, the two girls drove over to Nicki's house. They were sleeping there because they had promised to help Nicki's mother prepare for a children's Christmas party at the women's and children's shelter where she volunteered.

She walked home from the women's shelter on Saturday afternoon, leaving the party after Santa had arrived with the children's gifts. There was nobody home when she arrived there – her mother was Christmas shopping and Byron was playing hockey. After having a shower, Megan had second thoughts about the blue dress and tried various other combinations of clothes before coming back to the blue dress again. She experimented with her hair, trying to straighten out some of the frizziness that she hated, then decided to leave it loose to her shoulders in its usual style. When she heard her mother's car pull into the driveway she hurriedly pulled on her bathrobe and went downstairs. By the time her mother came into the kitchen from the mud-room which linked the garage to the rest of the house, Megan was drinking a glass of milk and reading the first section of the Saturday paper, nonchalantly unconcerned about her upcoming date – or, at least, that's how she hoped she looked.

· · · · ·

Alan was waiting for her as she came through the subway turnstile. She had arranged for him to meet her at the subway station, telling him she had a couple of things to do and would not be going home before meeting him. The real reason was because she knew that, if he came and picked her up at home when her mother was there, she'd feel like a little kid going out with a favourite uncle or something. She had assured her mother that Alan would be driving her home, however. While neither of them said anything, Megan was pretty sure that her mother knew why she had made this arrangement. She offered to drop her off at the subway, saying she had forgotten something and needed to go over to the supermarket anyway. Megan was glad because she didn't really want to walk that far in her shoes when you definitely needed boots if you were walking.

"Hi," she said walking towards him. "You're early."

He laughed. "So are you."

"That's because I was afraid of there being a delay on the subway. So I planned to get here early – then, if there had been a delay I wouldn't have been... late, that is."

"That's quite... brilliant," he said and they both laughed. "I'm just early in case you were early." He gestured for her to go ahead, then fell in step beside her. "The car's on a meter just along the street. I've made reservations, at the little bistro place I told you about, for six-thirty because I know – from previous experience – that they're a bit slow. There's a parking lot within easy reach of both the restaurant and the theatre. Here we are." He unlocked the passenger side door of the green Volkswagen Audi.

She got in as Alan closed the door and went round to get in himself.

"It should warm up again pretty quickly – it hasn't been left out in the cold for too long," he said as he started the car.

"Oh, I'm okay. It gets pretty hot and uncomfortable in the subway. How was your Little Brother's hockey game?"

"Surprise, surprise – they actually won. It was the first time. I was really glad for him."

"Does the equipment fit him all right?"

Alan had been a Big Brother for the last couple of years to a boy from the inner city public housing development at Regent's Park and Megan's mother had given Alan some of Byron's outgrown hockey equipment for the boy whose mother could not otherwise afford for him to play.

"Oh, he was the big hero when he told the other kids that he had Michael McGrath's nephew's skates."

"I didn't think kids that age would know Michael."

"They get most of their information from bubble gum cards – they're mostly too young to stay up and watch *Hockey Night in Canada.*"

"Yeah, I suppose so. Did you play hockey?"

"I wasn't much good, I'm afraid. My uncle – well, you know Dennis, he's your uncle, too – took me to Maple Leaf Gardens a few times to see Michael play, though, so I managed to maintain some dignity with my peers despite not being any good myself." Alan grinned. "I even got him to prevail upon your grandmother to talk Michael into doing one of those careers talks that schools are always trying to get kids' parents to do. That was just after the Leafs won their last Stanley Cup – so you can imagine how I basked in second hand glory then!"

"Danny and I were too young to benefit from that, but we used to play up the fact that Michael was our uncle for all it was worth. Danny even had his eighth birthday at the Gardens."

They had reached the parking lot by this time.

"It's about half a block that way," Alan said as he opened Megan's door, which she had remembered not to open herself and burst out of like a teenager.

They walked along to the restaurant without speaking because the cold wind was in their faces. At last, in the shelter of the restaurant lobby, they laughed at each other's breathlessness.

"Fortunately, the wind'll be behind us when we leave," Alan said, taking her coat.

"I think I'd better go and comb my hair," said Megan, removing her hat and handing it to him to give in at the coat check with her coat.

She wasn't even upset when she had to wet her hair to control the static which the cold air and hat had caused. They were so comfortable together that you'd think they'd know each other for twenty years. Life was so wonderful...

At dinner, they talked about everything from Andrew Lloyd Webber to skiing to tennis to the application Megan would soon be making to the Ontario College of Art and how her brother Danny liked being at Western. When Alan ordered a bottle of wine, the waiter made no attempt to question her age which would have been mortifying since she was three months short of her nineteenth birthday. It was an advantage of being with an older man – if she'd been with kids from school, they'd all have been asked for their birth certificates.

A couple of times she caught herself chattering about inconsequential things but found that he was as good – or bad, depending on how you looked at it – at talking nonsense as she was. But he could be very serious, too, and she found herself telling him all about how she planned to take advantage of the McGrath-LaPlante dividends to support herself while she attempted to establish herself as an artist once she was through OCA How she had expected to have to go commercial or teach the way most people had to. And how, once she had achieved a successful career, she'd donate the income she received from the shares each year to cancer research in memory of her grandmother.

Alan said he thought it was wonderful to have met somebody who felt the same way he did about using money you hadn't really earned for the good of other people, and that he hoped she'd find some time in the schedule she had set for herself to be his friend because like-minded people owed each other that. And he told her about how the growing threat of AIDS, of which she knew nothing except that it was some sexually transmitted disease that gays contracted, would impact on business at McGrath-LaPlante and that they must also use their resources to combat the disease. Nobody else in management, apparently, realised the implications yet, but, as dreadful as it sounded, the spread of the disease was going to make them all very rich and, more importantly, well placed to make a difference.

Megan scarcely remembered what they had to eat. Whatever it was, it must have been good. Her plate was empty. They decided to finish the bottle of wine and have coffee after the theatre.

After the theatre, they went to one of the new dessert and coffee restaurants which were coming into vogue and talked about *Cats* and theatre and Andrew Lloyd Webber again and planned to go to see *Les Misérables* when it opened at some unknown point in the future. Then Alan drove her home and they both agreed that it had been the most wonderful evening and he said she really must promise to make room in her life for him and he'd call her tomorrow and he kissed her gently at the front door and she walked into the house on air and floated up the stairs.

"Did you have a nice time, Megan?" her mother called to her.

"It was so wonderful... I can't believe it really happened," Megan replied.

# ALAN

"I do understand, Alan. Really I do. I think I'd want to be left alone, too, and it's a good idea to make amends to Adam. So, I'll butt out, except to ask you – well, for my Mom really – she'd really like you to come and have dinner with us tomorrow evening. There'll only be her and me here. Byron will be going to a New Year's party and Danny's going back up to Collingwood after the funeral."

"Okay, Megan. Tell her I appreciate her thoughtfulness and I'll be there. You can tell me what time tomorrow."

"I'll let you go. Stay in your own flat, though. It'll just be depressing going downstairs and your Aunt Selena won't appreciate you sorting things out – I expect she considers it to be a female-type thing to do and will think you're interfering."

"You're probably right. I'll talk to you tomorrow. 'Bye, Megan and... I love you."

"I love you, Alan. 'Bye."

"Bye-bye, sweetheart."

Alan put the phone down and picked up the mug of coffee that he'd let go cold. He poured it into the kitchen sink, ran the tap to rinse it away and poured himself a fresh cup. Then the phone rang again. He tried to remember if this was the fourth or fifth call since the first one had awakened him this morning – not counting Megan's. He'd been glad to get that one despite having turned down her offer to go for a long walk with her and her dog and let the crisp cold weather clear his head.

"Hello."

"Alan is that you, Alan?" said a very British voice, sounding as if it was coming through a long tunnel.

"Yes, Frank. How are you? We have a terrible line here."

Frank Hayward was the President of the British conglomerate which had begun acquiring North American prophylactic devices manufacturing companies back in the 1950s. McGrath-LaPlante had been co-packing for them for almost as long.

"I just got the news about your grandfather and want to say how sorry I am to see him go. He was a wonderful old chap and I'm so glad to have known him. We only just got home from spending Christmas in the wilds of Scotland with my sister-in-law's family. Phone's been out of order up there since Christmas Day – don't know how they manage miles from anywhere and the phone on the blink half the time. Anyway, I understand from Joel that his wife had an arrangement sent through InterFlora..."

"Yes, Frank. It arrived at the funeral parlour yesterday. Looks lovely – we appreciate your thoughtfulness..."

"I'll be giving your uncle a bell, too. How's he taking it? Okay."

"Oh yes. Fine, thanks. It's not as if it was entirely unexpected. He would have been ninety-one in March, after all."

" Marvellous fellow. Had those production lines of yours running like clockwork for fifty years, Old Denny did. Not to say things are any different now, of course. You must be glad you've got the fellows he trained though... Well, you're right – darned awful line we've got. Give my sympathies to Dennis and Laura if I don't get through. Cheerio."

Alan shook his head as he put the phone down once again and returned his attention to his mug of coffee and the *Sunday Star* which he had been downstairs to pick up earlier. His grandfather's cat was scratching at the door and he went to let him in. He'd refused to come up earlier, so he'd left the door of his grandfather's apartment open so that the cat could come up if he felt like company. He evidently did want company now, judging by the way he was butting his head around Alan's ankles.

"Poor old fellow – can't figure out what's going on, can you?" He picked the cat up and carried him over to an armchair. Sitting with the cat in his lap, he finally finished his coffee and thought about getting a refill but decided not to disturb the cat.

Alan's apartment had been created for him, out of the second floor of his grandparents' house, the year he had finished his undergraduate degree at Western. The plans had been his Christmas present, allowing for him to select furnishings and fixtures so that the apartment would be ready for him in the summer. They'd said, in explanation, that it was time he had some privacy when he was home and they were getting old now and hardly needed all the space downstairs for entertaining anymore and, at their age, a home all on one floor was far more convenient. He knew they were really thinking about down the road to when he'd finished his MBA and went to work full-time at McGrath-LaPlante. By that point in the lives of their sons, both had left the family home – were married with children, in fact – so they had determined, since young people were not in such a hurry to get married anymore, to encourage Alan to stay. His grandmother died the year after the house was redesigned and renovated, and two years later his grandfather broke a hip, which refused to heal properly, and was restricted to life in a wheelchair. So Alan stayed.

He was glad he'd been able to provide some companionship for his grandfather during the last few years, although he was aware that it was a very small return for all that they'd done for him. Coping with a young boy who'd lost his parents could not have been easy for a couple in their sixties but they had undertaken the task without the smallest hesitation and gone on to survive his turbulent teenage years while in their seventies and put him through university in their eighties. Committing himself to a career in his grandfather's business was the least he could do in return... as well as being his conduit to what went on in the office. He'd often thought about how he would extricate himself from the company after his grandfather's death. Now that the moment had finally arrived, he wondered how he should go about it. The timing was wrong right now, unfortunately.

Although he had never felt that he was temperamentally suited to the corporate life, he had felt reasonably fulfilled since he had become Director of Marketing a year ago. McGrath-LaPlante had never had a marketing department as such before. Marketing had always been regarded as part of the sales function because the company supported few proprietary products, being predominantly a supplier to the large pharmaceutical companies. The advent and spread of AIDS during recent years had assisted Alan in making a case for producing McGrath-LaPlante branded latex prophylactic and protective products to meet potential new markets which would result from the need to control the spread of the human immunodeficiency virus. Setting up its own distribution system and avoiding competition with the companies for whom it custom-manufactured, McGrath-LaPlante was now marketing surgical gloves directly to dentists and the fast-growing dental hygienist profession, the alternative health professions and paramedical areas where the product had not been considered entirely necessary before. Having successfully got this part of his marketing mandate off the ground, Alan was now working on a strategy to sell McGrath-LaPlante branded condoms in non-traditional areas. Quite apart from developing new business for the company, he saw the project as a duty – from a personal, as well as, a corporate viewpoint, as he had explained to Megan on the momentous evening of their first date a few weeks ago.

Yes, Old Denny, he thought, you couldn't have timed it better if you'd planned it, which, maybe, is just what you did do. Well, I'll stay and finish what I started, but I do not intend to give the rest of my life to McGrath-LaPlante...

"And you, kitty-cat," he said, aloud to the cat, "are going to have to move because I have to get down there and take that kid to the movies."

He picked up the phone and dialled the number of his Little Brother. He had missed the boy's Saturday afternoon hockey game, having been at the funeral parlour. Adam's mother had brought him to pay his respects in the evening which had impressed Alan who privately considered her to be something of an airhead. He had thanked them both and arranged to take Adam to a movie this afternoon to make up for not being at his hockey game. Adam picked up the phone on the first ring.

"Hello."

"Hi, Adam, it's me. Decided where we're going?" he listened to the boy's excited reply. "Okay, but only if your mother agrees. I'll be there in twenty minutes anyhow. See you then."

. . . . .

"So there we are – the sad tale of the reluctant shareholder."

Alan stopped walking as they reached the first lookout on the Rattlesnake Point trail and he and Megan both gazed out over the Nassagaweya Canyon. It was the following Sunday and they were finally taking the therapeutic walk which Megan swore would make him feel better. So far, it was mostly making him feel frozen, but he had faith in Megan's judgement and was prepared to give it time.

"You sound just like Mom did when she was told about Grandma McGrath's will," Megan laughed. "The last thing she ever wanted to do was to work at McGrath-LaPlante. The difference is–" and she became more serious "–she's only caretaking our shares and can forget the whole thing, I suppose, in a few years. Sorry – I'm rubbing salt into the wound, aren't I?"

"It's okay. It must be nice to be 'only caretaking'. That's really what I thought I was doing these last few years. I mean – just Sunday – I was thinking how I'd get the Marketing Department firmly up and running then consider myself free to start my own life. Now, I have to re-think the whole situation."

Old Denny LaPlante had left his complete block of shares to his grandson. Together with the twelve and a half percent he had inherited from his father, Alan now owned thirty seven and a half percent of McGrath-LaPlante stock and was the largest stockholder.

"You don't have to stay *in* the company – my grandmother held more than thirty per cent for years and sat on the board without being involved in management."

"She inherited her shares – she never worked for the company in the first place. I was brought up to take a place. I'm expected to take over as CEO when Dennis decides to retire and you could hardly blame him for deciding to retire right now."

"It's crazy – these people wanting to control things from the grave. I sort of understand why Grandma McGrath did what she did. I mean dividing the shares between her three children would have meant the risk of Michael and Aunt Frances selling out to Aunt Laura and that, to her mind, would have been selling out to Uncle Dennis – a dreaded LaPlante, no offence intended to present LaPlante company, of course." She squeezed his gloved hand between the two of hers. "Neither of them had ever been involved with the company and could hardly be expected to see things her way. But I don't get what your grandfather was up to at all. Why alienate Uncle Dennis – his son, his namesake even? And what about Cindi and Jayne – *they're* his grandchildren, too. And Jayne's in line to be VP Finance, so Mom says."

"Yes, she is. I'm afraid Old Denny wasn't like your grandmother, though. Women's Lib had not caught up to him. He –"

"–objected pretty violently to my mother's appointment."

"He did that," laughed Alan, remembering Old Denny's indignation at Isabel McGrath's will. "Come on, it's too cold to stand around. Let's get moving and warm ourselves up."

"Ben!" shouted Megan, "where are you?" The spaniel came bursting through the leafless brush. "Come on – this way, boy. Oh, look at all the burrs on you..."

They walked on in companionable silence. The icy wind was blowing in their faces making conversation difficult. Reaching the next lookout, they turned their backs to the wind while they caught their breath.

"Any buffalo out down there?" Alan asked, peering into the buffalo compound beneath them.

"I think they're all in the shelter."

"If they've got half a brain they are. It's a lot colder up here than I realized. I hope it's not too cold for Ben."

"Ben's tough – he's been coming up here most of his life, in all weathers."

"Your mom used to bring you all up here for hikes, did she?"

"Here and Kelso – we'd swim there in the summer, and we'd go to other places along the Escarpment – Mount Nemo, Hilton Falls – have you ever been there?"

"No. You'll have to take me there next. You can educate me on the Niagara Escarpment just like your mother did you. Deal?"

"Why not?" Megan smiled. "First lesson coming up – look up there. See them?" She pointed toward a pair of turkey vultures soaring above the trees on the other side of the canyon. "They're the Escarpment garbage men – turkey vultures. They should have migrated by now really."

"They look as if they have no heads," Alan said, as the birds come closer to the Rattlesnake side of the canyon.

"They tuck them in. They're very ugly – wrinkly like turkeys. We saw some close up once tearing away at a racoon corpse. It was pretty gross."

"Crawford Lake's that way?" Alan asked nodding in the direction of the opposite outlier.

"Ah-ha. That's where the Iroquois village was found. The plan is to reconstruct it completely over the next few years. Have you not been there either?"

"No. I told you I need educating."

"You know what we should do?" said Megan. "Take Adam to Crawford Lake one weekend. He'd love it! Can we? Or, maybe he'd resent me. Perhaps you should take him by yourself."

"Without my expert guide. No way. We'll tell him you're Michael McGrath's niece and he's bound to like you. Anyway, you and I are a team now. Right? So he's going to have to get used to you being around... just like everybody else."

They grinned at each other.

"You look frozen," Megan said.

"So do you." He hugged her tightly to him as they began to walk on. "If we walk quickly and if we survive the cold, we'll get back to the car and drive to somewhere I know – not too far from here – where they have the best French onion soup you ever tasted."

. . . . .

"To put it bluntly, Alan, you must have had him completely fooled." Dennis LaPlante stirred sugar into his coffee, took a sip and put the cup back on the saucer. "That's not meant as a derogatory statement, by the way."

"I know," Alan said, taking a sip of his own coffee. If, by some remote chance, he ever did become CEO at McGrath-LaPlante, this coffee in cups ritual would definitely be replaced by coffee in mugs. "But you know, as well as I do, that it was best to humour him these last few years. He wanted to believe that I lived and breathed the company just as he had done – just as he envisaged my father would have done... *And*, Dennis, just as you do."

It was Dennis's turn to nod, "I know".

"So why didn't he leave his shares to you? Why cut you out?"

"He didn't cut me out. I get the Holgates – Selena, by the way, tells me they need restoring and suggests the people she always used down there in Moncton. I hope she's not driving you to drink, by the way."

Selena LaPlante – Dennis's older sister – was a recently retired art gallery curator who lived in New Brunswick. She had flown to Toronto for the funeral and was currently staying in her father's apartment while sorting things out.

"No. I mostly keep out of her way. She did insist on taking Megan and I out to dinner on Saturday evening, and quite let her hair down after a couple of glasses of wine. She got very confidential with Megan, in fact, and told her all sorts of stories about her student days at OCA I never really knew her and always thought of her as an old lady – even when I was a kid she seemed old – so it was a bit strange to think of her as an art student. You'd never believe the things they got up to – bet you didn't know where she was when she told your parents she was staying overnight at her girlfriend's and the girlfriend told her parents she was staying overnight at your house. It's amazing – such a proper little old lady like Aunt Selena..."

"Not so much of the *old* – she's my sister and, by implication, it makes me old. Anyway, your father and I were barely into our teens when Selena was at OCA, and we lived and breathed hockey – whatever she was up to was the last thing we'd be likely to take any interest in. But it doesn't surprise me. Your cousins were out there to stay with her several times, remember?  It's only been during recent years – and they've still never split on her to their mother – but they've told me a thing or two about the high-stepping art world in Moncton."

They both laughed.

"This thing with young Megan," Dennis continued, "it's serious then. I mean, judging by the conversation, she did the staying overnight that got Selena started on her reminiscences."

"Yes," Alan replied. "It's serious. I'm going to marry Megan.

Oh, nothing's going to change just yet–" he said, hurriedly, in response to his uncle's surprise "–she's still going to Europe with her girlfriends for the summer and then to OCA in the fall, but we'll get married eventually."

"Bet Old Denny didn't catch on to that now, did he?"

"No, I never talked to him about it – mainly because I was afraid he'd get upset and have a heart attack... "Alan broke off. "You mean?..."

"Yes. He decided not to leave the shares to me because of what he saw as a McGrath comeback. To his mind the McGraths had made no contribution to the company since *old* Angus McGrath died – and he didn't count Megan's father's short time with us before he died. Yes," he said, holding up his hand before Alan could interrupt, "I know Isabel always sat on the Board right up until she died, but contribution to him meant *physical* contribution, hands-on working for the company. He resented the McGraths. He didn't see them for what they were – an old woman, a superannuated hockey player, his sisters and a bunch of kids. They were parasites drawing their dividends and never putting anything into the company – well, he didn't mind Laura because he still had the *what's hers is his* mentality of his generation. I imagine, after Isabel refused to sell out to him and then set up her own crazy will, he started to worry about the McGrath boys coming into the company – he knew Danny was working here and Marilyn, of course, and–"

Alan suddenly saw the light.

"–he was afraid that if you died and Laura inherited your shares, the McGraths together would hold a majority position."

"Exactly," said Dennis.

"Now I really do feel like a snake in the grass," Alan said slowly.

"No need. You're the guy who's taking the bottom line to new heights – you deserve the dividends. I know you're not interested in being CEO and I know your cousin, Jayne, is and will, I think, be ready for it when I retire in a few years – everyone will just have to put up with me a couple of years longer than I originally intended. My father will be turning over in his grave at the idea of a female CEO, but it won't be so unusual eight or ten years down the road."

"She's half McGrath, too."

"So he'll be turning over in his grave twice. What can we do? As you, yourself, keep pointing out circumstances have conspired to make our products highly profitable in the coming years. McGraths and LaPlantes – we'll be so busy turning down offers to buy the whole kit and caboodle, we won't have time to fight among ourselves."

"I still feel as if I got the shares under false pretences," Alan said. "Well, I did if you want to get technical, but I didn't hide my relationship with Megan for that reason. In fact I even thought about introducing her to him without telling him her last name, but decided she looked too much like her family – not so much Laura, but Frances... and Michael, too – anyway she looks too much like a McGrath for me to have been able to get away with it. Here I was, worried about giving him a heart attack and it looks like I was feathering my nest at your expense."

"He made the will months ago..."

"I know, but if I'd been honest, at least he would have had time to change it..."

"And take a page out of Isabel's will – threaten to finance the Cancer Society or, in his case, perhaps, the Heart and Stroke Foundation?"

"Okay, okay – it's not worth continually hashing over. Let's forget it. One thing it does change though, Dennis..."

"What's that?"

"I don't need to wait for Board approval of my condom shipments to Uganda. If you guys can't see that the PR angle more than covers the cost, I can finance it myself now." Alan grinned and stood up. "Well, I've got work to do," he said. "See you later."

. . . . .

Two days later, on Selena's last evening in town, Alan took her and the rest of the family out to dinner. Dennis and Laura pulled up beside them in the restaurant parking lot.

"How's that for timing?" said Dennis, getting out of his car.

Alan went to open the door for Laura.

"How are you, Aunt Laura?"

"Fine, Alan." The wind ripped away the light scarf she had over her head. "This wind is awful. I didn't realize it had become so strong."

"I should have let you off at the door, Laura," said Dennis, coming around the car with his sister. "Sorry – it didn't seem so bad when we started out."

They all hurried to the restaurant entrance. A car horn hooted as it was driven past them into the parking lot.

"There's Cindi and Robert," said Laura.

"Well, we're not waiting out here for them to park." Dennis said, pushing her forward. "Let's get inside."

They checked their coats.

"Coming along to the restroom with me, Selena?" asked Laura. "I'd like to fix my hair."

"Well, I don't think anything I do will help mine much, but I'll come along," replied Selena. "Here's Cindi now." She addressed her niece, "Isn't the weather dreadful, my dear?"

"Hello, Aunt Selena. It doesn't seem to be bothering you. You're just as spry as ever." Cindi hugged her aunt.

"Terrible word to use – spry. Something you might say about your grandfather before he passed on..."

"I'm sorry," laughed Cindi, as her husband, Robert, helped her with her coat. "I'll correct that – just as – as *perfect* as ever. I know what you're going to say now – *and they gave you a master's in education?* – right? Right. It was the first adjective I could think of in my windblown state. Were you on your way to the restroom with Mom?" Laura had continued on to the restroom while Cindi and Selena were talking. "Let's catch her up. Hi, Dad. How are you, Alan? Haven't seen you for ages – well, except for the funeral, of course. Let's go, Aunt Selena." She took her aunt's arm and they followed the direction her mother had taken.

Robert joined Alan and Dennis at the coat check.

"A mile a minute – that's Cindi," he said.

"That's okay," smiled Dennis, "I survived the twenty-five years before you took her off my hands."

"I reserved the table for seven-thirty. Jayne won't be here until then. So I'll let the *maitre d'* know we're in the bar," Alan said. "I think the ladies will find us all right."

They were seated, with their drinks, at a small table near the door by the time the ladies came looking for them.

"Here they are, Mom," cried Cindi. "We should have known we wouldn't get to eat right away and I'm starving. Sit here, Aunt Selena. Oh good, we have some peanuts to stave off the hunger pains."

They settled themselves and ordered drinks.

"It's your sister's fault we're later than Alan originally arranged," said Selena. "He was going to call you, but I said we may as well relax at the bar and wait for her."

"Oh, it's all right. I was only joking. So, Alan," Cindi said turning towards him, "what's all this I hear about you and my little cousin?"

"She might *once* have been your *little* cousin, Cindi," Selena remonstrated, "but she's quite grown up now and will be attending my old *alma mater* in the fall. Lovely girl..."

Cindi raised her eyebrows. "Wow. She certainly found favour with you. I never heard you talk about me being a *lovely* girl – or Jayne either. I must admit I haven't seen Megan or the younger boy since – oh, it must be since Grandma McGrath's funeral and their mother whipped them out of there as soon as it was over, anyway. We used to see Megan and the older boy – Danny, the one who was at Grandfather's funeral with his mother... we'd see *them* once in a while, at Grandma's, but I mostly remember them when they were little – before their father died. So I can be excused for thinking of her as little. I remember now – Megan used to draw cats and dogs – really well. Little cartoon things – I was quite envious. She was only about six or seven."

"That was when her father died. She told me that she spent months after the accident concentrating on drawing the perfect *Garfield*," Alan said. "I don't imagine you remember, but when my parents died, I used to draw *Huckleberry Hound* all the time. We were talking about it a while ago – when we first met. Drawing probably has a lot more value in helping children through crises than is generally acknowledged."

"You're right," Selena told him, "but it is being increasingly used now. Since I retired from the Gallery, I've been volunteering

– working one-on-one with troubled children at a local school. It was covered in the little training course I was sent on, but it's not being used as much as it should be."

"Talking of troubled children – how's your Little Brother? Adam?" Cindi asked Alan. "You should get him drawing *Huckleberry Hound* and I do remember yours – I stole one once and pretended I did it."

"Adam's doing pretty well – he's hardly a troubled child, though. You never saw a kid so well balanced, in fact, and I don't think he'd be into *Huckleberry Hound*. I'd have to update my skills to drawing something more contemporary – *Gremlins*, perhaps. The *maitre d's* trying to get my attention. Shall we go in and tell him to show Jayne to our table when she arrives?"

"I think so," agreed Selena.

"Is that okay with you, Dad?" said Cindi, breaking into the conversation on the other side of the table.

"Going in?" asked Dennis.

Alan nodded.

"May as well." Robert said. "We're all finished our drinks. Jayne can follow on."

"Here *is* Jayne, now," Cindi said, as her sister put her head around the doorway. "Stay there – we're just coming."

They eventually got themselves organized in the dining room with glasses of wine, meals ordered and some *hors d' oeuvres* to assuage Cindi's hunger. Alan found himself sitting between his two cousins.

"Did you know that Cindi just admitted to stealing one of my *Huckleberry Hound* drawings and pretending she had done it?" he said to Jayne.

"You mean when we were little? Sure, I remember that. I didn't believe her. We were both klutzes at drawing. You used to be able to do all those animal cartoons – *Yogi Bear and Boo-Boo*... How did you get on to that topic?"

"Oh, we were talking about Megan's cartoons..."

"Megan's. Oh, she had you beat by a mile! Remember Megan's *Garfield*, Cindi?"

Cindi was in deep conversation with her father on her other side.

"That's how we got onto the subject in the first place." Alan said.

"*I* thought seriously about stealing one of Megan's *Garfield*s, but I wasn't as corrupt as my sister. I got her to give me one instead and I pasted it on my binder and basked in reflected glory instead. I was in about grade eleven – old enough to be proud of my little cousin. It was a bit different with Cindi and you at age seven – she could hardly sing your praises. It's just not done – boys are considered most uncouth when you're seven! *Gross*, the kids would say now."

"Thanks. It's nice to know what you thought of me after all these years."

"Oh, I think we forgave you eventually. Fortunately you became more desirable by the time you were fifteen or so – funny how that happens with kids..." She turned her attention to Selena across the table. "What time is your flight tomorrow, Aunt Selena?"

"Two-thirty, but I'm getting a little worried about the weather, dear. They're saying this storm shouldn't get here until the next day, but the way that wind is out there, I wouldn't be surprised if they're quite wrong."

Alan applied his attention to the salad that had been set in front of him and let the conversation drift over him. Born within months of each other, he and his cousins had grown up together. His being orphaned early had probably resulted in their being closer than they would otherwise have been. As a child he was generally included in their family excursions in order to give his grandparents a break and they, consequently, had a more amicable brother-sister relationship than many actual brothers and sisters. Dennis had been a concerned surrogate father to him, particularly once it became obvious that he was not going to have a son of his own. Alan was relieved that Jayne was turning out to be the one to follow in her father's footsteps in the company. He had not wanted to disappoint his uncle by falling short of being CEO material any more than he had wanted to upset his grandfather so, now that Dennis could see Jayne's potential, it was a relief to be able to stand aside. Opposition to Jayne's climb up the corporate ladder would be coming from her mother not her father, he reflected. As the father of two daughters, Dennis, had readily adapted to the increasing numbers of women in senior management. Laura, however, was a throwback to her mother's generation. Cindi – being a schoolteacher – was acceptable, being married made her even more acceptable, but accountancy and business were for men. And, quite apart from her career choice, poor Jayne had also had to withstand a lot of criticism over breaking off two relationships, before they evolved into marriage, with what Laura considered to be very appropriate young men.

Their entrées were brought to them and their wine glasses refilled.

"You're very quiet, Alan," said Laura across the table, "or, perhaps, I should say, preoccupied?"

"He's in love," Cindi chimed in, before he could say anything. "Leave the poor boy alone." She patted his shoulder consolingly as if he were sick or traumatised.

"Why didn't you bring my little niece along with you tonight?" Laura continued.

He could hardly tell her the truth – that is, that there was no way he would want Megan to have to face them all at once, getting talked down to as the little niece or little cousin, whichever the case. Better to let them all get used to the idea of the two of them as a couple on an individual basis, rather than *en masse*. It was only very recently that Laura had stopped regarding Megan's mother as some kind of renegade. According to Megan, her mother had been considered responsible, by his family, for years after her father's death in a drunk driving accident.

"The poor girl is extremely busy working on her portfolio for her interview at OCA next week," Selena answered for him. "You've no idea how much work one has to put into it. I remember selecting things for mine – selecting, discarding... then deciding to do something else. Of course, it was in the middle of the war when I did it and decent paper was hard to come by. But, what fun – I'd love to do it all over again."

"Did Franklin Carmichael teach you, Aunt Selena?" asked Jayne.

"Oh yes. I was there when he died. Heart attack – he was quite young, too. Only in his mid-fifties. It was very sad."

"Imagine that – to have been taught by one of the Group of Seven."

"There were quite a number of us who were. Apart from Carmichael, several other members of the Group taught there, you know. J.E.H. McDonald was OCA principal at one time – way before my time, I don't hesitate to add. Why do you ask, dear?"

"Oh, I was talking to someone about La Cloche and the cottages – real cottages with no hydro or roads – that have remained that way up there. The Carmichael cottage up there on Cranberry Lake is still used by the family. It's real wilderness country – you have to get to it by boat...

"You young people have been spoilt – no stamina," said Selena. "Who wants hydro in a cottage?"

"Hey, Aunt Selena – I took an Outward Bound course last year – and survived!" Jayne exclaimed. "In fact, the reason the subject came up was because we were planning a winter camping trip up in La Cloche – the man, who was telling me about the Carmichael place, and me."

Laura's ears had obviously pricked up at this. "Who is this outdoorsy type then, Jayne?" she asked.

"Oh, you'd hate him, Mother. But, don't worry about it – we're not asking you to come winter camping with us."

After a momentary silence, everybody laughed.

"I suppose I asked for that," said Laura. "I shouldn't pry. I'm sorry, Jayne."

"And I shouldn't be so touchy. Sorry, Mother."

"So, who's for dessert?" asked Dennis to dispel any remaining awkwardness as the waiter began to remove their dishes.

. . . . .

"I'm afraid I don't like my sister-in-law very much, you know," said Selena when she and Alan were driving home. "One shouldn't really admit to such a thing, but I'm rather glad that my career took me away from Southern Ontario. I don't think we would have got along at all well. It's amazing that those girls have turned out relatively normal, although Cindi is rather highly strung."

"Robert told me she had a couple of drinks before they left home," Alan told her. "Apparently she figures a drink dulls the senses that react to her mother's nit-picking – her terminology, not mine."

"Well, I hope she doesn't go overboard with that particular cure. The McGraths have a bad history in that regard. It would have been nice to have had dinner with all you young people alone – Jayne could have brought her wilderness man and Megan could have come along – but I suppose you could hardly leave out Dennis and Laura."

Alan smiled. "No, Aunt Selena. Maybe another time, though. Next time you come, you must stay longer. The apartment is there for you any time, you know."

"You're not going to renovate the house, then? I suppose I should say re-renovate the house."

"No – not just now, anyway. What do I need a whole house for? I'll keep it as it is and the apartment will be available for visitors – actually, it could prove quite advantageous business-wise."

"It'll attract your British and European contacts looking to combine business and pleasure by bringing their families with them –" Selena said, astutely. "– a lot more comfortable than a hotel."

"Just what I was thinking. With such business smarts, you should have gone into the company, Aunt Selena."

"My father would hardly have sanctioned such a thing," she laughed. "He was only agreeable to my having a career in art because he saw painting as being somehow feminine. Goodness knows what would have happened if I had chosen anything else. He would have been about as set *against* me studying business and commerce as he was determined that Dennis and Drew – and later on you, too – *did* get business degrees. You know, I believe – even then – he was angling to get rid of the McGraths. And they made it easy for him."

"What do you mean?" asked Alan. "They couldn't help dying."

"Do you remember Angus McGrath – not the old man, he died before you were born – I mean *Isabel's* husband? No, I expect you were too young..."

"I think he died when I was about five. No, I don't remember him – I probably never even met him. I never knew any of the McGrath's except Laura and, of course, I made it my business – as any boy in the sixties would have done – to be, at least, on nodding terms with Michael."

"Yes, the hockey star," said Selena, reflectively. "It was his older brother, Angus – Megan's father – who was supposed to follow his father into running McGrath-LaPlante, but the boy never stood a chance."

"From what I've heard, he didn't want a chance. He did everything he could to stay out of the company!"

"That's the LaPlante version – created by Old Denny."

Alan had never heard her refer to her father as Old Denny before. "And you don't buy the LaPlante version?" he said. Having arrived home by this time, he drove the car into the garage. "How about you come up for a night-cap with me and tell me why?"

"Yes, I'd like that," said Selena. "And it will be good for you. You have to stop feeling bad about not living up to your grandfather's expectations."

"But I told you I talked the whole thing out with Dennis the other day."

"You're still feeling guilty though, aren't you?"

Alan shook his head and smiled. "You're probably right," he said.

They went inside and up to his apartment. His grandfather's cat was sitting on the front step and followed them up. Alan took his aunt's coat and hung it over the bannister, then poured them both a good-sized brandy.

"Whether or not Angus – Junior, that is – would have followed his father's wishes in other circumstances is, of course, debatable. The fact that he was still in university, when his father died, and Dennis and your father, Drew, were already well-established in the company, sent Father into action. He whittled the organization down to a powerful triumvirate operation with Dennis as President, Drew handling sales and Father continuing to rule over operations – although he was past retirement age, even then – and that's what Angus was faced with when he finished his MBA. Naturally he wasn't about to stick around. He took off to see the world. Isabel was furious, of course, but there wasn't much she could do about it. Each of her children had inherited company stock when their grandfather died so, with the odd job to supplement his dividend income, he was able to stay away from the whole situation. Later, after he married Marilyn and they came back to Toronto, Isabel tried again to get him to consider working for the company – by that time your father was no longer with us and even Father could see that the contribution of someone with a vested interest would have been beneficial – but he flatly refused. Just before he died, he did work for the company for a few months. Father, by then, was retired – or, at least, as retired as he'd ever be. Angus brought in a lot of business. He was very good with people – just like his father. But that, of course, was the whole trouble – with the two of them..."

"What trouble?"

"Wine, women and song," said Selena, raising her glass. "Angus Senior partook of a lot of wine, women and song before the *alone in a Montreal hotel room heart attack* of Isabel's story, and Angus – why was that family so unimaginative about names? Marilyn had the sense to put a stop to it but, I understand, Michael has carried on the tradition, though why I don't know – I thought hockey players were supposed to be very superstitious, or is that baseball players? Anyway, the problem with *all* the Angus McGraths was wine, women and song."

"I didn't know about that," Alan said. "I do remember when Angus was killed, but the drinking part was supposed to be because of his despondency over the break up with Marilyn."

"That was Isabel's story. That whole generation was expertly skilled in the art of cover-up and the science of opportunism. This is strong stuff you're feeding me, my boy. I hope you intend to see me safely downstairs."

Alan smiled. "Of course."

"Joking aside, you don't need to feel badly about your own treachery at all, you see. Your grandfather took his opportunities and locked out the McGraths, Isabel put one over on him and, in a few years, I think we'll see McGraths and LaPlantes working happily together again. Now, you just see me down those stairs–" she said, finishing her drink, "I have to get my beauty sleep."

"Aunt Selena," Alan said slowly, "how do you know all this?"

She put down her glass and looked at him, an amused expression on her face. "Let's just say that, in the mid to late nineteen-fifties, I was of an age that philandering husbands find highly attractive – old enough to know not to push for a more formal relationship – or want to, for that matter – but still young enough to be desirable. In later years, I suppose my curiosity was heightened by the experience and I naturally observed what was happening more closely than most."

"You..." Alan felt his voice trailing off. He gulped. "Did Isabel ever know?"

"If she did, I would have been the last person to find out."

## MARILYN

After his mother's funeral, Michael returned to Vancouver and did not come to Toronto again until three years later. We saw him once. After receiving the news of the children's inheritance and my enforced employment at McGrath-LaPlante, I decided to splurge and we visited my brother, in Australia, for Christmas. I arranged the trip out so that we travelled on a flight originating in Vancouver, and Michael and his son met us at the airport. Angus was eight then. Since he scarcely knew us, I expected him to be rather shy. He was hardly shy. On the contrary, he appeared to demand constant attention and completely exhausted my own three children who took it in turns to look after him when we drove down to Stanley Park for the afternoon. I privately thought that it was just as well his parents were divorced – it would be the only way to get any rest from the child!

I talked to Michael on the phone a couple of times after that. So did Danny. Then he moved without leaving a forwarding address. Danny was upset at losing contact for some time, but worked at McGrath-LaPlante for the first time that summer, then back at school, was soon caught up in improving his grades and applying for a university place, so did not remain feeling slighted for long. Now and again the subject came up and we'd wonder how Michael was and if Angus's behavioural problems had improved. I'd check periodically to see if Laura or Frances had heard from him, but there was no communication until a few weeks before Christmas three years after the one when we'd met him in Vancouver. He phoned and asked if he could bring Angus to visit us for Christmas.

"You're welcome, Michael," I said, "but won't you be upsetting your sisters staying here."

"Actually, I was hoping Byron might help me out with Angus. The other cousins are all so much older."

"Well, Byron's older now, too," I reminded him. "Maybe not *as* old but time doesn't stand still, you know. I never really thought of Byron as mentor material, either."

"He's still playing hockey, isn't he?"

"Oh yes. He's not expecting to follow in your footsteps any longer, but he still plays."

"I'd just like Angus to be exposed to a boy's life in Ontario, I guess. I sometimes wonder if he's not living in a vacuum over there in Victoria."

"Because they don't have enough ice and snow?"

He laughed. "No – just the academic environment with his stepfather on the UVic faculty... the whole association Victoria has with retirement rather than youth... Anyway can we come? I can't let him loose in my sisters' homes – you know that."

But it'll be okay in your ex-sister-in-law's, I thought crossly, then realised that this was really a cry for help. The child's behaviour problems evidently had not improved and his father was hoping that a couple of weeks in the company of his cousins might help.

"When do we expect you?" I asked.

"Judith wants me to pick him up the day school ends. She and Lawrence are taking the baby – they have a little girl now – to visit Lawrence's parents in California for Christmas. The truth of the matter is that his parents aren't exactly crazy about Angus – not that you can blame them since Angus hasn't exactly ingratiated himself to them. Anyway, I thought I'd go and fetch him and we'd stay here for the night and fly to Toronto the next morning."

"I take it school ends the same day there as here – the Friday?"

"Yes – we'll be there sometime on the Saturday afternoon. I'll book a car and give you a call before I pick it up. Okay?"

"I'll make sure that if I'm not here, Byron will be or maybe Danny – he should be home then, unless he just dumps his laundry and takes off somewhere–"

"He's at Western?" Michael asked.

"Yes – second year."

"And Megan?"

"Megan's at OCA but she's moved in with – with her fiancé. She says it's easier for school."

"You're right – time doesn't stand still. You approve, I take it? Is he a responsible type?"

I smiled. "Oh yes. Michael, Megan's going to marry Alan – Alan LaPlante."

"You're joking. When did that happen?"

"Oh – let's see... they met at last year's company Christmas Party and haven't looked back since."

"What about his grandfather?"

"Old Denny never knew – he died just after Christmas last year. Alan kept it from him because he was afraid he'd have a heart attack if he knew his precious grandson was involved with a McGrath. Then he had a heart attack anyway and left Alan his entire interest in McGrath-LaPlante because he was afraid that if he left it to Dennis, Dennis might die and leave it to Laura and then the McGraths together would be majority shareholders. Crazy – huh?"

"Wow – I'm really out of date. He's a bit old for her isn't he? I mean, there's a bit of an age difference, isn't there?"

"No more – less, in fact – than Charles and Di."

"What?"

"The Prince and Princess of Wales."

"Oh. Well, I guess you all know what you're doing. I'd better call Laura and Frances and let them know we're coming. How's Laura behaving towards you now?"

"Oh, no problem. I don't think we'll ever be best friends or anything, but she doesn't seem to actually hate me or anything, not that I see much of her."

"Well, I won't hold you up any longer and I'll call if anything changes. Thanks, Marilyn. I really appreciate your help."

"You're welcome. Hey – tell you what. Why don't we go and cut down a tree on the Sunday? He'd like that, wouldn't he?"

"Sure. Sounds like a good idea."

"Okay, then. 'Bye."

. . . . .

As it turned out their flight was delayed and they did not arrive until sometime after eight in the evening. Byron had eaten his supper and gone to a party at a friend's house, but Danny, who had arrived home from school for Christmas the day before, stayed to welcome them. I had made a casserole in case of the need to keep things warm and we had supper when they arrived.

This was not a good move. I'd have done better to have made Angus run around the block a few times to release some of the energy pent up due to spending the day in plane and airport, and then ordered in a pizza! As things were, he picked at his food, kept asking if he could give some to Ben and wishing aloud that we had let him unpack his suitcase first. Finally, when it turned out that he didn't like the fruit and granola desserts I had made, I suggested that Danny take him up to Byron's room and help him unpack and put his things away.

"Byron volunteered Angus sleep on the daybed in his room," I explained to Michael, "but, if it doesn't work out, we'll move him in with you. You're in Megan's room." I turned to Angus. "Is that all right with you, Angus? Or would you prefer to share with your dad?"

"No – with Byron," he said quite decisively. "It'll be like a sleep-over."

"Well, I don't know about that. Not if you mean staying awake all night. Byron doesn't do that any more. He used to, but he and his friends seem to be more into sleeping now. Anyway Danny'll show you the way and there are Atari games set up on the little television in Byron's room for you to play. Do you like video games?"

"Yeah? Why didn't you tell me before? Wow, Dad, Atari! Let's go, Danny!"

He raced up the stairs.

"Finally scored a hit, Mom," remarked Danny with raised eyebrows, as he picked up Angus's suitcase and back pack and followed the boy.

"We'll be having coffee in the living room when you come down," I said, hoping Angus wouldn't expect him to stay and play the games with him. "You go through, Michael. I left every thing ready in the kitchen, so I'll just be a minute."

"Lawrence won't let him have an Atari," Michael told me when I brought in the coffee. "He gets to play at his friends' homes, of course, but they all beat him because, naturally, they've sharpened their skills."

"He might beat Danny," I said, as we sat down with the coffee. "He's not that up on it. Byron got the new board for Christmas last year. Danny played a bit with him then, but it hasn't exactly been high priority when he's been home since then. Anyway, I'm glad it turns out to be something that'll keep him busy..."

"Yes, I'm sorry he was such a pain at supper. He is actually improving, believe it or not. It's just that – well, hanging around the airport all the morning, then not being able to move about too much on the plane and the time difference..."

"Oh, that's all right." I said, "I expected it to some extent – mealtimes get pretty messed up anyway, when you're flying. So what have you been doing with yourself, Michael? Everybody's been wondering what's going on with you – you *should* keep in touch, you know."

"You mean Laura?"

"Well – Frances, too. And Danny. I mean, let's face it, whether of not you keep in touch with your sisters is really nothing to do with me, but you and Danny seemed to get quite close after the time you took him out to lunch and told him all the family secrets..."

"Oh – he told you about that?"

"Not at the time – you had him pretty mixed up then – but later... Anyway, you could have let him know where you were."

"Yes, I should have. It's hard to explain. I just got into a really bad bout of depression – just the situation with Judith and Angus and – if I'm honest – not being a hockey hero anymore and... Do you know what happens when you get depressed?"

"Well..."

"Oh, I don't mean the blues – feeling blue... I mean real, *clinical* depression. You procrastinate – keep putting off even simple things like calling your relatives. You just don't feel equal to it, somehow. Then it gets to the point where you've left it so long, it becomes a major effort to figure out an explanation, so you leave it some more..."

"I'm sorry," I said. "I didn't realise..."

"Anyway, I'm over it now. Judith landing Angus on me made me realise that I had a responsibility and couldn't spend my life wallowing in depression. And, Marilyn..."

"Yes?"

"I appreciate you letting me use you as a stepping stone. There's no way I would even have attempted calling Laura without having the excuse that staying here would be good for Angus. Although, even then–" He poured himself more coffee and I held my own cup towards him. After he had filled my cup, too, and was sitting back in his chair again, he continued, "Even then, Laura couldn't see why I had to stay here. She thought I should leave Angus here with you and stay at her place myself. I said I'd see how he settled in – just to placate her. I wouldn't really do that to you."

"You'd better phone her. She called earlier and I told her the plane was delayed and I'd get you to call when you got here."

"Well, she's not to know when that was. I'll call her when I finish my coffee."

Danny came downstairs.

"He's honing his skills on that one with the long worm – Superworm or something? Anyway, it should be good for a little while. Did you save me some coffee?"

I poured his coffee. "I'll go and look after loading the dishwasher," I said.

"I can do it, Mom, if you and Michael are talking," said Danny.

"It's okay. You've earned yourself a rest, I think."

I went into the dining room and cleared the table, then stacked the dishwasher, turned it on and cleaned the kitchen. Just as I was wiping the counters, the phone rang. It was Laura. I wished I had given Michael another reminder so that he could have called her first.

"Yes, they're here," I said in answer to her immediate query. "Sorry – he would have called before, but what with unpacking and having supper and everything, he's only just this minute got to it..." I called into the living room, ensuring that she could still hear me, "Michael that's Laura on the phone now – I told her you were just about to call her... must be a case of great minds thinking alike."

I heard Danny telling him to get it in the study, waited until I heard him lift the receiver and put down the one I was using. I poured the remainder of the wine we had had with dinner into a glass and went into the living room.

"I'm finishing the wine," I said. "There's beer in the fridge, Danny, if you'd like to get it for you and Michael. Take the coffee things as you go, please. Angus is really into that Atari game, isn't he?"

Danny picked up the coffee cups and put them on the tray which I had originally served coffee from.

"He seems to have been going through a pretty bad time – Michael, I mean," he said. "I wish I *had* gone out there the summer before last now – I'd have been able to find him through the insurance agency he works for. He's still with them."

Danny had toyed with the idea of going out to Vancouver the summer before he started university but had, in the end, decided to go on a wilderness vacation with a group of his friends during the two weeks when he wasn't filling in for vacationing plant personnel at McGrath-LaPlante.

Michael came back from the study as Danny picked up the tray.

"Danny's just getting you a beer from the fridge," I said. "How did you make out with Laura."

He grinned. "Oh, so-so. She still can't understand why I'm not staying with them."

"Well, maybe Angus will decide he likes us and will settle down and you'll be able to."

"Perhaps," he said doubtfully. "I did try to make her understand that the problem with Angus was a bit more involved than I had admitted before – without going so far as to make her think he was a complete brat, I mean. I think I managed to communicate that I wasn't in the running to compete with her as parent of the perfect child. How are those two girls getting on anyway?"

"Oh, they survived," I laughed. "Jayne gives her mother as good as she gets and Cindi mostly avoids her. Cindi's about to make Laura a grandmother..."

"Yes, Laura told me."

Danny came in with a beer each for Michael and himself – poured into beer glasses, no less. I raised my eyebrows and he grinned a little sheepishly.

"Well, I thought I'd be a good host," he said.

"Cheers," said Michael taking the proffered glass and raising it.

Danny raised his own glass.

"Anyway, Jayne's going to become V.P. Finance next year when Harry Jameson retires and Laura still can't see a woman's career as being an accomplishment," I continued. "Cindi's being a teacher was a bit more acceptable, but poor Laura still can't understand her putting off motherhood so long. Dennis is quite the opposite – he's grooming Jayne to eventually take over as CEO"

"Wow, that's a switch. It's you, I think – it's you being there that changed him. Has to be... because three years ago he was having fits over my mother's will. So Dennis has become a women's libber in his old age! What about Alan – I thought he was the one being groomed for President..."

"Only while his grandfather was alive," Danny said. "You missed the LaPlante Last Will and Manipulation – it was even more dramatic than Grandma McGrath's!"

"I didn't even know Old Denny was gone until your mother told me," Michael told him, nodding in my direction. "What did he do – leave Alan out of the will for taking up with a McGrath girl?"

"No," I interjected, "I told you about it. He never knew about Megan – Alan was afraid it would give him a heart attack. It was Dennis that he left out of the will – from the McGrath-LaPlante viewpoint, I mean. He left him other stuff."

"Dennis? Right, I don't get it..."

"Well, it was Grandma's fault," explained Danny. "You see by setting it up so that we – Megan, Byron and me – became shareholders or will do, I suppose I should say, she put the McGraths in a position of holding the majority of the shares if anything happened to Uncle Dennis and Aunt Laura inherited his twelve-and-a-half per cent. He left all his shares to Alan and instructions for Uncle Dennis to do the same thing – you have to remember that *his* sons had actually inherited their stock from their uncle, who had no sons, and that Alan was closer to being a son than a nephew to Uncle Dennis, anyway – so it wasn't inconceivable that he should. In other words, Uncle Dennis was to follow the LaPlante tradition of keeping women out and McGraths in their place. The irony is that if Uncle Dennis actually did that and, down the road, Megan married Alan and he died and she inherited his shares, the McGraths would own the company completely."

"My God, Danny – you're beginning to sound like your grandmother and Old Denny yourself," I told him, "I'd never even have thought of that."

"I'm just joshing, Mom. Megan would have become a LaPlante anyway..."

"Well, none of this explains why Jayne is going to succeed Dennis instead of Alan," Michael interrupted.

"Oh, that's quite simple," I said, "Alan doesn't want to. I never knew any of this, of course, being blacklisted for so many years, and you were never around – or interested either, for that matter – but Alan only ever went into the company because he felt he owed it to his grandfather to do so."

"Back when Grandma McGrath died, we – well, it was Megan actually – way before she actually knew him – called him the Crown Prince of McGrath-LaPlante," said Danny. "All the time he was there under duress... You know, we haven't heard a peep out of Angus for ages – should I go up?"

"No, I'll go. I expect he's fallen asleep – it's eleven-thirty, you know."

I went up to Byron's room and found Angus, still clutching a joy stick, asleep on the floor. I switched off the television and game board and turned back the covers on his bed then called softly down to Michael to help me get him into bed without waking him. This accomplished, I took Michael across the passage and showed him which drawers I had cleared for him in Megan's room. He looked around the room.

"It's funny," he said, "The last time I was in this room it was inhabited chiefly by Barbie dolls and stuffed animals. Are you really happy with it?  With Megan being..."

"Of course, I sometimes wish we could go back to the Barbies and stuffed animals – I'd be lying if I didn't, but I don't have regrets about Alan. You see – maybe this sounds silly, but you know the old phrase about marriages made in Heaven?"

He nodded.

"That's how it is," I said. "you'll see. That saying must have originated with people like them. They just, somehow, go together..."

•  •  •  •  •

The next morning poor Byron, who – getting home just ahead of his midnight curfew in time to join the rest of us in bringing each other up to date on our activities – had crept quietly into bed so as not to disturb his little cousin, was awakened by Angus at seven thirty. This he did not appreciate and tried to doze while giving Angus instructions on playing the various video games.

Angus's rather shrill voice woke me in the next room and I got up, showered and dressed much before I liked to get moving on a Sunday morning. I went into Byron's room, reflecting that it was a long while since I'd been forced into early rising because of children being up and around.

"Hi, Aunt Marilyn," said Angus, "how did I get in bed in my underwear last night?"

"Your father and I put you there. We figured it was easier to leave you in your underwear than to get your pyjamas on. You fell asleep on the floor. Now, do you usually have a bath or a shower?"

"Shower, but I'm not dirty. I don't need one."

"Yes, you do. You were travelling all day yesterday – you can't travel clear across the country without getting dirty. You should really have had a bath last night before you slept in my clean sheets. I bet your mother doesn't let you go to bed dirty, does she?" I continued without giving him time to reply. "Now, come along and I'll see that you've got the water right and then I'll put your things away – how come you and Danny didn't do that last night? Anyway, decide what you're going to wear and come along."

My continual talking technique had the desired effect and the faintly mesmerised Angus was in the bathroom with his bundle of clean clothes before he had time to argue. I turned on the taps and ensured that the temperature of the water was adequate.

"There just pull the lever up when you're ready and there are clean towels on the rail," I told him. "and don't lock the door because you're in a strange bathroom and we need to be able to get in if you run into trouble. And clean up when you're finished and put your dirty clothes in the laundry basket. Okay?"

"Yes," he mumbled. "Don't let Byron change the game."

"Don't worry about that. I expect Byron's gone back to sleep by now."

I went back to Byron's room and put Angus's clothes away, without disturbing the shopping bag full of wrapped Christmas gifts in the bottom of the suitcase, then I went downstairs to the kitchen, let Ben out and in again and debated whether to make a full pot of coffee or just enough for myself. I knew the boys would sleep as long as they could but I wasn't sure about Michael. I decided to make half a pot, which I put on then emptied the dishwasher, which I hadn't had time or inclination to do the night before, and laid the kitchen table for everyone, putting out orange juice, cereal, fruit, milk and bread to cover all eventualities. I hoped, however, that Angus and I would be eating alone so that I could get to know him a little.

Surprisingly he came downstairs without going back to his room and the Atari, and waking Byron. He was probably hungry, I reflected, remembering the picked at supper.

"I left everything tidy for the next person, Aunt Marilyn," he said. "Wow – goody, you have *Harvest Crunch*. It's my favourite. Where shall I sit?'

"It doesn't really matter. I don't think any of those lazy guys are getting up anyway. Help yourself. Do you want me to pour your milk?" Watching him spill cereal all over his placemat, I had visions of milk spilt across the table. I poured it without waiting for a reply. "Have some orange juice first." I poured him some and served myself some cereal while he drank his juice. We both ate in silence.

"Do you have egg or toast or anything like that for breakfast?" I asked him, when he had finished the bowl of cereal. I leaned my chair back to reach the counter and put bread in the toaster.

"No thanks. Can I have some more cereal, though?"

"Go ahead," I said, finishing my own. I stood up and poured the milk on the cereal he had put in his bowl then poured my coffee and buttered my toast before sitting down again.

"You don't remember us when we came to Edmonton, do you?" I asked.

"I forget Edmonton. I know I lived there when Dad played hockey, but I can't remember it. I remember that time when you were going to Australia, though, and were in Vancouver for the day and I remember Megan looking after me. I liked Megan – when will she be coming?"

I had told him, at supper the night before, that Megan and Alan would be bringing Alan's Little Brother, Adam, over this afternoon and we'd all go out to a Christmas tree farm to cut down a tree. He hadn't known what a Little Brother was and Danny had explained about the organization and how Megan's friend was a Big Brother to Adam, a boy of Angus's age, who had no father or older brother to do guy things with. Angus thought it sounded cool and probably more fun than having a father and a stepfather, a comment which Michael obviously did not appreciate but let pass without saying anything. Actually it was Megan who had suggested getting the two boys together and the Christmas tree expedition had seemed like an appropriate occasion. Megan and Alan were intending to cut a tree for themselves and one for Adam's family, so they had every excuse to leave early if the boys weren't getting along with each other. If things worked out, however, everybody would be staying to trim our tree except Michael who would have to leave, as soon as we got back, to go to Laura's for a family dinner with his sisters' families.

"Not until after lunch. She's looking forward to seeing you again, but they have to get some other things done and pick Adam up and everything. I was asking you about Edmonton because I was sorting out the big cupboard downstairs where we keep all the sort of things – mostly junk, really – you know, things which you don't want to throw out but aren't really very useful – you probably have a cupboard like that at your house... Anyway, I was sorting things out and found this." I took down, from the top of the fridge where I'd left it, an old sketch book which Megan had had when she was eleven, the summer we went to the Rockies. "Megan was the same age then as you are now. She sketched our holiday – it was a kind of project." I moved his empty cereal bowl and put the book on the table in front of him. "The first few pages are at the airport and on the plane, then we stayed at your house for a few days. Take a look."

I refilled my coffee mug and sat down as he turned the pages.

"That's Mom and Dad. Megan was a good artist – I don't know any kids my age who can draw like this. And this is me, isn't it?"

"There's two or three of you in there and the tent the boys slept in your back yard – your dad slept in it, too, actually. Your mom and I figured he was recapturing his lost childhood or something..."

"I wish I remembered it," Angus said a little wistfully. "It sounds like it was a lot of fun. I guess I was too small to sleep in the tent. Oh look –" he turned another page "– me with Ben. I didn't know I'd seen Ben before – he must be quite old." Ben, in his basket in a corner of the kitchen, pricked up his ears when he heard his name. "Megan was a good drawer, wasn't she?"

"Well, she still is," I said, "that's why she's at OCA."

"What *is* OCA?"

"Oh, I'm sorry – how would you know? It's like you saying UVic to Byron – he wouldn't have a clue. Anyway it's the Ontario College of Art."

"I should have guessed that with looking at her drawings. I like this one of Ben in the water – he looks kind of puppyish."

"Actually he wasn't very old then – about a year or so."

"I wish I was an artist," Angus said, "then I could draw my trip – this trip, I mean."

"Well, I'm sure your dad's going to take lots of photos – and you, too. Do you have a camera?"

"I didn't bring it because Dad says it's better to take 35 mm pictures of important things – I mean, things that you want to keep. But he says I can use his and I can have all the pictures – he'll just get duplicates of the ones he wants."

"I see."

I finished my coffee and began to put our dirty dishes in the dishwasher while Angus went back to the sketch pad.

"We have a photograph album of that trip, too, if you want to see it later. And maybe you'd like to see our Australia pictures, too."

"Yes, I would – but I want to finish this first."

"Well, I didn't mean right this minute..." I smiled, "You'll be here for two weeks."

I had been hearing the sounds of somebody in the shower while we had been talking, but was not sure whether it was Michael or one of my sons. I put fresh coffee on. It turned out to be Michael. He came into the kitchen and looked surprised to see Angus engrossed in the sketch book.

"Good morning," I said. "Did you sleep well?"

"Like a log," he said, "I must have been completely beat after sitting up half the night talking with you lot. Did this one wake you up?" He nodded towards Angus.

"Oh, it's all right. I'm not really into sleeping in much. I've just put a fresh pot of coffee on – I drank all of the previous one. Help yourself to juice and cereal. Would you like eggs?"

He sat down at the table and poured some orange juice into a glass. "No thanks – cereal's fine..."

"Hey, Dad!" said Angus, looking up. "Have you seen this?"

"No – what is it?"

"It's Megan's – a sketch book she did when she was only my age. You're in it. And Mom and me when I was little. And Ben. I'll

bring it round there and I can show it to you while you're eating."
He moved round to the other side of the table next to his father.
"Just don't spill anything on it."

"What kind of slob do you think I am?"

Angus chuckled. "No... look – see, here's you."

"Oh, that was when they came to Edmonton and the boys and
I camped out in the back yard. I remember – Megan was going to
draw the whole trip."

"Well, she did – see how much there is. She's a good artist –
that's why she's at – what's it called, Aunt Marilyn?"

"OCA you mean?" said Michael before I could answer.

"Yeah – the Ontario College of Art. You didn't think I knew
what it meant did you?"

"No – but, then – if you don't know things, you have to ask
somebody. So I figured you were smart enough to have asked Aunt
Marilyn. Now, did you take your Beclovent this morning? – you
sound a bit wheezy to me. You'll have to take some Ventolin, too"

"No, I forgot." Angus stood up. "Sorry, Dad."

"I forgot, too," I admitted to Michael. "I should have reminded
him."

"No, Marilyn, he's supposed to be responsible for it – he's old
enough now. Where is it, Angus?"

"In my backpack. I'll go and get it."

He ran through the living room and up the stairs to his room.
I poured coffee for Michael and myself.

"We were getting along so well, I completely forgot to ask him
what the schedule was with his medication."

"Don't worry about it. He understands the importance of being
responsible for his asthma himself – he knows his mother will

never agree to me taking him away again if he ends up in the hospital. It's his short attention span that's the problem."

"He stayed interested in that sketch pad for a long time. In fact, except for bugging Byron about the Atari games first thing, he's been quite a pleasure to have around all the morning."

"That's good," said Michael, "I was feeling a bit guilty about sleeping in and leaving you to deal with him. Thanks. Think I should call him back down?"

I shook my head. "Don't worry about it. It's about time Byron – and Danny, too – got up anyway."

. . . . .

Angus kept us all on our toes for the two weeks that he and his father stayed at our house, although it was rather nice having a younger child around again for Christmas. He and Adam got along well together and, one evening the following week, Alan took him to see Adam's hockey practice and to MacDonald's afterwards. Michael, however, squelched the boys' plans for Angus to visit Adam and stay overnight at his Regent's Park apartment. I had realised too late – on the first afternoon, in fact – that Michael wasn't too crazy about his son's association with the inner city child. I wasn't quite sure whether he was motivated by concern for his son's safety in that part of the city, or by snobbery. I was so used to the boy being part of Alan's life and – by extension – Megan's, that I tended not to associate him with the tough neighbourhood in which he lived. Angus was, quite obviously, fascinated with Adam's world. His own comfortable, rather privileged background palled by comparison – not that he was about to let Adam know that. His transfer from the public school, which he had originally attended, to the private school he went to now – in reality due to his behavioural problems – was upgraded, for Adam's benefit, to an expulsion and poor Lawrence was turned into a dreadful stepfather who only cared for his own child and hated having to have Angus around. Mostly communicated during telephone conversations, none of this information, naturally, was imparted when Michael was within hearing. Asked why he didn't just go and live – as Adam stoutly declared he would have done – with his hockey hero father, he confided that he was afraid for his mother's life if he left.

Most of these revelations were made to Alan by Adam, a stolid, very honest kind of child to whom telling wild stories about his family would not have occurred, in the weeks after Michael and Angus had returned to BC. We discussed telling Michael, but decided that, since it was all quite obviously fabricated to compete with what Angus perceived as Adam's more torrid lifestyle, there was not much point in upsetting him. Alan and all three of my own children owned up to telling their friends silly stories about themselves, at various points in their lives, just to create an impression and I had to admit I'd done it myself. I did, however, get Judith's address from Michael and wrote to her explaining who Adam was and told her a little about his family just in case Angus's imagination was continuing to work overtime and his friends' parents began to complain about stories he was telling them about Regent's Park. I put an emphasis on the fact that we had introduced the boys because we thought it would be a good learning experience for them both since I knew this would appeal to Lawrence who, Michael had told me, was an ardent socialist and quite upset about Angus going to a private school.

The two weeks were hectic. Michael came back from dinner at Laura's house, that first Sunday evening, with an invitation for all of us to go there in the evening on Christmas Eve for a "family get-together". Since I wasn't a family member and, while I was on better terms with my one time in-laws now than in previous years, I was scarcely overjoyed at the prospect. I had been planning on a quiet evening at home... hopefully alone. Danny already had other plans, but I leaned on Byron to come with us to keep an eye on Angus. Alan and Megan were there and Laura's daughter Cindi and her husband – Jayne had gone away for Christmas – and Frances and her husband and daughter, Angela, who was now in her second year at McGill, having begun university at the same time as Danny. Angus had not seen either of his aunts since before his parents had separated, although communication had been maintained, until the last couple of years through the birthday cards and Christmas gifts, they sent him in care of Michael, and the required thank you letters. Once the initial introductions and small talk were over, he was restless until Dennis, thankfully, suggested Byron take him downstairs to play pool which kept him busy while the adults chatted. I didn't expect him to stay attentive for too long and was a bit worried about him damaging the pool table but, as it turned out, he was quite an expert with a pool cue and the younger men – Alan and Cindi's husband, Robert – joined them for a game before he lost interest. Laura brought out hot snacks at this point, after which we were able to graciously take our leave.

Megan and Alan, as well as my parents, came to have Christmas dinner with us creating a nice family atmosphere. As they had grown older, my mother and father had become far more open-minded than they had been when my brother and I were growing up. They, in fact, had accepted Megan's moving in with Alan far more readily than I had myself – apparently recognizing it as quite a normal stage of development, an attitude far removed from the days when I was engaged to be married and exhorted to save myself for my wedding night! Even having Michael staying in my house – despite the presence of our respective children – would have been looked at quite differently in those bygone days. It's sometimes said that grandparents relate far better to their grandchildren than to their own children and this was definitely the case here.

So, Christmas passed and, in the succeeding days Michael took Angus to see the various sights in Toronto including the Hockey Hall of Fame, where he could be shown first-hand evidence of his father's hockey days which, naturally, were far removed from reality for him – he was only four years old when Michael retired, after all. Megan and I went with them the day they went up the CN Tower and I talked Byron into coming to Niagara Falls with us on another. By the time they left to go home, I felt we had all established bonds with Angus and I hoped that, perhaps, with coming to know his father's family and developing feelings of belonging, his behaviour problems might stabilize. I also hoped that Michael would stay in touch and not let himself get dragged down by depression again. And, although I positively hate anybody doing such a thing to me, I manipulated the possibility of a new interest for him by asking him to drop off a belated Christmas gift to the child of a former neighbour and good friend who had recently returned to her Vancouver roots after the break up her marriage. I privately felt that if Michael stopped carrying a torch for Judith and became more open to a new relationship, both he and Angus might be happier. It was worth a try.

# BYRON

Byron was relieved to finally get out of the crazy penguin suit and hoped he'd never get talked into wearing one again... not for his own wedding, for sure, because he'd never have that kind of wedding if he ever married at all and he didn't think he would... no way would he submit to such a waste of time and money, and he hoped nobody would ever ask him to be a groomsman again... certainly not in an unexpected May heatwave, anyway.

He hung the suit on the hanger that had come with it, and put it in the bag ready to go back to *Tuxedo Junction*, and pulled on shorts and a tee shirt. He and Danny had left the Granite Club, as soon as the bride and groom had gone, and driven home. It was too warm a night to stay dressed up like a waiter for long.

Downstairs he found Danny sitting out at the patio table, in the moonlight, sipping beer from a can. His brother hadn't changed, but they'd both thrown off their jackets and ties and opened up their collars before even getting into Danny's car to come home. Byron poured himself a large glass of the lemonade he'd made from scratch that morning, over lots of ice. He didn't drink alcohol or caffeine or eat red meat. He joined Danny on the patio.

"It's weird, you know," said Danny, meditatively, "Megan hasn't actually lived here for the last three years, but it didn't seem as if she'd really gone until today."

"It's probably because you're only here at vacation times yourself – it doesn't seem that way to me. She left ages ago. But then I was the baby and the two of you always seemed so much older than me, so I wouldn't notice it so much, would I?"

"I guess not."

"I'm just glad it's over – the wedding bit, I mean. I still can't see why they needed all that phony shit. I know you explained how it was good for the company's image to do the Establishment type stuff, but I wouldn't do it."

"You've made that pretty clear. Even if it was Establishment," Danny said, sounding a little defensive, "Megan was a beautiful bride you've got to admit."

"Well, it's kind of hard to see your sister as beautiful – I mean, she's your sister – right? But I know what you mean – they looked like something in a wedding magazine."

"You know," Danny said, after a short silence. "I was ready to smash his face in – that first Christmas they started going together..."

"Yeah, coming on like some Victorian big brother. I remember."

"Well, I'd worked there – at McGrath-LaPlante – for the two summers before that."

"Mom was there, too. She knew him."

"Mom's a VP – she doesn't hear the office gossip... or worse, the plant gossip. Alan had a reputation as a regular Casanova. You should have heard some of the snide remarks when he got into all his marketing schemes to protect the world from AIDS. Of course I was upset when he started getting the hots for my sister..."

"He didn't get the hots for her... Jesus, you *are* Victorian," broke in Byron. "It was a meeting of the minds and souls."

"Where the hell did you get a phrase like that from?"

"Actually, Mom said it once – a long time ago. She was talking to Nana, eh? And, I guess, trying to reassure herself, though I didn't get it at the time." He shrugged. "The phrase kinda stayed with me – the poetry of the minds coming together and the soul being one already, you know? Hey – my name's Byron, what do you expect?" he added, in response to his brother's quizzical expression. "She was right, though – you just have to look at them."

"I guess so," Danny admitted. "I expect I'm just envious that I haven't experienced *a meeting of the minds and soul* with anyone. Hey, bring me out another beer, will you?" he added as Byron went back into the house to refill his glass.

"How do you know that the old gossips at McGrath-LaPlante don't say the same kind of stuff about you, anyway?" Byron asked his brother when he came back. "Here's your grossening booze." He slid the can across the table.

"They probably do. I was more impressionable then – took everything I heard as gospel." Danny grinned, pulling the tab on the beer can. "You'll see what I mean when you start working there."

Danny, after graduating with an Honours BA from Western, was finally taking the summer off this year and, travelling via Hong Kong and Singapore, to visit their relatives in Australia. Byron was going to work at McGrath-LaPlante for the first time. He knew, however, that it was not the place it had been when Danny first worked there five years before. The company had expanded more than anyone would have imagined, at any previous point in its history, with new assembly lines and personnel continually being added. Unlike his brother, Byron was not interested in operations and the last thing he wanted was to learn about the different aspects of production as Danny had done, and Alan, and all the McGraths and LaPlantes before them. He was fortunate in the fact that the unprecedented growth of the company had resulted in this system of "apprenticing" young LaPlantes and McGraths during their summer vacations becoming basically unrealistic. Byron wasn't at all sure that his future was going to be with McGrath-LaPlante, but he did know what he wanted to do... and there was no point in having stock in a family firm if you didn't make use of your resources, was there? Byron had talked his mother and his new brother-in-law into hiring him in the sales and corporate communications department for the summer.

Byron had followed his older sister into the local school board's School of Visual Arts program but his interest was design, not fine art. His mother had talked him into staying in the Grade 13 program, although he would have preferred to graduate this year. However, he intended to go – not to university – but to the community college, instead, and take one of the new computer graphics courses. Meantime, he'd found out that Alan was equipping his communications department with Macintosh computers and graphics software and, suddenly, after several years of finding excuses to avoid having to work at McGrath-LaPlante, Byron was clamouring for a summer job there.

Maybe it would be limited to inputting copy, rendering somebody else's layouts and proofing but it sure as hell beat packing safes into boxes on the assembly line, he thought, in the silence that followed the banter about gossip.

"Did people resent you when you first started working there, Dan?" he asked.

"Maybe some did a bit, at first," Danny replied, thoughtfully. "But most of them knew the story and were willing to give me a chance. It's not like it must have been for Dad, for instance, or Uncle Dennis – like, being the owner's son and going to private school, I mean... being from such a totally different background to the guys in the plant..."

"We *would* have been like that if Dad hadn't died, wouldn't we? Gone to Pickering College like Dad and Michael – right?"

"It was only because Mom refused to let Grandma McGrath pay the fees that I didn't! I remember them fighting about it – on the phone, of course. They never met face-to-face. Apparently the McGrath system was that you went to the local public school for the primary grades but by nine or ten you were supposed to associate with the kids who'd be your peers in later life."

"Sounds British..."

"Well, I suppose that's the idea – right? Anyway, Mom refused to take me out of Twin Oaks because she said I'd had enough trauma already and was happy there. She – Grandma, that is – tried again with Megan, using the fact that Angela was at Havergal as bait, but never tried it with you – guess she figured you were a hopeless case anyway..."

"Thanks," Byron said, with a grimace. "I'd have thought Mom would be home by this time – maybe we shouldn't have left."

"I think she's probably crying on Hugh's shoulder about now..."

"Lost her little girl, you mean? I expect you're right. Think she'll stay at his place then?"

"Probably." Danny rose and picked up his empty beer cans. "I'm going to bed, anyway. I want to leave early in the morning." He was driving up to a friend's cottage the next day for the rest of the Victoria Day weekend. "'Night."

"'Night, Dan."

. . . . .

Byron awoke, with a start, to the ringing of the phone the following morning. He closed his eyes, hoping somebody else would answer it, then looked at the clock and realised he must be alone in the house. He picked up the extension on his bedside table.

"Hallo?"

"Byron?"

"Yes, Michael," he said, recognizing his uncle's voice.

"Is your mother there?"

"No. At least, I don't think so. She wasn't when we went to bed, so I imagine she stayed at Hugh's."

"Oh."

"D'you want his number?" Byron asked, getting out of bed and reaching out to open his blind. He recited the number, without waiting for a reply. There was a short pause while Michael wrote it down.

"Thanks, although I don't think I should call her there about this... Maybe you can help me?"

"Sure. What's the problem?"

"It's Angus."

As if I couldn't guess, thought Byron. "What's he done?" he asked.

"Disappeared. We thought he was in bed – he's on the pull-out couch in the room that used to be the old man's den – but, figuring he was sleeping pretty late – for him, I mean – I went to check his room and found he wasn't there."

Michael, who had remarried last year, was in Toronto for Megan's wedding. He and his wife, Lise, her ten-year-old son, Justin, and Angus were staying in the ground floor apartment of Alan's house. Selena LaPlante, Alan's aunt, who usually stayed there when she was in town, was using Alan's spare room instead and, since Alan and Megan by this time were in England on their honeymoon, was alone in the upper apartment.

"Could he have gone upstairs? Did you check with Alan's aunt?"

"She hasn't seen him. I put off going up and disturbing her, but she was actually up hours ago. Laura and Dennis are picking her up shortly to go out somewhere – I wasn't really listening... Do you have that kid Adam's number?"

"No. Why would I have it? Ask the aunt – it's probably in the little book by the kitchen phone up there."

"I should never have brought Angus. He made out that he *really* wanted to see Megan get married and all the while he was planning to get together with that slum kid..."

"The modern term is inner city youth, Uncle Michael," said Byron.

"Don't get smart, Byron. Can't you see I'm worried sick? Alan needs his head tested – inviting the kid – and his mother and sister – to the church. It's a wonder he didn't ask them to the reception, too."

"He didn't because he didn't want them to feel out of place at the Granite Club, not because they'd embarrass us. He's been Adam's Big Brother for more than five years – they care about each other. Why shouldn't Adam come to the church?"

"Let's not argue about it, Byron. You're sure you don't have the number? – I don't want to bother Selena again."

"You can look it up in the directory. Their last name is Kinchen – and they're on Sumach Street."

Byron put the phone down. That's what a private school education did for you, he thought remembering the discussion he and Danny had been having last night, turned you into a snob. He shook his head and made his way to the bathroom.

Showered and dressed, Byron was eating cereal in the kitchen when his mother called.

"Byron, what did you do to Michael?" she asked.

"Sorry, Mom, but he really made me mad. He was knocking Alan for being Adam's Big Brother and having him and his family at the wedding and, generally being a snob..."

"It's not snobbery," she began. "Well, maybe it is a bit... But it's mainly Angus being down there – in that area – that he's worried about."

"It's snobbery, Mom. He doesn't want his little boy getting soiled by contact with the common people. He thinks Alan needs his head tested – his exact words – for letting them come to the church. I know he had the privileged McGrath upbringing, but you'd have thought being in professional hockey would have knocked that stuff out of his system. I mean aren't half the guys in the NHL supposed to be from tough backgrounds?"

"Not any more, Byron, It costs a fortune for kids to play hockey, today – you should know that. Kids like Adam only get to play when they have someone like Alan to help them."

"Michael was a Toronto Maple Leaf in the sixties, Mom. Those guys were tough... Anyway, did he call Adam?"

"He spoke to his mother – Adam wasn't home. He'd left to meet Angus at the Queen Street subway. His mother says the boys arranged – weeks ago, by phone – to spend the day together. She was under the impression that Michael approved... and Adam was, too. Adam's a responsible kid – I don't think he'd lie..."

"Nor do I," agreed Byron. "He wouldn't have gone for it if he knew Angus didn't have his father's permission – he's not like that. Angus spun him a line."

"Anyway, I think I put Michael's mind at rest about drugs and paedophiles, etc. I told him that whatever he thought of Adam's background, the boy's responsible and street-smart and Angus is not going to get himself in any trouble if he's with him. He was making noises about not knowing if Angus even got to Queen, but I told him..."

"... that you don't have to be a brain surgeon to figure out how to get over to the subway from Alan's house even for people not brought up to condescend to using public transit?"

"Well... I didn't say that... and don't be so judgmental. Anyway, I spoke to Lise and he's got her all upset – they have Jays' tickets for this afternoon and were originally planning to take the boys to Harbourfront first – the Children's Festival is on – and have lunch there before the game."

"I don't think the Children's Festival would have turned Angus on exactly. Michael seems to forget he's fourteen – not Justin's age," Byron pointed out. "They'd probably have lost him anyway..."

"That's what I thought, too, but I didn't say anything. Anyway, Michael wants to stay at the apartment in case Angus calls, so Hugh and I are going with Lise, instead. I'll be home to change shortly – I don't think my mother-of-the-bride dress is quite the right outfit... Danny's gone, I guess?"

"Yeah, he was gone before I woke up. How long were you there to, last night?"

"Later than I would have liked. You know how there are always people who don't know when to call it a night... and I could hardly leave. I'm glad I had Hugh – I didn't get much help from my sons, did I? Sneaking off like that..."

"Sorry, Mom. It was hot and boring and... well, Hugh was there with you. We thought you wouldn't mind."

"Well, I should be thankful you left rather than turn into drunken bores like some of those who stayed, I suppose. We'll be over in a while."

"See you, Mom."

He put the phone down, got himself another bowl of cereal and a glass of orange juice and took them out onto the patio. The dog, Ben, lying in the morning sunshine, looked up at him and flicked his tail but, evidently, considered him not worth getting up for. He sat at the table and finished his breakfast. He'd phone Michael and apologise for his rudeness before Mom got home and asked him to. Maybe he'd even try to explain to him that it was quite normal, at fourteen, to want to explore the city on your own. No... maybe not. He'd only get himself into another confrontation. He really didn't understand Michael, not that he really knew him all that well, anyway. As a small child, he remembered being told that his uncle played for the Edmonton Oilers. Danny had explained how Uncle Michael used to be a Maple Leaf but got traded to Edmonton. He remembered his uncle visiting them once or twice, but he only had shadowy memories of the visits – Danny and Megan being very excited and himself, gamely copying them. He did remember going to visit Michael and his family the summer he was seven. Later, when he got into minor hockey, he remembered cursing the bad timing – Michael had retired from hockey the year before Wayne Gretsky became an Oiler. Playing on Gretsky's team would have given his uncle a far higher profile in the eyes of Byron's own team-mates! After that, he hadn't seen him again until Grandma McGrath died. It was really only in the last couple of years – well, since the Christmas Michael had brought Angus to stay with them – that they'd had any real contact... and he was always so hyper about the kid that you couldn't really get to know him anyway. Whichever way you looked at it, this was not the big hockey hero Danny used to boast about so much – making Byron feel he'd missed out by being born too late!

He had to admit that, when Angus wasn't around, Michael was a lot more like the image Danny had painted for him when he was a kid. That was true. When he and Mom had gone out to visit, last summer, after Michael and Lise had phoned to say they were married, he'd been good fun – with a new wife and a new home and, basically, a new life, he should have been! Angus, thankfully, was away somewhere with his mother and stepfather. Megan and Alan had visited them at Easter and found the same thing. Megan said he was almost the fun person she remembered from her childhood until they'd gone to fetch Angus from Victoria for the Easter weekend – then he'd turned back into Mr. Paranoia again. Lise had actually confided in Megan, who had been Justin's baby-sitter for much of her early teens when Lise, during her first marriage, had lived near them in Islington, that she definitely would not have considered marrying Michael had he had custody of Angus.

Everyone found Angus a pain... Byron felt sorry for his cousin. It couldn't be easy being shuttled back and forth between two households, neither parent exactly overjoyed to have you around. He had been a problem, mainly due to his asthma and hyperactivity, way before his parents' marriage broke up, but having a stepfather – and a stepmother, too, now – involved in his life seemed to have made his behavioural problems worse over the years. Well, the term *behavioural problems* was just a label really, wasn't it? Angus's trouble was attitude – he'd never had the opportunity to develop family loyalties. As a result, he... well, basically, he just manipulated everybody for his own ends.

Wow, that's deep, Byron thought, maybe I should be looking at a psychology career instead of design.

"You know, Ben," he said, addressing the dog, "maybe you and I should get into my little old automobile and visit poor Michael... apologise in person, eh? – And see if we can cheer him up – well, stop him getting into the bottle anyway." He pulled a face. "Come on, boy." He collected his breakfast things and took them into the kitchen.

· · · · ·

Byron had to drop by his friend Mark's house with a book he'd promised to lend Mark, who had to study for an exam scheduled for the next day, then find a bank machine and get gas before driving over to the North Toronto neighbourhood where Alan's house was situated. Finally underway, he realised he had spent a lot longer than he'd intended at Mark's which meant that his mother had probably already picked up Lise and Justin. He should have left her a note then Michael would have known to expect him and Mom wouldn't be wondering why he'd taken off all of a sudden.

"Shit – they'll be thinking I'm as inconsiderate as – as... as Angus," he told the sleeping Ben who opened one eye and closed it again. "How can I be such a klutz. I know what we'll do – pick up one of those vegetarian pizzas from that place Megan orders from. It's past lunch time. Sound good?" Ben gave him a look of what appeared to be disgust. "Well, it's not meant for dogs anyway..."

He was feeling quite hungry by the time he pulled into the driveway of the big old house which Everton LaPlante had built in the early 1900s when his fledgling vulcanised rubber products company began making money. Michael looked surprised when he answered the door.

"I thought I'd bring you lunch to make amends for being rude this morning," said Byron. "I hope you don't mind – I brought the dog, too."

"That's okay." Michael said, stepping aside to let Byron pass, then calling the dog who was sniffing around in the bushes that separated the driveway from the neighbouring house. "Here, Ben... come here. Good boy." Ben ran in and he closed the door. "Why don't you take it through to the garden? – and I'll get some plates and stuff from the kitchen... and some beer. Oh no – you're a health nut now, aren't you? I think there's enough orange juice..."

"It's okay – I picked up a carton – it's in a bag hanging from my wrist under the pizza box – but I can use some ice."

Byron went along a passage, which ran the depth of the house, to a door which led out to the formal garden at the back. Ben followed him.

"Now you just stay right beside me, Ben. Be a good dog – if you start trampling tulips, Alan'll kill me – though it looks like they've all wilted in the heat anyway."

Ben lay down under the table as Michael brought plates, serviettes and a glass full of ice cubes out through the French doors of the dining room.

"Your mom was wondering where you'd gone..." he said when they were both settled and eating pizza.

"I expected to get here before she and Hugh did, but I had to go to a friend's house and ended up staying there longer than I meant to. Was she annoyed? Danny and I weren't in her best books to begin with – we kind of snuck out of the reception early and she thought we should have stuck around. Not early exactly – Megan and Alan had left – but, you know..."

"... there were still all the party animals sitting around talking about other weddings and things?"

"Yeah..."

"... like me?"

"I didn't mean..."

"I'm only kidding. We left about the same time. Justin was half asleep and Angus was sulking. He appeared to be attracted to some several times removed LaPlante cousin of about his age, but was too scared to talk to her. She obviously noticed him noticing her, and must have asked somebody else at their table – this was after dinner, when the tables had been moved back for dancing, so they were close together – anyway, she asked who he was and we all heard whoever answered tell her very clearly that he was Michael McGrath's bratty kid."

"Another kid?" asked Byron.

"No," replied Michael, "Female adult. Brilliant, eh?"

"Shitty thing to do. Had she been drinking?"

"I think she just had a permanently loud voice. Anyway, it was instant deflation. Lise tried to get him to dance with her, so did your mother and Jayne – your cousin, Jayne? – she was at the table on the other side and heard. But he wouldn't snap out of it and it was getting late – relatively speaking – so we left."

"Jerk woman – I wonder who she was?"

"Some distant LaPlante – I don't know half of them."

"Neither does Megan. Aunt Laura made us invite them all – made it seem like Alan owed them." Byron poured more juice from the carton into his glass. There was more room for juice now that the ice cubes had melted a little. "Angus was all right by the time you got home – back here, I mean, eh?"

"I talked to Lise all the way home – directing the conversation to her, but it was really for Angus's benefit – about how the last time I'd been in the company of so many unknown LaPlantes was at Laura's wedding when I was ten years old. I was the ring bearer and LaPlantes, who knew who I was, were apt to tell LaPlantes who didn't, that I was Angus McGrath's bratty kid."

"And it worked?"

"Oh yeah. He soon started giggling and he and Justin were fooling around with the idea of the LaPlantes referring to people as their father's bratty kids and they moved on from there – you were Angus McGrath's Angus's bratty kid because it got too confusing with there being two fathers called Angus... and by the time he went to bed, he was fine. We all seemed to be such good friends – so that's why it was so damned upsetting this morning when he took off like that." Michael stood up. "I'm going to get another beer – is there anything I can get for you?"

"No. I'm okay, thanks."

Michael returned. "Judith's had Angus seeing a psychiatrist for the last couple of years because kids like him – the hyperkinesis and short attention span – have severe problems with self esteem as they get into their teens and finally start to slow down. They start to look beyond themselves and find out what people think of them – i.e. what happened last night. So you see – until I talked to Mrs. Kinchen – I thought Angus had gone off because... well, because of bad feelings about himself. It's happened a couple of times before – once when he was with me in Vancouver. He got scared after he'd found his way to Gastown and called me to come and pick him up. The other time was when he was at home in Victoria – he met some street kids with a dog. Luckily they were decent kids and got him to phone his mother. So that's why I was so out of my mind until Mrs. Kinchen told me that the boys had planned this little exploit weeks ago. I wasn't so paranoid then..."

"Still pretty worried though?"

"Yeah, but not in the same way," Michael said. "I had no idea he still had Adam's number. I knew that he phoned him a few times after that Christmas when they met. I know that because Judith wanted to know who Adam was. Eventually the novelty wore off – speeded up by the cost of the calls being deducted from his allowance. But, I guess he must have kept the number and called him once he knew we were coming for the wedding." Michael grimaced. "So that's the story. Now I'll do you a favour and put it out of my mind – or, at least, to the back of my mind. I've hardly had a chance to talk to you – what with all your groomsman duties..."

"You nearly ended up being in the wedding party yourself," Byron told him. "We all figured Megan would ask you, since you're our closest male relative of the right age, to give her away, but she went all women's lib and wanted Mom to do it."

"I thought it was a nice idea. I never did see the sense of some male relative filling in for a deceased or absent father – it makes the role so meaningless unless, of course, he really has had a role in the bride's upbringing. I imagine it'll become quite usual, for the mother to give away the bride, in the future – with so many women bringing up their children alone."

"I guess. I wouldn't want such a stuffy wedding though – not that I intend getting married anyway. If I did I'd just do it and tell everyone afterwards – like you did."

Michael laughed. "That's all right for second marriages. It wouldn't have worked when Judith and I were married – people expected an extravaganza. Of course, in my case, it was turned into a public relations circus... television cameras and everything..."

Byron, less than three years old at the time of Michael's wedding, only knew what other people had told him about it. For Danny and Megan, as the junior members of the wedding party, it had been – except for Danny's eighth birthday party two weeks later – the last happy, memorable family event before their father died. He knew that – as Maple Leaf management had intended – it had given Michael a high profile which, a few weeks later, resulted in more attention than there would otherwise have been on his poor performance after his brother's death.

"I don't know why people have to get married anyway," Byron announced. "It just causes bad feelings when things go wrong."

"Not always... sometimes people live happily ever after, you know." Michael was silent. "So what do you think of Hugh?" he asked, after a few minutes.

"He's okay. I don't think Mom'll marry him, though, if that's what you mean. She thinks he has too much emotional baggage – I mean, she believes he cares about her, right? But, you see, his wife died of cancer three years ago – abdominal cancer which is really fast – and she says its going to take a long time for him to learn to live with it and she'd rather be his friend than a rival to the memory of his wife."

"Sounds like Marilyn talking."

"Well, it is – it's not like I haven't lived long enough to figure something like that out myself, eh? With Danny and Megan being away the last few years – well, Danny's home in the summer and a few days here and there – but, with there mostly being just Mom and me, I think we probably discuss personal things more than most parents and kids usually do."

"Well, he seems a nice enough guy," said Michael, "though I haven't really had a chance to talk to him. A wedding reception's not a great place to get to know someone..."

"Well, you'll be able to talk to him properly at our barbecue tomorrow. It's a pity you aren't staying longer. It's a long way to come just for a few days, but I guess you didn't want to take Angus and Justin out of school for too long."

"Have you finished school yet?"

"We just have a few exams to do and we'll be finished for the year... I could be finished for good, but I made a deal with Mom that I'd do Grade Thirteen even though I don't need it. She's afraid I might change my mind and decide I want to go to university after all..."

"So you're still set on graphic design?"

"Yes. I'm going to work in the advertising department at McGrath-LaPlante for the summer. Alan says it'll just be gopher stuff, but it's a start – is that the phone, I hear?"

Michael jumped up and ran into the house. Ben, asleep under the table, awoke with a start and barked.

"Okay, boy," Byron calmed him, "it's okay."

Michael returned to the patio a few minutes later.

"He's at Adam's apartment. I left this number with Adam's mother this morning. She made him phone. Congratulate me – I didn't do my paranoid act and tell him I'd pick him up. I told him to get himself back here – fast," he grinned. "You know what?"

"He was too surprised to argue, even?"

"Right."

Byron stood up and held his hand out in high five position, "Way to go, Michael!"

# MEGAN

Megan tilted her seat back when the seatbelt sign went off and closed her eyes. She floated in a sense of well-being among the images of their three weeks in Britain. She loved London which she had visited on two occasions previously on business trips with Alan and, for a longer period of time, three years ago when she and Nicki had spent the summer between high school and college travelling in Europe. Their honeymoon, however, had been spent in the north of England, Scotland and Ulster, from where her Scotch-Irish forefathers originated. Her mind travelled from the bed and breakfast cottage built in the side of a fell in the Lake District to the equally picturesque house where they'd stayed in County Antrim and the gothic hotel on the rugged Caithness coast. Idyllic was the word, she thought, for the enchanting three weeks. She smiled to herself.

"We'll come back," Alan said, taking her hand and squeezing it.

"I know," she replied, "we're going to have a wonderful life."

"We already have a wonderful life. What's the *going to* bit?"

Megan opened her eyes and laughed. "I know," she said, "we must be blessed."

They smiled into each other's eyes.

They had met an old man on the ferry from Arran who had told them they were blessed. He was fey by reputation, he said, and had the gift of second sight. He told them where the lords of the isles had battled the Norsemen and, travelling up the coast, after hearing him, they had felt almost like intruders in the domains of St. Columba, Somerled and the MacDonalds and MacDougalls of old.

"We *are* blessed," Alan raised his glass. Megan picked up hers and found it empty. "No wonder you're so relaxed..."

"I'm relaxed because I'm so happy. It doesn't have anything to do with gin and tonic," she replied firmly. "Do you think they'll think I'm English when I ask for gin and tonic when we get home?"

"Ask who?"

"In bars and things..."

"I didn't know you were going to be inhabiting bars and things..."

"You know what I mean."

The stewardess brought them fresh drinks in response to Alan's signal.

"*Now* we'll toast our blessedness," said Alan, raising his glass.

Megan clinked hers against it. "I love first class," she said. "I remember whenever we travelled economy as children, we'd get so impatient waiting for the stewardess to trundle the drinks up the aisle. We must have driven Mom up the wall with our whining. In first, you just signal the stewardess and she remembers what you're drinking. Even the food tastes better. This has been the most wonderful trip of my life." She was silent for a few minutes.

"There's a part of me that'll be glad to get home, though. I have so much work to do – my own work. No more OCA projects. I just hope I have the discipline to work on my own."

"I'll make sure you do – I didn't just marry you for your pretty face, you know. I'm expecting a return on my investment..."

Almost the entire attic had been converted into a giant studio when she moved into the house nearly three years before, the original tiny windows being replaced with large dormers. It had been the envy of her fellow students at OCA. Now, Megan was eager to start working on canvases of some of the places they had visited. She had been developing a unique landscape style, over the last few years, loosely derived from the effect which is created in a photograph when a subject is tightly focused, leaving a soft out-of-focus appearance to the rest of the picture. Her work was well-received among both students and faculty at the college and she had won two awards in her final year and had been critically acclaimed at the graduating students' show. The big test would be in finding a dealer and exhibiting her work, however. And, before that, she must find out – as she had just indicated – if she had the self-discipline to paint full time.

I'll approach it, she thought, as if I were actually going out somewhere. That'll be best – as if I were going to school or a job – instead of just upstairs to the studio. I just mustn't let myself fall into bad habits. I'll get up everyday and we'll have breakfast together before Alan goes to the office, then I'll get right down to work...

The going could get tough – it was easy to get distracted when your life was so wonderful.

. . . . .

"Alan's just been talking to Uncle Dennis and some deal has come through or something – you probably know what they're talking about better than I do. Anyway, they're having a meeting at the office in the morning, so I thought – if you're not busy, that is – I'd like to come over by myself. I'm dying to tell you about everything."

Megan was talking to her mother on the phone. They had finished supper, in the breakfast nook off the kitchen where they generally ate when alone, and were drinking coffee while sorting through the pile of mail that had accumulated during their vacation.

"I set the day aside especially for you, love," her mother replied. "I'm dying to hear about everything, so get here as soon as you can."

"Great," said Megan. "You'll never believe what Aunt Selena did, Mom. We'd only been in half an hour or so and were trying to decide whether to unpack first or go grocery shopping. We were too disoriented to decide – you know how it is at the airport when you get off the plane. I wish they'd do something about that crush in customs – it's always the same. You feel like your plane came in unexpectedly and they weren't prepared for you or something. Well, there we were – oh, first of all when we went into the kitchen, there was a bottle of champagne and a welcome home card, which was really nice of her – then the door bell rang and it was a man from one of those little gourmet catering companies with our welcome home dinner. Wasn't that just so cool? She's such a nice lady. Alan phoned her, but she's not in right now. Everything was so good, too. Did Danny get off all right?"

"That was a lovely idea. Yes, Danny phoned from Hong Kong the day before yesterday. The plane journey was tedious – same as going to Sydney, I imagine. Never-ending. Hong Kong's exciting, he said, really different. Hard to imagine how so many people can live in such a small space. He'll be moving on to Singapore on Tuesday and said he'd call you from there."

"Oh, good. Did he remember to take the two paintings for Aunt Jennie?"

"Yes. Did you have time to do much painting over there?"

"Oh, yes – a fair bit. Mostly just sketches to work from. I'll bring them over tomorrow. Is Byron there?"

"No – I'll get him to give you a call when he comes in, shall I? He's going camping somewhere tomorrow with Mark."

"Sure," Megan replied. "I just want to say hi. Was he okay with his exams?"

"Oh, yes," Marilyn laughed. "He's still complaining bitterly about going back to high school when he'd rather go to Sheridan. I'm going to find out more about these computer graphics courses – I have an appointment to see the department head at Sheridan, in a professional capacity, actually but, of course, I have a personal interest with Byron being so obsessed with it. Maybe he's right – the future is now!"

"Is that what he says? There were quite a number of people, who graduated with me, enrolling at Sheridan for next year, you know. I mean, it's quite normal for OCA graduates to take commercial courses, but these desktop publishing programs are attracting a lot of people..."

"Well, we'll see."

"How's Hugh? Did he survive meeting all the McGraths and LaPlantes all right?"

"Oh, he did more than that. Michael did what Byron calls his Mr. Paranoia act the next morning. Angus took off."

"What happened?" Megan asked.

"Everything worked out in the end, so don't worry. The first I heard about it was the phone ringing – I was at Hugh's and we were having breakfast, a long romantic-type breakfast. Oh – I know you kids think we're too old for such things, but we were. The phone rang and it was Michael looking for me."

Megan giggled. "That's hilarious – your ex-brother-in-law calling you at your boyfriend's house on a Sunday morning..."

"Oh, I tell you – Hugh really got the McGrath family full blast that weekend. To get back to Michael – he was all upset. Angus wasn't in his bed and he'd phoned me at home, but I wasn't there and Byron had been rude to him... he was a total wreck."

"Why would Byron be rude to him?"

"Michael was rather derogatory about Adam and Byron thought he was being snobbish... you know how socialist Byron is – sometimes I wonder if that's why he doesn't want to go to university. Michael wanted Adam's phone number and thought we had it and Byron got mad and told him to look it up in the book and hung up... or something like that. He went over there later and they more or less made up their differences..."

"What about Angus?"

"He, apparently, had set this up with Adam earlier. He still had Adam's phone number from two-and-a-half years ago when he came here for Christmas–"

"But Adam–" Megan began.

"I know – Adam wouldn't do something like that. That's exactly why Byron got so mad with Michael accusing Adam of God knows what. Adam didn't know that Angus hadn't cleared it with his father. All he knew was that he was to meet Angus at the Queen Street subway beside the newsstand and – well, generally hang out, I suppose. Eventually, Angus talked him into showing him where he lived although Adam didn't really want to – he phoned me, later, to tell me that he wanted to apologise for his part in the thing but was too scared to call Michael. Anyway, once they got there, Adam's mother made Angus phone his father right away."

"I'd better tell Alan," said Megan, "He'll probably want to call Adam and put his mind at rest. He bought him a Fair Isle sweater and a tee shirt from John O'Groats as well because he won't be able to wear the sweater until the Fall. So what did they do all day?"

"Went to that space thing in the bottom of the CN Tower – Angus had plenty of money with him – checked out how the dome stadium is coming along, wandered up Yonge Street..."

"I'd better go, Mom. Alan's hearing only my side of the conversation here and wants to know what's going on... See you tomorrow. 'Bye." She turned to Alan, who had been gesticulating wildly trying to get her attention. "It's okay. Just a kids' prank. None of it was Adam's fault – it was my fiendish little cousin leading him astray."

"Can you tell me what happened?" Alan demanded, picking up the pile of discarded envelopes and junk mail and putting it in the garbage container. "All I heard was something about Byron mouthing off to somebody and something about Angus and Adam..."

Megan, starting to clear up the remains of their supper, was in the midst of telling him what her mother had said when the phone rang. Alan picked it up.

"Hello."

Megan carried the dirty dishes across to the dishwasher.

"Whoa... slow down, Adam. It's all right. The McGraths aren't blaming you – Megan was just talking to her mother about it..."

She stacked the dishwasher and put the left over food in containers in the refrigerator while Alan continued to talk to his Little Brother. She shook her head as she thought about the boys' escapade and wondered how they had related to each other after two and a half years. The years between eleven and fourteen were years of change. As eleven-year-olds that Christmas, when they met, they had been children. Now they were high school students – at least Adam would be in the Fall. The BC system was different – high school started at grade eight, didn't it? Who knew how it worked at Angus's private school? The point was, the boys were at a point in life where, as students, they would begin to make decisions about the courses they took and, in theory, the direction in which they were headed. The fourteen-year-old Adam was far more aware of socio-economic distinctions than the eleven-year-old Adam had been. Whatever the extent of Angus's maturing outlook, the two would scarcely have had the spontaneous small boy relationship of their first meeting. Adam's reluctance to speak to Michael would have been less the result of shyness of the one-time hockey hero than of the certain knowledge that a kid from the city's most notorious low rental housing project was not the companion of choice for the hockey hero's son.

Poor kid, Megan thought, Angus probably lied because Adam would definitely have wanted to know that he was allowed before agreeing to meet him – and he'd probably been half afraid that he was being lied to... Angus, on the other hand, would have been fully confident that the other boy's perception of his more privileged position would preclude him from refusing to meet him.

She thought about her young cousin, as she went into the bedroom and began opening and unpacking the suitcases they had unceremoniously dumped there when they came in. She'd seen him twice since that Christmas visit. Her mother had admitted to engineering the meeting between Michael and Lise. Megan, too, had hoped something might develop. She had been thirteen when she'd answered the advertisement for a baby-sitter Lise had posted on the notice board in the local supermarket. Justin had been about a year old then and his parents needed a regular baby-sitter while they played badminton once a week. She had later found out that Lise, at this time, had been desperately trying to shore up a disintegrating marriage. During the five years before Lise had given up on her marriage and taken Justin back to Vancouver, where her family lived, she had become quite a close friend of both Megan and her mother. The friendship and eventual marriage last year of Lise and Michael had resulted in far closer ties with Michael and Angus who, previously had only appeared in the lives of Megan and her brothers at progressively lengthening interludes. Megan had twice gone with Alan to Vancouver on extended business trips in order to visit Lise and Michael, the last time just a little over two months ago. Michael had been almost the fun uncle she remembered from her childhood until they had gone to Victoria – partly to visit because Megan had never been there before and partly to pick up Angus for the weekend. Byron was right, Megan reflected, Michael really did become paranoid around his son. Maybe it was just the way people were with hyperkinetic children – always afraid to relax their vigilance in case the child spun completely out of control. Michael had taken her with him to pick up Angus at Judith's house, leaving Alan, Lise and Justin to wait for them at a nearby restaurant. While she had never really known Judith well, it was only polite that she should go with

Michael and renew acquaintance although she suspected that Michael's real motive in taking her was because he was not, even after eight years, very comfortable in his non-custodial parent role. Judith, laughingly wondering where the time had gone, congratulated her on her upcoming marriage and introduced her to Angus's four-year-old half-sister, Stephanie. Lawrence, Judith's husband, had not been at home. Angus, himself, had grown considerably and was almost as tall as Megan now. He seemed generally more withdrawn although this didn't seem to effect his constant need for action. He was as fidgety as ever. They had not stayed long and, after Judith and Michael had made arrangements for which ferry Angus would take to return on Monday afternoon, they drove back to the restaurant where they had left the others. Angus was quieter than he used to be – almost sulky, in fact. At first, Megan had thought it was because he was older but, observing his behaviour, she noticed that he seemed to have all his old confidence around his father and Justin, but with her and Alan, and to some extent, Lise, he was more diffident and less sure of himself. Talking together, later that evening when they were back in Vancouver, Lise confided to Megan that she definitely would not have considered marrying Michael had he had custody of Angus. He was a lot less demanding now than he had been when she first met Michael, she still felt – every time he visited – as if she were holding her breath waiting for life to return to normal.

"Hey, wake up there."

Megan was startled out of her reverie when Alan came into the bedroom. She found, to her surprise, that she had hung clothes in the closets, piled others in the corner of the room to take down to the basement laundry room and carefully placed souvenirs and gifts all over the bed.

"My God, I must have been on automatic pilot," she exclaimed, looking around her.

"So where were you?"

"Vancouver and Vancouver Island mostly," she said, "but, before that, I was thinking about socio-economics..."

"As applied to Adam and Angus?"

She nodded.

"Well, unfortunately there's not much you or I can do about it – however hard we *think* about it. We should never have brought them together in the first place. I should have foreseen the complications. Despite his years in hockey, your Uncle Michael is still a McGrath, a Pickering College *alumnus* and living in the nineteen twenties and I should have known it couldn't work. I guess I was so busy being the philanthropist that I forgot about real life."

"Is Adam all right? I hope it didn't upset him too much – at exam time, I mean."

"No. I mean he was upset, but he managed his exams okay. Since he doesn't have a father – well, not so's you'd notice, I'm allowed to go to his graduation at the end of the month."

"That's good. Take some good photos for them – his mother will be so proud..." Megan began to clear the things off the bed, putting some on top of the cedar chest and the rest on the floor. "I'll finish sorting things out in the morning. Do you realise that it's nearly five in the morning British time – no wonder my mind's only half here!" She pulled off her clothes and added them to the pile of laundry. "Did you turn everything off?"

"Sure. Except what you're turning on..."

"Fun-*ny*..."

. . . . .

Megan arrived at her mother's house just as a tremendous thunder storm broke. She left her sketches and the presents, she had brought with her, in the car and made a quick dash to the kitchen door which her mother, watching for her, had opened as she pulled into the driveway. They sat drinking coffee at the kitchen table, watching the storm through the patio door.

"Adam called just after I finished talking to you last night," Megan said, after having given her mother a précised version of their entire trip.

"Bit late wasn't it?"

"He'd been trying to get through all the time we were talking – and, quite likely, all the time before that when Alan was speaking to Uncle Dennis. He wanted to give his version of events to Alan before anybody else did, I think, poor kid. Talk about being put in a spot – I felt quite sorry for him. Alan's going to his graduation at the end of the month. It's hard to believe he'll be in high school next year – I still think of him as a little boy."

Her mother laughed. "Well, that's the way it is with children growing up. It seems like only yesterday that *you* were graduating from grade eight."

"Oh, I remember," said Megan. "Remember how you took me shopping for a graduation dress and Byron had to come with us because Danny didn't get home in time to watch him. Adam seems quite grown up, though – compared to me, then. I mean, I thought I was *so* mature, but I was actually quite ditzy, wasn't I?"

"I don't think so. You were quite normal for your age – it's best to *be* young when you *are* young. Responsibilities come far too quickly. I liked you being ditzy – as you put it. I was a little sad when you suddenly grew up."

"I don't remember it quite like that. When did I suddenly grow up?"

"When you met Alan, of course. You stopped being the ditzy teenager and became a young woman who seemed to know where the future was better than I did myself."

"Oh, come on, Mom. It wasn't as clear cut as that," protested Megan. "I did know that Alan was my future, though. I spent that whole winter floating on a cloud somewhere – it's a wonder I ever managed to finish high school and get accepted at OCA."

"Oh, you worked all right – like someone inspired. That's what I mean – you just suddenly couldn't wait to put high school behind you... Changing the subject to the really grown up, married you, we have the photos that Hugh took. I meant to show them to you right away and the storm put it out of my mind." Her mother got up a little hurriedly and went into the living room. "Help yourself to another cup of coffee."

Megan rose and poured them both fresh coffee reflecting on her mother's sudden obvious emotionalism. They shouldn't have got into that silly 'remember when' type conversation. The rain seemed to be easing up a bit at last. Maybe she could run out and bring in her things in a minute and bring Mom back to the present. Her mother came back into the kitchen, still looking a little weepy.

"Here we are," she said. "When will you be seeing the official ones?"

"The man's supposed to come round with them one evening next week."

They both sat down at the table and looked at the photographs.

"Wow, Hugh's composition is really good," Megan said. "I didn't need to have a professional... I look a bit goofy there."

"What? Don't be silly. I thought you were a beautiful bride."

"Thanks. The mother of the bride looked pretty good, too. Especially this one with tears running down her cheeks and smeared mascara."

"I meant to get rid of that one. I was mad when I discovered he'd taken it."

"Don't chuck it, Mom. It's sort of beautiful, you know. It tells a story, doesn't it?"

"Does it?"

"Yes, Mom. It tells a story of a woman who did a wonderful job bringing up three children to be responsible, contributing human beings all by herself. Not that any of us are actually contributing yet, but you know what I mean – the potential is there. Do you think this rain'll hold off while I run out and get my sketches? I really want you to see them so I can show you what I have in mind for a series of paintings. Sort of like the Acadian series I did after we stayed with Aunt Selina. Only it won't take me a two years to finish this time, because I can paint full time now."

"That was a really nice thing to say, Megan," said her mother. "Thank you." She squeezed her hand. "Yes, run out and get them quickly before it starts again."

# DANNY

Landing in Vancouver on his flight home from Sydney, via Honolulu, Danny was looking forward to staying with Michael and Lise for a few days before heading home and getting ready for graduate school. It was a surprise to find Lise and Justin waiting for him, after he cleared customs, instead of Michael as he had expected. Danny must have looked a little shocked because Lise started to explain before he could even begin to ask where Michael was.

"Angus has gone missing," she said. "I'm sure it's just the usual looking-for-attention-type stuff, but Michael's frantic, of course. He's at home in case Angus – or the police – call."

"He wanted Mom to come to the airport because he didn't want to leave you stranded if Angus called while he was on his way," chimed in Justin. "If he calls while Michael's out looking, you see, we're supposed to call him on his car phone. Can I carry something, Danny?"

"Sure, here – take my duffel bag. Can you manage it?"

"Yeah. I'm not a kid anymore, you know. I'll be in grade five this year."

"Okay... Look, Lise – maybe it's not a good time. Perhaps I should see if I can get a flight to Toronto..."

"No," Lise said, firmly, "You come and stay as we arranged. This isn't the first time Angus has done this... and I'm sure it won't be the last. Besides... we want to hear all about your trip."

"Well, if you're sure..."

"Of course, I'm sure. Here, let's get your stuff to the car and then we can talk properly."

In the car, driving from the airport to West Vancouver, Lise explained that Judith had called from Victoria the evening before. She had thought that Angus was at a neighbourhood friend's home and, when he hadn't come home for supper, she had phoned the neighbour and discovered that Angus wasn't there at all. An hour or so later, the neighbour had brought her dejected and tearful fourteen-year-old son to Judith's house and the boy had miserably admitted to planning to run away with Angus to Vancouver.

" He cried off at the last minute, apparently, because he figured that, because they both look a bit young for their age, the cops would know they were only fourteen and bring them home and they'd look like dorks," she said. "His words – not mine."

Danny grinned.

"Angus *is* a dork!" cried Justin from the back seat. "He's always causing problems."

"You stop that, Justin," said his mother, crossly. "It's not for you to make judgements. You don't understand."

"I do so. He's got no right to mess up people's lives. My parents live miles apart and I hardly ever see my father, but I don't go around acting like a jerk over it and I'm only ten and he's fourteen and should know better."

"Justin," said Lise, "we've discussed this before and I'm not about to get into a discussion about it again now. Please butt out while I finish talking to Danny."

"Hey, Justin," put in Danny, "try and guess what I brought you from Australia while your mom tells me about Angus. Okay?"

"Okay – hey, did you know I still have the koala bear Megan brought me back the last time you went?"

"You do? Well, it's not a koala bear, so keep guessing – but only in your own head, so's your mother and I can talk. Okay?"

"Okay, Danny. I'll be seen and not heard."

"So, Philip – that's Angus's friend's name – decided he wasn't going and Angus swore him to silence, but his mother knew something was up as soon as she asked him if Angus had been there during the day – she and her husband had both been at work all day. It didn't take her long to get the details out of him. Apparently, the plan was to get a bus, via the ferry, over to Vancouver before anybody knew they were gone, then they were going to find a beach to camp out on. Angus said he knew where street kids camped out on the beaches."

"Does he?"

"No – at least, I don't see how he could. He only ever goes to the beaches up our way. He hardly knows the city, really. I mean, if Michael takes him to a Cannucks game or we go to a show or something, we drive to wherever. We might walk a short way, but he's not gone anywhere on his own except for the time–"

"Michael told my brother about Angus running away and calling him from Gastown."

"Yes, that's what I was going to say. He actually walked from West Vancouver, over the Lions Gate Bridge, to get there and wasn't away long enough to have gone anywhere else – besides, his feet were too blistered. He was just trying to impress the other kid. The problem is – if he did find his way to wherever street kids hang out, they–"

"–they might take all his kit off him and whatever money he has and leave him where they found him or take him under their wing and do the same thing – less aggressively. And those are the better scenarios. What do the police say?"

"The police don't exactly have too much sympathy with teenage runaways. They're supposed to be looking for him both here... and in Victoria, too, since we don't know for sure that he actually did leave Victoria."

"I guess teenage runaways are a dime a dozen for the police."

"Sadly... yes."

"Chances are he'll turn up with no more damage than having lost his belongings, so let's be positive. Did the other kid say *why* they were running away?"

Lise smiled. "Does any runaway kid know why?"

"It's usually some imagined injustice or a bid for attention, although if any kid gets enough attention it's Angus..."

"That's really the problem, isn't it? Both his parents seem to be constantly on edge about what he's doing, what he's done, what he's doing next... Is this what happens when a child has a chronic condition like asthma – not that that's so much of a problem now that he's older – or is it the attention deficit problem or is it just the kid himself?"

"Bit of everything, I think." Danny told her.

. . . . .

Michael's car was not in the garage when they reached the house in West Vancouver which Michael and Lise had bought after their marriage the year before. There was a message beside the phone in the kitchen. Angus was at a downtown police station and Michael had gone to fetch him.

"Perhaps I was premature in discounting the police," said Lise. "Justin – help Danny take his things to his room while I get us all some cold drinks. Would you like a beer, Danny? We remembered to get Heineken especially for you."

"Thanks, Lise. Do you mind if I have a quick shower first?"

"No – go right ahead. Justin'll show you where everything is. And, Justin," Lise added to her son, "don't you bother Danny – let him have his shower in peace."

"I'm not a dork, Mom," Justin said, already halfway up the stairs. "Come on, Danny,"

Danny followed Justin on a tour of the second floor which ended with the spare room. "I think there's some clean underwear and shorts in that duffel bag you've been helping me with, Justin. So we'll just open that for now..." he began to unzip the duffel bag, "... and if you'll just point me to the bathroom again, I can freshen up and we'll check out the big suitcase. Okay?"

"Sure, Danny. I wasn't hanging around for my present or anything. I just want to help..."

"Thanks. You feel pretty grubby when you've been on planes for twenty-four hours..."

"I felt pretty grubby just flying from Toronto after Megan's wedding, but that was because I spilled my pop! The bathroom's right here..." He led Danny out onto the landing again and pushed open the bathroom door. "I cleaned it specially this morning – it's only used by me and Angus, when he's here, and visitors. Mom and Michael have their own – kinda like at your house – ensuite, that's what it's called."

"Looks good, Justin. I'll make sure I leave it as I find it..." Danny said, closing the door. He turned on the shower and shrugged out of his clothes wondering how it was that Justin had survived his mother's divorce and remarriage so much better than Angus had, then berated himself for such stereotypical thinking as he stepped under the refreshing water and began to soap himself down. Angus had been a hyperactive toddler long before his parents' marriage fell apart. There was no reason to think that his parents divorce had anything to do with his behaviour. The two boys had completely different natures. Justin had always been a placid, good-natured child – he remembered how Megan would bring him over to their house when she was looking after him for Lise. Even as a three-year-old, it had taken little to keep him happy, whereas Angus, at three, had been quite a different story. He'd only seen him for a couple of days, of course, that time when they'd visited Michael and Judith in Edmonton, but they'd all been quite happy to move on to Jasper National Park – even Mom, though she wouldn't admit it, of course.

Danny turned off the shower and towelled himself dry. Hopefully, he'd have a chance to talk to Angus – unless Michael took him straight back to Victoria. He hadn't had any time to spend with his young cousin when Michael and Lise had brought the boys to Toronto for Megan's wedding on the Victoria Day weekend. Byron had talked to him for a bit the day after his taking off escapade that weekend, but that had been at the barbecue his mother had had for them and was more in the nature of keeping both Angus and Justin occupied while the grown-ups talked.

He tidied up the bathroom, took his discarded clothes to his room and went downstairs. Lise and Justin were outside on the back porch of the house. Justin ran back into the kitchen to fetch his beer from the refrigerator.

"Do you mind, Justin," Danny said, when the boy returned, "if I wait and give you your Australian gift after Michael gets back with Angus? He didn't even know I was coming, did he?"

"He knew you were going to make a stopover in Vancouver, on the way home, but none of us knew when because you didn't know when yourself," said Lise. "Michael thought he'd wait until you arrived to find out how long you were staying before he committed to taking you over to Victoria to see him, or whatever..."

Danny shook his head. "I hope he doesn't think we weren't going to tell him. Anyway, Justin – you see what I mean, don't you? We should wait and see which way the wind's blowing – okay?"

Justin nodded. He tipped an ice cube from the bottom of his glass, into his mouth and sucked it noisily.

"Sounds like them now," said Lise, and Danny heard a car pulling into the driveway. "Sit down and stay here, Justin," she added as Justin jumped up. They heard the car come to a halt in the driveway in the front of the house. A few minutes later Michael came through the kitchen to the back porch.

"He's having a shower and I've told him to go to his room when he's finished," he said. "Hi, Danny. Sorry about all this. How was the flight?"

"I'll get you a beer, Michael," said Lise getting up and going into the kitchen.

"Flight was as good as it could be," Danny said. "It's not possible to pretend a flight that long is enjoyable – unless you're some kind of masochist, of course. I should sleep well tonight, though!"

Lise came back with Michael's beer and another glass of wine for herself.

"Justin," she said, "I think it's time for your *Gilligan's Island* re-runs..."

"I'd rather hear about Australia..." began Justin.

"Danny's going to save it all for supper time which will be barbecued pork chops out here in about an hour from now. Meantime, be a good boy while we figure out what to do about Angus."

"Okay, Mom." Justin went into the house, looking a little crestfallen.

"So what happened?" Lise asked when he had gone.

"Well, the police called, about half and hour after you left, from one of the downtown stations. Angus had gone in there asking for their help. Some vagrants had rolled him, early this morning, and taken his pack and all his money–"

"Was he hurt?" asked Danny and Lise together.

"A few cuts and bruises that's all. Most of the damage was to his pride. He seems to have been lost for most of the day, finally came across this police station and thought they'd help him get his things back. They told him the best they could do was take his statement and make a list of all the stolen articles. Of course, they wanted his address and telephone number. He tried to pretend he was eighteen and small for his age and would prefer to check back with them because he had no fixed address. They threatened to get a social worker to talk to him while they checked the missing kids reports so he tried to get out of there fast but, of course, they weren't about to let him leave. I think he was too exhausted to argue anymore, by that time, and gave them our number."

"Have you called his mother?" asked Lise.

"I phoned her from the car to let her know what had happened and that I was taking him home with me for now. We agreed that, since we were all pretty well exhausted, he'd better sleep here and we'd talk tomorrow."

"Did he have much to say for himself coming home?" Danny asked.

"He fell asleep almost as soon as I started driving. I had to wake him up when we got here. I thought of just letting him go to bed and sort things out in the morning, but he was just too grubby, so I told him to get a shower and stay in his room until I'd decided what to do about him."

"So what are you going to do?"

Michael shook his head. "I don't know," he said, running his fingers through his hair, "but, I think, before I do anything, I'll go and have a shower, too. I spent most of the night driving around the city and walking along the beaches looking for him." He grimaced. "Pretty useless really, but you feel you have to do something..." He rose and picked up his empty beer can. "I'll go and have a shower."

Lise got up, too. "I'll get supper ready," she said, following him into the house.

Danny sat finishing his beer, which was luke warm by this time. He was debating whether to give his mother a call or remain in his semi-somnolent state in the comfortable, cushioned rattan chair, when Justin came diving out of the kitchen door with a fresh can of beer in one hand and Coke in the other. He put the Coke on the table, pulled the tab on the beer and handed it to Danny with a flourish.

"My God, Justin, you must be the only person around here not suffering from lack of sleep." He took a sip of the cold beer. "I was half asleep – you gave me a scare."

"Sorry. Mom said to bring it out. She said would you mind

lighting the barbecue. You just have to turn on the gas and press the automatic lighting thing. I'm not allowed to do it, or I'd do it for you."

"Oh." It took a minute for Danny's sleepy mind to make sense of this. "Sure." He got up and went over to the barbecue. Having lit it, he went down the steps onto the lawn and picked up a football lying there. "Here, Justin, help me move some oxygen to my brain." He backed up and threw the ball towards the boy.

"How's that?" cried Justin, catching it as he jumped down from the porch.

"Pretty good. It would have knocked your pop over everything if you'd missed."

They threw the ball until Lise came out to put the seasoned pork chops on the barbecue and set the table. She passed Danny his beer as they came back to the porch and sat on the steps. Justin scrambled to retrieve his Coke as his mother spread the table cloth and began to lay places..

"Cheers," he said raising the can to Danny.

Danny held up his own can. "You're letting him come down, then?" he said to Lise, noticing that she was laying five places.

"We just talked it over and decided we'd only be making matters worse if we made him stay in his room while you're here..." – she interrupted herself – "Can you go in and bring out the salad, Justin, please?" and lowered her voice, as he went indoors, "– it'll just encourage jealousy if Justin gets to spend the evening with Angus's cousin and Angus doesn't, if you see what I mean..."

Danny nodded his understanding as Justin came back out with the salad. He was beginning to wish he'd never had the bright idea of stopping over to visit his uncle's family before going home.

He looked at his watch – yes, he'd be almost home by now if he'd got on the Canadian Airlines Toronto flight from Honolulu instead of the Vancouver one. Let's try the positive approach, he thought, being tired is making me negative. Since I'm here, I have to see what I can do to help.

Michael came outside carrying a platter of marinated vegetables ready to grill.

"I'll go in and get the dressings and things," said Lise. "You come and help me, Justin."

"Did you tell him I was here?" Danny asked Michael, who has lifted the barbecue lid and was turning the pork chops before organizing the vegetables.

"No – I told you he fell asleep as soon as we started driving and we've both been having showers since we got back and, assuming he hasn't been prowling around, he wouldn't know anybody was out here – both his room and the main bathroom are at the front."

"Yeah – Justin gave me the grand tour and I already used the bathroom. D'you mind if I go up and get Angus for supper?"

"Lise told you we decided to let him come down, then?"

"Yeah. I think it's the right thing to do. I just wish my timing had been better–"

"*Your* timing? Your cousin's the one with the timing problem."

Danny went into the kitchen where Lise and Justin were getting drinks and buns and butter together to take outside. "I'm going up to get Angus," he said. He went through to the hallway and up the stairs. There was no response to his knock on his cousin's door. Thinking he was maybe asleep, he gently turned the knob and pushed open the door. Angus was lying on the bed staring at the ceiling.

"Hi, Angus," said Danny, remaining in the doorway and leaning against the jamb.

Angus looked puzzled for a minute, then turned – half sitting – to the doorway.

"Danny? How come *you're* here?"

"I thought I'd make a stopover here on my way home from Australia and visit you all. I guess you've saved me the trouble of having to go over to Victoria to visit you..." He figured it was better to make it clear, right off the bat, that he had had every intention of seeing the boy before flying home.

"How long have you been here?"

"I arrived this afternoon. Lise and Justin came out to the airport to get me because, with having the police out looking for you, your father didn't want to risk being on his way to pick me up and getting a call from them, or you, and having to go pick you up instead."

Angus muttered something and flopped back on the bed, looking at the sky through the window.

Danny continued. "So what were you up to?" There was silence. "Well, supper's nearly ready. We'd better go down." Angus continued to study the sky. "It's a barbecue – outside. So let's go."

Angus rolled over on his side. "Okay," he said, "but I'm only coming because I'm hungry – I haven't eaten all day, you know. I was robbed and beaten up."

"Yeah, I heard about it." Danny decided to be blunt – it was time this kid woke up to reality. "What did you expect wandering around by yourself in the middle of the night? You want to be a street kid – you have to get yourself a protector and you've got to give a lot more than just your worldly goods to get yourself one at that level of society."

"What d'you mean? I had hash I'd have shared with them." Angus said, sitting up.

"Use your head, Angus. You surely didn't think you'd find some gang of vagrants to take you in because you're a nice kid with a bit of dope to share, did you? How do you think these people live?"

"You mean drugs and sex and stuff?"

"Right. And degradation and AIDS and all the rest of it. It's not fantasyland, Angus. It's the real world. So try growing up a bit before you run away again. Okay? Now let's go down to supper."

Angus stood up and walked towards Danny.

"You won't tell my dad, will you, Danny? I mean – about the hash?"

"Not unless it becomes relevant – and it's not right now. But – just so's we're on the same wavelength, Angus – I made the decision to say no to drugs when I was your age for the simple reason that, if you want to be a person that counts in this life, whether that's in some high profile career way or simply as a member of a family, you need exclusivity when it comes to use of your brain cells. Get it?"

"Yeah, I guess so," Angus replied, looking uncomfortable. "They'll be wondering what's keeping us..." He started towards the stairs. "How long are you here for, Danny?"

"I have a flight booked for Friday afternoon. So I'll be here all day tomorrow and Thursday."

"D'you think Dad'll be able to talk my mom into letting me stay? She'd probably be glad to get rid of me for a bit..."

. . . . .

Danny took the two boys over to the greenbelt, behind the house, after supper to show them how to throw the boomerangs he had brought for them, leaving Michael and Lise to discuss the situation. The next morning Judith agreed to Angus staying until the weekend on the grounds that his attitude might be positively influenced by being around his cousin. After breakfast, Danny suggested an all men's overnight expedition, to whichever provincial or national park they chose, leaving Lise, who worked as a freelance public relations consultant, in peace to finish a project she was working on. The boys enthusiastically got the camping gear together and Lise packed food for supper and the next day's breakfast – they'd stop for lunch, both days, at a restaurant.

They took the TransCanada Highway out of Vancouver and headed up the Fraser River canyon. Danny had never visited this part of the country before and received an extensive education from Angus and Justin who had, at various times, been taken on camping and skiing trips all over the province and generally considered themselves experts on the history and geography of British Columbia.

It was generally a pretty exhausting day and both Danny and Michael were glad to relax by their campfire when the boys had finally gone to sleep.

"So you're still headed for McGrath-LaPlante then?" Michael asked. "I thought you might change your mind once you got your degree..."

"No. I'm transferring to York for my MBA, though – that way I can combine work and school more effectively than if I stayed at Western. Dennis wants me working more closely with Sean Hennings – did you ever know him?"

"I never really knew anybody there – except for family members."

"He's Vice President Operations. He's been there forever – I'm expected to take over from him eventually."

"Well, you seem to be in the right place at the right time," Michael said, rather cynically, "there's a lot of money to be made in the business, now."

"Yes, that's true, but I think just about everybody associated with the business – with the industry, generally – feels badly about the reasons for that. McGrath-LaPlante is paying its debt to society, don't you worry about that! I can't even keep count of the number of projects Alan's got going for getting product to third world countries, inner-city clinics and hostels, kids' programs – you name it..."

"Sorry, I shouldn't have put it that way – it's my guilty conscience talking. I'm the one just sitting back and collecting my fat dividend cheques."

"Talking about fat dividend cheques, Michael, Megan and Byron and I want to give Mom her shares back – my father's shares, I mean. Do you know how that stands legally? I mean both Megan and I get ours out of the Trust now that we've graduated but, of course, Byron's third share stays in trust until he graduates... that's another thing, he doesn't want to go to university – will a community college diploma qualify him to get his stock? And, what happens if it doesn't?"

"I would imagine the university degree clause is there just to ensure that you each acquired post secondary education – rather than university education specifically, but I don't remember how all the other clauses went. I don't imagine there'll be any problem, though you'll have to wait till the Trust can be wound up to transfer the two point whatever per cent of Byron's third. Does Marilyn want to quit then?"

"No – nothing like that. It's just that when Grandma McGrath set this whole thing up, she made no provision for Mom to have that option, which isn't exactly fair, is it?"

"Well, my mother was never famed for being fair, let's face it," said Michael. "But, surely, if Marilyn did want to leave McGrath-LaPlante now that she's free to do so, she's not likely to have any problem getting a comparable position?"

"No, not right now, but a few years down the road she might – I mean, she's not getting any younger. That's not really the point, though. The six and half per cent of McGrath-LaPlante is hers – my father left it to her, in a will that was made *after* their separation. He wanted her to have it – probably to ensure that there was always dividend income to fall back on for bringing up the three of us, of course. Anyway, she had to change her own plans because of Grandma McGrath's will – I mean, to ensure that we did get our shares. It couldn't have been easy – going into the position over the heads of people who probably thought they were in line for the job, mutterings of nepotism, etc. She did it for us – so we want her to have her shares back – she could even live off the dividends now, if she wanted to..."

"I can't quite see Marilyn becoming a lazy bugger like me, living off her dividends. If she did leave, I'm sure she'd want something else to do. But you're right, she should have the option – she earned it. You'll have to discuss it with whatshisface – Connor, Merv Connor..."

"Megan set up an appointment for her and I to go in and see him next week for our share certificates to be handed over so, I guess, we can discuss the whole thing then."

Michael poked at the fire and adjusted the logs so that they would burn through before they went to sleep. "Sometimes I wonder where all the years went," he said. "Do you remember the campfires at the cottage when you were little kids? You and Megan and Angela roasting marshmallows and refusing to go to bed..."

"Sure. I was up there last year. It's a lot less rustic now – Aunt Laura's not really the type that's into a *cottage* cottage, right?"

"Right," agreed Michael.

"There's a phone and hydro," Danny continued, "and plumbing. Dennis asked me up, with Sean Hennings, to plan the future of McGrath-LaPlante operations management. Jayne was there, too. Sean and Dennis go way back – they were at Western together, I think. Dennis brought him into the company back when he became president – that's why I thought you must have met him at some point."

"Maybe I have – and forgot. Was he at the wedding?"

"Oh yes, but so was half of McGrath-LaPlante. I don't remember where he sat or anything... Anyway, they put a plan in place for their retirement in a few years, and handing over the reins to a new generation of McGraths and LaPlantes – their hyperbole, not mine. How come Laura got the cottage, anyway? She's the least cottage-type person I know."

The McGrath cottage, built on Lake Simcoe near Beaverton, by Danny's great grandfather in the early nineteen-twenties, had been a summer retreat for succeeding generations. Michael and his brother and sisters had spent most of their summers there as children and, until their father's death, Danny and Megan, and later Byron, had been accustomed to spending much of the summer there with one or both of their parents and their Aunt Frances and her family. Danny remembered Michael being there intermittently with hockey buddies and girlfriends.

"No idea," Michael replied. "You'd have thought Mom would have left it to Frances – she was the one who loved it most. She and Angus – your father – were always making plans to live there when we were kids. I used to trail around after them – my relationship to them was a bit like Byron's was to you and Megan – the little brother tagging along. They loved the cottage – Frances and Angus. I mostly remember Laura sulking because she'd rather be back in the city with her friends but, maybe, that's because she's nearly ten years older than me so I don't remember a heck of a lot about her before she was a teenager. It was a disappointment for Frances, though – whichever way you look at it. She should have had the cottage."

"I don't remember Aunt Laura ever being there when I was a kid – except for family parties but then, Cindi and Jayne were older than us – maybe they'd reached the age where it was boring, same as their mother when you were a kid..."

"No – even when they were younger, they went to the LaPlante cottage more than ours – who owns that now, by the way?"

"Alan's Aunt Selena–" Danny told him, "Dennis's sister."

"I thought she lived in New Brunswick somewhere. What good is a cottage in – it's in Muskoka, isn't it?"

Danny nodded.

"What use does she have for a cottage in Muskoka?"

"She does – live in New Brunswick, I mean, but Alan got the house and Jayne and Cindi got the money. Dennis and Laura already had the McGrath cottage, so Dennis got the paintings and Selena got the cottage – though it would have made more sense the other way around."

"I suppose she could have sold it." Michael suggested.

Danny laughed. "Selena's like Alan – part of the philanthropic element of the LaPlantes. She has some deal going with an organization in the city that sends needy families there for holidays."

"Oh, good for her. We didn't really see much of her even though we were staying in the same house for the wedding. Lise was upstairs with her and Megan during the afternoon before the wedding rehearsal, but I was in charge of the boys."

"Megan's very close to her. She really championed her when she and Alan first started going together which was a great help to Megan. Mom and I had got to know Dennis and Laura again by then because of working at McGrath-LaPlante but, you have to remember, after my father died, Megan and I only saw the rest of the family now and again so, by that time, they were virtual strangers to Megan and here she was making off with their nephew before she was even finished high school. You can imagine her reservations about them – especially after I'd already mouthed off at her and made my opinion known. I was pretty mean, you know..."

"Played the disapproving big brother, huh?"

"Well, it was in her own interests, I thought. I mean, Alan wasn't a saint exactly... even if he does appear to have become one now."

"Personally, I could have done without the saint stuff," Michael said emphatically. "Angus would never have got his taste for the low life if he hadn't met that Regent's Park kid. I don't like to sound like a snob... Oh, I know you and Byron like to think you were fortunate in avoiding going to Pickering College like the rest of the McGraths. Don't look so innocent – your brother isn't too big on tact, yet. But, be honest, Danny, would your mother have wanted you hanging out around Regent's Park? And Angus already has two strikes against him with the attention deficit and hyperactivity – though, thank God, that's not so bad now that he's older – he doesn't need the added complication of other kids' problems."

"I suppose you're right. But Adam really is a together kid despite his background – or so Megan tells me. I don't really know him. And it was Megan's fault they met in the first place, not Alan's. She just thought it would be nice for Angus to have somebody his own age around that Christmas – she didn't think about the difference in their backgrounds. She probably thought of eleven-year-old boys as a homogenous group. They were both really upset when they found out what happened this time – Megan and Alan, I mean."

"Oh, I know. Alan called me, as soon as they got back from the UK, to apologise for being the unintentional cause of the whole problem," Michael admitted, reaching into the cooler. "Here, let's split this last beer and get to sleep. I can't see to pour it into a can, though – that beaker there only had water in it, didn't it? It's okay, I'll have the beaker," he added, in response to Danny wrinkling his nose as he passed the beaker. "You can have the can."

"I had a bit of a talk with Angus before supper yesterday. I'll give it another go before I leave – being his older cousin might rate me higher than you in terms of being relevant to the world today. No offence intended – twenty-three is probably easier for him to accept advise from than forty-whatever you are now. Come on let's drink up and get to bed – I think we're the only people still up in the entire campground."

. . . . .

The boys woke too early the next morning for Danny and Michael who both would have preferred to sleep in. It was just as well since they'd been promised a trip on the Hell's Gate Airtram on the way home and were able, after a rather burned breakfast cooked by Angus, to get there before there was too long a line up. They arrived back in West Vancouver late in the afternoon. Michael had to go into his office to deal with a problem which had arisen that morning and Lise diplomatically created some chores to keep Justin busy, so Danny went for a walk with Angus along the nearby beach.

He had decided to say no more about the running away episode. Michael would be taking Angus back to his mother's, after his own departure the following day, and the kid would have trouble enough explaining his escapade to his mother and stepfather. He didn't need more static from him, too. Instead, he struck a deal for he and Angus to call each other regularly, intending for this to give the boy an anchor. He hoped that by showing a sincere interest in his young cousin's life, the boy would, perhaps, develop a sense of responsibility towards him as someone who cared about what he was doing, thinking, feeling...

They had a long talk about people and how behaviour impacted on different members of a family and about why it was important to think about the effect your actions could have on the people who loved you. He suggested Angus try and find himself a part time job – hoping that this would not be contrary to his parents' wishes – and told him about some of the jobs he'd had in his early teens. Angus loved the story about the crazy cat lady who continually cancelled and renewed her order for the community newspaper he delivered so that he never knew what his reception would be when he knocked on her door to collect. Byron had eventually inherited both the paper route and the cat lady when Danny moved on to more lucrative part-time employment as a stock boy at the local supermarket. Angus said he wished Danny and Byron were his brothers instead of his cousins because they'd be more fun to live with then his little sister. Danny reminded him that his sister had feelings, too. Hadn't they just been talking about not hurting people who cared about you? Angus grimaced and said he didn't think she cared too much about him. Danny looked at his watch and suggested they start walking back or Lise would begin to think they didn't care about *her* if they were late for supper.

# MARILYN

It was within the space of a few months that Megan graduated from OCA, was married and became a full time artist, that Danny finished his Honours BA at Western, enrolled in the MBA program at York, became Assistant Operations Manager at McGrath-LaPlante and bought a home of his own. Then Byron started his desktop publishing course at Sheridan College – yes, I finally gave in on that one! I was confronted with the fact that my children were no longer children. They were young adults. The realization came as a bit of a shock. It shouldn't have done. After all Megan had not lived at home for three years and Danny had been away during term time for four years. Byron was still at home – physically, that is. His mind appeared to be mostly buried in the Macintosh computer that had replaced the Atari and Nintendo game boards of earlier years. I had arranged for his McGrath-LaPlante dividends to be paid into his own bank account after his eighteenth birthday in the spring, as I had done earlier with Danny and Megan, and he was in control of his own post-secondary education funds. He made noises about being asked to share a rented, dilapidated old farmhouse near the school, but must have decided that it would involve too extended a social life – either that, or he contemplated that there would be too many demands for the use of his computer. Anyway, he ended up staying at home and driving to the Oakville campus each day.

Danny bought a condominium apartment in North York to give himself more convenient access to both the university and McGrath-LaPlante now that he was combining school and work. While this effectively saved commuting time, I was still concerned that he might be taking on too much. He assured me that lots of people took MBA courses and worked, too. It was a good time for selling real estate and, even after taking out the expense of his summer in Australia, the profit he made on selling the house he'd owned and shared with fellow students, during the university years in London, provided a hefty down payment on the condominium. He and Megan finally acquired ownership of their shares in McGrath-LaPlante – well, the ones that had originally been their grandfather's. They had their share of the stock that had been left to me by their father, and bought back by his mother, transferred to me. I knew none of this until they both came into my office, after spending most of an entire morning with Merv Connor, the lawyer, sorting out their affairs. They had decided not to mention their intention to return my shares until it was a *fait accompli* – not that things would be completely finalized until Byron was qualified to claim his. However, I did now own a little over 4% of McGrath-LaPlante which was worth a great deal more than it had been when my husband owned it – due, in part, to the creative marketing of my new son-in-law but also, sadly, to the demand created for our products by the current need for protection from contracting HIV.

I made a conscious decision not to feel depressed about the fact that my children were already concerned about ensuring that I had enough to live comfortably on in my old age. Essentially I was, once again, at a point of transition – as I had been six years before when Isabel McGrath died and I was catapulted into a senior management position at McGrath-LaPlante. The difference, however, was that my children's welfare was no longer a priority. While this gave me freedom, it also created feelings of rootlessness. I was relieved when Byron decided to remain at home. It allowed me to continue to have an identity. Oh, I wasn't kidding myself that I didn't have to move on from, primarily, being a mother. I was just delaying it until I literally became an empty-nester. I also had myself convinced that, as long as I had the house to maintain, I need not make the crucial decision, which I knew I would soon have to make, about whether or not I should marry Hugh.

I had met Hugh Johnston the year before at a human resources seminar. As a single parent of three children, I had had little time to cultivate personal relationships while the children were growing up. While there had been two or three what are known, today, as meaningful relationships, these had not lasted long because, let's face it – the chances of three children bonding with what they perceive to be a replacement for their dead father are pretty remote. Danny had been especially prickly and, even as recently as last Christmas, had been slow in accepting Hugh as part of my life. Byron, who had been the first to meet him when I invited him to dinner one weekend, had talked a mile a minute throughout the meal. They found common ground in the potential of computer software to completely change business and industry. This was shortly after Byron had discovered Apple's Macintosh and graphic software and decided on the direction his career should take.

An industrial psychologist, Hugh had been one of the speakers at the seminar and, unable to find a mutual acquaintance during the short lunch break to do so, had introduced himself to me, then spent the rest of the remaining time with me. The next day he called me at the office and asked me out to dinner. He was a widower whose wife had died of abdominal cancer two years before. Outwardly he appeared to have adjusted to his loss, but I didn't need his psychology degree to know that he was really still numb with shock at her sudden death. My own marriage had been over for several months when my husband died and our entire relationship had been for less than half the time of Hugh's marriage, but I knew that hopeless numbness that sudden death brings – the total disbelief that it really happened, the nights of waking from the false security of dreams of earlier days and the raw pain of the memories brought by photographs, possessions and even certain words and phrases. It takes years to adapt to living with the emotional upheaval of sudden death – even if you are a psychologist. In fact, in Hugh's case at least, that made things harder rather than easier – people expect psychologists to have some kind of mystical control of their emotional responses and he tended to stretch himself too far rather then dispel such assumptions.

I had come to care deeply for Hugh and, I believed he cared for me – well, he *had* asked me to marry him so I could hardly believe otherwise. But I was not ready to give up my house and my independence. It was not the starry-eyed, all-encompassing love I had felt for Angus more than a quarter of a century before or the marriage-made-in-heaven love of Megan and Alan. Instead, it was a comfortable, more mature kind of commitment and I needed time before I was ready to risk replacing the partner for whom Hugh once had – still had – one of those other kinds of love. I knew that Hugh, himself as a psychologist, perceived this response in me as insecurity, Perhaps, it was, but I was in my late forties – approaching fifty – and entitled to have a need to find myself, wasn't I? Besides, his own two children – away at university for most of the year – still counted the house they had grown up in as their home and were no more ready to lose that home than I was to lose mine. I had convinced Hugh, when he first proposed marriage, that it was better – for everybody involved – for us to maintain our separate households until all the children were comfortable with us as a couple and, more importantly still, until we were both individually comfortable about selling our homes. Selling one and keeping the other would place far too much stress on both of us and leave all seven of us open to building resentment. I think he had assumed that we'd live in his house and sell mine – while certainly no throwback to the fifties or sixties, Hugh was still of a generation of men who had to be reminded that women were people, too, and that this one was not exactly falling over herself to occupy his late wife's home.

With Hugh and the question of marriage put firmly on the back burner for the time being, I continued to work at McGrath-LaPlante, paying special attention to grooming my successor. This was a young man – well, not so young anymore really, but I guess I had reached an age when everybody under forty seems young – who I had hired, shortly after my arrival. At that point the Personnel Manager, a gentleman who had expected to be promoted to the vacancy into which I was being parachuted, decided to move on to greener pastures. At the time, I felt badly for him and even wondered if he had a case for the human rights commission despite the fact that I was not unqualified for the position and the board of directors of a private company is quite at liberty to appoint who it chooses to replace a retiring officer. He has, since, swiftly climbed the corporate ladder in a multinational corporation in the medical devices industry and we are on good terms. I hired Peter Dailey to replace him and, fortunately, was able to demonstrate my personnel expertise with a perfect match of person and job. Peter stayed and proved himself highly effective in middle management. He would soon be ready to take his place as a member of the senior management team and I would be leaving the company's human resources department in good hands.

Hugh, meantime, decided not to renew his contract with the large motor corporation for whom he had worked on a consulting basis for many years. He was in great demand as a seminar speaker and had been talked into teaching a post-graduate course at York University, in addition to the two he already taught there. For a while, he really did free up some time but, once word spread that he had done so, demands for his services began to come in thick and fast. By January, he had to hire a secretary/bookkeeper to keep things organized and was soon talking about creating a full service operation which would include executive recruitment and career counselling once I left McGrath-LaPlante to join him. I wondered whether I should be annoyed at his presumption or flattered by his visualization of me as his business partner. Six years before, my desire for a career change had been thwarted by Isabel McGrath's death and the necessity to continue in what was basically an extended area in the same field. I had, of necessity, extended my knowledge of the human resources function as applied to the corporate world and increased my own income while entitling my children to receive their stock dividends and safeguarding their inheritance. There was no question that I had benefited from the circumstances and, despite my restlessness at the time, if I were honest, I'd have to admit that I probably would not have risked changing career direction at that particular point.

Now, in a recovered economy, my chances of succeeding at something of my own choosing were better, but I was six years older...

All the indecision rattled around in my mind for several months. Sometimes I thought that being business partners would help both Hugh and I to decide whether or not marriage would work. At other times I indulged myself in the dream of the brilliant career in cultural anthropology which I had intended for myself before getting side-tracked into marriage and becoming involved in the personnel industry by accident. It was hardly productive to dwell on might-have-beens and my twenty-five-year-old degrees and the experience in a very tenuously related area hardly qualified me to begin that career now. I was hardly unique. After all, very few people ever really managed to spend their lives working at what they wanted – or were even qualified – to do. I remembered a lunch-time conversation I once had with my son-in-law, Alan. It was at the beginning of his relationship with Megan and I did not known him well at the time.

Concerned about his interest in my not-yet-nineteen-year-old daughter, I had asked him to lunch – to some extent to play the heavy-handed parent wanting to know what his intentions were. I thought that Alan had probably been chiefly concerned with impressing upon me his sense of responsibility when he told me how, despite never really wanting a corporate career, he was becoming reconciled to the fact that he was in the right place at the right time and had to finish what he had started at McGrath-LaPlante. He did not mean in terms of the company's unprecedented marketing success, which he had orchestrated, and the consequent impressive increase in the income of the various stakeholders, but in being positioned to play a part in fighting the dreadful, infectious disease that was becoming rampant throughout the world. After his grandfather's death, he had abandoned his previously planned intention to free himself from McGrath-LaPlante because he knew that, in later years, he would never be able to forgive himself if he turned his back on the opportunity to have a positive impact on something so destructive. The years that followed had shown that he meant what he told me that day and my respect and admiration for him had grown accordingly. People ended up where they never intended to be for all sorts of reasons. Perhaps my destiny was to impact on people's lives at the personal occupation level rather than at the mass socio-cultural level that I had once envisioned. You have to maintain a sense of humour about these things.

At the beginning of April, I made plans to leave McGrath-LaPlante at the end of June, retaining my seat on the board until the next annual general meeting and claiming the company as my first client.

. . . . .

Hugh was delighted when I told him I had finally come to a decision about my professional future, at least. I was surprised when he agreed with me in wanting to look for office accommodation for our joint venture. I had expected him to try to persuade me to share the premises which he had created on the ground floor of his home. It was his secretary, Anne-Marie, to whom I found I was indebted for impressing upon her employer the need for an expanding business to be located with other businesses. We jointly purchased one of the new condominium units which were becoming the vogue in office accommodation. The brand new building would be ready for occupation by the middle of July. Meantime, we would have a vacation while Hugh was free of academic commitments.

I had not seen my brother, Jamie, and his family since the children and I had visited Australia the Christmas our lives were changed by my mother-in-law's death. Danny had spent the previous summer there and my parents had gone – probably for the last time, since they were now in their eighties – for the past Christmas season. Jamie and his wife, Jennie, had planned to come to Canada for Megan's wedding, but their youngest son had been involved in a serious traffic accident the day before they were due to leave. Andrew, apparently, was now fully recovered, albeit with a pin in his left leg.

"Hugh," I said, at the congratulatory dinner to which we treated ourselves after our offer was accepted for the condominium, "would you be interested in visiting Coffs Harbour in July?"

"Coff's where? Oh – the place where your brother lives." He looked surprised. "Really?"

He made it sound as if it were the next thing to my agreeing to marry him.

"I'd really like you to meet my brother and we *are* planning to have a vacation..."

"Marilyn," he said, taking my hand, "I can't think of a nicer holiday. I've never been to Australia. I'd love to go. In fact, why don't we plan on going for the whole of July so that we can do all the tourist-type things. Okay?"

"I don't suppose the building will be ready when they say it will, anyway..."

"I'm not just thinking of that. It's time we had a – a mega-type holiday. We can really relax and have fun."

"I thought it would be a good idea to take advantage of everything falling into place for us. I mean, Anne-Marie can have her own vacation then start getting ready for the move and Janice is going to be living at your house for the summer and Byron is there to take care of mine..."

Janice was Hugh's daughter. She was graduating from McGill this year and, intending to return to school for her master's in the fall, had a job for the summer in Toronto.

"Speaking of Janice," Hugh said, "she asked me, last night, if I thought you'd come to her convocation next month."

"Really! That's wonderful, Hugh. I'd love to. That really is a surprise."

Janice had been in her last year of high school when her mother died. Surprisingly she had not lost the year as her father had expected. Instead, she had adjusted and been accepted, a few months later, for McGill. Her brother, Ian – a year younger than Janice, had experienced more difficulty in finishing high school. He had eventually managed to improve his average and was now enrolled in pre-med at McMaster. Neither of them had been eager to accept a new woman in their father's life and Hugh and I had tacitly agreed to take a hands-off position and let them adapt to the situation at their own pace. Janice's invitation for me to attend her convocation was the first time either of them had shown a desire to include me in a family occasion – even Christmas Day had been celebrated, both years since we had met, in our separate households.

"I didn't expect that... It's-it's great... I'm so glad," I continued, aware that I was babbling. "Shall I call her? She really wants me to come?"

"Hey, slow down. If she were to see you acting so dizzy, she'd change her mind..." He squeezed my hand and I could tell he was probably even more impressed than I was. He raised his wine glass. "Here's to the future and our – eventually – getting it together. We've bought a property together, I've been asked to accompany you to the other side of the world and meet your brother and my daughter's asked you to her convocation – things are starting to move at last."

I laughed and clinked my glass to his. "To a day to remember," I said.

. . . . .

It turned out to be just that – a day to remember. But not in the way I intended. Byron's car was in the garage and the lights were on when I arrived home. I had scarcely put my key into the lock of the kitchen door when Byron opened it.

"Mom," he said, "Michael just called and Angus has run away from home – for real this time."

"Hey, come on," I said, "you're starting to sound like Michael himself. Aren't you over-reacting a little?" I knew immediately that he wasn't. Byron was the last person to catch Michael's paranoia, the first person to play down hysteria, in fact. I put the milk, I'd stopped to pick up, into the refrigerator. "What happened?"

"He's been gone since Friday. They didn't call before because they were expecting him to show up during the weekend. You know how he is – expects the world to fall in with his plans and can't handle people looking at him the wrong way. Like last year when Danny was there and he went to the police expecting them to find the bums who rolled him. Well, it didn't happen this time. Nobody knows where he is."

"Where was he – at home or at Michael's?" I asked.

"At home. That was the trouble at first – he was supposed to be going to Michael's for the weekend, so they thought he had just skipped school to get over to Vancouver early. He's done that before, apparently – regularly, in fact, ever since he's been old enough to travel back and forth on his own."

"I know. Judith doesn't like to punish him by not letting him go to his father's because that would be like punishing Michael, too. Though – quite honestly – it's equally likely that Judith and Lawrence don't want to have to give up their skulking teenager-free weekends and prefer Michael to look after the punishing."

"Well, that's what they thought he was up to, but when he still hadn't shown up by the late evening, they knew it was another one of his runaway stunts. The police were called but, you know how they are with teenage runaways – they don't actually do anything..."

"So, how did Michael sound?"

Byron grimaced. "Oh, you know – the usual. Taking it out on everybody else. Oh, don't worry–" he stopped me as I was about to speak, "–I played it very cool and didn't blow – even though the casual observer would definitely have thought it was all my fault the way he was coming on."

"Good for you," I said, patting him on the back. "Now, how about putting the kettle on for a cup of one of your herbal teas before we go to bed? The one that helps you sleep for me – I drank too much wine at dinner and I know darn well that I'll develop insomnia two hours after I go to sleep."

He filled the kettle and put it on to boil, then got out mugs and tea bags. I sat down at the kitchen table and rifled through the mail that Byron had put there earlier.

"What were you celebrating?" he asked, after watching me check to see if there was anything other than bills and junk mail. He leaned against the counter waiting for the kettle to boil.

"What?"

"The too much wine?"

"Oh," I added the phone bill to the hydro bill and put the envelope on the junk mail pile, "our offer was accepted for that business condo unit and Janice wants me to go to her convocation. What do you think of that?"

"The condo or Janice?"

"Janice, of course. I always thought it would be Ian who came round first."

"I think they're both pretty immature. When is it? The convocation, I mean."

"You know, I was so stunned I forgot to ask. I imagine sometime in the middle of next month. Maybe we should ask them to your birthday dinner next week..."

"Ian's hardly going to want to drive over from Hamilton just for my birthday, is he? Not that I blame him – I can't honestly say I'd want to bother to go to any trouble for my maybe-eventually-step-brother's birthday." He picked up the now boiling kettle and finished making the tea. "Besides, Alan's going to be in France, so I kind of thought it'd be nice if it was just us. You, me, Danny and Megan."

He passed my mug of tea to me and stayed at the counter dunking his tea-bag with a teaspoon.

"Yes, that would be nice," I said. "Okay – it's *your* birthday. It would probably have been putting them on a spot anyway and they might have resented it." I picked up the spoon, that Byron had put in the mug, and squeezed my tea bag, thinking about the fact that it would also be Angus's birthday. "What am I going to do about Angus's birthday card?"

"Maybe he'll have shown up by then," said Byron. "Here, I'll take that." He held out a dirty glass he'd taken from the sink and I dropped my teabag into it. After repeating the procedure with his own tea bag, he sat down opposite me. "You may as well think positive and send it. What with your desire for tea and your proposed trip to Montreal, I didn't finish the story. Angus has been telling kids at his school that he planned to hitch to Toronto this summer, so Michael thinks he may show up here."

"I don't really think that's likely."

"That's what I said – politely, though. The kid just doesn't have that much staying power. Actually, Mom, I'm more worried about weirdoes..."

"Which kind of weirdoes?"

"Perverts, pimps, paedophiles, whatever..." he took a sip of his tea. "I know I haven't seen him since last year, but he's always looked young for his age..."

"He's probably changed enormously since last year," I said. "Boys do between fourteen and fifteen. You did. So did Danny. It's a very tough age for parents to have to cope with – all that burgeoning male ego that's so easy to damage..."

He looked at me as if he thought I was being flippant, then decided to ignore it if I was. "Danny told me that Angus said he had hash with him that time last year when all his things got stolen and he went to the police station. It's usually drugs that turn a runaway into a full-time street kid. That's if some pimp gets hold of him in the city. If he gets out of the city and really does try to hitch across the country, God knows what kind of people he'll get involved with."

I was silent. I really did not know what to say. Byron was too old now for me to play down his fears – he probably knew more than I did about the dangers facing runaway kids. I slowly drank the rest of my tea thinking back to the end of August last year when Danny had come home from Australia, stopping to visit Michael and Lise on the way. He had told me how he had tried to mentor his young cousin and the deal they had made to stay in touch. It had worked for a while. I had talked to Angus myself – several times – when he called Danny. Then, after Danny had bought and moved into his apartment, he had made sure Angus had his telephone number, but found Angus calling him increasingly less frequently and he, himself, having to make the calls progressively more often. Eventually, figuring the telephone company to be the only beneficiary, he had given up the whole project. He'll be mad at himself, I thought, when he finds out.

"We'll tell Danny tomorrow," I said. "We can say it was too late to call him. Okay?"

"Good idea," replied Byron. "He's going to be pretty mad at himself for giving up on the kid. You can only do so much, though. He did his best."

"Of course he did," I agreed. "Did you say I'd call Michael?"

Byron nodded. "You could hold off until tomorrow and say you came in after I'd gone to sleep."

I grinned. "No, I'd better do it now. Poor Michael."

"Lise is the one I feel sorry for."

. . . . .

Angus was not found. Michael called every day. It was almost as if he thought Angus would appear, momentarily, on my doorstep. I called Judith who confirmed that Angus had indeed informed several friends that he was hitching to Toronto. I had hoped that this part of the story might prove to be some chance remark which had become exaggerated in Michael's mind but, no – Angus had been working on his friend, Philip, to leave with him – Philip wasn't about to trust Angus to find their way clear across the country, however. Philip and Angus had been friends since they were six years old when Angus first moved to the neighbourhood after his parents split up and he moved to Victoria with his mother to live with Lawrence. Since he did not go to the same school, Philip did not know that Angus had actually left until he arrived home from his school and Judith called him. By that time it was just another confirmation of Angus's plans. After receiving the call from school informing her that her son was not in class, Judith had checked his room and found clothing, other than the school clothes he had left the house in that morning, missing. She had an arrangement for the school to inform her if Angus was not at school, but this morning it had been her turn to work at the co-operative nursery school her daughter, Stephanie, attended and the school secretary had not got hold of her until she and Stephanie came home for lunch. She'd immediately called Michael who had left his office and gone to the ferry dock to check out the bus passengers coming off from Victoria. Lise, fortunately working at home for the day, had been put on alert in case Angus showed up there. And police in both Victoria and Vancouver had been informed. Their efforts were all too late, however, and Angus had slipped through to who knew where? Judith was crying.

"I wish I understood why he does these things, Marilyn," she said. "Nobody could love him more than I do – and Michael, too – yet, it sometimes seems that he's just determined to hurt us as much as he can."

"It just seems that way. He doesn't think things through and consider other people – boys are like that at his age."

"It has nothing to do with his age. Well, not the way people mean when they say that. I know that bringing three children up by yourself wasn't exactly easy, but they weren't like this, Marilyn. This is something else. It's psychological – dysfunctional... I don't know how to describe it, although – from the ADHD angle (that's what they're calling the condition now), it does have to do with his age. Impulsiveness, refusal to think things through... they're the symptoms, which are more likely than hyperactivity, to get the child into trouble in the adolescent years. Sometimes he's almost reclusive – nothing like the hyperactive little boy he was. Other times, he's almost manic and drives us all berserk. I suppose I'm describing mood swings, aren't I?"

I agreed that she was.

"He's been seeing a psychiatrist for three years now. We've all been involved in counselling – even Stephanie. And Michael and Lise – and Justin – have met with him. Nothing seems to help..."

"He seemed to be doing quite well last fall," I said. "I talked to him on the phone, myself, two or three times before Danny moved into his own place."

"Yes, Danny did a wonderful job with him – right up until about February, it must have been. That's when he seemed to change again. Even John – the psychiatrist – said that Danny was doing him far more good – more good than *he* was, in fact! But Angus just seemed to lose interest and was either out or wouldn't pick up his phone when Danny called. I felt awful – I mean, Danny must have more than enough to do..."

"Danny was only too pleased to do something to help. He feels terrible now about giving up."

"Oh, please tell him not to. There was no point in continuing to spend the money making telephone calls for nothing."

"He knows that, Judith, but he still feels badly. We're just hoping that Angus remembers – if he gets here, I mean – that Danny is his friend. I don't suppose he has the McGrath-LaPlante number, does he?"

"No, not unless he's hoarded it for some reason, though he doesn't know anything about the company as far as I know, so I can't really think of any reason for him to..."

"Nor can I. It was just a thought. It would be nice to know that he was able to make contact with one of us at any period of the day. We've told Adam Kinchen in case he tries to contact him and he has everybody's phone numbers so that he can call one of us right away. And he's a very trustworthy boy."

"It's all right, Marilyn," she laughed at my emphasis on his being trustworthy, "I haven't been influenced by Michael in that regard. I trust your judgement."

This was just one of the conversations I had with Judith as I tried to help her keep her hopes up. She knew that she owed it to her daughter to try to maintain the normal routine of their lives and she was not – as she put it, herself – about to cave in under the stress and dump more problems on Lawrence. He'd born all the problems with Angus right along with her and she felt she had to bear up for his sake. It was a tremendous strain on all of them and I felt the least I could do was to be there, on the other end of the phone, to listen and offer encouragement. She handled herself far better than Michael did – he did not have the same compulsion to refrain from dumping on his family as his ex-wife did and, consequently, I found myself offering a sympathetic ear to Lise, too.

Byron, despite his still rather ambiguous attitude towards Michael, flew out to Vancouver the following weekend. His exams were finished and, although Alan was employing him in McGrath-LaPlante's marketing department again for the summer, he was not due to start work for a couple of weeks. He scoured Vancouver's parks, streets and beaches on foot, questioning street kids and vagrants without coming up with a clue to Angus's whereabouts. He took Justin along after school and at the weekend which helped the boy to feel that he was doing something positive. Michael set off to drive the Trans-Canada Highway to Toronto the day after Byron arrived. Lise was both relieved to get a break from his continual preoccupation and agonizing over the situation and worried in case he got himself into trouble questioning less than sympathetic travellers along the way. He made the journey without getting physically aggressive as Lise, in her worst nightmares, imagined he might if he fancied some teenage hitch-hiker or long distance truck driver was holding out on him. Unfortunately, however, a couple of aging, ardent hockey fans in a bar in Winnipeg recognized him and, by the time he reached Toronto, newspaper headlines were proclaiming, "Ex-Maple Leaf's teenage son disappears" and "Have you seen Team Canada hero's runaway son?"

We were all hounded once media archives were checked and Michael's McGrath-LaPlante connections remembered. Budding human interest journalists dug deep and came up with the story of the fairy-tale wedding of the runaway's parents and Michael's subsequent failure to lead the Leafs to a Stanley Cup win after the sudden death of his older brother. Megan came and stayed with me until Alan returned from France. Alan's position at McGrath-LaPlante and his AIDS prevention activism resulted in he and

Megan being relatively well-known in Toronto establishment circles and, using her own name, she was increasingly becoming accepted as an up and coming artist. It did not take long, therefore, for the connection between Megan McGrath, McGrath-LaPlante and Michael McGrath to be made. She had tried leaving the answering machine on, not answering the door and cancelling the house-cleaning service, but was caught by an enterprising young journalist when she sneaked out to buy milk and bread. After that, she decided confronting journalists was easier in groups of two or more than as a solo act and repossessed her childhood room for a few days.

Michael, like the rest of us, was in two minds about the value of the publicity. On the one hand it virtually prevented him from searching downtown streets as he had intended to do. On the other, if Angus were on those streets, surely somebody would alert either the press or the police after recognizing him from the pictures in the paper, which Judith had handed over when the story broke – supposing it potentially more useful to co-operate and get current photographs printed in the papers, than to refuse to speak to the reporters and have them dig up out-dated ones from other sources. Michael stayed in Danny's spare room. Danny – ever the diplomat of the family – had decided that it would be uncomfortable for me to have Michael stay when I no longer had a houseful of children and did have a potential fiancé. He had invited Michael to stay with him as soon as Michael, in touch with everyone either by car phone or pay phone, told us that he was attempting to track Angus by road. While reports did come in from people who reported seeing Angus on the bus and on the ferry, the day he disappeared, and some sightings of a boy answering his description attempting to hitch a ride in Burnaby that evening, the media stories did not help us to find him. Within a few days of arriving in Toronto, Michael called a press conference and announced a ten thousand dollar reward for any information leading to the discovery of Angus's whereabouts and hired a national security company to follow up on the responses. A week later he increased the amount of the reward, but the resulting calls continued to be either cranks or sightings of wandering teens in various parts of the country, none of whom turned out to be Angus.

Judith called me a couple of days after that to tell me that the Vancouver police were beginning to talk about the possibility of foul play.

"They can definitely trace him to the bus station, so there's no doubt that he did get to Vancouver and they feel that if he were camping out with street kids somewhere, somebody would have recognized him by now and come forward – if only to claim the reward. Nobody's come forward with any more information about the boy seen hitch-hiking in Burnaby and they'd like to confirm one way or the other if it was him or not, so they've been checking the bus routes trying to find out if anybody saw him on the way to Burnaby since it's not likely that he hitched in the city. It's difficult because school was out by that time and there were hundreds of kids around. They want to know when Michael is intending to go home. I've given them Danny's number so I imagine they'll be calling him." She finally paused. "He *is* still there, isn't he?"

"Yes," I said, "he's talking about going home, since he's pretty well convinced that Angus is not here in Toronto. You know, Judith, I think he really wanted him to have got himself here because, despite all the worry it caused, it would have been an accomplishment that would have really boosted his self confidence."

"I know what you mean. I've kind of thought that myself in between times of being worried sick. Now that the police are getting serious, I wish, more than ever, that it could have been so."

"Did you tell them that Byron spent two weeks tracking down street kids?"

"Yes. Did he get home all right? I meant to ask you before, but... well, I had other things on my mind. We all really appreciated what he did. Tell him the police were pretty impressed when Lise told them of all the areas he'd covered. I was just talking to her – I called earlier to see if she knew when Michael was coming home, then the police were there to see her and she phoned me back to tell me."

"I'll tell him. He's out at the moment. He just started his summer job today and went to Megan's for supper. He was only too glad to be able to do something – that's the whole problem, Judith, everyone feels so helpless. Byron was able to do something practical and, even if it didn't get results, at least it was doing something. I wish I could do something..."

"You are, Marilyn," Judith said, huskily, "you're the one who's listening to us all – me, Michael, Lise..."

"Danny's the one who's been doing all the listening to Michael," I said, "and studying for exams at the same time."

"Oh, no – I hadn't thought of that. Is he managing all right?"

"He had the last one today. Michael's taken him and a couple of his friends out to supper to celebrate. Danny didn't really think that was such a good idea but, of course, the other guys realise that Michael wants to show his appreciation to Danny for being a sounding board the last couple of weeks. They're pretty good at limiting their conversation to hockey and revolutionizing the business world – generally keeping Michael talking about other things, you know..."

"Well, *I* really appreciate all your family's help."

"We're glad that we can at least be supportive. Is that Stephanie I hear? How's she bearing up?"

"It's pretty hard being five and trying to figure out what's going on, I guess. She's missing Angus. It's funny, despite the age difference and all the problems, she's really very attached to him. I'd better go. I'll talk to you later. 'Bye, Marilyn."

"'Bye," I said.

At the office the next morning, Danny told me that Michael was flying home that evening and he was going to drive his car back for him the following week. The Vancouver police had called when he and Michael arrived back at the apartment the previous evening and told him they were now investigating Angus's disappearance as a possible case of foul play. I told him about my conversation with Judith.

"How did Michael react?" I asked.

"Well," said Danny, "he was the best I've seen him since he got here until the police called. First reaction, of course, was that he thought it might be good news, then he just practically collapsed. I mean, he's still – well, I guess we're all still hoping that Angus has just found himself some friends and either hasn't heard or read the news or is deliberately ignoring it – right?"

"It's hard to know what we're hoping – at least, that's how I feel..."

"Anyway, he went from the best he's been to the worst in thirty seconds. Personally, I don't think the police action indicates the worst any more then before – it's more likely somebody there has a guilty conscience about treating it so lightly before it got the media attention."

"I think you're probably right."

Jayne came into my office.

"How's Michael?" she asked Danny. He told her what had happened. She shook her head. "It's hard to believe this is really happening," she said. "You don't expect things like this to happen so close to home. I wish the police had some other way of putting it – *suspected foul play* sounds so final."

"Danny and I were just agreeing," I said, "that the Vancouver police are probably being so melodramatic because they feel badly about not taking the case seriously in the first place. Fifteen-year-olds running away from home are every day events for them – they don't exactly go looking for them. Now, with all the media – it's a different story. Somebody's looking to get his name in the papers."

"You could be right. What happens to the reward if the police find him?"

"I imagine Michael will have to give it to some police charity or something," Danny said. "At least, if some bunch of vagrants or superannuated hippies have got hold of him and are waiting for the reward to go up in price, they'll be flushed out."

"There's a lot of weirdoes down the west coast and on some of those islands in the Gulf there..." Jayne murmured.

"Better for him to be there than for some pimp to have taken him over the border or something," Danny said grimly.

"Let's try to be a little more positive, guys," I said, getting up and shepherding them both towards the door. "See you later."

· · · · ·

Byron and I drove up to the airport, after supper that day, to see Michael off. It was hard trying to keep his spirits up and I was glad that he was flying back because just the thought of his driving across the country in his present, preoccupied frame of mind would have had us all sick with worry. Laura and Dennis came over to the airport, too. And Jayne. Dennis took us all for a drink at the Constellation Hotel afterwards and we tried to persuade each other that Angus would soon be found and everything was going to be all right. It was a dismal evening.

Lise called me the next morning to let me know Michael was safely home and that she and Justin were looking forward to seeing Danny when he brought the car back next week. She hoped that he would stay for a few days. I told her that Hugh and I had arranged our tickets so that we would be stopping over in Vancouver for a few days on our way to Australia next month. I had previously discussed, with her, the possibility – under the circumstances – of postponing the trip. She said she was glad we were still going because, as she had said before, my first priority should be myself and Hugh. Danny, Megan and Byron were all available to Angus should he show up in Toronto. We both hoped, of course, that Angus would be home again by then. But, he wasn't.

## ALAN

"Alan?"

"Adam – is that you? Is something wrong?"

Something evidently *was* wrong. Adam would soon be sixteen and had known Alan since they were matched as Big and Little Brothers when he was eight years old. He had long ago outgrown being hesitant and knew that he could always find an attentive, non-judgemental listener in Alan – whatever the problem. Alan could remember only two occasions, since the first few months of getting to know each other, on which Adam had been ill at ease with him. Once, just a few weeks ago, when – after bringing his girl friend to meet Megan and himself – he'd initiated a discussion about sex, in reality seeking Alan's opinion on whether or not he and/or the girl were ready for sex. The other time was when Megan's cousin, Angus, had inveigled Adam into showing him around Toronto, conveniently forgetting to discuss the expedition with his father and causing a subsequently, constrained relationship between Michael and Alan, who Michael resented for having introduced Adam to Angus in the first place. That was all water under the bridge now, with Angus having been officially a missing person for nearly a year. Alan stiffened in response to his racing thoughts.

"What is it, Adam?" he asked, alarmed now at Adam's prolonged silence.

"Alan – Angus just called me."

"What?"

"Angus – he called me."

Alan was at a loss for words. If it had been anybody but Adam, he would have thought he was the victim of a cruel joke. Adam had looked to him as a mentor all these years. He was a good kid and he sounded about as stunned as Alan, himself, was feeling.

"What's the matter?" Wrapped in a bath towel, Megan came through the connecting door from the bathroom into the bedroom. Always an early riser – even on a Saturday – she had been having her morning shower while Alan continued to sleep.

"It's Adam," he said and handed her the phone.

"What's the matter, Adam?" she asked, sitting down on the side of the bed beside Alan.

"Megan," Adam made a supreme effort to control his own shock now that Alan's passing the phone to Megan necessitated him telling *her* that her missing cousin had called him. Alan, himself, had no idea why he had given Megan the phone but, listening to Megan's side of the conversation, he knew that it was making it easier on both Adam and Megan.

"Megan," Adam continued, " your cousin, Angus, just called me. I know this must be a big shock for you, but – well, it was for me, too."

"You're sure it was Angus?" Megan asked, appearing to recover from the shock faster than either her husband or Adam. "I mean, it wasn't somebody playing a joke or something..."

"Why would somebody do that? I've never talked about it to anyone other than Alan and you and your family, anyway. It was Angus for sure – his voice was deeper, naturally, but he still sounded, basically the same as the last time I talked to him."

"What did he say?" Somehow, she knew it would be pointless to ask where he was.

"He said, 'Hi, Adam, I hope you remember me – Angus McGrath? Megan's cousin?' Then I was so stunned I couldn't seem to say anything, so he said, 'Adam, are you there?' So, then I asked him how come he was calling me and he said he wanted to make sure I remembered him. Excuse me for saying so – but he sounded sort of spaced – stoned..."

"But it was definitely Angus?"

"I told you. Yes, it was him. For sure."

"So what did you say," Megan asked, leaning back against Alan and holding the phone so that he could hear, " after he said he wanted to make sure you remembered him?"

"I said, of course I remembered him – how could I have forgotten him? Then I started to ask where he was and he interrupted and asked me if I still saw you and Alan. So, I said yes, why wouldn't I see you and he said he had expected I would have been more mature by now. 'What's that supposed to mean?' I said and he said I'd find out when I lightened up and stopped taking life so seriously. I was getting a bit pissed off – annoyed, that is – and asked him if he'd woken me and everyone in my family this early just to insult me. I'd answered the phone, but it had woken my mother and sister, too, of course. Then he asked what time it was so I said nearly six and he said, 'Oh, you mean Hogtown time – did you know that's what they used to call it – Hogtown?' So I said yes and started to ask where he was again and he said he'd better let me get up for school – sort of – well, a bit sort of sneeringly – since I hadn't learned yet that that's not what education is all about and would I say hi to you because you're the only one of his relatives with guts enough to live your dream and he respects that – then he hung up. I was about to say it was Saturday, not that it really matters..."

Megan was silent. Adam's voice came over the phone. "Megan, are you still there?"

Alan took the phone from her.

"It's okay, Adam," he said. "Look – don't worry about it. We'll figure out what to do – not that there's anything that can really be done, but we'll decide what to do about telling his father and, hopefully preventing him from feeling the need to interrogate you... okay? I'll talk to you later and... thanks for calling us. I'm sorry he had to upset you and your family – apologise to your mother for me..."

"Don't worry about that. I just wish I'd had time – or been on the ball enough – to keep him talking and find out more, but you know how it is when the phone wakes you up and you feel all shaky and disoriented?"

"Yes, I know what you mean. Don't worry. I'll talk to you later. 'Bye."

Alan shifted his position to lean over and put the phone on the bedside table. Megan came out of her reverie and jumped up.

"Shit – I feel awful," she said, looking totally wretched. "I never bothered with him – I think I wrote him off as a little nuisance. My brothers were far more involved with him – and concerned about him – than I ever was... I should have shown more interest..."

By this time Alan was out of bed and holding her tightly against him while she continued.

"Guts! I always had somebody to champion me – Danny, my mother, you. I had it easy... I didn't have to have guts to live my dreams – why does he think that? Oh God, I should have spent more time with him..."

"Look, sweetheart," Alan said, taking her shoulders and gently pushing her back to face him. "This isn't the time to let him put you on a guilt trip. The kid probably had a crush on you and everything you stood for was exaggerated in his eyes – how were you supposed to know? You hardly ever saw him – how could you have helped him. Don't you see? The Megan-who-lives-for-her-art was a figment of his imagination. It wasn't you." He slid his hands down her arms and caught hold of her hands. "You're the Megan who lives to make her husband some breakfast while he has a shower, I hope."

He pulled her towards him and kissed her forehead. She relaxed a little.

"I think I see what you mean," she said slowly. "but I should still have done more."

"No – you couldn't. Not the last few years, anyway, and before that you hardly knew him. There was no way you could have nurtured him after we made the big boo-boo – in his father's eyes – of introducing him to Adam. It was much better that we kept our distance. This – well, maybe not his actually disappearing, but something like it – would have happened regardless of who tried to help Angus. Look at Danny – Danny bent over backwards for him and it didn't help in the end."

"You're right," she said. "I shouldn't take it as a personal condemnation, should I? Let's put that part aside and decide what we are going to do."

"Good girl." He turned her around in the direction of the door and patted her behind. "You get dressed and be Megan-who-lives-to-make-her-husband-some-breakfast and I'll get my shower and shave and then – and only then – we'll discuss it rationally. Okay?"

Megan smiled at last. "Okay."

Megan managed to come down off her guilt trip while she prepared breakfast and, afterwards they decided to drive over to her mother's house and see what she thought before they did anything. They both agreed that this was not something to discuss by telephone and it was better to get more input before telling Michael, especially since neither of them – under the circumstances – was really the ideal person to break the news to him.

As it turned out, not only was Byron there, but Danny and Hugh, as well. Hugh's and Marilyn's secretary, Anne-Marie, was getting married the next weekend to – by a strange twist of fate – to an old neighbour of the McGraths. Hugh, Danny and Byron had all been at a stag given for him the previous night. Hugh was drinking coffee at the breakfast table when Alan and Megan arrived, but neither Danny nor Byron had yet put in an appearance. Marilyn was on her way up the stairs from the basement, where she had just put a load of laundry into the washing machine, when Megan tapped at the kitchen door. She let them in, explaining about the stag and the less than up-and-raring-to-go state of the menfolk.

"Is something wrong?" she asked. "This is a strange time to come visiting. Embarrassing, too – with your brothers both dead to the world still and Hugh trying to wake himself up with coffee. I'd better put a fresh pot on... What's happened?"

She said all this while guiding them both in the direction of the kitchen table where Hugh sat grinning at them a little sheepishly and Byron's dog, Ben, limped towards them, wagging his tail.

"Hi, Ben – how are you, you poor old man?" Megan stooped down to pet the old dog.

"How are you, Hugh?" asked Alan, sitting down at the table.

"It's not as bad as she makes it sound," Hugh said. "We were just being responsible citizens walking back here for the night rather than driving when we'd been drinking – that doesn't mean we all got polluted."

"We would never dream of thinking such a thing," said Megan, laughing. "In fact, we're only too glad you're all here. We need all the help we can get on the problem *we* have."

"What d'you mean?" asked her mother, coming to join them at the table after putting on fresh coffee.

"Angus called Adam Kinchen this morning," said Alan.

"What?"

"Now you know why we hot-footed it over here so early," Megan said, taking off her jacket and hanging it on the back of a chair before sitting down next to Alan. "We don't know what to do."

"You haven't called Michael?"

"Are you kidding? Anyway, it's still only six thirty there and – well, we're both too chicken to do it. We thought we should talk it over first."

"She just means that Michael is likely to get a bit hostile, Marilyn," explained Alan. "You know – the shoot the messenger syndrome. So we just need some advice and, maybe, a volunteer to tell him."

Marilyn grimaced. "Actually, he's going to have a bird no matter who tells him."

"Right!" said Megan. "That's precisely why we're here."

"Perhaps," suggested Hugh, quietly, "you should tell us just what happened before we decide what to do."

"Good idea," Alan said and proceeded to tell them how Adam had called them after the early morning phone call from Angus. He repeated Adam's story, including the first part which he hadn't actually heard himself but which Megan had told him afterwards. "Megan went on a bit of a guilt trip at first over the last bit, but I think she's all right now–" he took her hand and looked at her until she smiled and nodded. "So, anyway, we decided not to do anything too hasty and came over here."

"We decided not to phone because it didn't seem like something we should lay on you on the phone," added Megan.

"I see what you mean," said her mother. "It won't be too easy laying it on Michael on the phone either."

"Right," Megan nodded.

Marilyn got up to pour the coffee. "Well, Danny's the closest to him," she said. "Should we wake him up? Do you want a refill, Hugh? Can you come and get yours and Alan's, Megan?"

Since nobody knew which question to answer first, Megan silently went and picked up the two filled mugs and Hugh held his mug up to be refilled. Marilyn replaced the carafe and brought her own coffee to the table.

"Sounds like one of them is up and about," remarked Hugh in response to sounds of the toilet flushing followed by the shower being turned on in the bathroom overhead. "Most likely Danny – it's still a bit early for Byron, isn't it?"

"You're probably right," Megan agreed. "The last time Byron stayed over at our place he slept till eleven-thirty. I don't know how people can do that."

"Well, not everyone wants to rise and shine at six on a Saturday morning like you do, either," retorted her husband, "I'd probably still be asleep myself if this hadn't happened."

"Okay – so I'm the weirdo." Megan turned to her mother. "D'you think Danny'll do it, Mom?"

"I expect so." Marilyn said. "He'll probably agree that he's the best person – though even he hasn't really been getting along too well with Michael the last few months. Since Michael turned into a sort of modern day Dan Peggotty, I mean."

"Have you heard from Lise lately, Mom?" asked Megan.

"Yes," Marilyn replied. "Have you?"

Megan nodded. "She thinks it might be better if she and Justin left."

"I know. It must be hard to live with someone who's so completely obsessed. At least, Judith – however upset she really is – is doing her best to keep their lives – hers, Lawrence's and Stephanie's – as normal as possible. Maybe, once he knows for sure that Angus is definitely alive, he'll settle down a bit..."

"More likely to get worse," said Hugh.

"Not necessarily," Alan said reflectively, "but he will take it personally – Angus phoning Adam, I mean – not even somebody in the family, let alone Michael, himself."

"That's what I mean. If he gets offended, it might bring him to his senses and make him see that life must go on."

"It's more likely to put him into a major clinical depression, actually," Alan told him. "Although it might put an end to the Peggotty act. By the way, we think it better not to tell him the bit about Angus telling Adam to say hi to Megan for him because she's the only one he respects – okay."

"Yes," agreed Marilyn. "It's best not to rub salt into the wound."

"I should have spent more time with him," Megan said, shaking her head. "I could have done. Remember that Christmas when he was here and he was fascinated with that old sketch book – you made photocopies for him – remember, Mom?" Marilyn nodded. "I was so selfish – wrapped up in myself. I could have helped him to sketch – with him being interested, I mean. I could have let him mess around with paint or something. I never thought of it..."

"I don't think it was drawing so much that attracted him to the sketch book," said Marilyn.

"What d'you mean?"

"It was the pictures – your drawings of him and Michael and Judith. The idea of being three years old again and safe with his mother and father – no teachers and schoolmates to make him feel like a nuisance, no step-father getting impatient with his thoughtless behaviour, no feeling different..."

"You're right," agreed Hugh. "I don't know Angus – I only met him on one occasion, the weekend of your wedding–" he nodded in the direction of Alan and Megan "–so I don't know the individual case, but I do know about ADHD because it's not just a childhood problem as most people seem to think. It's still a problem when the people, who have it are grown up and in the work force – that is, it's still a problem if they haven't learned to control it or turned it into a positive, which can be done – it's where all the high energy achievers spring from! So it's my job to know about it. In young children, the motor overactivity is the major problem which is why, until recent years, such children – Angus included, so I understand – were usually diagnosed as being hyperactive or hyperkinetic. But, by its very nature, the disorder is also characterized by a deficit in attention and concentration abilities and by impulsive behaviours which is why, today, the term attention deficit disorder with hyperactivity or ADHD is used. What has been most misunderstood over the years is the notion that ADHD features disappear as the child grows older when, in fact, inattention, impulsivity and hyperactivity continue into adolescence and that's when – even if they do disappear or the adolescent learns to control or compensate for them – low self esteem becomes a major factor. And, of course, that's not so surprising in the face of the under achievement, difficulties in relationships with peers and poor relationships with adults caused by the disorder over the years. Following that come the drug and alcohol problems..."

"You think that's where Angus is at?" asked Megan.

"I don't know. We know he was, at least, experimenting with hash the summer before last when Danny was there," Hugh replied, "Anyway, the reason I delivered the lecture was because the problem's not one which a single person's interest and concern will make or break, so there's no point in berating yourself, Megan. Treatment of ADHD is multi-faceted – cognitive therapy for the attention deficit problem, diet control, remedial education, behavioural therapy to increase self-esteem, family and child counselling, family support generally – and it all needs to be consistent and ongoing. You have to be there all the time, so there's nothing anybody here could have done to help and I think you should all remember that, and refrain from feeling guilty over what's happened, because I don't imagine we've heard the worst yet."

They were all silent.

"I guess I was being rather arrogant really," said Megan, "acting like I could have been the answer when you only have to look at poor Judith struggling with the problem all these years..."

She was interrupted by Danny coming down the stairs and into the kitchen.

"What's happening?" he asked. "You all look like you're having a council of war..."

"Angus called Adam Kinchen," Megan told him.

"What? Really? What happened?"

Megan told him.

"Has anyone told Michael?" he asked as soon as she was finished.

"No," said Alan, "We've been waiting for you to wake up."

"Oh. You mean you want me to do it? Why didn't you wake me up?"

"We do all think you're the best person to tell him, Danny," said his mother, "but they're three hours behind us remember?"

"But he'll want to know..."

"I think it's better to tell him in a calm and composed way – not without thinking it through first. It's going to be tough enough dealing with his reaction as it is."

"You're right," Danny agreed. "Is there any coffee left?"

"There's a bit in the carafe," Marilyn said. "Why don't you put some more on? And I think maybe I'll call Judith while you're deciding how to go about the Michael problem. It's still a bit early – for a Saturday, I mean – but I think we've left it long enough. And the police will be wondering what took us so long – not that it really matters as I hardly imagine they'll continue to treat it as being a possible case of foul play now. He's been gone for ten months, he'll soon be sixteen and he's made a telephone call apparently of his own free will. They'll be back to writing him off as just another teenage runaway. Poor Judith." She stood up. "I'll use the study phone – I can't handle you all watching me."

. . . . .

"I don't think I want to have children," Megan said, as they were driving home later in the afternoon, after staying for a protracted lunch. "I couldn't handle all the heartbreak."

"Oh, I imagine the good times usually make up for it," Alan replied gently. "I don't think you should get negative about having children just because of Angus. It's not the general rule for things go *that* wrong."

"It could be genetic..."

"Genetic predisposition possibly..." Alan paused as he concentrated on trying to see around an oncoming truck making a left hand turn, before turning left himself. "And that needs environmental conditions to trigger whatever the child's genetically predisposed to – or so I understand. Actually, if I'm honest I don't know what I'm talking about, but I don't think it's something to worry about. We hardly need make decisions about having a child in the middle of all this, do we?" He glanced over at her. "Hey, don't get upset, love."

Megan blinked back tears. "I'm sorry. It must be delayed shock or something. I just keep thinking about when he was a little boy – the time we visited them in Edmonton, I mean. They had this big home with their own little woodlot at the back and Michael and Danny and Byron pitched one of our tents – we were on our way to Jasper and Banff for a camping holiday – out there and had a camp fire with no girls allowed. Danny was so happy. You see, Uncle Michael was his hero and we hadn't see him since he was traded and everything. Anyway, I was in the house with Mom and Judith and, of course, they spent most of the time gabbing, so I played with Angus. I was eleven – just coming up to baby-sitting age – at least, I thought so and it was good practice for me. He was a cute little kid – never stopped, of course. The doctor was advising that he go on Ritalin and Judith didn't know what to do. She'd been working hard at controlling his diet – watching the sugar and not letting him have anything with colouring or preservatives, etc. She didn't want him on more medication – he already had to take stuff for his asthma – and she'd heard that Ritalin turned kids into zombies and thought the hyperactivity was preferable. Michael, of course, just tuned out. Men usually do – no offence intended."

Megan stopped speaking and glanced at her husband.

"It's okay," he said, "I'm not about to take it personally. You're quite right – fathers usually are the last to admit that there's something wrong with a child. I expect it's the male ego, as usual..."

Megan smiled. "I expect so," she agreed. "Anyway, I got the distinct impression that Michael wasn't exactly co-operative and his basking in my brothers' hero worship those few days wasn't madly helpful to Judith. Michael expected his son to be like Danny had been when he was little. You see, my father would take him to Leaf games to see Michael play from – well, from as soon as he was out of diapers, I guess. Pretty silly really – right?"

"I've never really been able to understand people taking small children to games – unless they can't get a baby-sitter or something..."

"That wasn't the case – Danny could easily have been left at home with Mom. She was stuck at home with me. But, that's beside the point. Michael couldn't accept the fact that Angus just did not have the same temperament as Danny and the really silly part of that was that Danny was the exception rather than Angus. I grew up in The Perfect Child's shadow, so I know! But I'm going off on a tangent, here. I looked after Angus, while Mom and Aunt Judith did their thing and... that's how I tend to think of him – as he was then. It's so difficult to accept that he's grown up to become a druggie street kid."

"We don't know that for sure," Alan said.

"It's not as if there's another explanation that comes to mind." Megan looked out of the window and blinked back tears. "Sorry. I didn't mean to snap," she said after a short silence.

"Is there a suit in your locker at the club?" Alan asked.

She nodded.

"How about we go over there for an hour or so, then?" he continued. "You'll feel better after a few laps. And if I can't get a squash game, I'll work out then join you in the pool."

"Do we have time?" Megan asked. She knew it would do the trick. She always found swimming good for working off stress and she had to make an effort to get the problem of Angus back into proportion before they went out to dinner with her friend Nicki and Nicki's new boyfriend who they hadn't met before. Nicki had been working on an education degree since graduating from OCA and had met the man while on a co-op assignment at a program for emotionally disturbed children. Between the assignment and her course work, Nicki had been pretty busy during the last few months. Megan, working hard on paintings for her first exhibition scheduled for September, had not seen much of her and, consequently, knew little about the new man in her friend's life. She and Nicki had known each other far too long, however, for Megan not to know that the man was important to Nicki and that she was eager for him to meet her friends.

"Lots of time – as long as you weren't intending to spend a lot of time deciding what to wear..."

"When do I do that?"

"Oh, I can think of a few occasions..."

"Not very many," she said smartly, than realised he was deliberately provoking her. "Oh, where would I be without you to bring me back to earth?" She smiled, leaning over and kissing his cheek. "Let's go – we'll dazzle Nicki's social worker friend with all our vibrancy and good health... or something like that."

. . . . .

The social worker was not the intense, bespectacled, over-nice social worker stereotype. His name was Brian and he was a cheerful, sturdy, good-looking man in his early thirties and Alan immediately felt annoyed with himself for expecting otherwise. He'd worked with enough social workers, after all, over the last few years, on AIDS prevention programs. The hour they had spent at the club had succeeded in helping both he and Megan to recover their usually good spirits but, once Nicki and Brian began talking about their work with emotionally disturbed children, naturally the latest news of Angus had to be told, including Megan's guilt at not having done more to help her cousin.

"What you're telling us about the painting therapy you're doing with the children proves I could have helped him," Megan told Nicki.

"With you here in Toronto and him in Victoria?" Nicki responded. "I don't think so."

"What Nicki means, Megan," said Brian, who was the Chief

Social Worker at the residential children's facility where Nicki had met him, "is that it's a lot more involved than just encouraging kids to paint. I agree that it sounds as if Angus might have benefited from art therapy, but – just because he admired you and your work – would not necessarily have meant that you encouraging him to paint would have helped him. Have you talked to his mother about it?"

"I don't really know her. His parents separated when he was six, you see, and we didn't have a lot to do with my father's family when I was growing up – there were problems after my father died – and they were out west – Michael, I mean..."

"Angus's father, Michael is Michael McGrath, the hockey player – ex-hockey player, now," Alan explained to Brian. "It's all very complicated. Michael only kept in touch with Megan's family spasmodically and he was the non-custodial parent, anyway. Then, more recently, when the two families were seeing more of each other, we messed things up by introducing Angus to Adam – my Little Brother who he called this morning – who lives in Regent's Park." He grinned. "The McGraths are Pickering College alumnae going back to the last century, so Michael wasn't too impressed at us for thinking that a boy, he perceived to be a slum kid, should be a playmate for his son. So, even though Michael's now married to a good friend of Megan's, we tend to keep our distance."

"Mmm," said Brian. "Complicated. I was a Big Brother too, by the way. He's eighteen now, and thinking about being a Big Brother himself, but we're still good friends."

"Adam is almost sixteen, and I think we'll remain friends, too. At the time, the boys were both eleven and it was Christmas and..."

"Michael had brought Angus to stay at my mother's," Megan continued the story. "He wanted him to have a family Christmas and was afraid Angus would be too disruptive at either of his sisters' homes, so he talked my mother into having them, even though my poor mother's not even a relative except through my father who died seventeen years ago. My father's family was – is – quite spread out age-wise and Michael is the youngest, so his eldest sister's children are – well, Alan's age. In fact, my cousin, Cindi – who's also Alan's cousin because her father and his father were brothers, was about to have her own first child at the time – she has two now. My younger brother Byron is the closest to Angus in age, but he was fifteen then and into hockey. He really didn't have much time for Angus, so we took Adam over to play with him. It was the wrong thing to do as it turned out and Michael's never really been too crazy about us ever since. Actually, Michael's so hostile towards Alan that we had to get my brother, not Byron – my older brother, Danny, who's close to Michael – to phone him and tell him about Angus calling Adam this morning."

Brian did not look as if Megan's explanation had clarified the situation to any large extent and Nicki started to laugh.

"Maybe I shouldn't be laughing at you, Meg," she said, "but this really takes me back. When we were little," she explained to Alan and Brian, "she'd go into great long explanations like that in class and the teacher wouldn't be able to stop her. One teacher just avoided choosing her, when we put our hands up, so we fixed it so that none of us would put our hands up and she had to ask Megan – remember that?"

Megan grinned. "I thought I'd improved since then," she said.

"You have," Nicki told her. "If you'd made that explanation ten years ago, you'd have had Brian thinking your family was totally incestuous. As it is he just thinks it's confused."

"It's okay, Megan," said Brian. "You made your point – your uncle clutched at all kinds of straws rather than admit that his son needed professional help and then thought he knew better than the therapists anyway – right?"

Megan nodded slightly but did not reply.

"That's the way it usually is," he continued. "The mother often ends up working overtime to offset the negative effects of the father's lack of support in these cases – especially when the parents are living apart and the mother has no control over what's happening when the child is with the father."

Knowing that Megan, while quite ready to defend her husband against Michael's hostility and to discuss her uncle's shortcomings with him, was not quite so prepared to be otherwise disloyal, Alan replied for her.

"I think it became easier for Judith after Michael married Lise," he said, "because that gave Angus a family environment when he was with his father instead of the boys-together-type situation that had existed whenever Angus visited Michael prior to that. But it was also after that that the running away episodes began, though I think that was more likely his age than his father's remarriage – he seemed to accept Lise and her son. I mean, I ran away a lot or thought about running away at thirteen, fourteen..."

"You didn't try to run away to the city streets, though," said Megan. "You just stayed at your friends' houses and didn't tell your grandparents where you were – lots of kids do that or something like it. Angus was really obsessed with living on the street."

"That's what happens with kids who have low esteem," Brian agreed. "Alan's right – the running away part is not so unusual and it was probably just as much his age as it was his father's remarriage. It used to be thought that so-called hyperkinetic kids got better in their teens but, in fact, low self esteem becomes the major factor. After years of under achievement, difficulties in relationships with just about everybody, it's not really surprising. What is surprising is the fact that it took educators, the courts, etc. so long to make the link between hyperkinesis in childhood – or ADHD, as it's called now – and truancy, petty thievery, assault, etc. in adolescence."

"Hugh said the same thing – about the low self esteem, I mean," Megan began.

"Who's Hugh?" Brian asked.

"My mother's friend – my soon-to-be stepfather, I think. If my mother ever makes up her mind, that is. He's an industrial psychologist."

"Hugh Johnston?"

"Yes, you know him?"

"I did my master's at York. I took one of his courses."

They had been toying with their coffee for some time and Nicki, taking pity on the hovering waiter, asked for the bill.

"Why don't you invite us back to your place to finish this discussion?" she asked Megan.

"Of course. I'd love you to – you'll have to excuse the mess, though. We haven't been home all day – except to change."

Alan was glad to see Megan back to her normal self. The conversation with Brian had been good for her, especially his reinforcement of the points Hugh had made that morning. He was sure she would take to heart now the fact that, despite the implications made in Angus's remark to Adam, she really had never been in any position to help the kid. He watched, with amusement, as Nicki grabbed the bill which the waiter tried to give to Brian.

"Has he not heard that, today, women are people too," she muttered, as he finally took away the bill along with her credit card.

Alan grinned at Brian. One day, he thought, women won't have to go through this hassle every time they host a dinner or lunch and, by the same token, men won't have to feel the waiter perceives them to be some sort of gigolo letting the woman pay. "Thank you for asking us to dinner, Nicki," he said.

"Thank you, Nicki," Megan and Brian said almost in unison.

"You're all very welcome," she said, pleased to be acknowledged as the host, by her friends, at least. "Actually it's been a really great evening, hasn't it? Despite the sombre topics of conversation, I mean."

"Of course," said Megan. "That's why we're not ready to let it end yet, right? Where did you guys leave your car?"

"Brian's car. I'm not so feminist that I insisted on driving us. It's in the lot around the corner – probably where you left yours."

"No, actually somebody pulled away from a meter just as we got here, so we took it quick."

The waiter came back and Nicki signed the credit card voucher. They collected their coats and went out into the street. Alan's car was almost immediately in front of the restaurant. He unlocked the passenger side door for Megan.

"We're just along here," said Nicki, gesturing towards the street corner, "so we'll be right behind you."

"Okay, we'll see you shortly," Megan replied getting into the car.

"Did you really want them coming over?" Alan asked, after getting in and starting the car. "Aren't you tired. It's been a draining day – emotionally, I mean."

"Yes, I know, but I haven't seen Nicki for ages and I didn't have the heart – or the wit – to make an excuse. I've got sort of beyond feeling tired, anyway, you know how you get – too tired to be sleepy..."

. . . . .

Megan did eventually get sleepy but not before she'd quizzed Brian in depth about painting therapy and the possibility of volunteering at the centre. He gave her his telephone number and told her to give him a call on Monday or Tuesday and he'd arrange to show her around.

"The problem is," Alan heard her say as she brought him a mug of coffee in bed the next morning, "I didn't get his last name. Did you?"

"Megan, how come you're up making coffee. Couldn't you sleep in for once?"

"I did, my love. It's after eleven. And you didn't hear a word I said, did you?"

"Something about calling Brian about volunteering at the children's place..." Alan sipped his coffee and wished she hadn't woken him. "You didn't get his last name. So – ask Nicki."

"I can't do that – it's insulting. I should have been listening."

"You know – I don't think she actually told us. I remember her saying, 'Brian, this is my best and oldest friend, Megan. And her husband, Alan. Meg, Alan – this is Brian.' She didn't say his last name, I swear."

"That's good. I can ask her, then. I won't call right now, though, in case they're sleeping in. He's nice, isn't he? I hope they stay together."

"I liked him, too," Alan said, feeling more awake after a few sips of coffee. "We'll have to ask them over for supper – make sure we do our part to keep the relationship going. Is Nicki doing special education then? I thought it was a straight education degree."

"It's one of the options, I think. Kind of an obvious for somebody with a fine arts background, I suppose. I just hadn't thought of it before – painting as a therapeutic tool, I mean. I should have done – I remember Aunt Selena talking about it once, although I thought it was just an informal thing that was not particularly recognized by social workers, you know?" Alan nodded sleepily in response. "Are you going to get up?"

"I guess so. Why? You've already had your shower."

"I jogged before I had my shower and I'm hungry and I'm going to make breakfast – well, brunch – and I didn't want to make yours if you weren't going to get up."

"What's wrong with breakfast in bed?"

"The last time I did that you went back to sleep and everything congealed on the plate."

"Okay – I'm not apologising for that incident again. I'm apologized out on it. I'm getting up anyway." Suddenly he was wide awake. "Oh-oh – d'you know what we forgot – I forgot, I shouldn't extend the forgetting to you..."

"What?"

"I didn't get back to Adam."

"I'm sure he'll understand," Megan finished her coffee and rose from the bed where she had been sitting. "He must know what a flap it put us all in. I'll go and start cooking so get up after you've called him."

She grinned and held her hand out for his empty mug.

"I promise I won't go back to sleep, okay?" Alan said, handing her the mug. "In fact, I'll actually get out of bed before I dial the number."

He pushed back the bedclothes, swung his legs over the side of the bed and picked up the phone as Megan left the room. Now who's on a guilt trip, he thought ruefully. He really did feel awful for not having remembered to call Adam before going out to dinner last night. Adam's mother answered and, after accepting his apologies for Angus's thoughtless behaviour the previous morning and telling him that it was a relief to know that Angus was alive after not hearing from him for all this time, she called Adam to the phone.

"Hi, Adam," he said, "I'm really sorry I didn't get back to you yesterday. We went over to Megan's mother's before deciding what to do about telling Angus's parents about him calling you. We stayed for lunch and into the afternoon, then fitted some exercise in before going out to dinner with – you've met Megan's friend, Nicki – she and her new boyfriend took us out to dinner or, at least, Nicki took her new boyfriend and us out to dinner. You must remember Nicki? – the feminist one, Megan's *person of honour* at our wedding?" – this had been a joke at the time which he knew Adam would remember – "They came back here afterwards and I've been asleep since they left, so I can only apologise for being such a jerk."

"It's okay," Adam laughed. "When you didn't call, I figured there must be some family conference going on. I knew I'd eventually find out how things went. How were his parents?"

"Megan's mother told Angus's mother. She was calm and

rational about it – the way she's been all along. Of course, she was pretty emotional, at first – relief that he was definitely alive and hurt and pain that he had done this to her, then she talked about this being, perhaps, the first step in a reconciliation."

"That's what puts me off most about what Angus did," said Adam. "However much I blamed my mother for my problems – which I don't, of course, and I don't have any problems, anyway – I could never hurt her like that. I thought he cared about his mother. I know most of what he told me about his stepfather wanting to get rid of him and everything, when we were kids, was made up, but the way he made things up always seemed to show that he wanted to be with his mother. I may not be making much sense, Alan, but I can sort of see him wanting to hurt his father – it must be hard to not to have the talent to follow in your father's footsteps – right?"

"I don't think either of them ever really thought about it, did they?"

"It might not have looked like they did, but they must have done. Angus never said anything about his father being disappointed in him, but he made a big deal about his stepfather thinking he was a loser. Don't you think that could have been transferring, or whatever it's called?"

"Transference. You mean perhaps he attributed all the things he thought Michael felt about him to Lawrence because that way he wasn't being disloyal to his father and he wasn't crazy about Lawrence, anyway – in fact, he may even have considered Lawrence to have taken his mother away from his father. So turn him into the villain... that sort of thing?"

"Exactly," Adam replied. "I mean, I don't know a heck of a lot about psychology, but it would make sense wouldn't it? When he used to tell me that Lawrence might kill his mother if he wasn't there to protect her – he actually got that particular idea from a story I told him about a woman in our apartment building whose husband really murdered her – it was a sort of cover because he knew really that living with his father would never work out even if his mother did agree. It's sort of fascinating really, you know – all the silly things he told me about his family, well – they were all fantasies based on his real feelings – do you see what I mean?"

"My God, Adam, what is this – have you been reading Freud or something?"

"Maybe I've got it all wrong..." Adam sounded a little deflated.

"No – no, I wasn't putting you down," Alan said hurriedly. "I was just surprised at the intensity of your – your analysis. You've been doing a lot of thinking."

"I haven't really thought about the stuff he used to say to impress me for years. I didn't even realise he said it to impress me – he was the kid from the wealthy family and with a father who had played in the NHL, why should he think he had to impress me? I just started thinking about his mother and that made me remember about him saying he couldn't go and live with his father because he had to protect her from his stepfather – I think I knew that wasn't true even at the time – but the point was that it sort of showed he loved his mother. Anyway, I was trying to figure out what changed – why he should hurt her because that's the very worst of what he's done, isn't it?"

"Yes, I would agree that it is. The thing you're missing from your analysis is the self esteem angle. I'm no psychologist myself, but I think the biggest problem that low self esteem brings is the honest belief that life will be better for the people you really love if you're not around. That's why kids leave home, take to the streets – commit suicide, even – without a thought about the pain they're leaving behind."

There was silence at the other end of the phone as Adam obviously digested this.

"That's it, isn't it?" he said thoughtfully. "That *is* why kids hurt their parents – they don't set out to do it. They don't know they're doing it. I'm really glad you told me that – it's been bugging me ever since Angus woke me up. I'm glad, too – not just because of Angus, but other kids, too. I mean, I'm glad they don't do it on purpose."

"Look, Adam, I'm going to have to go. I'm supposed to be having my shower while Megan makes some kind of super brunch and she's not going to be too pleased if I'm not ready when *it's* ready. How about bringing Karen over for supper one night this week?"

"Yeah? She'd like that – she really liked it when we came before and, you know what, Alan?"

"What?"

"We talked about it rationally like you said and she doesn't think we're ready for it, but she respects me for discussing it like she was a human being and not just being out for myself like most guys are. So I won't be joining your consumer base for a while yet, but maybe not too long – eh?"

"Fun-*ny*," said Alan. "How about Wednesday for supper? I'll call you back later if that doesn't check out with Megan. I must get moving or I'll be in a lot of trouble. 'Bye."

He put down the phone.

"I heard that last bit," Megan said, putting her head around the door. "It's ready – so you'll have to get showered after. What on earth took so long?"

"Adam's growing up," he said, shrugging into his bathrobe and making for the bathroom. "I'll be there in two ticks, I promise."

# BYRON

A green Audi pulled out from a parking meter ahead of him as Byron drove through the Arrivals level at Lester B. Pearson International Airport's Terminal Two. He quickly steered his Isuzu Rodeo into the spot, hoping that Danny would not be delayed at Customs for too long. He'd used his cell phone, a birthday present from his mother and stepfather two months before, to check that the Air Canada flight from New Delhi was on time, but there was no sign of Danny outside the terminal building where they had arranged to meet. The attendant came into sight and Byron got out of the car to feed the meter. If Danny wasn't out by the time he had to pay for a second fifteen minutes, he'd have to run in and get some change. He leaned against the car, keeping an eye on the two possible exits Danny would use after reclaiming his luggage, and wondered idly how sun-bleached and baked his brother would look after first six months in Uganda, then six in India, where McGrath-LaPlante plants were now up and running. He didn't envy his brother the tough job it must have been to win the respect of employees, many of whom were twice his age, in countries where – in the eyes of many – a Canadian was probably not far removed from the colonialists of earlier years. Of course, all the company's senior management people had spent periods of time in both Kampala and Delhi during the year, but it was Danny who had been responsible for getting both new plants into operation.

Byron was now working full time in McGrath-LaPlante's advertising and marketing communications department which had expanded considerably since his brother-in-law first employed him for the summer four years before. Alan had encouraged him to start working on a marketing communications diploma program, at night school, to complement his graphic design education and, while he had not, at first, been entirely enthusiastic, he was glad now that he had accepted Alan's guidance. He was a far better team player now that he understood the strategy behind the creative direction he was given by his immediate boss, the advertising manager, and was faintly embarrassed when he remembered his former arrogance, knowing that he would probably have been fired that first summer if he had not been a family member and future shareholder. He grinned to himself – Danny would be surprised to find his little brother had finally matured. And Danny, he thought, scanning the exits again, had better hurry up because feeding the meter again would mean using up all his change and having to go into the terminal and up to the departures level to get more – without missing Danny – *and* getting back before the meter expired. He couldn't risk using the change and counting on Danny showing up, then having the meter expire and getting waved on by the attendant. Why didn't they give you longer on these meters? Obviously, said the logical side of his brain, so that people didn't abuse the pick-up spaces. The red flag clicked up in the meter – shit, that was a fast fifteen minutes. He decided to hang on to his change until the attendant actually came into sight again. This didn't take long. He put the money in and nodded to the man.

"Hey, Byron!"

Danny was finally through. Byron dodged between a taxi and a shuttle bus and arrived on the sidewalk beside his brother.

"Hey, great to see you, Danny!"

The two brothers hugged and slapped hands.

"Which d'you want me to take?" asked Byron, regarding the piled up trolley. "You must have had to pay extra baggage."

"Lots of it," Danny agreed. "It was that or courier it. You can't spend a year abroad without collecting a few extras. If you take that suitcase and the duffel, I can manage the rest and we won't need to trundle the trolley across the road."

With the luggage stashed into the Rodeo, they made their way out of the airport and headed along the highway towards Danny's North York condominium.

"So you haven't actually destroyed my apartment or anything, then?" Danny asked.

"It's probably in better shape than you left it. I was always a better housekeeper than you – so Mom says."

Danny had asked Byron to move into his apartment to avoid having to leave it empty for the year he was away. Their mother and Hugh had finally married, shortly before Danny left for Kampala, and moved into a house new to both of them, ending the previously ongoing debate about whose house to keep and whose to sell. It was while Byron was still camping out in their old family house with the 'For Sale' sign on the lawn, that Danny had suggested his putting off getting a place of his own and moving into the empty apartment for the year.

"You're probably right," Danny agreed. "How is everybody?"

"Mom'll be on the phone as soon as we get in, I expect. She called to tell me the plane was on time before I left – like I'm too stupid to check for myself... Meg says to call her as soon as you feel like it – she doesn't want to be a bug but she'd like to welcome you home or whatever. She's agreed to do an exhibition next spring."

"She has?"

"Ah-ha."

"She said she wasn't going to. She didn't think she'd have enough new stuff ready in time."

"That was when they wanted her for the fall – this coming fall," Byron explained. "They've persuaded her that she shouldn't leave it longer than the spring or, at this stage of her career, she'll risk getting written off as a one-exhibition wonder – in the art world, it seems to be exhibitions that count, not what you sell outside of them. Alan wasn't too crazy about the idea, at first, because he thought it would stop her going to India, after all, but she says she wants to work there. If they're going to be there for six weeks, she should have enough feel for the landscape there to at least have some presentable water-colours, maybe even a couple of canvases as long as there's nothing to interfere with her working on them until the baby's born – and after too, I guess. Meantime, she's working on canvases – mostly from her Australia sketches."

"Well, let's hope her pregnancy stays healthy..."

"There's no reason to think it won't. Alan wanted to cancel the whole India thing at first – well, he has to go himself, of course, but he could get away with being there for a shorter time. Then Meg got her doctor to bring him up to date on contemporary attitudes towards pregnancy..."

"Yeah, she told me about that," Danny said. "She got me to

help her convince Alan that India was no longer... well, the jewel-in-the-crown-India, and that she'd be perfectly all right. But I talked to her two weeks ago and she didn't say anything about the exhibition. That must have happened since then."

"I think she was mulling it over for a while before she said anything to anybody – even Alan. Anyway, she's got lots of work really – it's just her own perfectionism that makes her think there's not enough for an exhibition and, of course, the fear of not living up to the promise of the first one." Byron pulled into the underground parking area of the apartment complex. "Here we are – home sweet home."

The phone could be heard ringing as they finally manhandled Danny's luggage along the passage from the elevator to his front door. Byron put his key in the lock as the answering machine clicked in.

"It'll be either Mom or Shelley. Shelley's coming over to make your supper, by the way. Bianca'll be over, too, in a while."

He opened the door as the machine's message ended and Danny's neighbour and sometime girlfriend, Shelley, began to speak. Danny picked up the phone in the foyer.

"Hi. We just got in the door," he said. "And my charming brother has only this minute told me you have supper planned – thank God, I thought I was going to be stuck with his vegetarian junk. Come on over and help me unpack."

"Thanks. I went grocery shopping so you wouldn't have to come home to nut cutlets or whatever and I've had steaks marinating all afternoon all for the pleasure of being invited to help you unpack...?"

"Well, why not?" Danny asked with mock seriousness. "Come on over – I'm not even going to bother to unpack until tomorrow.

Bring the steaks, though. See you in as long as it takes – okay?"

"I'll be right over and welcome home, Danny."

Byron brought in the luggage while Danny was speaking to Shelley and had it strewn across the floor and bed in the master bedroom by the time Danny put the phone down.

"Shelley's on her way over, but I want to have a quick shower, so talk to her will you?" he said to Byron. "And thanks for the obstacle course," he added hopping over suitcases to get to the ensuite bathroom.

Byron went into the kitchen and took a beer from the fridge. He put the front door on the latch so that Shelley could get in and picked up the phone to call his girlfriend, Bianca. There was no answer – despite wholeheartedly embracing technology insofar as graphic art was concerned, Bianca objected to the impersonality of the answering machine. Deciding she must be on her way over, he took his beer out onto the balcony. He leaned on the railing and soon spotted her car pulling into the visitors' parking area. Bianca was his soul-mate, he was sure. What he wasn't so sure about was whether living with her was going to work out. He was committed now. Next week they'd be moving into the townhouse they were buying together.

He had know Bianca for several years. They had both been enrolled in graphic arts courses at Sheridan College, but did not actually start going together until after graduation last year. As Bianca had pointed out, there was no adjective short of arrogant to describe Byron when she had first met him. It had taken his nineteenth birthday and being of legal drinking age for Byron to give his home-made, healthful lemonade up for beer like the rest of the kids – albeit, microbrewery brands only. While he still chose to be a vegetarian, he had eventually mellowed in his condemnatory attitude to people who were not. At a graduation party, Bianca had told him that now that he was on the way to being a human being, she'd really like to see more of him and they'd been going together ever since.

He remained leaning against the balcony railing until, eventually, there was a soft tap at the door.

"It's open," Byron yelled.

The two girls came in together. They had met in the passage and Bianca had been co-opted into helping Shelley to make the transfer of the prepared supper dishes and groceries in one pass instead of two.

"Hi!"

"Where *are* you guys?"

Byron rose and looked in at the balcony door.

"Danny's having a shower," he said. "He'll be out in a minute. Help yourselves to a beer and come on out here. Or d'you want me to open a bottle of wine?"

"Beer's fine for me," said Shelley. "I'll just organize this stuff. You go ahead, Bianca."

Bianca joined Byron on the balcony.

"So everything was okay?" she asked.

"Oh yeah. I even managed to get a meter in the short term parking – soon as I got there. His luggage seems to have multiplied since he went though – he must have had to pay a fortune in excess baggage."

"Did you have to wait long? Customs at Pearson is such a pain."

"It wasn't too bad. I allowed for the Customs problem – you have to be pretty dumb not to. I'm getting to be a pretty experienced picker-upper at the airport – I pick people up a hell of a lot more than I actually travel, but I live in hope that, perhaps, one day...." The phone began to ring. "That's probably my mother."

"I think Danny's out of the bathroom," said Bianca, who was nearer the door.

Danny came out a few minutes later.

"You didn't tell me Mom was having a family dinner tomorrow..." he said to Byron. "Hi, Bianca. How are you?" He kissed her cheek. "Byron?"

"Sorry. I forgot. We got talking about Megan, remember? Anyway, you surely guessed she'd want to see you and it *is* the weekend. Is Shelley ready for me to put the barbecue on?"

"Please," Shelley said coming to the doorway. "Anybody need another drink?"

"No thanks," said Byron.

"Bianca?"

"I'm fine – thanks, Shelley. So tell us about India, Danny."

. . . . .

Byron did not get a chance to talk to Danny about the latest news of their cousin Angus until the next day. He and Bianca had left after supper to go to a birthday party for Bianca's sister and he didn't return to Danny's apartment until the following afternoon. Danny was ready to leave for their mother's house but agreed to wait while Byron showered and changed so that they could go together instead of taking two cars.

They went in the Danny's Toyota sports car which Byron had 'exercised' once in a while during his brother's absence.

"Did you call Megan yet?" Byron asked as Danny drove out of the condominium complex and headed for the highway.

"Yes. She was surprised you hadn't told me about Angus..."

"Sorry. I didn't think you'd want to discuss it with the girls there yesterday. Do you agree with her?"

"About not telling Mom?"

"Yeah."

"Well, she's not exactly against telling Mom," Danny replied. "She wanted to discuss the situation. In fact, she feels terrible about not wanting to tell Mom–"

"But figures Mom'll insist on telling Judith and Michael."

"I told her that I didn't think Mom would do that – especially when there's no guarantee that Angus'll show up anyway – if we fully explain the situation and convince her that the whole thing can look unplanned by the time they're told."

"How d'you figure that?"

"Well, they both know – Michael and Judith, I mean – they both know that Angus has been calling Adam intermittently – right? And we've all become pretty sure, due to the times he makes these calls, that he's on the west coast somewhere – more likely south of the border than north, okay? So we just tell them what is basically the truth – Adam told Angus that his girlfriend had won a weekend in San Francisco and tickets to a Blue Jays-Oakland game in a contest and Angus had finally admitted that he was in San Francisco working as some kind of attendant to a disabled man and offered to meet them at the hotel and show them around. Adam told Alan and they agreed not to say anything to any of us about it until it actually happened in case he didn't show up – which he probably won't do anyway. And, after I'd got through saying all that, Megan tells me Alan had said the same thing – he figures Michael can't think worse of him than he already does, so he may as well be the fall guy if it gets to that stage."

"Oh – well, she hadn't talked to him about it when she called me," said Byron. "Alan was in Montreal and she didn't want to bother him with it until he got home."

"He got home late Friday night so they slept on it and came to that decision at breakfast yesterday, but she couldn't get hold of you when she tried to call you and they had to go to some highland games thing with the Daileys and the Brits. That's another thing you didn't bother telling me – that *they* were here. Well, were here – Alan's dropping them at the airport before coming on to Mom's."

"Well, I didn't think you'd want to talk shop as soon as you got home. Anyway it was only Joel McCallum and his wife – they're always making excuses to come over here on so-called business trips. He went to Montreal with Alan and poor Megan was stuck with entertaining his wife most of the week and couldn't get any work done."

"Okay, never mind," said Danny. "It's just as well I didn't know or I'd have felt obligated to go over and see them last night. I got away with just talking to Joel on the phone instead."

They were both silent for a while thinking about Angus rather than Joel McCallum who was one of the directors of the multinational British-based company which was McGrath-LaPlante's largest co-pack customer.

"Maybe I should go with them," Byron said eventually.

"I thought of suggesting something like that," replied Danny. "Not necessarily you – any one of us. But, if he does show and something positive develops, or even something negative, for that matter, it kind of blows a hole in the story we're intending to give his parents and the most important thing is to have news, of some kind at least, to give to them. It doesn't matter which way you look at it, after more than three years now, nothing is going to happen that'll turn the clock back – right?"

"Yeah – the most we can really hope for is that we can tell them that he appears to be getting along okay, although I hate to think what the so-called job's all about – like, I'd rather not think about it, you know? So, anyway, whatever we do, we can't risk jeopardising the meeting between him and Adam. If Adam can win his trust this time maybe we can get more ambitious another time and eventually get him making contact with his mother, even if whatever he does for a living is as bad or worse than we think it is. Whichever way you look at it, I can't really see Angus and his father being reconciled. I mean – shit, I feel bad saying it, Danny, but – well, Michael didn't cause Angus's problems, I know, but he sure as hell didn't help..."

Danny didn't reply. He was busy navigating the traffic lanes around an accident.

Once past the accident scene, Byron began to wonder if his brother's continued silence meant he was annoyed at what he'd said about Michael. Surely Danny had got over his childhood hero-worship of their uncle – for God's sake he was an MBA just returned from setting up operations in two of their company's third world plants, he surely must be able to see beyond the hockey hero of twenty years ago. Byron, himself, had not seen Michael in the three years since Angus had run away from home but his mother and sister had both maintained their friendship with Lise and had visited her and Michael when travelling to or via Vancouver. Lise had come to Toronto for his mother's wedding last summer, and she and Justin had stayed at Megan's. She had admitted during the 'welcome Lise and Justin' supper Megan had put on for them that, while she was embarrassed about Michael not coming with them, she was kind of glad to get away from him for a while. It was tough living with someone who was continually clinically depressed, she said.

While she had not talked much about it to him, he knew she had discussed the problem in more detail with Megan. He learned a bit more when he had taken Justin to a Blue Jays' game. The kid had grown up since that summer when he had insisted on tagging along with Byron as he searched the city streets and beaches for Angus. He still looked for his stepbrother on the city streets, he had told Byron. They all did. But he didn't think he was there. He was pretty sure he'd gone across the border with one of the gangs of street kids that continually worked their way up and down the west coast.

Bright and talkative as ever, Justin had recounted his hockey successes of the previous season and confided his determination to remain his team's top scorer when he played bantam in the fall. He had played well enough last year for people to forget that Michael was his stepfather, not his father. He figured Michael was pretty pleased with him, but guessed it didn't make up for his own kid running away...

"Did you know young Justin's becoming quite a hockey player?" he asked Danny, breaking the silence.

"Yeah, Michael told me – I talked to him a few times while I was away. He'll be playing bantam now and was top scorer again last season."

"How's Michael feel about it? I got the impression that Justin's more concerned with making Michael happy than being a good player for his own satisfaction."

"I think you're right," Danny replied. "Michael's proud of him but – let's face it – it's not the same as if it were Angus. I hope Justin doesn't get hurt." He turned into the Oakville street where their mother now lived. "Looks like we're here before Megan and Alan."

"So we *do* discuss it with Mom?" Byron asked as Danny pulled into the driveway.

"Mom'll see it our way, see if she doesn't."

# MEGAN

Megan placed the sleeping four-month-old Steven James LaPlante in his crib, switched on the intercom they had installed so that she could hear the baby from her studio if he wakened, and tiptoed out of the nursery. After putting her lunch dishes in the dishwasher and switching on the rinse cycle, she was just about to climb the stairs to the attic studio when the door bell rang. She changed direction and ran down the stairs to the ground floor, deciding that this would be quicker than going back into the kitchen to use the intercom – she certainly didn't want the caller ringing the bell again and waking the baby. She didn't recognize the shape of what looked to be a young man though one of the panels of mullioned glass that framed the front door of the house and, assuming that it was somebody selling something, quickly opened the door before he could press the bell again.

Dressed in jeans and a worn but once not inexpensive suede jacket, the boy – in his late teens – was immediately familiar – a little like her younger brother, Byron, in fact. She stared at him in disbelief.

"Angus?"

"I didn't think you'd recognise me."

"Why ever not?" Megan was not about to admit to almost not having done so. "You're taller – I used to look down to make eye contact, now I look up." She grinned. "You've grown yourself some stubble there... but, essentially, it's you." She took his hands and drew him inside. "I'm so glad to see you at last, Angus," she said, hugging him.

"You really are?" Angus asked, when Megan finally took a step backwards.

"Of course I am. Surprised – stunned, in fact, but definitely happy to see you." She closed the door. "Come on up," she said, still holding his hand.

Angus followed her up the stairs. "I thought you'd have changed it back into one house by now," he said.

"Oh, we're going to," she replied. "We left it because – well, we actually preferred living in the apartment, so we left things as they were but it's different now, of course..."

"With the baby?"

"Yes. Come on into the kitchen. I'll make some tea – or would you prefer coffee?"

"Tea's fine. Is it a boy?"

"Yes. You mean Adam hasn't filled you in?"

"I haven't talked to Adam since last summer when he came to San Francisco. He told me you were pregnant then."

"Oh. Well, yes – it's a boy. Sit down." Megan filled the kettle and plugged it in. "Steven James. At first we thought, perhaps, he should be named after Alan's grandfather, but decided the world – well, the world as applied to McGrath LaPlante, at least – wasn't ready for another Denny LaPlante. Then we considered naming him after both our fathers, but decided not to tempt fate."

"Have him turn out like me, you mean?"

"What? No, of course not. I meant that they both died relatively young. Anyway, I don't know what you've turned out like, do I? I haven't seen you for years – and you've been virtually incommunicado for most of them. Anyway, Steven's sleeping right now but he'll be awake later on for his bottle. Are you hungry? Have you had lunch?"

"I don't usually do lunch," said Angus. "But if..."

"...there's something handy for a sandwich, you'll have it. Right?"

Angus grinned. "Thanks."

"There's some ham – or are you vegetarian?"

"No, no – that's cool. Great."

Megan took a French stick from the bread box and cut off a large portion which she sliced horizontally and spread with butter and Dijon mustard before making a large ham and lettuce sandwich.

"Here you are," she said, placing it before him just as the kettle began to whistle. "Go ahead – I'll just make the tea."

"Thanks, Megan."

Angus was halfway through his sandwich by the time she put the tea things on the table and sat down opposite him. She poured milk into the mugs and waited for the tea to brew. Angus suddenly smiled. "You do it the way your mom does. I'd just started drinking tea when I stayed there with my father that Christmas – remember?"

Megan nodded.

"So when I went home, I'd pour the milk first and they'd kid me about trying to pretend I was English."

"I don't really know what's so English about it. My mother's parents actually came here from England which is, I suppose, why she does it – and taught me to do it – but *most* people do it when they serve it properly. You only do it the other way around when you shove a teabag in a mug. You remember my mother's parents, don't you?"

"Yes, they came to Christmas dinner. I liked them. They didn't keep on at me to behave –" he grimaced "– the way my own grandparents did."

"My grandfather died just before Christmas. Nana's still very grief-stricken – they would have celebrated their sixtieth wedding anniversary this year and, of course, he didn't see Steven, their first great-grandchild – she was very upset about that – and my cousin's wife – in Australia – just had a little girl. Back in the summer, they were both so looking forward to the next generation arriving... It's sad, isn't it?"

"I'm sorry – he was nice."

Megan poured the tea while Angus finished his sandwich. She decided that it would be best to let him lead the conversation rather than to question him. While she had no idea why he was here, the fact that he'd come to visit her indicated that he wanted some contact at least, with his family and she wasn't about to scare him off. She passed his mug of tea to him.

"Do you take sugar?"

"Please," Angus spooned sugar from the proffered bowl into his tea, then sipped it. "Thanks for the sandwich. It was good." He put down the mug. "I went to your exhibition," he said.

"You did?"

"You sound surprised. Did you think they'd throw me out or something?"

"No, of course not. I just didn't know you knew about it, that's all."

"I saw it in the paper. We're staying with my friend's brother and someone had given him the arts section because there was something about somebody he knew in it. Anyway, I saw the ad and before I could stop myself, I said, 'Hey guys, that's my cousin – my cousin Megan.' Then I had to bullshit them that we were related on my mother's side."

"What d'you mean?"

"Think I'm stupid? – I haven't used my real name for years. I just pretend I have no family. It would be okay with people my age – I mean they'd make the connection between Michael McGrath and the Summit Series or the old Maple Leafs and might make a crack, then think no more of it, but older people would remember all the shit in the papers that time. It was the surprise of seeing your name that made me blurt it out without thinking."

"I see."

"So then Scott says, 'That's just around the corner. We'll go this afternoon.' So we did. That was yesterday."

"So what did you buy?" Megan asked dryly.

"Scott thought the Indian stuff was cool. So did Ange – he's really into Zen."

"Good for Scott and Ange. How about you?"

"I liked everything. I told them I was your number one fan from years back. Then the owner – or manager, whatever – figured we were vagrants trying to hang out in there and told us to get lost. Angie told him I was your cousin but he just said, 'Yeah, right. Anymore bull and I call the cops.' So I wasn't about to get into a scene about it and told the others we'd better go. So now they think I was lying."

"And that's why you're paying me a visit?"

"No, of course not. I wanted to see you. And the baby, too. Steven..."

"And Adam – are you going to see him?"

Angus took a deep breath. "No, not Adam," he said.

"Why? I thought he was your friend. It was Adam who you always called. Not any of us – your family, I mean."

"I know, but you see... last summer when Adam and Karen came to San Francisco... well, I had a job then and kind of built it up a bit and now..."

"Now you don't?"

She remembered Adam and Karen coming to supper after their trip to San Francisco last summer and how they kept looking at each other for reassurance as they told her and Alan about meeting Angus there. Angus had taken them out to dinner at a restaurant where he was obviously well-known and where they were served wine, despite the fact that they were all only eighteen and certainly did not look any older. He had explained his surprisingly prosperous lifestyle as being due to his job as a live-in nurse to a wealthy man who had multiple sclerosis. The man wanted someone who could be a friend in preference to a professional nurse and he'd hired Angus through a social agency which helps kids find jobs to get them off the street. None of them liked to think about what a street kid, adopted by a disabled man and set up as his nurse, really did – even if it was through a social agency – and there was an embarrassed silence into which Karen burst out that they had tried to figure out something else to tell them but decided the truth was better in the long run. Alan had thanked them for being honest and started asking them about the rest of their stay. She remembered how, after Adam and Karen had gone, she had cried long and hard, although she was, of course, perfectly aware of what runaway kids did in order to survive. It was just, she told Alan, that all the time you didn't know the truth for a fact, you could skirt around the issue and pretend to yourself that it wasn't really happening. She'd become a mother since then and felt a pang for Judith as she watched her cousin finish drinking his tea.

"No," he said, "we're just hitching around – me and Scott and Angie. Angie's never been out of BC before. He –" he changed his mind about continuing on the subject of Angie. "Adam wouldn't understand. He's all into going to college and being a social worker. We've nothing in common anymore..."

"I don't think you ever really did. In my innocence, I figured all eleven-year-old boys had something in common and introduced the two of you. It wasn't until later that I found out just how wrong I was."

Megan shared the rest of the tea between them and, after sipping her own, said, "It's not too warm. You don't have to drink it if you don't want to." She paused. "So where are these friends of yours now? Scott and Angie?"

"Still crashed in Scott's brother's apartment, I think. They're more night people than day people..."

He, obviously, wasn't about to go into details. Megan nodded. "So, how come you're awake?"

"Me? Oh – I'm not really into sleeping much." He grinned. "I'm the hyper one, don't forget – your Uncle Michael's bratty kid. How is my father, anyway? Do you ever hear from him?"

"He married one of my best friends, remember? Of course I hear from him – well... from Lise, anyway. You know that your antics haven't exactly made Alan and me your father's favourite people, so we don't actually see as much of them as we would do otherwise. Since you asked, I'll tell you – he's not doing too badly now, but he's had an incredible battle with clinical depression over the last few years because of what you did. And it's not been exactly easy for your mother – nor, come to that, for Lise and your stepfather, either."

She stopped, wondering if she'd said too much and scared him off. He just grimaced slightly, however, and shrugged his shoulders.

"If it hadn't been me, it would have been something else, Megan. My father's prone to depression – like all old hockey players. They can't handle life when they're no longer every kid's hero – so they take to the bottle or popping pills or whatever..."

Megan privately tended to agree with him, but decided a change of subject was in order. She stood up and picked up the tray of tea things.

"Bring your plate and mug over and leave them in the sink," she said. "I think I hear sounds of Steven waking up, so I'd better put a bottle to warm."

She put the tray on the counter and took a bottle of formula from the refrigerator. Angus watched her plug in the bottle warmer and put the bottle into it.

"My mom had one of those when Stephanie was a baby," he said. "She must be eight, nearly nine now – Stephanie, I mean. I wonder what she looks like..."

"You could always go home and see."

"Maybe one day. Not yet. Does Stephanie know that you named your baby Steven?"

"Oh yes. I never even thought about it at the time, but Stephanie wrote a little note, on the card your mother sent, saying what a good choice it was. She missed you a lot, you know. Little kids think a lot of their big brothers – even if the big brothers scarcely acknowledge them. Little stepbrothers do, too. Justin still looks for you on the Vancouver streets and beaches. He played bantam this year, and his team's in the quarter finals, Lise told me on the phone the other night."

"Good for him," said Angus. "So Dad has a hockey player kid, after all."

Megan did not respond. Hearing the familiar sounds, from the nursery, of the hungry baby waking, she picked up the bottle and tested the milk on the inside of her wrist.

"Go and sit in the living room," she said. "I'll change the baby and bring him in there – it's not very comfortable feeding a baby on a kitchen chair."

Angus was sitting on the living room couch looking at a photograph album when she brought in the freshly diapered baby a few minutes later.

"Here we are, Steven," she said. "Here's your long-lost cousin Angus come to visit."

She held the baby so that he faced Angus and sat down in an adjacent armchair. The baby fixed Angus with a puzzled blue-eyed stare, then puckered his little face and looked up at his mother. Megan cradled him comfortably and offered him the bottle. He eagerly sucked the nipple and made soft slurping noises as he fixed his gaze, once again, on Angus.

"He looks like Alan, doesn't he?" Angus said.

"Yes," Megan agreed. "I feel like a traitor – producing a LaPlante instead of a McGrath." She laughed. "Old Denny must be chuckling in his grave. You never met him, did you? Alan's grandfather?"

Angus shook his head.

"I never knew much about the McGraths and LaPlantes," he said. "I knew there was a company, but I didn't realise what prophylactic products were until I read the manufacturer's name on those condoms they have in the high school dispensers. That was one of the things that pissed me off about my father – he should have told me what the company made instead of letting me read my name on a condom wrapper."

"We didn't know either until your father told Danny when he was fifteen. Anyway, they don't only make condoms..."

"I know – it's just that it was embarrassing at the time. It's not something I give a shit about now – one of the growth industries of the nineties, why should I? I just have to make sure I get back in favour with my father before he kicks off, so that I can inherit his shares..."

"Angus! That's awful."

"Sorry. I guess I'm a what do you call it? A cynic."

"You certainly are," Megan said, putting the bottle on the table beside her and lifting the baby to her shoulder and gently patting his back. "Your father probably didn't know about the condoms in your school. Those machines in the high schools are a fairly recent innovation – in fact, Alan worked on it for several years before schools and school boards finally bought on to the idea. McGrath-LaPlante had to design in special unobtrusive dispensers..." She stopped talking. He obviously was not interested.

"Pretty good burper," he observed, when Steven spat up some milk onto the folded diaper on her shoulder. "Is this where you got the idea for those banana tree paintings in the exhibition?" He pointed to some photographs in the album Megan had made of the pictures they had taken when she and Alan visited her uncle in Australia the Christmas before last.

Megan nodded. "They all sold, you know," she said. "Did they have stickers on them?"

"I didn't notice. I just thought they were a little weird, but I can see how you arrived at them when I look at these."

"You can?"

"Being a street kid doesn't mean I'm dumb you know?"

"That's not what I meant, Angus," Megan said, gently. "That series of paintings is about the most abstract thing I've ever done. I don't expect people to be able to interpret them very easily. In fact, I think it was very observant of you. Don't be so defensive."

They sat in silence while Angus finished looking at the photographs and the baby sucked his milk. Megan recognized that her young cousin was being far more open and honest with her than he had been during the three years of intermittent contact with Adam. His attitude towards Adam had been one of arrogance, albeit born of feelings of inferiority, that communicated his belief in his lifestyle being free and unfettered by comparison with Adam's conventional school-dominated life. Here, with her, he was allowing the chinks in his armour to show. She wondered whether it was because she was older than he and had once been a hero figure to him... or whether he really had believed in the way he was living and was now becoming disillusioned. She wanted to help him, but was not very sure about how to go about it without scaring him off again.

Last summer, they had told Michael and Judith only that Adam had met Angus in San Francisco and that he appeared to be happy and in good health. While they appreciated the fact that Angus's parents were not about to fool themselves into believing the version of Angus's life told to Adam, nobody wished to elaborate on what their son's lifestyle must really involve. She fleetingly wondered what she would tell them about this unexpected visit, then figured she'd better concentrate on how to handle things now that he was becoming distracted. It was too late, however. He was already getting to his feet.

"Have to get back downtown," he muttered, moving to the doorway.

She put the baby's bottle down and stood up, holding Steven upright and gently patting his back again.

"How about bringing your friends to supper tomorrow evening?" she suggested.

"I'll see what they think," he mumbled, already on the landing.

Megan followed him down the stairs. "Alan will want to see you while you're here... and Danny and Byron. And my Mom, of course..."

"I'm not bringing Scott and Angie to some big *family*-type thing," he said emphatically.

"No-no... I didn't mean tomorrow. There'd only be us – Alan and me – for supper. I meant my mother and Danny and Byron will want to see you... sometime. Whatever's convenient..."

"I'll see." He opened the front door while she was still only halfway down the stairs. She could hardly run after him with the baby in her arms. "Thanks for the lunch. 'Bye."

He slammed the door behind him before she could reply. She debated going after him and decided there was no point in pushing him. It was still too cold to go running outside without stopping to dress Steven properly. Spring was taking its time about arriving this year.

· · · · ·

"You didn't get a phone number or anything?"

Her mother's voice, over the phone, sounded incredulous.

"I didn't get a chance," said Megan. "He just suddenly upped and decided to leave. There was no stopping him. It was like when he was little, you know – forget this scene, time to move on... We were getting along like a house on fire, then he started getting irritable and argumentative all of a sudden."

She had finished feeding the baby after Angus's departure and after putting him in the playpen rather than back in his crib, since he did not appear to be very sleepy, she had called Alan at McGrath-LaPlante only to be told that he was in a meeting. She debated whether to ask for one of her brothers, then decided to phone her mother first.

"Was it something you said?" Marilyn was asking.

Megan thought back over the conversation.

"I don't think so," she said. "I was feeding Steven – he'd specifically said he wanted to see Steven – and he remarked on how like Alan he is, so I just said my usual line about Old Denny chuckling in his grave..."

"He wouldn't have understood that..."

"I know. He said he'd never known much about the company and rather cynically – coolly admitted it, too – said he'd make sure he got back in favour with his father before Michael kicks off – his words, not mine – so that he could be sure of inheriting his shares..."

"Little brat..."

"I thought so, too, but I don't think I over-reacted. I was being careful not to let anything he said shock me because I wasn't about to scare him off... It wasn't anything I said, I'm sure. I think he just got bored with me."

"Well, there's nothing we can do – other than hope he'll either phone or show up on your doorstep again. You're the only one of us living in the same house you lived in before he ran off. I wonder if he still has Danny's phone number. We'll just have to wait and see what happens, I suppose. 'Course he may show up there for supper, with these other kids, tomorrow..."

"I doubt it," Megan said. "It was obvious that the idea didn't exactly turn him on."

"Well, you did your best, love," her mother told her. "There's not much more you can do. What does Alan say?"

"I haven't told him yet. He's in a meeting. I said not to bother telling him to call me back – I'll wait and tell him when he gets home, I think. He won't appreciate hearing the latest on Angus coming out of whatever the meeting was. I'm going to wait till he's home before I call Michael, though – in case I need a shoulder! It's still only lunch time there anyway, so it'll be better to call when they're sure to be home."

"At that rate you'll be putting it off until quite late. I think I'll call Judith and tell her about it. I'll let her know you're telling Michael yourself – okay?"

"Sure," Megan agreed. "Now, I guess I'm committed. Hopefully Lise'll answer the phone and Michael will be out."

"Coward."

"I know. Do you hear Steven gurgling away?" She held the phone over the playpen. "Hear him?" she asked, putting it back to her ear. "He didn't seem very sleepy after his bottle, so I laid him in the playpen. He's watching the mobile and laughing and kicking – having a great time. I guess I'll have to give up on the idea of working this afternoon now. Oh-ho, Mathilda's eyeing the mobile again – she jumps up at it and I'm afraid of her landing on Steven. Talk to you later, Mom. 'Bye."

She caught the cat in mid air. The baby watched them solemnly for a moment, then turned his attention back to the mobile over the playpen.

"I wish you would learn not to do that, Mathilda," Megan said, stroking the cat's head. "I don't like having to shut you out, but I can't have you falling on the baby, can I now?" She held the cat up and looked into her eyes. Mathilda let herself go limp and Megan snuggled her against her chest. The clockwork mobile began to run down. "Now, I'm going to wind it up again and I'll give you one more chance. You jump again and you're outside – okay?"

She put the cat down and re-wound the mobile, while Mathilda purred and rubbed against her ankles. She stooped down and Steven twisted himself around to look at her and the cat beside him. "I think this silly cat just wants some attention, Steven," she said. "Won't it be nice when you're big enough to play with her? 'Though I suppose, by that time, she'll be too grown up to play..."

The cat was young, having been acquired the year before. The old cat which had belonged to Alan's grandfather had died some months before and, while they were trying to make up their minds whether to get another cat or buy a dog, a neighbour's child had brought Mathilda to Alan with the sad story that she'd been given to him by an aunt whose cat had had kittens, but his mother had decided that his sister was allergic to Mathilda. He figured Alan and Megan must be missing their cat, so would they like to have Mathilda and let him come and play with her now and again? So, for the moment, the decision was made for them, although Megan had been leaning toward getting a dog. Before Byron's dog, Ben, had died two years before, they would often pick him up and take him for walks with them. So, she rather missed having a dog with them when they were hiking. By the time the cat had settled in, plans for a dog had been put on hold – first because of their stay in India, then there was her pregnancy and all the preparations for the exhibition, then the new baby himself. Maybe by the summer, they could start thinking about it again...

Megan straightened up and walked over to pick up Mathilda's catnip mouse from under a chair on the other side of the room. She threw the mouse to the cat who soon became engrossed in pouncing on and batting the toy.

"There we are, Steven," she told the baby, "that's given her something to keep her busy."

The baby chortled and kicked his legs in reply. Much to Megan's relief, he was a happy baby who rarely cried. Working as an art therapy volunteer at the children's mental health centre where her friend Nicki's boyfriend, Brian, was now Director of Casework, she had learned a lot about emotional, cognitive and behavioural problems in children since the day three years ago when she had rather hysterically informed her husband that she didn't think she wanted to have children. However, throughout her pregnancy, she had still intermittently worried about passing on some corrupted gene, so that now one of her greatest joys was to watch her little son demonstrate his serenity. Sometimes she found herself watching the baby and brimming over with happiness, hardly able to believe her good fortune in life. Did she really deserve her wonderful husband, beautiful son and successful career? It was not a question she could answer. Today, after the visit of her cousin Angus, the question – or, really, the question in a broader context – was an even more difficult one... Circumstances had favoured her – serendipity, if you will. How would she ever have met Alan if her grandmother had not made that crazy will and involved their, previously renegade, branch of the family in the family business once again? Yes, she *would* still have gone to OCA – her mother had immediately invested the proceeds of the sale of her father's McGrath-LaPlante shares to his mother, in an education fund to ensure that whatever happened money would be available for post-secondary tuition fees for the three of them. But, without the dividend income from the shares her grandmother left to her, she would have needed a job during and after those college years when, instead, she had been able to devote both school hours and free time to sketching, painting, continually improving and growing... Without Alan, she would never have had the huge studio to work in or have made the contacts among people, financially able to invest in the works of young artists, that came her way strictly through being Alan's wife. She could never have hoped for the huge success of her first exhibition, this critically important second one, the recognition of her talent, the media interviews and the demand for her work if Grandma McGrath had not mounted her crusade against old Denny LaPlante. And, while her life had been so propitious, her cousin's could not have gone more wrong! He surely didn't *deserve* that...

The sudden ringing of the telephone snapped Megan out of her reverie. Little Steven stopped fractionally then continued his intense study of his own kicking feet. Megan picked up the phone.

"Hallo?"

"Megan, it's me – Byron. I'm not interrupting anything, am I?"

"What? Oh, you mean work? No – I didn't get upstairs today. Guess who showed up? Or, have you been talking to Mom?"

"What d'you mean?"

"Oh, nothing. I called Mom a little while ago to tell her that Angus had been here."

"What? You're joking."

"I'm not," Megan replied. "I'd had my lunch and Steven was asleep – we were out this morning and he overdosed on fresh air – so I was just about to go up and finish sketching in something I started working on yesterday and the doorbell rang. I dashed downstairs before whoever it was could ring the bell again and wake the baby. I opened the door and there was Angus – he looks a lot like you now, you know."

"Well, what did he want? How did he get there?"

"I'm not terribly sure what he wanted but, I imagine, he got here on the subway."

"That's not what I mean. How did he get *here*, to Toronto?"

"He hitched with two characters called Scott and Angie, who's into Zen. They went to the gallery last night and couldn't figure out why Zak asked them to leave."

"Did Zak call you then?" Byron asked.

"No, he didn't believe them when they told him Angus was my cousin – thought they were just vagrants looking to keep warm or, more likely, something worse than that – surprisingly enough! Anyway, I made some tea and gave him a sandwich and we were talking and everything was going along fine, then he started getting irritable and eventually just decided he'd had enough of me, I guess – just got up and left. By that time Steven had woken up and I was giving him his bottle, so I couldn't even keep up with Angus and show him out properly – he was gone before I was even halfway down the stairs. So, as I was telling Mom, I don't know where he's staying or anything – except that they're staying with the brother of one of the other kids and it's somewhere in the vicinity of the gallery because that's how they happened to go there. I asked him to bring his friends to dinner tomorrow, but he didn't seem all that crazy about doing so."

"Didn't you ask him where he was staying?"

"Believe me, if I had known he was going to take off like that, I would have done or, at least, attempted to. As things were, I was more concerned about gaining his confidence, so I wasn't about to risk him – doing what he eventually did do anyway – by having him think I was prying."

"D'you think he'll show up tomorrow?"

"I doubt it. All we can do is hope he'll make contact again."

"What about Adam?" asked Byron. "Has he seen him?"

"He says he has nothing in common with Adam anymore – not that they ever did have anyway, except us, I suppose. Anyway, that's the story of my hopeless failure and lost afternoon... What were you calling about anyway?"

"I was going to invite you guys to dinner on Sunday – if you're not doing anything..."

"What's the occasion?" Megan asked, flippantly.

"It's not an occasion." Byron sounded a little embarrassed, she thought. "Look, you won't hate me for this, will you, Megan?"

"Hate you? For what?"

"It's Bianca's parents... they want to meet you?"

"Oh God, Byron, that's embarrassing."

"I know. They only just found out that my sister Megan was *the* Megan McGrath."

"*The* Megan McGrath – they didn't really *say* that?"

"They saw you on the *Canada AM* interview... and they read the *Globe and Mail*. They eventually figured out that you were my sister and, yes – that's how they put it. Bianca had already invited them to dinner when all this came to light and she got a bit carried away and said that since we owed you guys a dinner, we'd see if you could make it on Sunday, too. She was showing off a little about knowing you – you're going to have to get used to that sort of thing..."

"I know," said Megan. "I didn't really expect it of Bianca, though. She always seems to be so practical, feet on the ground – you know..."

"The thing is – she had a bit of a problem with her parents about buying the house with me and not getting married – they're sort of old-fashioned – and it's only been recently that they've come around to accepting it. This'll be the first time they've been here. So when her mother began talking about you, she figured that inviting you would really solve the problem."

"Maybe it would have been better if you hadn't told me all this, Byron. Like, just invited us to dinner... Look, I'll do it because you're my brother, but if I end up looking like a self-conscious idiot who doesn't impress anyone, don't blame me."

"You won't. Anyway, aren't you getting used to being a celebrity?"

"I'm not a celebrity. I'm getting all the press right now but, once the exhibition is over, I'll be forgotten except for the occasional article on OCA grads, the young mother angle, establishment wives, etc. you know how fickle the media is..."

"Megan, you've made it now – you're Canada's most exciting young landscape painter. Next stop – the world."

"Fun-*ny*... Anyway, we'll be there on Sunday. Seven-ish?"

"Thanks, Meg."

"You're welcome. Byron, can you get hold of Danny and tell him about Angus before you leave the office. I haven't told Alan yet, either – he was in a meeting when I called."

"Sure. Give Steven a hug for me and I'll see you Sunday. 'Bye."

"'Bye."

· · · · ·

"So we have to go out both Saturday and Sunday evening?" Alan said, not terribly enthusiastically.

Megan had waited until she had given Steven his last bottle of the day and settled him for the night before telling him about Byron's dinner invitation. Byron had told Danny about Angus, and Danny had told Alan when they were both on their way out of the building at the end of the afternoon. That, then, had been the major topic of conversation at supper time. After supper, Alan had looked after Steven – and the dishes – while she went over to the club for a swim. She'd called Michael, on her return, and told him the story. To her relief, he'd sounded more resigned than upset at the news.

Now, over a cup of decaffeinated coffee before going to bed, she told Alan of Byron's dilemma.

"I could hardly say no, darling, could I? It's not as if he makes a habit of asking favours of me – in fact, I can't even remember the last time he did." She got up from her chair, put down her mug and moved over behind the end of the couch where Alan was sitting. "Lean forward," she said and began to massage his neck and shoulders. "Anyway, we don't have to stay late. We can always say the baby-sitter has to be home early."

"Who's baby-sitting?"

"My mother and Hugh, but they don't even know Bianca's parents so they're hardly likely to tell them. I called Mom and told her about Byron and why he was asking us to dinner and she offered to come over and baby-sit."

"That feels good. Sorry for sounding like such a grouch..."

"It's okay. It's been a tough two weeks having to be out somewhere all the time, but the exhibition will be over next week and we can go back to being normal again and as dull as we like."

"I know I was complaining about all the action but, I think, *dull* is going a bit too far... I object to being called dull. I'm not really getting dull, am I?"

"Oh, dull as ditchwater. But much better looking..."

"Well, let's be thankful for such small mercies, shall we?"

Megan stopped massaging, picked up her mug of coffee and sat on the floor in front of him. "My turn," she said.

"Oh, I forgot to tell you," Alan said, beginning to massage her shoulders, "the official retirement party's going to be June 25th."

"How come? I thought it was going to be earlier."

"I don't know. I thought so, too – that it was going to be earlier, I mean. Peter Dailey's looking after it – your mother's protégé. I think there was a mix up. His secretary forgot to confirm or something. Anyway, mark it on the calendar so that we don't screw up and make some other arrangement that weekend."

"It *is* a Friday, isn't it?"

"Ah-ha. I meant, we can't make a weekend commitment involving that evening. Are you going to watch the news?"

"I think so..."

"Can you reach the remote, then. I wouldn't want to interrupt your massage."

"You'll interrupt it anyway if I have to lean over there."

"Only on one side." He bent over and kissed the back of her neck.

Megan picked up the remote and turned on *The National*. Turning her attention to the television set on a lower shelf of one of the two big oak wall units on either side of the stone fireplace, she was suddenly aware of something missing from the adjacent shelf. She jumped up and examined the shelves.

"What's the matter?" asked Alan.

"You – you didn't move any of the musical boxes, did you?"

"No. Are you sure you didn't change things around and then forget?"

"Alan – they're not here." She turned to face him. "They're not where they're supposed to be or on any of the other shelves either. Three of them – snuff boxes." She sat down heavily beside him on the sofa. "I can't believe it. How could he do it to me?"

When she was five her father had given her a little wooden jewellery box, which played *You Are My Sunshine* when the lid was lifted. He had been away somewhere and brought gifts for Danny, Byron and herself when he came back. Byron's gift was a large stuffed Winnie-the-Pooh and, since Byron was a baby who didn't even know who Winnie-the-Pooh was, while she was able to read all the Pooh stories by herself, she privately considered herself to be a more suitable owner for the bear. Danny had received some kind of unbreakable hockey stick for playing street hockey in the driveway and, since she was the person he mostly played with, she couldn't quite see why she had been given a silly girl's gift instead of a hockey stick like her brother. She had argued about it and eventually been sent to her room, where she had used the chair from her desk to reach the shelf at the top of her closet and thrown the jewellery box to the very back of the shelf. Later, as a twelve-year-old, she had re-discovered the rejected gift, remembered her dreadful behaviour and, after indulging in a guilt trip over being such a scruffy little tomboy instead of the pretty little daughter her dead father had wanted, had begun to collect musical boxes, eventually moving into antiques as she got older. They were mostly jewellery boxes and snuff boxes, but she also owned a Victorian parasol with a musical box in the handle and little silver Mozart-playing powder box, dating from the Regency period which Alan always said must have belonged to some hooker with a royal lover.

Alan put his arm around her. "How long did you leave him alone?" he asked.

"Only while I was changing Steven's diaper. I was rather stupid – I should have left him in the kitchen. Instead, I told him to make himself comfortable in the living room and I'd be right there with the baby. I wasn't thinking... but, of course, I didn't know I should have to... Oh, Alan, one of them's the first gift you ever gave me..."

"Don't worry, sweetheart. We'll call the police – we'll get them back."

"No – we can't call the police," Megan turned towards him, horrified. "What about Michael? He won't be able to handle it."

"Megan, you're not Michael's mother. You're his niece. What he can and can't handle is not your problem. His son is a common thief and has stolen from us We have to accept that and so does he."

Megan was silent.

"It's not just Michael..." she eventually said in a small voice. "I can't handle it. I feel like such a fool. I mean it would be different if he'd broken in or something – though, of course he wouldn't have been able to. The alarm would have been on. We can't tell the police that I let someone steal things from right under my nose."

"Meggie, it's not just a matter of getting the snuff boxes back. Angus has to be stopped for his own good. And the rest of your family's. If he gets away with it this time, who's to say Danny won't be next, or your mother, or Byron. Don't you see? We have to report it. He's a drug addict, sweetheart. He doesn't care who he hurts."

"You don't know that for sure." Megan said. "Maybe it was just done on impulse – being here, seeing our beautiful home and possessions, resenting his own lifestyle. Maybe he figured he could get enough for the snuff boxes to get a place to stay, look for a job – something like that..." she finished falteringly.

Alan put his hands on her shoulders and turned her to face him. "Look," he said, "go over, in your mind, everything you told me about this afternoon. Think about the way he acted, what he said to you, the sudden mood-swing and leave-taking. He'd told the other kid you were his cousin. Right?"

Megan nodded.

"These homeless kids hanging out together come in – to put it bluntly – packs. There's a leader who holds the purse strings, the drugs... controls the other kids. The other kids steal, sell their various sexual favours, roll their clients, mug old ladies – do whatever their leader tells them to do or risk being beaten up, disfigured, starved or – worst case – not getting their fix. That kid sent Angus here..."

"He sounded as if he was really glad to see me," Megan said, sadly.

"I'm sure he was – any one would be glad to see you, love. You're a nice person – a wonderful person –" he hugged her to him and stroked her hair, "– he was really happy to see you, but his need to satisfy his addiction was greater. He had to get something for his pal to sell and get out of here and back to his friends. They've probably sold the snuff boxes, taken the night off and are all as high as kites by now."

Megan shuddered slightly at the reference to taking the night off. She pulled away from Alan so that she could look directly at him. "Let's just keep it to ourselves for now... No, no, I mean the family," she explained, as he was about to interrupt. "We'll report it to the police, but we don't need to tell anybody about it, do we? Until they charge him, at least. If they do..."

"I suppose. At least we'll avoid having Michael descend on us with all sorts of accusations if we keep it to ourselves. And you're right, the police are not all that likely to find them, although getting hauled into court and sentenced would be the best thing for Angus – get him away from the – the other kid and into drug rehab…"

"You were going to say pimp, weren't you?'

"Yes," Alan admitted.

"I have to accept it, don't I? Now that the whole situation's here – right on my own doorstep, I mean"

"Yes," he nodded.

"I wish he'd stayed wherever he was. It's a lot easier to block it out when you're not actually confronted with the reality." Megan stood up. "Are you going to call the police now?"

"No. I don't think it works that way anymore – unless it's something major. You have to go into a police station and make a report, sign a statement, etc. now. I'll do it in the morning and they'll probably send an officer over sometime during the day to see you, okay?"

She smiled. "Okay. So let's get to bed. I feel completely exhausted and, even if Steven sleeps through, five o'clock'll be here in no time."

## DANNY

"Is Jayne bringing her wilderness man?" Selena LaPlante asked Megan.

"His name's Niall, Aunt Selena. You shouldn't call him that – it's catching. We all end up doing it. I imagine he's coming – if Jayne can drag him out of his canoe. What am I saying? You see what I mean? We've got to stop doing this. *Is* Niall coming, Danny?"

"As far as I know."

Danny held his index fingers up for Steven James LaPlante to grasp in a concentrated effort to pull himself into a sitting position. He had dropped by his sister's home earlier in the afternoon and been persuaded to stay to supper and welcome Alan's Aunt Selena who was making one of her regular visits to Toronto in order to attend her brother's upcoming retirement party. Alan had since returned with his aunt, after picking her up at the airport, and was now grilling chicken breasts and vegetables on the barbecue while Megan was bringing out the salads and dressings and setting the patio table. Selena had inspected her grand-nephew, remarking on how he had grown in the two months since she had seen him when Megan and Alan had taken him to visit her in Moncton at Easter, then requested the details of the retirement party.

Only half listening to the conversation, Danny studied the baby who stared right back at him with the dark blue eyes he had inherited from his father, then turned his attention to the cat, Mathilda, who had materialised from the shrubbery near the barbecue, proceeding to rub herself against Alan's ankles, no doubt more interested in what he was cooking than in him. Danny had taken to dropping in at his sister's home quite frequently during recent weeks. Megan had made light of the surprise visit of their cousin Angus. She laughed about his lack of response to her dinner invitation. And she claimed not to be concerned about his whereabouts – whether in the city or wherever he might have moved on to. Danny was only a year older than Megan and they had been very close as children growing up together. Outside of Alan, he probably knew her better than anyone despite their relationship having, naturally, become more distant in adulthood. His sister was compassionate to the extent – for a long time – of actually feeling that she had not given Angus the help which she thought she could have done, given his childhood admiration for her. He had expected her to have them all combing the city for him after his failure to either show up for dinner or contact her again. Instead, she had played down the entire affair and, quite obviously, had no wish to discuss Angus or his situation and whereabouts.

Danny had found Alan equally unwilling to talk about Angus and, when he'd asked his mother if she thought there was more to the story than either Megan or Alan was ready to discuss, she had laughed and said that they were both so wrapped up in the baby that neither of them had much interest in anything else just now. There had been comments on the office grapevine recently about a sudden increase in Alan's phone calls to Megan during the working day. On one occasion, Danny had actually been so incensed that he'd warned the executive secretary who he'd overheard exchanging crude comments on the fact with somebody on the other end of a telephone conversation, that he wouldn't be contributing any favourable comments when her next salary review came up. It was not just the office gossip that was bothering him, however, so much as Alan's obvious concern, in the weeks since Angus's visit, about Megan when she and the baby were alone. Except for the period when his sister had first become involved with Alan LaPlante and resented Danny doing the over-protective big brother bit, he and Megan had always confided in each other and shared their problems, trusted in each other's judgement and known when something was wrong. Danny knew that something was wrong in Megan's life now and he was quite sure that Angus was at the source of it.

Not knowing that Selena LaPlante was expected today and that Alan would be picking her up at the airport, he had expected to find his sister and brother-in-law together and intended to attempt to coax the story out of them. Instead, Alan had just left for the airport and Megan was busy with advance preparations for supper. She had talked him into staying for supper and he'd surprised himself at his dexterity in feeding baby food to his little nephew while she marinated chicken and prepared salad ingredients. This, Megan told him, would ensure that Steven would sleep while they ate their supper. Looking at the baby energetically rolling over and performing a series of what looked like push-ups, in order to get a better view of the cat, Danny had a feeling that her strategy wasn't going to work.

"Unfortunately that was the image I had of him long before I ever met him and that's how I think of him," Selena was saying. "You remember, Alan, dear... you and I went out to dinner with my brother's family – it was when Father died – and Laura was giving Jayne quite a hard time about this new young man of hers. Outdoorsy – that's what she said... very Laura-like – condescending. And Jayne said something like 'You'd hate him, Mother. But, don't worry – we're not asking you to come winter camping with us.' Oh, I forgot – Laura's your aunt isn't she...?" She looked at Danny a little uncertainly, although Danny – while he didn't know her terribly well – was pretty sure she was putting him on.

"It's all right," laughed Megan. "We spent our childhood doing Aunt Laura imitations. Have some more wine." She picked up the bottle of wine which Alan had placed in a clay wine cooler after pouring them each a glass. "There's just enough for you and I. Danny can run up and get another bottle from the fridge – d'you mind?" She turned to her brother. "I've been up and down too many times..."

"No problem." said Danny, getting to his feet.

"You'll be glad when you finally get this house renovated – I should say re-renovated, I suppose," observed Selena, while Megan filled her glass. "I can't think why you haven't had it done before now."

"Mainly because we really liked our little apartment... or, maybe, we're just procrastinators... Anyway, it'll all be done by the next time you visit. The whole kitchen-breakfast-dining-room area and small bathroom will be going back to, basically, the way they were when that part of the house was your nursery – no, I guess you'd have been too old, wouldn't you? Your little brothers' nursery, then. Anyway, it'll be a self contained suite – so you'll still have privacy when you're here – how's that? We'll show you the plans later – you don't mind waiting, do you? They're in the study."

"Don't worry about it, dear. There's plenty of time – I'm here for a week."

Megan poured the rest of the wine into her own glass, put down the empty bottle and walked over to pick Steven up as Danny went into the house.

By the time he came back with the new bottle of wine, Selena was gently rocking the baby, who – transfixed by one of his great-aunt's dangling earrings – was finally beginning to look sleepy, and Megan was placing platters of barbecued chicken and grilled vegetables on the table. Alan picked up the cork screw and handed it to him.

"Here, it's the foolproof kind," he said. "But I'll do it if you prefer..."

"Good. Here–" Danny handed over both bottle and cork screw "–there's nothing more embarrassing than getting bits of cork in somebody else's wine."

Alan proceeded to open the bottle.

"There, I told you it was foolproof," he said, removing the cork. "Sit down. I think we're all set." He filled Danny's glass and his own.

"I think I'll just take Steven up, Aunt Selena, now that you've almost got him to sleep," Megan said. She gently took the baby from Selena. "You guys go ahead. I'll be back in a few minutes." She carried Steven into the house.

"Here, have this seat, Aunt Selena," Alan said, guiding his aunt to her place, then sitting down himself. "Sit down and pass the potato salad, Danny."

"The chicken looks lovely..." said Selena, placing chicken on her plate and adding some of the grilled vegetables.

"Alan's becoming quite the barbecue gourmet. He's been taking lessons from my stepfather – we all have," Danny told her. "Before Hugh came into our lives, we'd throw our steaks or chicken or chops on the barbecue, slap on some seasonings or barbecue sauce and be happy to eat the result. Now we're all marinating and basting, like a troupe of James Barber clones, trying to compete with Hugh."

"Well, I'd say it looks like Alan's winning," said Selena, "this is really good..."

"Megan did the marinating to be honest – I can't pretend otherwise because Danny probably arrived when she was in the middle of doing it and I'm not about to have him catch me out in a lie. The McGraths would never let me live it down – right?" He waited for Danny's nodded assent. "I really only slapped everything on the barbecue."

"Team effort, then," Selena amended. "I'm really enjoying it. You did a wonderful job on the vegetables, too. Keep it up and you'll never have any trouble with little Steven eating his vegetables. People usually tend to let them dry out too much when they do them on the barbecue. How's your brother, Danny? Still trying to convert everybody to vegetarianism?"

"Oh, he's less of a crusader these days. When did you last see him? It must have been..."

"He dropped by on some errand the last time I was here, but had a car full of people and couldn't stop. I was in the living room downstairs and he knocked on the door to say hello. That was this time last year when you were in India."

"... well, you'll find he's becoming quite a responsible human being. Quite normal, too. No more long lectures on the human body not being designed for carnivorous activity, etc. Thank God."

"He finally realised that the human *mind was* designed for freedom of choice?"

Danny and Alan both laughed.

"That's one way of putting it," Danny said.

"What's the joke?"

They all looked up as Megan came out of the house.

"Aunt Selena was asking after Byron and we were talking about how he's matured," Alan said. "Sit down and get your chicken while there's still some left. It's very popular stuff and going fast."

Megan put the lemon meringue pie and pot of coffee, she'd brought out with her, on the table and sat down. She helped herself from the platters being thrust at her by both her husband and her brother and suggested they finish things off as long as Selena wanted no more. Selena shook her head and said she hoped she had enough room for some of the delicious-looking pie. They finished eating in companionable silence except for murmurs of appreciation when the pie was served. Over coffee the conversation focused on the success of Megan's exhibition three months ago and the proposal to market a series of three limited edition prints, featuring British Columbia rain forest scenes, to raise funds for an ecological organization there.

"Why three?" asked Selena.

"They *are* a series," Megan explained, "and it's actually all the idea of the company that bought them. That's really why they bought them. Not because they think I'm a wonderful artist or my work will improve the ambience of their boardroom, but for the PR value of associating themselves with environmental issues. A little ego-deflating to say the least, but there you are. Anyway, they figure marketing them individually *or* as a series'll bring in more money."

"The problem is that it'll also commit Megan to being associated with the whole enterprise and, of course, she doesn't have the time to get too involved," said Alan. "So we're trying to work out a compromise that'll make everybody happy."

"So you're going to become another Bateman?" Selena raised her eyebrows at Megan.

Megan sighed. "That's the whole problem," she said. "*He's* old enough to have lots of time to spend being an environmentalist *and* an artist. I'm only at the beginning of my career and I'm a mother and a wife..."

"Poor soul..." said Alan, shaking his head. "You're lucky it's rainforests they're saving and not rubber plantations or you'd really be in trouble."

"Ha ha. Very funny," Megan replied.

Danny started laughing. "Can you imagine? *'Buy a signed McGrath print and help protect our rubbers'*..."

"Shut-up, Danny!" said Megan. "I've heard it all before..."

"Byron?"

"Yeah. I guess if he's maturing, you must be regressing!"

Selena stood up. "Well, I'll leave you to your sibling squabbles and get on with my unpacking."

Megan grinned. "Sorry. Here, I'll come in with you and take some of this stuff up."

She began piling dirty dishes on to one of the large platters that had contained barbecued chicken and vegetables.

"Why don't you go in with Aunt Selena," Alan said, getting up and putting his hands on her shoulders, "and have a chat with her while she's unpacking. Danny and I'll take care of cleaning up out here..."

"And stack the dishwasher?"

"... and stack the dishwasher."

"Deal," said Megan, giving him a quick kiss and picking up the wine bottle. "I'll take what's left of this." She followed Selena into the house.

"Wino!" Danny called after her.

"Come on, Danny," said Alan, " get moving – you heard the deal."

. . . . .

Danny and Alan relaxed, in the comfortable cushioned rattan chairs on the balcony off the living room, companionably drinking cold beer, after taking care of the dirty dishes and leftovers and cleaning up the patio.

"I suppose really that it was only a matter of time until somebody came up with this kind of proposal for something of Megan's..." Danny said.

"Actually Zak was keen to get something like this going after her first exhibition – it's quite usual for dealers to advance these kind of opportunities – but I talked him out of it. At least, out of initiating anything. To be truthful, I resorted to threats to stop him. You'd have done the same thing. As you say, it was only a matter of time before somebody saw the possibilities anyway – a young landscape painter of, more often than not, environmentally threatened areas, reputation growing by leaps and bounds – it's an obvious..."

"... but, like she said, timing's wrong."

"In a way, it's even worse now than it would have been three years ago – there was no Steven then. It's all right for her to say that her work will be continually evolving over her lifetime, but she really should have had more up-front time to develop. With first me, now Steven complicating her life, getting her first solo exhibition too early – it's not a really sound foundation."

"Hey, I know years of starving in a garret, before bursting forth on the art scene, is the politically correct way to go, but aren't you being a bit over-zealous? Surely a bit of early recognition can't hurt that much?"

"If I am, there's not much I can do about it anyway. She makes her own decisions and you know Megan – she has her own agenda. I just worry that later on she'll regret the time not spent working..."

"She won't. And she's hardly likely to regret the time spent with you – you're her whole world. You have been from the day she met you. It's not as if you knew you'd be hampering the course of a genius's career..."

"It's okay for me worry about that possibility," Alan said, with mock dignity, "but I don't expect other people to accuse me of it – least of all, my brother-in-law." He got up from his chair. "Want another beer?"

"Sure. Cut me off before I end up having to stay over though."

Danny stood up to take some deep breaths and do some stretching exercises while Alan went in for the beer. He shrugged and leaned on the balcony rail, looking out on the darkened garden below. He though Alan was nuts to be worrying about Megan's career. He agreed with Megan's thinking that she had the best of both worlds and wouldn't want it any other way. Who wanted to be a genius anyway?

Alan came back out with the beer. "We forgot to feed the cat," he said. "And Megan's on her way up. At least, I heard her saying goodnight to Selena when I was in the kitchen." He handed Danny his beer and sat down.

They heard Megan call softly from the kitchen doorway. "Where *are* you guys?"

"Out here. On the balcony," Alan called softly back to her.

"D'you want some more coffee? I'm putting some on for myself."

"No thanks, love. We've moved onto beer."

"I hope Danny's not thinking of driving home then," Megan observed as she went back into the kitchen.

"Looks like you're sleeping over," Alan said. "You may as well. I shan't be staying up for another hour to keep you company, anyway – too sleepy. And you won't be able to drive until then."

"I guess you're right. So when are all these renovations scheduled to begin?"

"Oh, don't ask. It's going to be a nightmare. We were really stupid not to have had it done while we were in India. Well – stupid for not having it done long before that but –"

"– particularly stupid for not having it done then."

"Right. I just hope there won't be too many hold-ups. It'll be all right for me, of course, camping out with the place in tatters around me when I have to be here, but Megan's not going to want to stay at the cottage forever. The plan is for Megan and Steven to go up there next Sunday with your mother and Hugh – they're going to stay for the week. Selena will have left by then, too. She's going with Dennis and Laura up to their cottage. I've got a couple of guys from the plant coming in to move everything, from the areas where things will be happening, into the rooms which won't be affected. Then the construction people will move in. Everything's supposed to be finished by the second week in August, but we haven't actually given the cleaning people a firm date – don't want to jinx ourselves by being overly optimistic."

"So Megan's going to do the old Mum and the kids at the cottage for the summer bit – doesn't sound like our Meg somehow..."

"What doesn't sound like me?" Megan came out onto the balcony carrying a mug of coffee. She sat down, sipped the coffee and, deciding it was too hot, put it down on the table beside her. "Aunt Selena said to say goodnight. So *what* doesn't sound like me?"

"We were just talking about the plans for the summer," said Alan. "Danny doesn't think playing 'Mom at the Cottage' is quite your scene."

Megan grinned. "I'll survive," she said. "I've got everything set up in my boathouse attic studio now – so, as long as Steven co-operates, I'll be able to get a fair bit of work done. There's a young girl who's family has a cottage just along the lane. She's at the stage where being at the cottage with the family becomes a bit of a bore, I guess. Anyway, she's really good with Steven and wants to look after him while I work... so we'll see. You should see Steven in the water – we were up there last weekend and it was the first time it was warm enough for us to really play with him in the lake. He couldn't quite figure out the wet sand, but decided he liked it anyway. I hope you'll be able to come up this summer some time – you didn't really get to see it last year, with the summer being almost over by the time you got home."

Megan and Alan had bought the Muskoka cottage during the early summer of the year before, when Danny was in India. Most of last summer had been spent decorating and furnishing it. They had had the family up for the Labour Day weekend as a kind of combined housewarming and *bon voyage* party since they were due to leave for India themselves a few days later. It was not the kind of place that fitted Danny's perception of what a cottage ought to be and he had found it rather surprising that Megan should prefer something that was basically a second home over a log cabin far away from telephone and power lines like his own Haliburton retreat. He had concluded that pregnancy must have some hormonal influence on one's taste and refrained from questioning her on the subject.

"Sure," he murmured.

Megan picked up her coffee and sipped it slowly. "I realise it must seem to be a bit of a switch from the wilderness hermitage-type cottages that we always said were the only holiday homes worth having when we were kids..." she said, as if reading his thoughts. "The thing is that, because of this house being divided, McGrath-LaPlante has sort of relied on the downstairs apartment being a sort of *pied-à-terre* for customers and whatever since Alan's grandfather died. But, now that it's going to become a single family home again, with Steven – and, hopefully, other children – running around, and with Uncle Dennis retiring and Jayne not really being into the business entertaining thing, we have to be able to have other options and you can hardly take people like the McCallums, for instance, who turn business trips into family holidays, out into the wilderness somewhere."

"I hadn't really thought about it," Danny admitted.

"That's the whole trouble – you and Jayne and all the operational-type people think that marketing and communications is all fun and games. You can go off and play *voyageurs* or mountain men or what-have-you at the end of the working week, but we have to plan around the marketing function..."

"Megan," Alan interrupted her, "don't come on to Danny about it. It's me that made the choices..."

"I'm sorry. I just felt that I was getting sneered at for appearing to be becoming all the things we abhorred when we were children. I guess, I have to admit to being a bit on edge just now – super-sensitive... Anyway, we felt that, for the present, we had to have a cottage that was multi-functional rather than for our own amusement. So that's why we're on millionaire's row and not at the back of beyond."

"I'm sorry, too, Meg. I *was* being arrogant and I do appreciate the fact that, whatever titles the rest of us bestow upon ourselves, Alan is the one who is pivotal to McGrath-LaPlante's success and, as such, to the well-being of the rest of us," Danny said. "Forgiven?"

Megan nodded. "I shouldn't have been so touchy," she said.

"Which brings me to another point..." said Danny, not failing to notice the quick glance that passed between his sister and brother-in-law. "...why are you feeling – as you just put it yourself – so super-sensitive?"

Alan cleared his throat. "I think we're going to have to tell him," he said, looking across at Megan and nodding in response to her brief nod. "We didn't want to worry the rest of the family with this but – well, we realise that your sudden desire for our company isn't motivated only by our delightful camaraderie or free-flowing booze or whatever..." They all grinned at each other and visibly relaxed. "Anyway, we decided we were going to have to tell you but would wait until you actually brought it up."

"So now that I've brought it up?"

"Well..."

"It has something to do with Angus, doesn't it?"

Alan nodded.

"His visit?"

"He stole things," said Megan, "while I was changing Steven..."

"What...?"

"Some of my snuff-boxes."

"It's okay – we got them back," said Alan. "We went to the police–"

"We thought it would be best if he were caught and charged – that it would get him away from the-the people he was associating with..." Megan explained.

"That part didn't work, unfortunately, but we did get Megan's snuff-boxes back or, at least, we will do eventually. They're in police custody right now."

"An undercover agent – a women pretending to be shopping for a gift for a collector – found them in an antique shop on King East," added Megan. "It was a bit like being in a detective story."

"It wasn't Angus that sold them to the antique dealer, though," continued Alan, "which, of course, figures. These people he's with must be experienced at this sort of thing – something I didn't take into consideration. I just assumed they were all kids, but – according to the antique dealer – a perfectly presentable-looking guy in his thirties sold them to him. He had a story about how they'd been in the family for years and he was sorry to see them go but, in this economy you have to do what you have to do – or words to that effect. Angus had told Megan he was staying somewhere in the vicinity of Zak's gallery but the police weren't able to trace either Angus or the man who sold the snuff-boxes. So either they'd all moved on or that was just part of the story they'd primed Angus to tell." He stood up. "I have to visit the can. Want another beer on my way back? May as well since you're staying anyway."

"Sure," said Danny, addressing Alan's back as he went inside. He turned to Megan. "I'm sorry for being such a jerk, Meggie," he said.

"It's okay – you weren't to know. It was me who decided we wouldn't tell anyone – partly because I felt like such an idiot for letting it happen and partly because I didn't want Michael to have to know and, of course, I didn't want everyone having to worry about it. The silly part is that the thing that we really wanted to happen – for Angus to be caught and charged, I mean – didn't happen. I guess we were naive to think it would be as easy as that to get someone rehabilitated. The biggest problem is that we have no means of knowing if they're still here – in Toronto, I mean – or if they've moved on or gone back to wherever they came from... Or if they really were living where Angus said they were and know – or have some other means of finding out about the police looking for them and so..."

"So you're worried about them finding out you put the police onto them and, maybe, coming after you or something...?"

"Sort of. That's why we've been up at the cottage so much – even before the weather was really good enough. Alan's worried about Angus bringing these other people here and – well, something awful happening. He's relieved that Steven and I will be permanently up at the cottage, for the summer, after next weekend, but I have to worry about him being here, on his own, for part of each week."

"And you don't need to worry so much now that Danny knows, right?" asked Alan, coming back out with two beers and the coffee carafe. "I brought the rest of the coffee out." He indicated the carafe and Megan held up her mug. He poured coffee with one hand while handing Danny his beer with the other. "I turned the air conditioning down – it feels quite chilly in there after being out here."

"I think – once you realised this was a bit more than just a bunch of street kids you were dealing with – that you should have told the rest of us," Danny said, when Alan was seated again. "I mean, they could pull the same thing on any of us."

"Not really," said Alan. "For one thing Angus doesn't know where any of you live – you've all moved since he was last here and you're not terribly accessible from public transit. For another, they'd have to assume that, once we found out what they were up to, we'd warn you so they could hardly risk pulling the same thing and getting caught and, of course, that becomes even less likely if they know that the police are looking for them."

"Angus had my phone number and there aren't a hell of a lot of D. McGraths in the phone book anyway – they could find me easily enough and what's to stop them trying a little break and enter."

"They're hardly likely to be into breaking into a twenty-four hour security protected condominium. Their being 'a bit more than just a bunch of street kids' doesn't mean they're organized criminals – just that they're more savvy – streetwise, if you like – than I originally assumed. They're druggies – the thing that's far more likely to happen is Angus approaching Megan again and playing on her sympathies to extort money. Maybe bringing his pals along – um, that kind of thing..."

"So that's what all the panic buttons are about."

"Yes, there haven't really been any break-ins around here," Megan said. "We just say that so that people won't think we're paranoid. Anyway, that's the story and I'm relying on you and Byron to keep in touch with Alan when he's here alone on weekday nights."

Alan smiled. "I keep telling her that they're no more likely to show up here in the middle of the night than they are to break into your apartment," he said to Danny. "They have other things to do at night."

Megan grimaced but remained silent. She rose, picking up her mug and the coffee carafe.

"He's right, Meg," Danny agreed. "It's you who's most vulnerable, you and–" Alan caught his eye. "And there's no need to worry about Alan," he hastily amended. God, he must have had too much to drink. Even mentioning Steven in the same context as the possibility of Megan being threatened by drug-crazed street kids would have been unthinkable otherwise.

Megan looked at him, as he turned away to finish his beer, but made no comment. She opened the balcony door and went in. "I'll go and make up the couch in the study for you," she said, closing the door behind her.

"Did you think of visiting some of the gay bars?" Danny asked Alan.

"I thought of it – but I don't have the time or the inclination to play detective and what exactly could I do if I did find him? The kid's in the hands of a pimp, Danny – the only way you can break up that kind of relationship is to get him arrested and jailed or into some kind of rehab program and then there's no guarantee that it'll work... He's hardly going to wait around while I pull out my cell phone and call the police, is he? Apart from that, I'm not madly comfortable in gay bars... I feel kind of noticeable – like I had 'heterosexual' stamped on my forehead or something."

"Jesus, Alan, come out of the dark ages. You don't have to be gay to go to a gay bar nowadays. It doesn't even have to be a gay bar as such – there are lots of regular singles-type bars that are frequented by gays and bi's and people who haven't come out.

And they're often the kind of places where sex is bought and sold – and where druggie kids are likely to sell quick sex."

"You mean hanging around the washroom type of thing? Danny – how come you're an expert all of a sudden?"

"I was wondering when you were going to ask. Shelley – you know, Shelley Fowler, my journalist friend? Well, she had an assignment to do a piece, for the Sunday Star, on people going alone to bars. You maybe even read it." Alan shook his head. "Anyway, I got co-opted into helping with some of the research – she could hardly check out the men's washrooms herself, could she? I'm only kidding – she didn't really get into that stuff, but when you're actually surveying bars, that sort of thing becomes strikingly obvious." He paused. "*I* might give it a try – looking for Angus, I mean." He leaned forward and grinned. "I can take Shelley along for protection..."

Alan looked at him, consideringly. "I don't think it's really worth the time, Dan. We don't even know if he's still in the city and – if he is – there's every chance he's into something more organized than that by now. Remember the man the antique dealer described was not a street kid – not even an obvious transient." He stood up and stretched, then picked up the empty beer bottles. "Come on, let's sleep on it."

. . . . .

At Dennis LaPlante's retirement dinner, Danny sat with the rest of the McGrath-LaPlante senior management team – except for Alan and Jayne who, as members of the immediate family, were seated at the head table – and the various guests of honour. He'd brought Shelley as his escort and, having attended a number of company functions with Danny, she knew his co-workers and their spouses. Introductions were necessary to some of the guests, however – mostly older people who had been associated with Dennis for most of his working life.

"Shelley Fowler – I know that name, don't I?" said John Keating, a now retired, long-time executive in the Health Protection Branch of the Ministry of Health.

"Shelley's quite a well-known freelance journalist," Danny told him.

"That's right – you're the gel who did that piece on the singles bars in the Star," cried Mr. Keating, heartily.

Danny flinched inwardly. Shelley would not take kindly to being referred to as the 'gel' and the article having earned quite a lot of acclaim among her peers merited a more desirable description than 'that piece'. He willed her to have patience with the old boy. Shelley was his best friend and he admired her accomplishments, but was not blind to her faults. She was not patient with men – particularly the old guard types – who persisted in refusing to see women as contributing members of society. He would actually have preferred to come alone, in view of the fact that duty called him to entertain these guests. He had explained the situation to her, stressing the need for diplomacy. At the time, he had found himself remembering, quite enviously, the concern Megan and Alan had expressed for one another's careers last Sunday evening. He glanced, now, at the head table where Alan, as master of ceremonies, was checking that his notes were in order, and saw the smiles, of respectively encouragement and gratitude, that flashed between he and Megan as he stood up and walked over to the podium in front of and to one side of the head table. He tried to imagine, without success, Shelley doing the supportive wife bit for him, then – just as everybody fell silent ready for the speeches to begin – realised that she was actually in deep conversation with John Keating. She caught his eye and grinned as Keating turned his attention to the head table. He smiled back at her. Perhaps things were destined to work out eventually, although he knew there was no way he would ever have priority over her career.

Of course, Megan had been like that before she met Alan. No way would any relationship ever interfere with her career aspirations. Yet, look how she had willingly supported Alan in, increasingly, taking over corporate entertaining responsibilities as Dennis wound down his long term of office. He thought back to Megan's comment, in response to Selena's wondering why they hadn't had the house renovated before now. They really had procrastinated because they liked the little apartment which, of course, was not little at all in relative terms. The house was being returned to all its former glory not because they needed the room, but because it was about to re-enact the role it had played more than fifty years ago when Old Denny ran the show during and after the war when the second Angus was in frail health and his son, Danny's grandfather, was fighting in Europe. He smiled as he drew, for the first time, the parallel between Old Denny capitalizing on the demand for McGrath-LaPlante products during World War II and his grandson doing the same thing over the last few years. Funny how he'd never made that observation before...

Shelley suddenly poked him in the ribs and he automatically laughed and clapped along with everybody else.

"I missed the joke," he told her under cover of the applause.

"He was talking about the healthy competition, in the past, between McGraths and LaPlantes, which should never be mistaken for feuding, and that upon following Dennis's example, he had discovered, for himself, that McGraths were, in fact, quite marriageable. Then he asked Megan to bear with him for the moment and kick him in the shins later."

Danny made more of an effort to pay attention as Alan introduced Jayne – the new company president and a true composite of McGraths and LaPlantes who would, as such, bring the best qualities to be found in both families to the job and, for the first time in the company's history, the ability to add two and two and make four. Shelley smiled approval as the applause began again and Danny reflected that just a few years ago, instead of making the quip about her being an accountant, Alan would probably have applied that first time reference, patronisingly, to the fact that Jayne was a woman. Well, not Alan personally, but a man introducing a female CEO

As Jayne began her tribute to her father, Danny found himself wondering why somebody didn't straighten her and Niall out – make them get married... well, of course, that wasn't a hundred per cent necessary these days. Make them adjust their lifestyle, at least, and take some of the heat off Alan and Megan. Why should Jayne spend weekends kayaking and white water rafting while Megan had to create a studio out of a boathouse loft so that the cottage, which was everything she really disliked in a cottage, was always in shape for entertaining business associates. And that, in addition to having to renovate her house around the same purpose. He resolved to talk to Jayne about the situation and to do something about getting his own life in order so that he could handle some of the work himself. Down the road, he knew that Alan's plan was to resign his management position and act as a marketing consultant to the company, giving himself more time for working on his various philanthropic projects and, of course, on marketing Megan. So the rest of them really should start developing some social skills. It would make things a lot easier if he could ever talk Shelley into marrying him... he wasn't asking her to put her career on hold or anything like that – just integrate her life with his a bit more. Maybe her little conversation with old John Keating had shown her that corporate social etiquette wasn't such a big deal. It just needed a little self-restraint – same thing as interviewing someone she didn't much like for a story, if you thought about it. It wasn't as if he was proposing she should hold everything and do a June Cleaver...

Shelley nudged him again as Jayne ended her speech to enthusiastic applause, gave Alan a quick hug, then hugged and kissed her father before making her way back to her seat.

"Where do you keep going to, Danny?" she said. "You certainly aren't doing much of a job of staying on planet Earth."

"Just thinking..." he replied. "Is it that obvious?"

"Well, it's not obvious that you're thinking – more like you're dreaming..."

"I am. A great dream where you and I get married and live happily ever after."

The applause had died down and the words "live happily ever after" sounded loud to his own ears and he fervently hoped they didn't to anybody else. One or two people looked in his direction, but that was probably because they knew he was next to speak. He checked his breast pocket for his notes as Alan mounted the podium again and talked about how his great grandfather had ensured his sons' fitness to follow in his footsteps by having them work in every area of the business before getting a permanent position. When *his* sons grew old enough, the second Angus McGrath had followed his example and the tradition was established. There were a couple of anecdotes from Dennis's student years, then he introduced Danny as the latest McGrath to work through the 'apprenticeship' program before taking his place on the company's management team.

Danny stepped up to the podium. He decided to discard his prepared speech and pick up, instead, where Alan had left off and talk about the value of knowing how to do the jobs of all your employees. He talked about his first summer job at McGrath-LaPlante on the assembly line and how Dennis, who he knew only as the husband of his late father's sister and father of his cousins, had called him into his office and reminisced about beginning his McGrath-LaPlante career in the same spot thirty-five years before. For Danny, the fleeting image of his austere Uncle Dennis shoving packaged condoms into boxes had forced him to see his previously remote uncle as a person. It had been the beginning of a prized relationship with the mentor who had guided his development to becoming a key contributor to the company's recent international growth.

Danny found himself telling anecdotes which he had not, for the life of him, been able to think of when he was originally putting his speech together and, finally, ended saying how pleased he was to have this public opportunity to acknowledge Dennis's impact on his own growth, on that of the strong management team that Dennis had put into place and on every employee in the company.

"Great job, Danny," Alan whispered, pumping his hand as they exchanged places at the podium. He made his way over to shake hands with Dennis accompanied by as much applause as Jayne and Alan had received which really surprised him.

"You were good," whispered Shelley, taking his hand as he settled back in his own seat. "No notes – impressive."

"Nice speech, Danny," said John Keating, reaching over to shake his hand. Others smiled agreement before dividing their attention between Alan who was speaking again and Peter Dailey who was next up. Danny kept Shelley's hand in his own while Alan elaborated on Danny's references to Dennis putting together a strong management team, creating introductions for Peter, and – following him – Bruce Findley, the Sales VP, and Paul Chin who was replacing Jayne as VP Finance. Previous management staff and current and past business associates followed them in making their tributes to Dennis. Finally Dennis, himself, made his farewell speech which he ended by saying that he expected to see all those present gathered together again in a little over two years to celebrate McGrath-LaPlante's centenary and that he had every confidence in the relatively new, young management team's ability to guide the company into its second century and into the new millennium.

"So, do you think we can be married before we celebrate the centenary?" Danny asked Shelley when the applause was over and Alan had thanked everybody for attending and handed the balance of the evening over to the dance band which had been patiently waiting for the speeches to finish.

"Let's go and dance," said Shelley.

They began to make their way to the dance floor, stopping to talk to people at various tables on the way.

"You see, we're getting pretty good at it," Danny said, as they began to dance.

"Dancing?" Shelley asked, puzzled.

"Corporate socializing."

"Come again?"

"You were getting on with old John Keating like a house on fire."

"Well, I wouldn't be that enthusiastic..."

They were interrupted by Byron and Bianca dancing up behind them.

"What are you trying to do, Danny?" asked Byron. "Taking a shot at beating out Alan for the MC job at the centennial party? I never knew you had it in you."

His mother and stepfather danced past them.

"Way to go, Dan," said Hugh.

"You did a good job, Danny," his mother told him.

"Thanks," said Danny. "Is this party changing your image of me as much as it's changing my image of you?" he asked Shelley, swinging her away from his family who all seemed to have converged on the dance floor at once.

"What do you mean?"

"Well, don't you think I've become a bit more exciting than the serious, dependable, diplomatic old Danny who you could always rely on but was never really likely to make it in high society circles?"

"I'd hardly call McGrath-LaPlante high society and what d'you mean about your image of me changing?"

"I discovered you can be a diplomatist, after all."

"You weren't really worried that I was going to tell some old lech that... well, that's what he was, were you?"

"Of course not. I was just afraid you wouldn't come at all and I want you with me. I love you, Shelley. I want to marry you."

"Well, my love," said Shelley, "you're definitely improving – you forgot to mention the loving me bit the last six times you asked me to marry you."

Megan, dancing with Michael, steered her way towards them.

"Well done, Danny. I thought you did a great job – you sort of set the pace for the people after you."

"Thanks, anyway, but I think it was your husband who did

that. I certainly wouldn't have got off to such a good start without his intro and I think it worked for other people, too." He turned to Michael. "Hi, Michael, I'm glad you came. You haven't met Shelley, have you? Shelley, this is my uncle, Michael – he usually steers clear of company functions but, now and again, figures he should do something to earn his dividends."

"Glad to meet you, Michael," said Shelley. "I've heard a lot about you."

"I hope it was more flattering than what we just heard," replied Michael.

"Hey, time to switch partners," said Megan, as the band changed tempo. She grasped her brother's hands and swung him towards her as Shelley was led away by Michael. Megan called after them, "I forgot to tell you to watch what you say, Michael. She's a journalist."

"Shit, Megan," gasped Danny. "Did you have to do that. I was trying to get her to marry me."

"What here? Now?"

"Don't be an idiot. I think she's coming round – I think I'm getting better at it."

"Congratulations, then. Only I think you'd do better to talk to her about in some less public venue. What d'you mean – getting better at it? Do you make a habit of proposing marriage?"

Danny laughed. "Only to Shelley," he said. "Is Justin making out okay?"

Lise's son Justin, who – along with his mother and Michael – was staying with their mother and Hugh for the week, was baby-sitting Steven. Danny had spotted Megan, a couple of times, using her cell phone to check in with him.

"Yeah. I thought it was really sweet of him to want to do it. I thought, when neither of the girls who sit for me, was available tonight – there's a school dance – that I'd have to call the agency we sometimes use... I told you about the woman who got into the booze, didn't I?"

"Alan did," said Danny.

"Well, after that experience, I haven't been too keen to use them again, so I was really pleased when Justin suggested he come over. He's getting tall, don't you think? It's funny, isn't it? I mean, it doesn't seem so long ago that *I* was baby-sitting *him*."

"He's a good kid."

"Actually, Danny, it's reassuring to have a muscular young man there rather than one of the girls. Alan and I never actually say it to each other but, I think, we both worry about Angus or his druggie friends showing up. I told Justin – just as I always tell the girls – not to answer the door unless, well – in the case of the girls – they've arranged for homework help or something like that. And we leave the outside alarm activated, of course."

"How's Michael?" Danny asked, changing the subject.

"That's the first I've seen of him. He was dancing with Mom and we switched partners. Lise and Justin came over to see me on Wednesday – they arrived on Tuesday evening – Mom was taking Michael to a lunch that some old friends of his were going to be at, and Hugh was working at home and gave Lise his car for the day. I'd just discovered my mistake about Kathy and Donna having their school dance tonight – for some reason, I thought it was last week – so Justin sent Lise and me out for lunch so that he could practise baby-sitting..."

She was interrupted by her cousin Jayne.

"Time to change partners – hi, Megan. You know Paul, don't you?"

Danny found himself dancing with Jayne as his sister was whisked away from him by Paul Chin, the new V.P. Finance.

"Jayne," he said, "d'you mind dancing in utter silence for a few minutes? I have to recover from my mile-a-minute sister."

"You're lucky you got me, then, and not *my* mile-a-minute sister who, incidentally, is bearing down on us, let me warn you."

Danny whisked Jayne past his cousin Cindi, who was dancing with her father, in a sudden demonstration of almost professional waltzing.

"I need to get back to Shelley," he explained. "I was in the middle of getting her to marry me when this partner-switching started. That reminds me – you and I need to have a talk–"

"About what?"

"Entertaining..."

"Really? Song and dance? Comedy?"

"Entertaining customers. We don't have to get into it now but I'd like to discuss it with you in the not-too-distant future."

Jayne looked a little puzzled. "Let's do lunch sometime next week, then," she said. "Alan was fantastic, wasn't he? He's so good at that kind of thing..."

"There's Shelley – with Niall. You don't mind if we switch now?"

"Of course not," Jayne shrugged. "Hello, Shelley, how are you managing with old Two-Left-Feet here?"

"Niall's a good dancer compared to some I've known..."

"Well, I'm relieving you of him now. Your wanna-be fiancé, here, wants your company."

They changed partners.

"Danny–"

"Okay, okay..." Danny stopped her. "I'm going to shut up about it for now – wrong venue, I'm told. They're starting a line dance – let's get in there."

· · · · ·

"To be perfectly honest with you, Angus, I don't *know* where we go from here."

Danny heard Alan close the trunk and watched him wait for a car to pass before moving around the car to let himself into the driver's seat.

"We'd better take him to your place," he said, starting the car. "We don't need him getting an asthma attack, on top of everything else, from all the plaster dust at mine. Okay?"

He turned to Danny who was sitting alongside Angus in the back seat. Danny nodded and Alan pulled out from the curb in front of the dingy boarding house where Angus and his friends had been staying. As soon as he had negotiated the narrow strip of road left between the legally and illegally parked cars on the street and reached King Street, he called his doctor on the car phone. The ringing tone sounded on the hands-free microphone. Alan switched off the hands-free mode as the call was answered and picked up the phone.

"I'm really sorry to do this to you, Andy, in the middle of the night, but you won't actually have to get out of bed... No-no – it's not the baby... He's fine – he and Megan are up at the cottage. It's something else... I need you to find me a detox bed... probably before morning, I should think... Megan's young cousin. He's nineteen, so you're not limited to adolescent places, though one of those would be better if it meant he could move straight on into a residential program... Yeah, I understand... Yeah... yes, I know... Well, do whatever you can. We're taking him to my brother-in-law's apartment... Ah-ha... Well, let's hope it doesn't come to that..."

Danny listened as Alan explained the need to go to Danny's because of the renovations at his own house and gave the doctor his car phone number and Danny's number. He looked past Angus and out of the window. They had driven up a pretty deserted University Avenue and were now rounding the Legislature. He realised that they had never really expected to find Angus and consequently had no plans for what they would do if they did. God, what assholes they were – you'd think a couple of successful business strategists would have more brains...

He'd checked out downtown bars several times since Alan and Megan had told him the full story of Angus's visit to their home, sometimes in the company of Shelley or Byron and – when Alan was in town – with him. This evening, he and Alan had attended an industry dinner at the King Eddie and, driving up Church before jogging over to Jarvis to get onto Mount Pleasant, had decided to check out a couple of the gay bars in the area. One was the sleazy kind of place which attracts half-in-the-bag, curious straights after a night on the town and he and Alan, obviously, passed as such people and didn't attract any attention. While being mistaken for voyeurs was not something that exactly made them feel good about themselves, they had to admit that they really had stumbled on a good location for non-discriminating addicts to prostitute themselves for drug money. They still hadn't really expected to find him, though, and certainly hadn't envisioned themselves withdrawing cash from a nearby bank machine to pay off the pimp and his brother who controlled Angus and, then, driving Angus and the pimp to get the kid's possessions from the crumbling basement room where several young people appeared to be living. So, when Angus had asked where they were going from here, he really did have no idea. Alan, obviously, had been thinking faster...

"He's going to phone round right away," Alan said, putting

down the phone, "but probably won't have anything for us for an hour or so because he wants to try and line up something whereby he can move straight into some kind of program from the detox unit and that means picking up a place that somebody else has reneged on. There are waiting lists for this kind of thing. Either that, or what's probably more likely he'll have to get him detoxed then, if the dependency is fairly minimal, put him into one of the long-term, non-medical recovery places."

"Sounds expensive."

"Well, we'll have to get into that later. The other option is to take him into the police station where we made the report on his stealing from us, and regardless of what we told his friends about not putting the police onto them for receiving stolen property, get him charged. The problem there, so I'm told, is that the police aren't likely to be falling over themselves to book him and are quite likely to try to talk us into dropping charges because he's family and they don't need the aggravation. My original idea for getting court ordered treatment, apparently, is little better than a pipe dream at this stage of his criminal career."

"I kind of figured that, but didn't like to disillusion you," said Danny.

"D'you guys have to talk about me as if I wasn't even here?" complained Angus.

"You think you deserve any better?" asked Danny, sharply.

"Not really. But you either don't know, or are forgetting if you do, that you can only get drug rehab treatment as a voluntary patient and, so far, nobody's asked me if it's what I want!"

"You mean you'd rather stay with the scummy lifestyle you've got yourself into?"

"Well, no – not exactly..."

"So you thought we paid a small fortune to your grotty friends with every expectation of coming up with more money to support your sordid drug habit in some more comfortable fashion?"

"Okay, okay. I'll co-operate, but you could just include me in the conversation... It's my life you're talking about."

"We'll get your opinion where it becomes necessary," Alan interrupted him. "Right now, you just damn well co-operate or you'll be detoxing all alone in a police cell – family or no family."

Angus was silent. Alan pulled into the driveway of Danny's apartment building a few minutes later. "Go into the underground parking," Danny told him. "You may as well use my spot. I'm not going to be able to get my car from your place until we've got all this sorted out."

They could hear the phone was ringing as they reached the apartment. Danny quickly unlocked the door and turned off the security system while Alan picked up the phone in the foyer. He motioned Angus to follow him through to the living area.

"Hi. Nick?" he heard Alan say. "I see... No, no... Don't worry, we'll manage... Yes, I will... Listen, I really appreciate your efforts. Thanks... We'll have him there then and thanks again." He hung up the phone and came into the living room. "He's got you a detox bed," he told Angus, "but they can't admit you until ten in the morning, so you'd better tell us what to expect in terms of behaviour from you between now and then."

# MARILYN

The year that Angus spent in drug rehabilitation was, to some extent, a time for renewal for the rest of us, too. I suppose that, while we had become used to the idea of having a missing person in the family, the worry about whether he was alive or dead – healthy or sick, happy or depressed – was always there at the back of our minds. I know that both Danny and Megan felt that they had failed him, despite knowing that neither of them could really have done anything to prevent the situation. Byron suffered no such delusion. He didn't remember his own father and was, therefore, more objective about father/son relationships. Nor, despite wanting at one point to follow in his uncle's footsteps, had he ever developed the hero-worship of Michael that had been encouraged in his older brother and sister throughout their early childhood. No, Byron didn't expect Angus to put his father's feelings ahead of his own because, to his mind, respect was something that was earned not owed and Michael had not earned it from his son. Not that he approved of what Angus had done. He just wasn't about to go on a guilt trip when there was nothing he could have done that would have changed anything. But even Byron worried about his cousin, so that the year-long respite from worrying about Angus came as a welcome relief to him, too.

Alan and Danny never admitted how much they had paid the pimp to free Angus and Alan had insisted on paying, in advance, the treatment centre costs which were – to say the least – substantial. While he never told Michael what he had spent, he convinced him to agree to his taking the financial responsibility on the grounds that he and Megan needed, and could afford, the peace of mind it brought. He told him the whole story – which I didn't learn myself until the evening after they had had Angus admitted to the detox unit of a treatment facility near Guelph – from the theft of Megan's snuff-boxes during Angus's visit, and their subsequent fear of the possibility of Megan or the baby being harmed by his drug-crazed friends, to finding Angus hustling to support a drug habit, in a Church Street bar. He did not spare Michael any details, despite Megan's request otherwise, because, after spending three months worrying about the safety of his wife and child in their own home, he said he was just too angry to apply the usual kid glove treatment that everybody tended to employ when dealing with Michael. None of this happened overnight, of course. Michael wasn't actually told what was going on until Angus was detoxified and admitted into the rehabilitation program, where – to everyone's surprise – he progressed quite quickly and was soon working hard on an academic bridging program to qualify him for a high school graduation certificate and college enrolment when he finished the residential portion of the program.

Alan drove up to the cottage, after he and Danny had taken Angus to Guelph that day. Danny had picked up his car and gone back to his apartment to get some sleep but Alan, after being up all night, was hardly able to sleep at the house with construction people all around him. He had called the office and told them to call him if they needed him then summoned up the energy to drive to Lake Rosseau with his phone turned off so that they couldn't call him. He stayed awake long enough to tell Megan what had happened and slept, from early evening, through to the following morning. Megan, after settling Steven for the night, phoned to tell me the news, find out whether I wanted to call Judith or whether she should and to solicit my opinion of how best to deal with Michael.

Michael, after recovering from Alan's anger and revelations, was quite amenable to tailoring his involvement to the level recommended by the social worker responsible for Angus's treatment program. He stayed either with us or at Megan's on the occasions of his visits, the first time – towards the end of August – bringing Justin, who was eager to see his stepbrother again.

Judith, Lawrence and Stephanie were with us during the earlier part of the month. Stephanie was too young to visit her brother at the centre and it would be some weeks before he became eligible for weekend passes, but her parents felt that coming with them would prevent her from feeling alienated from the situation. Besides Stephanie had never been to Toronto and they could turn the two weeks into a vacation trip to some extent. Hugh, at heart an academic, related well to Lawrence and the two spent much of the time at one or other of the universities. Lawrence had, during his postgraduate days, spent some time at U of T but knew little about York; he and Judith were essentially west coast people. There were, however, many transplanted British Columbians to look up. Judith and I took Stephanie to all the tourist spots, including a day at Niagara Falls, then took her up to Lake Rosseau where we left her to spend a few days with Megan and the baby, who she considered to be her namesake. At nine, she enjoyed being with the baby and was quick to make friends with children at neighbouring cottages. She developed the same fascination for Megan and her art as her brother had done as a child and exhorted promises from her mother that she could stay with Megan again. Plans were made for them to come again at Christmas which, when the time came, we had to juggle with the visit of Michael and Lise. It was fortunate that Megan and Alan had decided to maintain the small separate suite for visitors, when they renovated the house. It provided a self-contained place for Michael and Lise to stay and enabled Megan to keep her promise to Stephanie and have her to stay at the same time without everybody falling over each other. Justin, fortunately, made an overdue visit to his father in Ottawa that Christmas and only had to be accommodated for the night before he flew home with Michael and Lise. Angus spent the Christmas weekend with his mother and sister at our house and the following weekend with his father at Megan's, where they had a small New Year's party to which all the younger generation McGraths were invited, reinforcing the sense of family that Angus was finally developing, while Michael and Lise went to a dinner theatre. Michael had bought the tickets during his previous visit with the idea of the two of them having their own New Year celebration to mark a new beginning for their battered marriage.

Notwithstanding a few remarks about me constantly providing parking places for former in-laws and in-laws-by-marriage, Hugh didn't really mind the constant flow of visitors and it was good to see the long-time breach between Michael and Alan finally beginning to heal. Byron said Alan should have straightened Michael out a long time ago but, then, he was my *un*diplomatic son.

Angus made steady progress with the help of the daily cognitive and behavioural therapy, that formed the basis for the treatment program, and which was designed to assist in gaining control of impulsive behaviour and thinking things through. He was given weekend passes after the first four months and went to the homes of either Danny or Byron at first. Being closer to the downtown area, Megan was a little concerned that the impulse to hop on the subway might prove a little too hard to resist if he stayed at her house. She had Danny and Shelley bring him over to supper on the first weekend to ensure he understood that there were no hard feelings and invited Adam and Karen. Adam was enrolled in the Child and Youth Worker Program at George Brown College and Karen had just started her first year at Ryerson. Since Shelley was a Ryerson graduate, conversation soon focused on the changes in the years since she had been there. This eventually, according to Megan who gave me a rundown on the entire evening the next day, led to discussion on what Angus should do when he had finished his academic upgrading and was ready to apply for college. He had talked about, perhaps, taking a graphic design course. Adam and Karen were both quite knowledgeable on the programs offered at the city colleges, but Megan had suggested he talk to Byron about going to Sheridan. She told me she figured he'd be able to continue with some of his therapy programs then because he could board somewhere recommended by the treatment centre, Guelph being reasonably accessible to Oakville and vice versa. He'd have to have a car, of course, but he had a California driving licence, apparently, so he wouldn't be stuck with the graduated licensing system and the restrictions it imposed on new drivers during the first year. And he'd need a computer...

I wondered where she was planning for the money for all this to come from and hoped that they weren't considering financing college and a car for Angus next year. Personally, I felt that, by the time he finished the year long program in July, my family would have provided enough emotional and, on the part of Megan and Alan, financial assistance and he should go to college in Vancouver or Victoria and live with one or other of his parents. Or, I imagined, the centre would have the contacts to find him some kind of sheltered accommodation there and he could be directed to whatever programs either of those cities provided to support drug rehabilitation. However, all three of my children continued to have Angus at weekends although, apart from the New Year weekend, Megan and Alan didn't have him to stay unless they were going to the cottage.

The first time they took him up there, on a weekend at the beginning of February when Hugh and I were invited, we drove over to Guelph to pick him up. We hadn't seen him since Christmas and I was impressed by how much healthier he was looking now. I hadn't agreed with Megan when she had said he looked like Byron, but now I could see she was right. They were very much alike – in fact, to the point of almost being clones of their respective fathers as they were, over thirty years ago when I first met them.

Driving up to Lake Rosseau, he chatted enthusiastically about everything from the good grades he was getting for his school work to his belated interest in hockey, and the possibility that the Leafs would make the play-offs this year, to the Muskoka winter scenery which he was seeing for the first time. Once there, he built a snowman and tobogganed with little Steven and helped Alan clear the ice near the dock for skating. The next day, he quickly adapted to cross country skiing – he had only ever skied downhill in BC – and we took a picnic lunch and all skied a local trail with Steven in a pack on Alan's back. It was a wonderful weekend for all of us and Angus became quite emotional in thanking Alan and Megan for the both the weekend and for all they were doing for him.

Perhaps I was wrong to have misgivings about Megan's plans for his future.

. . . . .

Around Easter Angus was ready to start making decisions about school and seriously discussed with Byron the possibility of enrolling at Sheridan. Byron's first question was the same as mine – who did he think was going to pay his fees? My youngest may look like his father but he's his mother, all the way, when it comes to practicalities. Our minds were put at ease, however. Judith had kept his registered education savings plan in tact and was going to transfer the money into an account from which tuition fees would be paid, as well as a regular allowance for living expenses, books and equipment, to Angus himself.

"They really are teaching him to think straight, Mom," Byron said when he told me. "He's actually talked the whole thing over with his counsellor and there's apparently a registry of people who can provide room and board – sort of like a halfway house kind of thing and they'll probably be able to find him accommodation so that he can get to school and to the support groups easily. As far as a car goes, Michael's going to get him one as a combined birthday and – I suppose you can call it – a graduation present. It'll be way after his birthday, of course, because he doesn't finish the program until July. He just has to get good grades in this bridging program he's doing and he's all set."

That particular piece of news was overshadowed the next morning by an excited call from Danny. Shelley had, at last, agreed to getting married and they'd set the date for mid-July.

"Danny and Shelley have finally named the day," I told Hugh. "Not for any romantic reason, though – as far as I can make out – but because Shelley has decided that her biological clock is running down."

"What's that supposed to mean?"

"That she wants to have a baby, I suppose."

"How old is she?"

"I'm not really sure. A bit older than Danny, I know, but I don't think, from the biological aspect, the situation's that desperate. I expect she meant it as a joke. Also I'm warned that they don't intend to have the sort of wedding that Megan and Janice both had. It'll be in a small church, that her family practically owns from the sound of things, somewhere over near Fergus."

Hugh's daughter, Janice, had been married three years before to the son of a high profile Member of Parliament in a St. James Cathedral ceremony and was now about to have her first child.

"Well, I suppose it's about time for another wedding," Hugh said. "At least they're giving us time to recover in between. It must be tough on parents when they all happen close together."

I laughed. "Making the adjustment to being a grandparent is harder, believe me. You'll see this time next month! I have a feeling that being a step-grandparent is nothing to the way you're going to feel when Janice has the baby."

Becoming a grandparent had been quite a shock for me. It was funny – all the time Megan was pregnant, it didn't bother me. Then, after Steven was born, I suddenly realised how much of my life had already gone by – that by the time this child graduated from university, I would be an old lady. It was a sobering thought that stayed with me for a long time.

"Hey, don't go turning into an old lady on me, again," said Hugh, knowing exactly what I was thinking. "Have some more coffee." He got up from the breakfast table to pick up the coffee carafe from the counter. We heard a car pull into the driveway.

"That must be Megan already," I said.

Megan was bringing Steven over for me to look after for the weekend. She and Nicki were running a dinner and silent auction that evening to raise funds for the children's mental health centre where Nicki's husband worked and where the girls both volunteered. As I went through the mudroom to the side door, I could hear Megan telling Steven to go and knock on the door so I waited for the scrabbling sounds of Steven, banging on the lower portion of the door with the palms of his hands, before opening it carefully so that he didn't fall in. I picked him up.

"Well, aren't you clever knocking on the door all by yourself."

"Mumm..." he said, waving vaguely in the direction of Megan and the car.

"She can manage," I said, unzipping his jacket, "she doesn't need us. Let's go in and see Grandpa Hugh."

"Doesn't need help – I'll have you know you're talking about a pregnant lady," said Megan struggling in with two large carry-alls full of clothes, diapers, toys and books.

"Really?" I pulled Steven's arms from his sleeves and put him down at the kitchen doorway. "That's wonderful." I went back and took one of the bags from her, hanging the jacket on one of the hooks by the door at the same time. I hugged her with my free arm, kissing her cheek. "When did you find out?"

"This morning. For sure, I mean. I bought one of those pregnancy tests and did it myself."

"What does Alan say?"

"I haven't told him yet. He ended up having to stay in New York for the night and should be getting on a plane just about now, I think..." she said, setting down the carry-all on the kitchen floor. "'Morning, Hugh – don't tell me you guys are still eating breakfast."

Hugh had Steven seated on the counter and was taking off his shoes.

"Hi. It's not a matter us still eating breakfast. We just haven't been able to finish because certain offspring have chosen this morning to keep giving us their good news. Give me Steven's slippers."

Megan took the slippers from the bag I was still holding and took them over to him. Keeping Steven from falling with one hand, Hugh gave her a one-armed hug. "Congratulations, dear." He put Steven's slippers on and fastened them. "Now, who's going to be an airplane?" Steven held his arms out and Hugh swung him horizontally to the ground, standing him upright at the last split second.

"'Gen, gar," the little boy shouted, tugging at Hugh's trousers. Hugh repeated the manoeuvre.

"What's the other good news?" asked Megan.

"Danny called and said he and Shelley are getting married," I told her.

"They are? When? Why hasn't he called me?"

"In that order," said Hugh, "Yes, they are. In July. And he most likely has but you're not there."

"Right!" said Megan. "How does my poor mother manage to live with such a literal person?"

I grinned. "Oh, she survives," I said.

"And very well, too," added Hugh. "And as for you, young man," he said to Steven, "I think that's enough airplanes for today. How about a drink of orange juice? Do you want some coffee, Megan. Your mother's so busy babbling about weddings and babies, she's forgotten all about the cup that's going cold here."

"Thanks. I've got Steven's cup here somewhere," Megan said, searching in one of the bags. "Here we are. Steven, don't pull Grandpa's legs when he's pouring coffee." She went to the fridge and poured some orange juice into the baby's drinking cup and gave it to Hugh who was now sitting down again with Steven on his knee, then sat down herself.

I passed her coffee to her and sat down with my own. "You're not picking Alan up, are you?" I asked her.

"From downtown? No way. He left his car in the Park and Fly because he'd have been really late if he had come home last night. So, what did Danny say exactly?"

"Not much at all really," I replied. "Shelley wants to get married and it'll be in the church where she grew up..."

"Fergus... or somewhere over there. Right?"

"Ah-ha..."

"Don't forget the bit about the biological clock," Hugh prodded me.

"What?" asked Megan.

"Danny said that Shelley finally agreed to marry him because she thinks she shouldn't put motherhood off any longer," I explained. "I imagine it's a joke."

"Sort of," said Megan. "She's been doing an article on women putting off having children until they've established themselves in their careers and then having difficulty in conceiving. She probably said it sort of tongue-in-cheek but with an element of concern, too. I'd better get a move on or they'll be wondering where I am. The Queen E. and Gardiner shouldn't be too bad on a Saturday morning, should they?"

"Not unless there's something on at the Ex and I don't think there is. We're going to be going over to see Janice this afternoon. She needs cheering up a bit."

"It's not much fun at the really feeling ugly part, is it? I'll get the baby seat out of the car before I go. And I brought his wagon over, too. I thought you might want to go for a walk and it's more fun than the stroller."

"For Steven or for us?" asked Hugh.

"All of you. I have to go," Megan finished her coffee and stood up. "Thanks for the coffee. Now, Steven – you be a good boy for Grandma and Grandpa." She stooped as Hugh stood Steven on the floor. "Give Mommy some kisses..." Steven obliged and Megan stood up wiping orange juice from her cheek. "You be good, now, till Daddy and Mommy come to get you tomorrow. Bye, bye." She waved her hand as she moved to the door and Steven imitated her. "I'll phone you later, Mom and I'll keep my cell phone turned on. 'Bye."

· · · · ·

Shelley succeeded in keeping the wedding small although half the village appeared to be gathered outside the church after the service. Her family had been well-known landowners and farmers in the region for several generations and, while the little church could not accommodate more than a few people outside of immediate family and friends, there were many more wanting a glimpse of the bride. The reception was at the Elora Mill and was also restricted to close friends and family.

Michael, Lise and Justin stayed with Hugh and me for the weekend and Angus flew back to BC with them afterwards to spend time with both his parents before driving back across the country, with his father, in the used car Michael had bought for him. They dug out their old camping equipment, which – apart from being used once or twice by Justin more recently – had lain forgotten in the basement storage space since the summer before Angus left home, and took time out for a mini-vacation in the Rockies. They both seemed to enjoy the father-son experience and did not have any major disagreements during the week in each other's company.

Alan and Byron had created a summer job for Angus at McGrath-LaPlante and he stayed at Byron's house for the interim. The job was a combination of the time-consuming fundamental tasks generally associated with summer jobs and delving into the company's archives for material to be used in some of the projects being developed for the centennial celebrations only a year away now. When it came time for school to begin, Byron helped Angus move his possessions, including a computer that McGrath-LaPlante had written off after upgrading their equipment, into the house in Milton where he would board for the year.

Alan's idea, in having Angus work on assembling research material, was to make Angus aware of his place in the history of the company. He admitted, however, that having Angus McGrath, a direct descendent and namesake of one of the company's founders, on the creative team developing centenary communications materials, also had great PR value. The plan had, actually, been formulating in his mind for some time but he said nothing to Angus. The terms of his summer job, and any future part-time work he did for the company, were basically those of any temporary graphic arts student's position. Hugh and I were up at his cottage for the Civic Holiday weekend when he first brought up the subject of Angus working on the company's centennial materials.

We had had supper and I was loading the dishwasher – something I found a little incongruous in a weekend cottage – while Megan was bathing Steven. Hugh and Alan were sitting out on the lawn overlooking the lake. I filled the detergent dispenser and turned on the machine then wiped the kitchen counters. Picking up the glass of wine which I'd brought in with me and then forgotten to drink, I went outside to join the men.

As I sat down, Hugh was saying, "It really all depends on how he handles the combined pressures of school, keeping up with his therapy sessions and working on anything you give him to do in the meantime..."

"The social worker fellow said, basically, the same thing," Alan agreed.

"I take it you're talking about Angus," I said. "Am I allowed in on the conversation or should I make myself scarce..."

"Of course not," said Alan, "I was just taking advantage of having an industrial psychologist in the family. By the way, Hugh, you should give Peter a call sometime – plant management is going to need some help in getting people's heads around all the re-training and new equipment impact."

"No redundancy involved?" Hugh asked.

"No – we'll be hiring soon, in fact. The polyurethane products will be coming on line before the end of the year. It's just the whole automation thing – so many of them find it intimidating and it's best to be a few steps ahead of what they're going to think. Doesn't your wife tell you what goes on at board meetings? We kept her on so that she could feel you out on these issues on the pretence of having a general 'How was your day, sweetheart?' conversation."

"I believe you," I said. "You're famous for having hidden agendas."

"Oh, come on, I'm not that obvious, am I?" Alan said, sounding quite shocked.

"I'm only kidding," I answered, surprised at his reaction.

"But you don't really think that, do you?"

"Not on a personal level – of course not..." I floundered until Hugh came to my rescue.

"I think what Marilyn means," he said, "is that she'd be lying if she said she didn't recognise that you do make very purposeful decisions that are not always exactly overt in nature, but it's not a personal thing and it's only obvious to other people with business acumen. In fact, that's the best way to describe it – acumen. And you are famous for it. And the phenomenal growth and continued independence of McGrath-LaPlante, during the last few years, are due to your having it. And that's a compliment – okay? Your ego back in shape now?"

"That brings us back to the Angus thing," Alan replied, "On a successful hundred years of a family business image level, giving his name – the fifth Angus McGrath – a little play would be impressive, but..."

"But, on the personal level, any number of things could go wrong and you could end up looking like a schmuck."

"Exactly."

"Could one of you tell me what this is about?" I asked.

"Alan wants to give Angus the job of researching the company archives and working under Byron's direction on developing centenary literature on the history of McGrath-LaPlante."

Hugh was interrupted by the flying figure of Steven James LaPlante in his yellow pyjamas. He scrambled up onto his father's lap.

"'Nite, dada," he said, planting a wet kiss on Alan's lips.

"Who taught him to do that?" I asked.

"His mother – who else? By example, no less. You should have seen us – if it had been taped we'd be strong contenders for America's silliest video, believe me. Go kiss Grandma goodnight, Steven."

He lifted Steven down and pointed him in my direction.

By the time Megan came out to take him up to bed, he'd repeated the manoeuvre on both myself and Hugh and was having 'The Gentleman's Ride' on Hugh's knee.

She waited until Hugh had finished the rhyme, then picked him up. "Come on, it's bedtime. Did you kiss everyone good night?"

The little boy's face lit up. "'Nite, mama." he said, giving Megan one of his wet kisses.

"Oh, he's so sweet," I couldn't help saying and he suddenly became bashful, hiding his face in his mother's shoulder.

"I'll be back in a bit," said Megan, turning back towards the cottage. "Are we all ready to go when Denise gets here? I think I'd better change – I look a bit grungy..."

We had all been invited to a party at a neighbouring cottage.

"Well, they said come as we are," said Alan, "So they'll have to put up with the way I look..."

"You always look right, anyway," Megan said, opening the screen door. Steven peeked over her shoulder at us, then hid his face again when I waved.

"I don't know if that was a compliment or an insult," Alan remarked with a grimace.

"I think she's just feeling fat," I said. "Your timing's all off – she'd feel better being pregnant when it wasn't bathing suit weather."

"I'll try to do better next time, mother-in-law. You've really got it in for me tonight. Can you throw me another beer, Hugh, please?"

Hugh reached into the cooler beside him and pulled out two cans of beer. He passed one to me to pass on to Alan. "Let me freshen up your wine, Marilyn," he said, taking an opened bottle of the wine we'd had at supper from the cooler. "You can't go to a party at the Sanderson's stone cold sober – they'll throw you out. I hope they'll make allowances for Megan in her current condition."

"Thanks, dear," I said. "So, can we get back to Alan looking like a schmuck."

"What!" exclaimed Alan. "Oh, that... Yes, my centenary project for Angus." He was silent, then went on, "If things were otherwise, we could go the whole hog and get all sorts of PR out of the fifth Angus McGrath developing a corporate video and brochure – even a book, perhaps – on the history of the company. But the problem with that, of course, is–"

"–all my fault."

"*Your* fault?"

"Well, if *Danny* had been named after his father and grandfather, etc., you wouldn't have the problem..."

"I hadn't really thought of it that way, although you have a point. Seriously, it's the kind of thing that would have got us all kinds of human interest journalism but..."

"It'll get tied to the all those old 'ex-hockey star's kid goes missing' stories," I finished.

"That wouldn't really matter since it has a happy ending – we're talking human interest, not superheroes. Even the drug problems are acceptable today. No, the trouble lies in whether or not he really lived the way he obviously did without telling anyone who he was and, even if he really didn't tell anyone, is somebody going recognise him and come forward with some big exposure story on him? Ordinarily, you just say 'no comment' and survive till you live down that kind of thing, but a hundred-year-old business, continuously run by two families, who've never fallen out, is newsworthy and we don't need some *exposé* on... well, you know what I'm saying. I'm not going to spell it out."

"Well, as we agreed before," said Hugh, "there's no reason why he shouldn't start doing the preliminary research while he's there over the next few weeks. Position him clearly as Byron's assistant and give him the goal of working with Byron to develop the material – it's a long-term project, after all, and Byron's not going to be really getting into it just yet – and then see how he manages school. If you just gradually work into it, there shouldn't be any danger of his feeling pressured and, God forbid, relapsing." Megan came out as he finished speaking. "Hi there, Megan. Is that little sixth-generation-McGrath-cum-fifth-generation-LaPlante asleep finally?"

"What did you call him?" asked Megan, shaking her head.

"It's all right," I said, "these guys figure the Sandersons throw sober persons out of their parties, so they've been busy making sure they're not sober and have reached the point of starting to sound a little silly to say the least."

"Well, they'll have to put up with me not drinking," Megan said, raising the glass of orange juice she was holding in a toast. "Here's to Patrick, then."

"Patrick?" I asked.

"She's calling him Patrick because we seem to be hitting this very fertile period sometime around St. Patrick's Day," explained Alan.

"I see," I said, raising my glass, "to Patrick."

## BYRON

"It's no good," Byron told Bianca, "I'm going to have to tell Alan. I can't wait for the little shit any longer – I'm running out of time."

With his foot, he yanked the door from the garage closed behind him, dropped his case, duffel bag and jacket on the kitchen floor and headed for the fridge. Bianca waited until he'd brought a can of beer into the living room, paced up and down for a bit and flung himself into chair before speaking. Despite his frustration, Byron had to stop and admire her serenity. If he were her, he would have been mad at him for acting like such a boor.

"He didn't show, then? Did you try calling him?"

"Yup. His landlady knows my voice now... I told her to tell him he was off the job."

"You've done your best, Byron, and – like you say – you're running out of time. You're going to have to finish it yourself and tell Alan it was a great idea, but it didn't work out. Can you use any of his work?"

"I'd rather start over, to tell the truth," said Byron, "but I think I'd better work from his layout so we can keep the fiction going..."

"I take it you really meant he's off the job..."

"He's going down the tubes, Bianca. I haven't pressured him. I haven't even complained about him standing me up three times in a row before tonight and countless other times before that. I yelled at him the one time, then felt bad because it turned out that he *had* been working, though not as much as he claimed. But I'm the one who's going to be under pressure now and there's no way I can prevent myself from communicating that – so, when I finally do get hold of him, I damn well intend to tell him what I think of him. It's not going to make any difference now, anyhow – he's well on his way back to where he came from, if you ask me."

"You don't have any proof of that – he could just be goofing off because he's discovered..." Bianca shrugged, "well, that he doesn't have what it takes..."

"He does... have what it takes, I mean. But he's doing drugs again. I know it. Hopefully, he's not back into the hard stuff yet, but here's nothing I can do about it if he is – is there?"

"No – no, there isn't. Have you said anything about it to Danny?"

"That's the whole problem – how do I tell Danny? Even worse, how do I tell Alan? He really wanted Angus to be part of the company in time for the centenary... and look at all the money he spent on him."

"Well, at least it's not like he can't afford it," Bianca said, realistically, "but – yeah, I know, that's not the point. Did you get anything to eat?"

"No – stupid ass that I am, I was all set to take him out for a late supper after we'd finished working. I don't know why we all bothered being so nice to him. I, for one, totally refuse to walk on eggshells any longer."

"I was busy working and forgot to eat myself, so I'll go and make us both some soup and sandwiches," said Bianca, getting up to go to the kitchen. "I bought a herb baguette when I went shopping. Just calm down and think it through before you decide what to do – I'll help you when I've got the food ready." She went through the archway into the kitchen.

Byron put the beer down, leaned back and closed his eyes. How could Angus have screwed up so soon? He'd had his suspicions before, but there could be no doubt about it now. He'd known for some time that the kid was partying more often than he was going to the support groups which he had attended regularly during the first few months of the school year. Things had started to go wrong just before Christmas – right around the time he'd brought a date to the McGrath-LaPlante party at the end of November.

The girl had been pretty spaced out although Angus, himself, appeared to be maintaining his abstinence. Nobody had actually made any comment on the girl's condition but, later, as the school term wound down and Angus was working with him again, Byron had learned more about her. Her name was Caitlyn, Angus told him, and she was the only child of a wealthy insurance broker who didn't believe in keeping her short of money, so she was the sort of girlfriend a student – on the sort of budget he was on – was glad to have around. Byron was surprised that Angus should suddenly consider his budget tight – he had an allowance from his mother and a job, his father had bought him his car, his mother paid for both his tuition fees and his board and Alan had given him a written-off company computer. He didn't say anything, however, asking instead whether she was a design student or doing something else. In reality a second year student, she was in some of the same classes as he was because she'd flunked the courses last year. Sure she did some dope from time to time, Angus had told him. There was nothing wrong with loosening up before a party. Byron didn't disagree. He did wonder, however, if it didn't make things a bit difficult for Angus – being around people with that kind of attitude when he was still working on turning around a drug habit. Angus had replied – and, of course, it was quite true – that he could hardly go to school and expect *not* to encounter people doing drugs and what did Byron think his continued therapy was all about if it wasn't to help him deal with these unavoidable situations. Byron privately thought that coping with being around people who did drugs was one thing, but getting intimately involved with one – and one who had shown up at your company's Christmas Party, on what he was pretty sure was a coke high – was another. He just shrugged, however, and muttered something about guessing Angus knew what he was doing. There was no point in making him think he didn't trust him. Hopefully he would tire of the girl before she did him any real damage. Meantime he suggested Angus bring her over for supper sometime over the holiday season.

Unfortunately he neither tired of her nor brought her over to supper. For Byron, this was ominous. Angus had stayed with Bianca and himself for more than a month last summer and he was sure he had been happy in their company. During the first few months of school, he had come over for supper, at least once a week, and talked about the course and how he was progressing. Byron had given him a couple of jobs that McGrath-LaPlante didn't need too urgently to do as class projects, remembering how – when he and Bianca had taken the program – real projects were always so much more fulfilling than course material, and everything seemed to be working out fine.

At Danny and Shelley's first Christmas dinner, Angus had excused himself early saying that he had turned down an invitation to dinner at Caitlyn's so that he could be with his own family, but had arranged to go there for the evening. Alan, also leaving early with Megan, little Steven and the eight-day-old Patrick John, had taken Byron aside and asked him to see what more he could find out about Caitlyn.

After Christmas, against his own better judgement, Byron had given Angus direction on developing the corporate brochure and video as part of the McGrath-LaPlante centenary communications program. While he had not expected Angus to get beyond the preliminary layout stage over the few working days between Christmas and New Year's, he had expected him to be in the office and working with the various materials he had retrieved from the company archives, back in the summer, and the draft copy which Jim Houston, the advertising manager and department supervisor, had prepared from them. Instead, the day after Byron had given him the project, he had phoned, at mid-morning, to say that he was working on some ideas at home. Looking across the office at all the materials still piled on his cousin's desk, Byron had decided to proceed with caution and said that was fine, but he'd like him to be in with whatever he had the next day because he needed to make sure he was on track. But Angus had not come into the office the next day. Byron had finally caught up with him on New Year's Eve when, presumably, he had gone home to change, the previous two days and three nights appearing to have been a continuous party. Of course he'd been working, Angus had said, sounding quite offended that Byron should think otherwise – he just hadn't been able to make it into the office. Byron had blasted him then and told him to get his priorities in order and meet him in the office the next afternoon. Surprisingly he'd shown up there, apologised and pulled a layout pad from his carry-all. He really had been working on the project and had prepared thumbnails of a themed video storyboard and brochure. It was Byron's turn to apologise.

In the two months since then, Angus had pleaded pressure of school work almost every time Byron had phoned him with requests for updates but had brought the basic design elements of the brochure and a storyboard, with mostly written descriptions of the contents of each frame, into the office one evening on floppy disks. He had remained long enough to add the copy to the brochure pages, print it out and show Byron how the elements fitted into the video version. Byron hadn't seen him since.

"Hey, wake up, Byron – I've called you three times and your soup's getting cold."

Bianca's voice, from the kitchen archway, intruded on his reverie and he sat up startled.

"I'm sorry – I was miles away," he picked up his can of beer and joined her in the kitchen, where she had set out the soup and sandwich supper on the kitchen table. "I just travelled all the way from the company Christmas party to this evening in ten minutes flat," he said, laughing. He sat down, adding, "Not that it's really funny. I think I'm going to call Danny after we've eaten and tell him what's been happening, then tell Alan first thing in the morning or as soon as I can see him – whatever... What do *you* think?"

"Oh, I agree," Bianca said. "I think you should have told them before. The stupid kid doesn't deserve a project that you or I would have given our eye teeth for when we were students. Well... let's be honest – I'd give my eye teeth for it now!"

"You'll get your wish, then. I'll need help, anyway," Byron gave his attention to his soup. Bianca worked freelance. She found it suited her temperament better than the permanent job she had had, when she first graduated, in the design studio where she had done her co-op internship. "That's the real reason I let it go on so long. I knew I could fall back on you to help me with it, but I didn't want to risk anybody thinking I was manipulating the situation so that you *could* work on it."

She nodded. "I understand that. I just hope Keri won't see it as nepotism."

Keri O'Brien was Byron's mechanical artist and, while she appreciated the fact that she was a technician rather than an art director, she had not been slow to comment derisively on the irony of a first year design student getting to work on the creative for such an important project.

"I wouldn't worry about that," Byron said. "Keri's going to be needed and when Keri's needed, Keri's happy. Besides she likes working with you – more than she likes working with me, in fact." He finished his sandwich. "Is there more tea?" he asked.

Bianca looked startled. "Yes," she said. "I made it in the pot. I just didn't pour you any because I thought you were drinking beer." She started to get up.

"I'll get it," said Byron. "I went off the beer almost as soon as I opened it." He got up to get himself a mug and the teapot. "Grabbing a beer when you're frustrated is a pretty stupid male reflex action."

Bianca nodded enthusiastically until he caught her eye and they both grinned. They sat comfortably drinking tea together.

"The one thing I haven't done," remarked Byron, "–and which I should have done – before going to Alan with the story, is to find out about that girl."

"Angus's girl?"

"Yeah – he asked me, at Christmas, to see what I could find out about her."

"He probably just meant how into drugs she is..."

"I would imagine big-time, but I don't really know. I didn't tell him anything about all the partying between Christmas and New Year's. He wasn't in the office much those two weeks, with the new baby and everything, so he didn't know that Angus was only there the one day. I was hoping the whole thing was just a glitch and Angus would get himself back on track and nobody need know. Keri suspected something was going on, but she was busy nursing her own grievances and not talking to me so I didn't even sound off to her as I might otherwise have done. Anyway, Alan hasn't brought up the subject since – other than to ask if we're on schedule..."

"And you've said 'yes'?"

"Well, it's not as if we've really been *behind* schedule..." The telephone rang. "Maybe that's him now." He jumped up and grabbed the kitchen phone. "Hello."

"Byron?" It was Alan. Byron mouthed this information to Bianca while Alan was speaking. "What have you been doing to Angus?"

What the hell was that supposed to mean, thought Byron. He asked, "What d'you mean what have I been doing?"

"He just called here complaining that he could hardly be expected to get passing grades if he had to be at *your* beck and call all the time."

"He what? The nerve of the little bastard..." Byron spluttered.

"What's going on, Byron?" asked Alan. "You sound like you need to take a deep breath – so, do it and tell me what this is all about."

Byron followed his advice and inhaled deeply. "I was going to see you first thing in the morning about this," he said, exhaling slowly. "I didn't want to tell you before because I was hoping he'd work his way through the problem, but – look, I don't know for sure but it looks as if he's got himself in with a bunch of kids who are at school to party rather than to work. If he's struggling, that's the reason why – not anything to do with me! This is the third evening in a row that he's done a no-show on me. I finally told his landlady to give him the message that he was off the job, so I don't know whether he got home, and she told him, or whether he decided to call you, anyway, and whine. It doesn't really matter what the reason was, I've had enough. I'm getting static from Jim, who developed the copy and theme months ago and wants to know what my problem is and I'd appreciate it if you'd let him know that you're my problem with your idiot plans for "the fifth Angus" – shit, Alan, I could understand your position if he were a LaPlante – but he's one of ours! Anyway, it's the beginning of March already and we have to develop advertising materials extending from the corporate brochure design which he's shown up with exactly twice since he was given the job. I decided I'd clear it with you in the morning and clean up what he's done so far, then go over it with Jim for his input and approval and get moving on it."

There was a long pause. The Alan asked almost cautiously, "Got it all off your chest, buddy?"

"Yeah... Sorry, I didn't mean to come on like that. I just couldn't stop once I got started."

"It's okay. You have every right. I just wish you'd told me what was going on earlier. I'm sorry, I should never have put you in such a predicament." Alan paused again, then continued, "He didn't say anything to me about the landlady giving him your message. I don't think he was at home anyway – I thought, well, *hoped* he was maybe using one of the public phones in the foyer at the centre because he did have a Group on Thursday nights. I was being overly positive and convincing myself that the poor kid must have so much to do, he was scarcely able to get to therapy but, now that I think about it, the acoustics sounded more like a bar..."

"I'm sorry, Alan."

"You don't have to be sorry. You did your best – same as the rest of us. I've known things were falling apart ever since he showed up with that girl at the Christmas party – I just didn't want to admit it. Did you ever find out anymore about her?"

"Only that she's not exactly hard up – he led me to believe that that's the main attraction, she does drugs – like we didn't notice, and her father's in insurance – a broker. I don't even know her last name..."

"It's Brewer – he introduced her to Megan and me as Caitlyn Brewer that night."

"You're honoured. He just said, 'This is Caitlyn,' to the rest of us," Byron told him. "So, it's okay to go ahead without him? Sorry to be so blunt, but I was totally pissed off with the little jerk when I finally got home tonight..."

"Yes, talk it over with Jim as soon as you can tomorrow – we'll just use the pressure of schoolwork excuse to explain why. Pull in any other help you might need design-wise. Sorry to have bothered you so late. Go to bed and get your beauty sleep. G'Night."

"'Night, Alan."

Byron hung up the phone. Bianca had cleaned up the kitchen while he'd been talking to Alan. She came up behind him and put her hands on his shoulders. "What's he say?" she asked.

"He sounded pretty upset. I'll tell you in bed – if I can stay awake. I suddenly feel so-o tired." He closed his eyes and let his chin slump onto his chest. "Must be all the tension draining out of me..."

. . . . .

"I spoke to Thelma Graves, the landlady, and she told me that she and her husband have attempted to talk to him several times – just about every time he's actually been home, in fact. Unfortunately, of late, that hasn't been too often."

Alan had called a family conference – at least, that's how he jokingly referred to it when he'd called Byron the day before and asked them over to Sunday dinner. It would be early, he'd said, because Danny and Shelley had tickets for the Toronto Symphony. They had originally intended to eat on King Street, but agreed to come as long as they could leave by seven-thirty. Byron had said, sure – he and Bianca were always available for a free meal as long as it didn't involve eating dead animals and how early was early?

Their mother was helping Megan with the dinner and Shelley and Bianca were chatting and playing with Steven in the family room. Alan settled Byron, Danny and Hugh with drinks in the living room and, after telling Hugh and Danny about Byron's problem with Angus and the events of Thursday evening, was updating them all on what he had found out since.

"I don't know if you remember, but Thelma is approved by the treatment centre – meaning that she and her husband are experienced in dealing with boarders who've been through the rehab program."

"How come she didn't tell Byron when he was calling all the time? About Angus goofing off, I mean," asked Danny.

"Mainly, I guess, because I didn't ask," Byron told him. "I didn't really think it was any of my business – at least, that's what I thought she'd think. She knows who I am from when I helped him move in and knows I'm not a senior member of the family or whatever you want to call people over the age of thirty. For all she knew, I maybe didn't even know about his drug rehab, whatever..."

"There's no system in place for contacting relatives in a relapse situation?"

"Well... it's the same as any kind of recovery..." Alan began, looking to Hugh for a more professional explanation than he obviously felt capable of himself.

"The basis for recovery programs," Hugh responded, "– and this is true whether you're talking drugs, alcohol, emotional, social behaviour, whatever – is that the patient is submitting voluntarily. Relapse prevention and assistance works the same way. The point of his living there is to receive support and encouragement, not for the landlady to be some kind of stoolie for the family."

"The problem is that he's got himself involved with this girl and seems to be completely under her influence," said Alan. Indicating Byron with a nod of the head, he continued. "Angus did talk to Byron a bit about her earlier on and *he* discovered that, supposedly, the primary motivator in the relationship was money – she's got lots of it–"

"Guess that's the first requisite for a coke habit..." Danny put in.

"I imagine..." Alan said, shaking his head. "Anyway, I did a bit of digging through certain insurance types of my acquaintance and got the low-down on a broker, rumoured to be heavily into recreational drugs, named Tim Brewer – her father."

"Bloody kid's sure a winner when it comes to choosing his friends," remarked Danny.

"I said basically the same thing back at Christmas time when he was still talking to me," said Byron, "I said it to him, I mean. His response was – what did I think the point of his therapy was if it wasn't to help him deal with being around these people without getting into the stuff himself? Now, it seems he's not even going to the Groups..."

"I finally caught him in this afternoon," Alan told them. "Thelma had told me he tended to come home on Sunday afternoons. She figures he probably gets bored and restless – she said, she spotted him for ADHD right off the bat – she figures he gets restless at that point of the weekend with all his friends sleeping off Saturday night. So I took her advice, phoned this afternoon and caught him while he was in. I told him that Byron, Jim and I had sorted out the brochure and video problem and not to worry about it–" he broke off as he caught sight of the rather aggressive questioning expression Byron could not keep off his face "–okay, Byron, I know it's not as simple as that, but I wasn't about to get his back up when I trying to get him to talk to me."

"Yeah, I guess..."

"So I told him that we'd all like him to come over since we were having a family dinner today – bring Caitlyn if he wanted to..." Nobody commented. "He basically gave me the brush off, so I said that I had been worried about him after he called the other night and would really like to talk over the school thing – was he into coming over later this evening?"

"And was he?" asked Hugh.

"He claimed to have work to do, but thought he might make it – he'd have to see how it went. So I won't hold my breath, but I'll have to throw you all out early because he's less likely to drive on by if the driveway's *not* full of cars."

"Shelley and I came on the subway, actually," said Danny. "We ride the rocket all the time now that we're downtown – it's easier." They had bought a huge, expensive townhouse near Casa Loma, after their marriage, which Byron found amusing given Danny's previous disdain for materialism.

"You're leaving anyway," Alan pointed out. "You don't mind, do you, Hugh? Byron? I don't mean *early* early. If he does come it won't be till, probably, close to ten – he likes to look unconventional."

"We'll be gone by then anyway," said Hugh. "I've got a lecture in the morning and I'm getting old enough to need a good night's sleep if I want to look good, which I'm still vain enough to want to do."

They all chuckled.

"Byron?"

"I've got a heavy week coming up so I wasn't intending to be up late either. By the way, Bianca's coming into the office after Tuesday to work on the storyboard – she's tied up with something Monday and Tuesday. We should have everything ready to present to you early next week."

"That's good. I appreciate it. Will Bianca co-ordinate the production then?"

"Yeah. She's much more experienced than I am with video production."

"Sounds good."

"So, to get back to the number one problem..." said Danny. "*What* is the strategy with Angus?"

"That's what we're here to decide," answered Alan.

"I don't think there's much we *can* do, unless he wants us to," said Hugh.

"That's why I want to get him alone."

"Evaluate the situation?"

"I guess... Do you have any suggestions, Hugh?"

"You can only feel things out as you go along. I wish I could be of more use, but with a relationship as removed as his cousins' stepfather, I don't think I'm exactly positioned to win his confidence. You may all feel pretty discouraged right at the moment but, with all the effort you've put in over the years, you do – each of you – have some chance of reaching him before he regresses all the way back to where he was two years ago. But there's no right way or wrong way to go about it. The one thing you'll have to try to do is stay right away from anything that'll put him on a guilt trip."

Alan nodded. "That's probably why–"

"–it's best you talk to him first? Yes. You're least likely to put him on a guilt trip. Oh, I know that it was you who footed the bill for his treatment, but I don't think money means much to Angus – other than as a means to an end, I mean. He's not about to feel bad about letting you down – he knows as well as you and I that you were mainly concerned with getting him out of the company he was in and removing the menace that it was constituting to your own life."

"That's the way I see it, too," agreed Alan. "He just perceives me as Megan's husband – not someone whose feelings he need worry about, whereas, Danny and Byron have both worked on an emotional level with him and could end up, at this stage of the game, making him feel guilty enough to feel that there's no more to lose so he may as well give up working at it. I can almost see his telephone call as being a cry for help and, despite the excuses this afternoon, he may just show up this evening."

"I suspect you're right," Hugh said. "About the cry for help. He may just be feeling overwhelmed by now, though, so I wouldn't count on getting him one-on-one that easily..."

· · · · ·

As it turned out, Hugh was wrong in thinking that Angus wouldn't show. The next morning, at the office, Byron had only just organized his day and directed Keri, on hers, when Alan called and asked if he had twenty minutes or so to spare. He didn't but went over to the executive suite anyway, taking a very early draft of the brochure with him so that, for anybody noticing, it would look as if that's what he was going to discuss with the Director of Marketing.

The executive secretary, Mary – she was one of the vanishing breed of career secretaries who would never dream of calling themselves PAs or executive assistants – was bustling about with coffee in a pot on a tray, with cups and cream and sugar, when he tapped on the open door of Alan's office and stepped inside.

"Ah – here's Byron now, Mr. LaPlante," she said, nodding at Byron. "Good morning, Byron, how are you?"

"I'm fine, Mary. How are you? Hoping Spring will eventually arrive, like the rest of us, I guess?"

Mary shook her head. "You can say that again," she agreed.

"That's great, Mary. Thanks," Alan said.

"Don't let him sit there talking till the coffee gets cold, Byron," she said, as she left, closing the door behind her.

Alan rolled his eyes. "Sorry," he said. "One day she'll retire and we'll be able to have coffee in mugs up here like everyone else." He waved in the direction of one of the chairs in front of his desk. "Sit down and help yourself... and try to drink enough for two so as not to upset her. I'm already swimming in the stuff and just can't handle another one. Megan and I drank a whole pot of it at breakfast and didn't even notice till we'd finished. Angus *did* show up last night, after all, just as we were about to go to bed and Megan was asleep before he left, so she needed filling in."

"He did?" Byron exclaimed, pouring some coffee into one of the cups and sitting down.

"About eleven. We couldn't believe him showing up at that time. Megan had just fed the baby and put him to bed and was wondering if he'd sleep through so that she could, too – we take it in turns if he needs a bottle in the night and it was her turn last night. I guess he must have done or, knowing her, she'd have woken me up then to find out what happened–"

"He had the nerve to ring the doorbell at eleven o'clock?"

"Yeah – said he hadn't realised the time until he was halfway here and figured I wouldn't mind. Hugh would probably interpret that as him testing me – right?"

"Probably. Have you talked to him?"

"Hugh? No," Alan shook his head. "I wanted to talk to you first – well, first after Megan – because I felt I owed it to you after putting you in such an awkward position. I realise, now, that it was not one of my more intelligent ideas – I was putting pressure on him, despite giving him the opportunity – as I saw it – to contribute to the company, repay his debt because, after all, I might have made the investment in his rehab, but the money ultimately came from McGrath-LaPlante."

"That's a little deep, Alan," said Byron. "I mean, I'd find it difficult to come up with that interpretation and I'm older, have completed a fair number of post-secondary education programs, achieve reasonably well in my job and didn't have my intellectual development arrested by drug use..."

"Okay, okay, I suppose so, but aside from all that, I took the liberty of making some commitments in your name."

"Oh, thanks..."

"Nothing involved. Anyway, getting back to him showing up on the doorstep, Megan excused herself after having him creep in and see the children and went to bed."

Byron didn't think Angus was terribly interested in his once removed cousins or whatever you called the relationship, but could imagine Megan going to great lengths to make him feel like one of the family even if it was eleven o'clock at night.

"Megan's worse than the rest of us at making allowances for him," he said.

"I know. It did seem to deflate the sense of challenging us that I think was the real reason for his turning up so late, though. I asked him if he wanted a cup of tea or coffee, but refrained from offering anything alcoholic. So, naturally, he asked for a beer and I said I was right out, after having had company, which wasn't true but there was no way I was having him treat the whole thing like relaxing with a buddy at the end of the day. I think he got the point – at least, he didn't ask for anything else. I asked him about the problems he had said he was having with his school workload and he said he'd just panicked a bit because he had let himself get into the position of having several overdue assignments and that he was getting himself sorted out now."

Byron poured himself some more coffee and sipped it while Alan went on to tell him that, while Angus had maintained his 'everything's cool' act for some time, he had eventually let some of the cracks show and Alan had got him to volunteer the information that he'd let his therapy groups slide because of his involvement with Caitlyn. He realised that this had been stupid but you hardly impress a girl by telling her you need the support of group therapy to prevent yourself from getting too influenced by her lifestyle. Alan asked him why it was so important to impress her anyway and he said because he cared about her, so Alan pointed out that he'd told Byron that he was only interested in her money. He said that he only told him that because he wanted to look cool and Alan had said he'd do better to stop working on this cool image and get real.

"So the end result," Alan finished, "is that he says he's not doing drugs – beyond  derivatives of the marijuana plant, that is, but the girl and, by the sound of things, most of her family and friends can't operate without a few daily snorts of the white stuff. At least it doesn't seem to be worse than that. Sick isn't it?"

"Yup. Did you tell him that he can hardly expect to hang out in that environment and not expect to end up the same way which, for him, would present one short step back to where he was when you and Danny rescued him."

"Not quite so bluntly. I asked him if he'd ever seriously talked to Caitlyn about drug use and his own experience."

"Had he?"

"No, it wouldn't have looked cool."

"Oh," Byron said, sighing sardonically. "Right..."

"I suggested he'd be better to forget about being cool and tell her that he'd been in drug rehab and needed to get back into his Groups. If she was worth having as a friend at all, she'd respect him for it and if she laughed at him – which is what seems to worry him most – then he should try analysing what exactly it is that's so attractive about her because whatever it is can't be worth throwing over all his own hard work for. I suggested that he was at a cross-roads and that was the real reason he had phoned me and the real reason he was here tonight. If he hadn't been, he would hardly have come complaining to me about his cousin overworking him when he knew I'd find out it just wasn't so. He agreed – about being at a cross-roads, I mean. He knows that he's going to have to make some changes if he wants to carry on with the design course and work here. He apparently likes and wants to work with you, which may be hard for you to believe, but he seems to think he's telling the truth..."

"And this is where we get to the commitments?" Byron asked.

"Yes. I told him that you were bringing Bianca in to work on the corporate video, so it wasn't as if the entire workload that he was supposed to have shared would be dumped on you..."

"So, I'd have time to help him out with some direction on the overdue assignments?"

"Exactly," said Alan. "You will, won't you?"

"I suppose so – as long as he's for real and it's not all just an elaborate charade to prevent himself from failing..."

"No, it's not and to safeguard that, I told him that, after the way he'd treated you, there's no way you'd want anything to do with him unless he undertook to get back into group therapy. He wavered a bit about going to the one tonight – the Groups he's in are Mondays and Thursdays – but I convinced him that they'd probably all had relapses at one point or another and nobody was going to think any the less of him for it. The other boarder at Thelma's, his name's Craig – was originally car-pooling with him on Monday evenings, according to Thelma, so I told him to talk to Craig this morning about getting that arrangement together again. That way, we can always check that he is really going. For now, he's to tell Caitlyn that he needs some space to be on his own and get his work caught up, then to get some advice on how best to deal with her from the other people in both tonight's Group, and Thursday's, before actually telling her the truth. I suggested he appeal to Caitlyn's sense of fair play – assuming she has one, of course – by explaining that he doesn't want to upset his mother by failing which, I think, is basically true. And, the final part of the deal was that he was to call you and apologise for being a jerk. Then, hopefully – I didn't really make it a commitment, you'd ask him about school and he'd have his opening to ask for your help." Alan paused, then said, "So what do you think?"

Byron did not really have the same faith in Angus's genuineness as his brother-in-law, but slowly nodded in agreement. "Well, you got him to open up, anyway," he replied. "At least we know for certain, now, that we're competing for his respect and affection with a bunch of cokeheads..."

"Don't be so cynical – it doesn't become you."

"God, you sound like my mother – she was always saying that to me when I was a hostile teenager–"

"I guess that's where I got it from," Alan grinned. "It doesn't sound like something out of my own vocabulary."

"No, it doesn't – yours is less poetic and more MBA," Byron said, getting to his feet and starting towards the door.

"Ouch."

"You deserved it. Well, I'll wait for his call. Meantime, I have work to do, so I'll leave you to your executive lifestyle – coffee in cups and all! See you."

# ANGUS

The bone-chilling sound of metal scraping against metal at high speed continued to echo in his ears as he struggled to wake from the recurrent nightmare. Finally awake he shivered in the sweat-drenched bedclothes as he rolled over onto his back from the semi-foetal position he'd been sleeping in. He pushed aside the duvet and exercised the numb right leg – the one that had been smashed in the accident – the way the physiotherapist had shown him until he could feel it again. He continued to exercise the leg while he fought off the despair that threatened to engulf him, then rose from the bed and slipped his feet into his slippers. First tentatively testing the strength of the leg, he stood up, picked up the cane and walked, shakily, into the adjoining bathroom where he drank several glasses of water and shrugged out of the wet pyjamas, sponged himself down and put on his bathrobe.

Moving as quietly as he could in his still shaky state, Angus went through the still dark house to the kitchen. He watched dawn breaking through the east-facing kitchen window while he made a half pot of coffee, then half-filled a large mug and let himself out onto the patio. It was warmer out here than in the air-conditioned house but not yet heat-wave humid, although he knew it wouldn't be long before it was. He walked down the garden to the wrought iron table and chairs that were surrounded by Marilyn's rose garden and sat down to drink the coffee. Gradually either the coffee, the scent of the roses or just the outside air – he wasn't sure which – helped him to calm down and he stopped debating on whether or not to wake Marilyn and ask for a tranquilliser. He leaned back in the cushioned chair and breathed deeply.

Angus had been living at Marilyn's and Hugh's house since he'd been released from hospital in May with a strapped leg and crutches. At the time he had felt only bitter resentment and spent a lot of time visualizing the family conference that they must have had that would have included his parents who had both flown to Toronto as soon as they got word of the accident. He would imagine them figuring out who would get stuck this time with the once-again detoxed Angus who couldn't be shoved back into the drug abuse treatment centre again because of his physical injuries and needed somebody to take charge of his medication while his suicidal thinking persisted. He pictured Byron saying yes; he probably was the closest to his cousin, but he and Bianca were career people and, even if Bianca did work mostly at home, you couldn't expect her to play nurse to him. Then Shelley would have pointed out how entirely unsuitable their house was for someone who would be an invalid all summer and, anyway, she had an assignment from *Macleans* and would be up to her eyes in work and no; her nanny was employed to look after the baby, not a full grown man with a broken leg, internal injuries and a drug habit. And Megan – yes, Megan would have found a way to cope. She could take him up to the cottage where everything was on one level and, therefore, ideal for someone on crutches, and hire a nurse – there were probably lots of new graduates around who'd jump at the chance to spend the summer there. But her husband most likely had put his foot down fast. He'd finally had Jim Houston take over from him as Marketing and Communications Director and had succeeded his uncle as Chairman of the Board, getting himself out of being at McGrath-LaPlante full time – and this summer was reserved for family time. Yeah, he'd say some goofy yuppie thing like that, and would no way cancel his plans to cart their two little kids off to Australia for the first half of the summer.

His parents, of course, would be out of the running – it wasn't wise to take him to BC, much better to keep him under the care of the doctor at Trafalgar who had patched him up and... well, there was always the drug problem. No, much better for him to stay in Ontario where his friends were – well, the ones that hadn't been killed in the accident, of course. Then Marilyn, looking apologetically at Hugh, would finally speak up and say – well, they were right in Oakville, near the hospital and not a long drive to Guelph – yes, he should attend those therapy groups to keep motivated – and they had the big ensuite spare bedroom, a split-level house – so not too many stairs to worry about and they knew of a nurse who would be available to stay with him when neither she nor Hugh could be around.

The nurse had turned out to be not a bad old girl. Her name was Wendy and she had worked as a private nurse for most of her working life – most recently looking after an Alzheimer's patient during the day when his wife was working but he had finally had to be institutionalized. Discovering that Angus was Michael McGrath's son had made her day and she was full of questions about his father whose career she had followed as a teenager. She was glad to hear that he was not one of the players involved in the Eagleson rip-off because she wouldn't like to think of him living in penury with next to no pension and hardly able to walk. Angus had assured her that his father's financial affairs were quite in order and it was shoulder injuries that had ended his hockey career, so he could walk fine. She was eager to talk about her memories of the Toronto Maple Leafs in the sixties and Angus was constantly having to remind her that he hadn't been born until after his father was traded to Edmonton. When Megan – back from Australia – brought her two little boys over to visit him, she was bombarded with questions about her memories of her uncle as a Maple Leaf. Megan had talked about how popular being Michael McGrath's niece and nephew had made her and Danny, as young children, and how he'd lost it after her father's death in a car accident. It was after this conversation, to which he hadn't really been paying much attention because Steven and Patrick were busy inventing a game which involved his having to hook them and reel them in with the cane, to which he had graduated the week before, that he understood the *déjà vu* that his car accident must have created for the family. It was also then that the nightmares had started...

"Want some more coffee?"

He looked up startled to see Hugh with a mug in one hand and the coffee carafe in the other. He sat down opposite Angus at the table and poured coffee into the mug. Angus passed his own mug over.

"Thanks," he said.

"Wake up with another nightmare?" asked Hugh.

"Yes. I didn't wake you guys up did I? I was trying to keep quiet, but–"

"–it's difficult when you're shaking and have a gimpy leg anyway."

"Right."

"Don't worry about it – I think I was just about due to wake up and Marilyn's still sleeping. Are you okay now?"

"Yeah," Angus said and sipped his coffee. "Hugh?"

"Yes?"

"D'you think the nightmares are caused by a guilty conscience?"

"Well, to be blunt – taking your chequered career into consideration, I wouldn't be at all surprised. Why do you ask?"

"Because I feel like such a jerk, Hugh." He paused, trying to pull his thoughts together. "You see, at first – after the accident, I mean – I just felt depressed... Once all the toxins were out, that is." He grinned sheepishly. "I was screaming inside about the injustice of-of them all dying and leaving me stuck with the police and all the questions and their families wondering why their kids had died and I survived and-and... why couldn't I have died, too? You know?"

Hugh nodded.

"Then I felt so shitty about there being nowhere for me to go. I thought Alan would have come up with the money to dump me in some kind of nursing home until I could walk again, but you and Marilyn took me in instead..."

"Would you have preferred to go to a nursing home?"

"No, that's not what I meant. It wasn't fair on you – you're not even my relatives. Why should you be stuck with me? It makes me feel guilty."

"And you wouldn't feel guilty about Alan paying for nursing home care?"

"That's different – his money comes out of McGrath-LaPlante and I'm a McGrath. If my father hadn't been a hockey player, maybe he'd have made all the money out of McGrath-LaPlante instead of Alan." Hugh didn't comment, but Angus could tell he didn't think it was a very healthy way to look at things. "You remember when Megan came over? After they got back from Australia – not the first time on the weekend... later when she came, with the kids, just to see me." Hugh nodded. "Wendy was still here then and she started bugging Meg about my father and the old Maple Leaf days and that..."

"And?"

"Megan was explaining that she was only very young and it was mostly Danny who was taken to games, anyway, because he was a boy. Then she told her about her father – my uncle, my Uncle *Angus* – getting killed in a car accident and my father being traumatised or depressed, or both – who knows, since nobody recognised such things then; especially not in hockey – and being forced to play and playing badly and getting traded and... Hugh, I didn't know any of that. I mean, I suppose I knew sort of way back in my subconscious somewhere but I didn't consciously know – d'you know what I mean?"

"I think so. You never really made the connection between your uncle in the car accident and your own accident and your both being named Angus and history repeating itself, except he didn't have cocaine and heroin in his blood stream – just a lot of alcohol."

"You mean it wasn't the same?"

"Just pointing out the difference – he was driving, you weren't – luckily, because if you had been you'd be up on manslaughter charges. Your accident probably did bring back the memories of your uncle's death for your father and for Marilyn and, to some extent, for Danny and Megan, but the last thing any of them would want is for you to get on a guilt trip over it. They just want you to get well."

"It's not just the accidents, though. Meg told Wendy that my father had clinical depression for years after his brother died. Did he?"

"I didn't know him then, Angus, but I know he's had a lot of depression so I would think it quite likely. And Megan's right, it wasn't something that was supposed to happen to macho hockey players – in fact, it wasn't something anybody, particularly men, owned up to much back then."

"Why did I never know? I must have spent half my childhood thinking my father didn't like me when actually he was depressed and it was nothing to do with me. Well, I imagine my asthma and allergies and stuff probably depressed him, but that was him dealing with them – not me, myself. I'm not making sense..."

"I know what you mean. Children are self-absorbed – it's quite normal for them to blame themselves for the things that go wrong in their parents lives. Usually, as they get older they're able to put things into perspective – as you just said, the way your father reacted to your childhood health issues was his problem, not yours."

"Self-absorption – they carry on about that when you're in rehab. I guess that's why it never really worked – I never figured out what it really meant till now. Dumb, eh?"

"No," Hugh shook his head. "There are people who live their whole lives so totally self-absorbed they never notice that other people have lives, too."

"Is that how people see me?"

"Yes," Hugh said levelly. "Let's be clear on this – I'm talking to you as a psychologist, not your cousins' mother's husband. Okay?"

"Okay," Angus nodded. He'd only really come to know Hugh during the last few weeks. He remembered him vaguely at Megan's wedding years ago and had stayed with him and Marilyn a few times in more recent years, but he'd never really noticed him much. He had known he was some kind of psychologist – maybe subconsciously he'd kept his distance because of that – and taught courses at York University. He also reminded Angus, for some reason, of his stepfather – possibly another reason for keeping him at arm's length. Hugh had been home quite a lot since Angus had been staying in his house and had turned out to be an okay guy after all. He never probed but was always there when Angus felt like he wanted someone to talk to and Angus surprised himself by telling him all kinds of things he'd never have believed he'd find himself talking about. He was the only person he'd told about the nightmares – except for the guys in Group, but that was different – and here he was talking about feeling guilty when he'd never expected to feel guilty about anything, let alone tell someone about it!

"It's self-absorption, you see, that lays you open to drug addiction, alcoholism... kills relationships and hurts the people who count. And you've done a lot of that, Angus. To be fair, it's not entirely your own fault – you didn't ask to be born with a hyperactivity and attention deficit problem for which treatment was in its infancy. The feelings of guilt, that are causing the nightmares, indicate that you recognize that you're finally seeing beyond yourself – you can't feel guilty if you have no perception of other people's hurt."

"Yup. You might see it as a breakthrough but I'm not so sure that self-absorption isn't preferable to the bloody nightmares..."

"They'll pass. Think of the positive effects – they're a great lesson in consequences for a start!"

"Oh great! The next time I feel like getting myself smashed up, I remind myself of the guilt trip it'll put me on...?"

"No, the next time you do something you shouldn't or don't do something you should, you think about who else it'll effect..."

"... and I might achieve sainthood yet!"

"You might at that!" Hugh said, rising. "Feel like getting some breakfast?"

. . . . .

Surprisingly Byron had agreed with Angus that it would be better for him to work permanently at McGrath-LaPlante rather than repeat his final year at Sheridan for the second time. Back in April, before the accident, the reorganisation of the department and the promotion of Byron to Advertising and Communications Manager had been made with a view to Angus's part-time and summer position becoming permanent, so it would have meant hiring another graphic designer if he went back to school. Angus had expected that Byron would prefer to take this particular route since he had never made any secret of the fact that his cousin's unreliability was a source of constant irritation and annoyance to him. Perhaps his agreement meant only that he expected Angus to screw up so that he'd be justified in dumping him for good!

While he was still in hospital, Hugh and Byron had gone over to Thelma's and picked up his computer, along with the rest of his belongings and his car, and set it up in his new room. Now that he had the doctor's okay, Hugh or Marilyn were driving him to the office once or twice a week. He found the combination of getting direction, input and materials for a project at the office and developing it at home, preferable to being in the office all the time and understood why Bianca liked working freelance. Maybe that's what he'd do eventually – when he had a home, of course. He'd need more in his portfolio than the packages and product information and education leaflets he'd designed so far, though.

Today, he had worked in the office and was staying for the plant versus office baseball game which was taking place this evening. There was a barbecue afterwards and he had a ride back to Oakville lined up with David Richardson, from Quality Control, who lived in Burlington. It was the first time he'd attended the company baseball game since the first summer he'd worked at McGrath-LaPlante – when he'd even come off the bench to pinch hit. Last year he'd been in BC visiting his parents and, the year before, in residential treatment again. Except for the game that first year, the centenary dinner and the Christmas party the year before that, he'd found some excuse to avoid going to every one of the company's social events. He couldn't really have said why... well, sure, he'd told himself that he wasn't into boring company things and had told his cousins that he couldn't forego a therapy group or a school thing and his friends that he had nothing lined up for the evening... In reality, he had a confidence problem. See, he was okay when he'd come through treatment and was attending groups and he was damn right okay if he'd smoked some dope or done some drugs. It was the in-between times that he had a problem – like, he didn't have the confidence to take his place as a McGrath. That was it really, wasn't it? It was a vicious circle – he'd feel good about himself for a bit, then decide this wasn't how he wanted to live his life and fight the need for support in keeping clean. And, sooner or later, he'd be into the drugs again. Maybe finishing with school would help – if he could make new friends who weren't into drugs...

"So where are you?"

"What?"

Keri O'Brien was standing beside him. "I've asked you three times if you're nearly finished," she said, "but God knows where you were. Obviously not here."

"Sorry, I was thinking..." Angus said.

"About?"

"About me. Nothing exciting."

"So – you nearly ready?" Keri asked. "I'm just shutting down, and I'll wait for you if you are."

"I'm not going to be able to get this finished tonight," he replied, looking up from his computer screen where he had been updating the company's website, "so if you don't mind waiting..."

"That's why I was asking," Keri looked at his computer screen. "When're you going to teach me HTML, then?"

"You could teach yourself..."

"I could, but it's a question of time." Keri went back to her own desk and turned off her computer. "If you could show me the basics..."

"Won't Byron send you on a course?"

"He might if *you'd* just get a move on with your convalescence–"

"I didn't exactly smash my leg up on purpose, you know."

"I'm only kidding. When *do* you think you'll be in full time?"

"The main problem's driving," Angus told her. "You can't drive without your right leg. Well, I suppose you could learn... but it's not like it's going to be forever. I was thinking of making a deal with Dave – Dave Richardson. I'm getting a lift from him tonight. I have a doctor's appointment tomorrow – so, if he says it's okay and Dave agrees to pick me up, I might be in everyday as early as next week."

"Sounds good," said Keri. "I think we're the only ones left in the building, so shut it down and let's get out of here."

Angus closed the open files and shut down the computer. He stood up, picked up the cane which was wedged into the corner formed by the desk and the wall and followed Keri out of the office and along the passage.

"You going to go on living at Byron's mother's place, then?" asked Keri, adjusting her usual loping walk to his slower pace.

"Well, for the time being – so long as they don't decide to kick me out. I'll be able to pay board once I start working properly then I won't feel like such a mooch, but I won't be able to get a place of my own for a bit. I'm not one of the rich McGraths, you know. I have to take what I can get."

"Maybe, though you don't exactly give the appearance of being destitute," Keri said, pointedly. "Surely you'll be getting paid a proper salary now – why wouldn't you find someone to share with nearer the office?"

Angus laughed. "It's all too complicated to explain... Perhaps I will one day."

"Explain or find somebody to share with?"

"Maybe both, you never know. Looks like the game's started."

They'd arrived at the side door of the building, used by most employees coming in from the parking lot. The baseball diamond was on the other side of the parking lot, adjacent to the far end of the plant. The bleachers and the nearby wooden picnic tables were full. Some people had brought folding chairs to sit on, while others sat on blankets on the grass.

"I hope somebody saved you a seat," said Keri, as they made their way across the parking lot. "You can hardly sit on the ground..."

"I could, but I doubt I'd ever be able to get up again. It's okay, Byron had Angie set up chairs for the art department, so we just have to find them. Angelo – I had a friend called Angelo, once."

"Back in BC?" asked Keri.

"Yeah, we hitched across the country..."

"Wow, cool. Did he go back?"

"Angie? I don't know. I guess, we lost touch." He thought of the weeks he'd spent strung out on heroin with Angie and Scott after they'd arrived in Toronto and hooked up with Scott's brother. God, what a jerk *he* was – how could anyone pimp the services of his own kid brother? "Another life – I've had several."

"And you're not about to tell me about them?" Keri said, not expecting an answer. "There they are, over there. Did you know Bianca was coming?"

"No. She's okay – I don't know why you don't like her."

"Who says I don't?"

"Nobody. I just got that impression."

"God, I hope everybody else doesn't–"

"No, they don't. They think you like her."

"It's not that I *dis*like her – it's just that she's always there to save the day whenever I – or you, too, for that matter – screw up. Doesn't it piss *you* off, too?"

It did, but Angus was not about to admit it to Keri. Bianca was Byron's partner, companion or whatever the current term was when people decided to be a couple but not to marry. She was family, whichever way you looked at it, and you didn't knock the family in front of the employees. Bianca, herself, saved him from having to reply.

"Hey, Angus. How are you? There's a seat for you here and a beer. Hi, Keri. We kept a seat for you, too. Are you okay, Angus."

Angus sat down heavily, suddenly feeling very fatigued.

"I'll be all right in a minute. It's what happens when you're out of shape and walk across a parking lot in the heat. I'll pass on the beer for now..."

Byron, dressed to play, stood up. "I'll get you some water. There's a case over by the dugout – they expected that was the only place it would be wanted. Just relax – you're white as a sheet."

Keri was looking quite miserable. "I'm sorry, Angus," she said. "I wasn't thinking... I should have got my car and driven you over."

"It's okay, Keri. I'm all right. I have to put up with being a ninety pound weakling for a while – it comes with the territory. Have a beer and watch the game."

"I think you're a bit more than ninety pounds. Like sixty, seventy pounds more," scoffed Bianca.

"I was speaking figuratively," Angus replied. He was actually feeling invigorated now that the weakness had passed. Almost like an adrenaline rush...

Byron came back with the water.

"You look better already," he said, handing Angus the bottle. "I'm due up to bat sixth if everybody gets on base, so I'd better get back over there. Take it easy."

"Thanks, man. Good luck."

"Show them how the pro's play, Byron," said Bianca.

"Go give them a run for their money, bossman," Keri shouted after him. "Gotta bring honour to the Art Department." She turned to the summer student, Angie. "Aren't you supposed to be in the dugout, Ang?"

"I'm only on the bench."

"You should be over there – prepared to bring honour to the department." Bianca agreed with Keri.

"Leave him alone. You'll have him completely demoralized by the time he does get to play." Angus told them.

"Right," said Bianca. "Angus should know. Did you know

that Angus came off the bench to be the hero of the game once?"

"God, Bianca, when did you start getting into the sauce?"

"I've only had one actually, but it's on an empty stomach. I forgot to have lunch."

"It's gone to my head a bit, too," said Keri. "I think I'll go over and get us something to nibble on."

She walked towards the plant end of the field where finger foods had been set out, along with a makeshift bar and several large barbecues which would be used to grill hamburgers and hot-dogs when the game was over.

"So when do you think you'll be back at work properly?" asked Bianca.

"I was just telling Keri that if I can arrange a lift with Dave Richardson and the doctor agrees, I can maybe start next week," Angus replied. "Why?"

"I'd like for Byron and me to have some time together before the summer ends. It's been impossible to go away for more than a weekend ever since he was promoted, mainly because he insisted on waiting for you to get on your feet rather than hire a new designer and has ended up doing two jobs – except for the projects that I've looked after. He wants both you and Keri firmly in place – with Angie to help you, of course – before he'll take time off."

"I knew he was keeping the job open for me, but–"

"You hadn't stopped to think about the extra load it put on him. I tell you, Angus – you'd better not screw up again after Byron's gone to this much trouble for you..."

Angus resented her talking this way while the student was still sitting with them, although his attention seemed to be on the game. Bianca, like Byron, was not big on tact. Probably what attracted them to each other in the first place, he thought, wryly.

"I'm sorry I wrecked your summer, Bianca," he said. "I'll make sure I *am* in next week and Keri and I will set up a system for handling the workload and get Byron's direction on everything and you guys can go away the week after. And, since we're being honest with each other, I think Byron would have much more faith in Keri's abilities if you'd stop putting her down all the time. She might not have your kind of confidence but she's perfectly capable of running things while Byron's away."

Bianca was about to respond, but Keri was approaching with two paper plates of various *canapés* and other appetizers to share between them.

"Here we are," she said. "This'll help sop up the booze. Bianca?" She held the two plates in front of Bianca first. "Those things with the sun-dried tomatoes on top are supposed to be out of this world."

Bianca took one of the phyllo pastries. "Thanks, Keri," she said.

"You're welcome. Are you okay now, Angus? Can you eat? Here, Angie – help yourself. You seem to be the only one paying attention to the game. Byron's up next and it's two out, two on, for the information of the rest of you..."

"You're kidding," cried Bianca, jumping up. "Show them how, honey!" she yelled.

Angus turned his own attention to the game. Despite his new-found realization that his screw-ups had ripple effects on the lives of the people around him, he resented Bianca's accusation and knew he was right about Keri deserving to count for more in Byron's estimation. Maybe if he and Keri could really get things running smoothly in future, they'd both earn Byron's respect and Bianca's services wouldn't be called upon so often. He joined in the cheering as Byron batted in the first of the two players ahead of him and watched the next man up strike out, ending the inning with his cousin on base.

. . . . .

Dave Richardson was an amiable middle-aged man who had spent most of his working life in the McGrath-LaPlante laboratories and had been Quality Control Supervisor during the last fifteen years. Angus didn't really know Dave, never having had any reason for knowing people in Quality Control. His cousin, Danny, had made the arrangement for Dave to drop him off on his way home to Burlington.

"So we beat you guys again, though I must admit I thought it was going to go the other way right up to the bottom of the ninth – expect you did, too. It's not often the plant gets beaten by the office, so it's not such a big disappointment as the other way round, eh? It was a darn close game, so I'm not about to pretend that I was counting on the two hits from those kids. Didn't even know them, let alone if they could play – both new since last summer. Of course, Joey Agnelli's been playing on the industrial league team all summer. The Sullivan boy's a student, just like you... though, I guess you aren't a summer student now, are you?"

Dave's monologue began as they pulled out of the parking lot and Angus wasn't quite sure whether he expected a reply to the question or not and waited before attempting an answer.

"Did they graduate you? The few weeks after your accident didn't make that much difference, did it? My son, Andrew, missed a final exam last year – he has Crohn's disease and was in hospital – we were able to arrange for an invigilator come to the house."

"I was failing, anyway, so it wasn't worth getting into that," Angus said, deciding that a reply was expected this time. "I'm sorry about your son. How is he now?"

"As well as can be expected. That was his BA. He's doing his Master's now – well, not *right* now, of course. He's a counsellor, for the summer, at a camp Sick Kids runs up near Collingwood, for kids with digestive diseases. He's been doing it summers, since he was in high school. So, you going back, then?"

"No," Angus replied. "I'm going to start working full time, as soon as the doctor says. Guess I'm lucky – Byron's willing to take me on without a diploma. With the way graphics software continually gets upgraded, it's not terribly important – the diploma, I mean. You have to keep learning new stuff all the time, anyway. I don't really think I could handle going back after what happened."

Angus didn't really know what made him add that last sentence. Sympathy bids were not his style – not after the years of living on the streets. Maybe the fatherly way in which Dave was speaking of his son was making him revert to the days of his childhood, after his parents' divorce, when he'd complain about his father to his mother, and vice versa, in order to get attention. As soon as he said it, he wished he hadn't.

"Must have been pretty tough – your friends getting killed like that," Dave said. "It's probably better you don't go back if you don't have to..."

They were on highway 401 now, heading towards 403 and Oakville – just as he and those dead friends had done the night of the accident. He didn't imagine Dave knew that. If they even knew at all, people didn't remember where other people's accidents happened.

"... better to have real challenges to get your teeth into. Case studies are all very well, but they're not like real work, right?

Not that I know a lot about your area, except that most marketing or advertising communications programs seem to involve figuring out how to do things that have already been done. That, or pretending you've got some new product to launch – whatever. Must all seem a bit futile, after a while. Yes, you'll be better off working. You'll be able to play on the company hockey team when your leg's better – imagine your dad made sure you played hockey, eh? He was playing for the Maple Leafs, your dad – back when I first worked for the company. Still young enough for his mother to force him to attend the occasional shareholders' meeting, though. Truth to tell – he probably liked the idea of all the girls trying to get a peep at him. Regular old battle-axe your grandmother was..."

Angus had only vague memories of his grandmother and flying to Toronto, from Edmonton, with his parents to visit her when he was little. He remembered the big old house in Richmond Hill better, and being sent to his room for climbing the fence at the bottom of the garden. There were fields behind and a small muddy creek which older kids always seemed to be in the process of damming. The fields had given place to a large subdivision now, but kids probably still played at damming the creek. He hadn't thought of that visit to his grandmother's house for years...

By the time he brought his thoughts back to the present, Dave had progressed from Grandma McGrath and his father to Grandma McGrath and his late Uncle Angus.

"...It wasn't till your aunt chucked him out that she got him into line. You never knew him, did you? No, because your father had only just got married – and, for the most part, people were still marrying, *then* having kids at that time – when he died. You must have been born the next year – you look like him though.

More so than his own kids. Byron, now – he looks like *your* father. Funny that..."

He couldn't see why it was funny. Since their fathers were brothers – was it so odd he and Byron should look like their respective uncles? The thought of Byron reminded him of Bianca's outburst at the game. Did she really resent him so much? So okay, maybe he'd screwed up a few times, but he'd also come through with some good stuff. Look at the company's web page – that had been his project from day one and it was good. It had won awards, hadn't it? Everyone had congratulated him, including Bianca herself. He could understand her being pissed off at him on the occasions when he'd failed to meet deadlines and screwed things up for her and Byron but, while he truly appreciated having the job, it had been Byron's idea right from the very beginning. It was Byron who had encouraged him to explore the idea of a career in graphic design – and Bianca had been right behind him.

He suddenly realised that Dave had stopped talking and was taking quick questioning glances in his direction as he continued to drive along the highway.

"Sorry, Dave," he said, "you reminded me of something that was bothering me. I guess I tuned out..."

"It's okay, kid," Dave laughed. "I talk too much. I was just saying it'll be something to see three McGraths on the industrial league hockey team this winter..."

"I hate to disappoint you, but I'll be lucky if I get as far as walking without a limp – my whole leg had to be rebuilt..."

"That's pretty tough – I didn't realise it was that bad..."

"It's okay," grinned Angus. "To further disillusion you, I was never any good at hockey anyway. Byron was the one they all thought would follow in my father's footsteps, but–"

"–he fell in love with a computer?"

He laughed. "No... before that. Before I knew him really – he says he discovered he wasn't good enough when he was a bantam. My stepbrother's the one who could have made it professionally – and he's not even related."

"Could have? Why didn't he?"

"He still could, I guess. He was eligible for the Junior A draft, you see, but he's in his first year at UBC – this was in the spring – and could have ended up getting drafted to just about anywhere and he wants to stay in Vancouver and finish at UBC. He doesn't think they'll wait around for him but he's staying in Junior B, so it could still happen in a couple of years."

"What's your father say?"

"He can't figure why Justin worked so hard and then chucked it – not that he's exactly chucked it, but that's how Dad sees it. Justin really only got himself this far because, as a kid, he thought it would make up for Dad's disappointment in me. He's a lot more mature now and thinks his education's more important."

"Why did he think your father was disappointed in you?"

"He didn't think so – it was common knowledge. I was a problem child. It was generally kept quiet, but – hey, you must remember the newspapers the summer I was 'missing'?"

"Well, yes... but it was just a teenage prank, wasn't it? That's what I understood."

Angus knew, of course, that his years on the street and his heroin addiction were not common knowledge at McGrath-LaPlante. He supposed rumours had gone around the company, particularly over the last few years, but his problems were never discussed beyond the family. While nobody had ever actually told him not to discuss his drug rehabilitation or the subsequent relapses, he never had. At least, not around the company. He'd started off at Sheridan that way, too, and had only eventually admitted to attending therapy groups when he became involved with Caitlyn Brewer that first year. Since then, he had come to discover that admitting to an addiction, whether as a user or as a person in successful recovery, usually resulted in negative attitudes from people. While his family's motives might not be the same as his own, he had to admit they were right – it was better not to talk about it. Mostly, he convinced himself that, despite all the shit he'd put them through, their joint motive for keeping the problem to themselves was because they cared about him and wanted to increase his chances of coming through. Other times, he figured he was just a skeleton in the cupboard. He wished he hadn't brought the subject up with Dave.

"Yeah, I guess so," he agreed, finally.

"Kids all go through these rebellions – how old would you have been? Fourteen? Fifteen?"

"Fifteen."

"Well, there you are. All fifteen-year-olds are problem children. Don't put yourself down... and we can't all be good at hockey. I'm sure your father appreciates that we all have our limitations..."

Obviously his father's clinical depression was also a well-guarded family secret, Angus thought, or Dave wouldn't be talking as if Angus had had a normal upbringing. He wondered what Dave would say if he told him that the great hockey hero, Michael McGrath, had so totally refused to accept his son's limitations that he had driven his wife into the arms of another man and himself into a quagmire of booze and depression. Quagmire – where the hell had that word come from? Good word to describe both himself and his father, though! Shocking the complacent Dave with the story of his own life before Alan and Danny had bribed Scott's gangster brother to let him alone, was a great temptation. Best shut up, though. He was the poor relation and needed his job. The company was definitely his best bet now... What did you do with your life? He imagined himself answering the question at the pearly gates or wherever the hell he ended up. Well, I contributed to saving mankind from disease and death, he would say. I designed packages and information leaflets for condoms and surgical gloves and, perhaps, a brilliant, landmark advertising campaign eventually...

They were approaching the ramp to the Queen E. when the transport trailer passed Dave Richardson's car on the right, although Dave was travelling at the limit and Angus figured there was no need for the driver to be so arrogant. The tyre broke free and bounced once before plowing into Dave's car.

To Angus, it appeared to fly towards him in very slow motion and he knew he'd have to forget the bit about the landmark advertising campaign when he reached the pearly gates.